CRAZY HAWK

ISBN: 979-8-9895048-2-4 (Hardcover)
ISBN: 979-8-9895048-0-0 (Paperback)
ISBN: 979-8-9895048-1-7 (Ebook)

Published by Hovartus Books

Book Cover Design by Lídia Puccetti
Formatting by Stone Ridge Books
Printed in the United States of America

First Printing Edition 2024

CRAZY HAWK

R.J. STEWART

For Danny

CHAPTER ONE

Her horse had one eye. He was a beautiful animal in every other respect, a rich golden buckskin with a jet black mane and a broad, well-muscled chest. His good eye, the left one, was deep brown, speckled with light discolorations, but where his right eye should have been there was an empty black socket.

"Your horse is near blind," Jube said. He stood a few feet in front of the animal and its rider.

"He sees what needs to be seen," the woman said, letting her right hand rest on a revolver stuffed into a holster dangling from her belt. "I asked you a question."

Jube shifted his weight slightly. He didn't want to answer that question, at least not yet. He noticed she had a lever-action rifle in a sheath running along the left side of the saddle, passing under her lower leg. "I heard about a woman who rides around with weapons like the ones you've got. Word is she kills folks for hire."

"What's your point?"

"Are you that woman?" he asked, trying to appear strong without the taint of belligerence.

She took the faded black baseball cap off her head and wiped the sweatband with a rag she had tied to the horn of the saddle, indifferently releasing her grip on the lead line to her pack horse, a stocky paint who drifted toward a manzanita tree to nibble on the leaves.

Jube figured her age as mid-twenties. She wore her auburn hair in a ponytail. High cheekbones, a jutting jawline and a crooked nose might have given her a harsh appearance if it weren't for the big, liquid brown eyes that softened her face.

She sat on her horse with a bold confidence that spoke of a lifetime in the saddle. Her skin was almost as dark as his own, but he was pretty sure she was a white girl baked into brownness by many long rides in the sun. Her patch-covered pea coat looked ancient, probably pre-Breakdown, maybe even from before the Great Virus. He recognized her ornately beaded, shin-high moccasins as Nations-made, but he was sure she wasn't from the Nations.

She dropped the cap back on her head carelessly so it sat at a rakish angle, tipped slightly to the left. "Well, either way, I don't see how it should stop you from telling me where your friend is. If I'm not that killer woman, it couldn't hurt." A smile tugged at the corners of her mouth. "And if I am her, you damn well better tell me." No smile now. The palm of her hand hovered a couple of inches over the butt of the revolver.

"He's not my friend," Jube said. "I just took his picture."

"Then tell me where I can find him." That hand moved a little closer to the revolver butt.

"If you mean to do him harm, I'm not telling you."

"That's the stand you want to take? For your non-friend?" Her eyes burned, and her body was as still as one of Jube's pictures. The buckskin seemed to understand what was going on, his one eye focused relentlessly on Jube.

"You never know when your time is going to come." He hoped he sounded more philosophical than scared.

The woman's face maintained its ferocity but her eyes now seemed to sparkle rather than burn.

What happened next surprised Jube. She dropped her hand onto her leg and her entire body appeared to relax, a smile breaking onto her dusty face like the sun bursting through storm clouds. She laughed, not mocking or cruel, more of a girlish giggle as if she were genuinely amused.

"Damn, I like a man who can call a bluff." She casually slid off the buckskin, who suddenly cared only about a clump of buffalo grass to his good-eye side.

"Name's Deirdre." She extended her hand as if it was the most normal thing to threaten to kill a man one moment and then want to shake his hand the next.

Her grip was stronger than expected for a woman who couldn't be more than five-two. Calluses pressed against his palm as the tips of his fingers closed on the back of her hand, which was smooth and warm. It'd been a long time since he'd touched a woman. He held the handshake a little longer than was customary.

"Jube," he said, releasing her hand.

"I'm no killer," she explained. "I carry those guns as a deterrent."

He wasn't sure what a deterrent was but he didn't let on because he cared what she thought of him from the moment he touched her. "I understand."

"Sorry about that stunt I pulled," she said sheepishly. "When I realized you thought I was a professional shootist, it seemed like a shortcut to some info. But you saw right through me. I guess I'm not much of an actress." Another laugh—hoarse, generous, loud and charming.

"So, will you tell me where he is?" The question had none of the intimidating tone of her earlier inquiry. Now she was simply a young traveler asking for directions. But she *was* a good actress. She had just convinced him she would gun him down if he didn't tell her what she wanted to know. She might still be acting.

As if reading his mind, she said, "Damn, now you don't trust me. I screwed that up, didn't I?" She kicked at the dirt.

"What do you want with Carlyle?"

"He's got a mule that's mine."

"He stole that mule?" asked Jube. It didn't seem likely.

"No…well…kinda. We traded. He needed a mule and I needed to move some feed." She waved her hand toward the north. "I got a load of oats waiting for me back there because that son of a bitch stuck me with a pickup wagon that had a broken axel patched together with tar. He had to know it was gonna break down the first time I hit a bump."

"So he cheated you."

"Yes, he did."

Jube toed a rock around in the dirt before he spoke. "Well, I guess I can't blame somebody for wanting to right a wrong. What if he's not prepared to give you satisfaction?"

She sat down on a dried-up cottonwood trunk that lay across the rock-studded earth like a body on a battlefield. "I don't know," she said as her big eyes blinked three times in quick succession, apparently an expression of frustration. "Haven't really thought it out that well, I guess. I just can't stand being ripped off."

"I wouldn't try bluffing him like you bluffed me. That could turn ugly real fast."

"Of course not," she said, her eyes widening as if shocked at the mention of gunplay. "I just want to confront him and see what he says. Maybe he can give me that wagon that's in the picture you took." She pulled a four-by-six photo from her coat pocket and handed it to Jube. "He must have picked that up after we did our trade."

Jube recognized the photo as one he had taken four days earlier. Carlyle, a raw-boned, angular white man, sat on a chestnut mule standing next to the bed of an old pickup truck that had been detached from the cab and turned into a horse-drawn wagon. On the flatbed sat four children, three boys and a girl, ranging in ages from about seven to around twelve. The photo had a deep fold in the middle, which meant Jube had discarded it as an unsatisfactory print.

"Where'd you get this?" he asked.

"At Sam's Livery in Tucson. I was asking questions about Carlyle. Sam told me about you and your picture taking. Said you threw away some photos. It was Sam who told me you were headed out to Carlyle's place. Anyway, I fished that pic out of the garbage. Hope you don't mind."

He shrugged. "No, I don't mind."

"There's something I don't understand," she said, pinching the tip of her chin with a thumb and forefinger. "If you took photos of them in Tucson, why do you have to cart your whole kit out there to take more?"

"He and his people have a lot of kids." He squatted down to draw lines in the sand with a twig. "Carlyle said he'd make it worth my while if I came to his place and photographed all of them."

"Huh. He's got a soft spot for kids. Wouldn't have supposed that." She stood and stretched, reaching behind to massage her lower back with those strong hands. "It's close to dark. Is it all right if I camp close to you? There's strength in numbers. This is Mountie country, you know."

He did know. He wasn't afraid of them because they'd never given him trouble but he'd heard they liked to grab females. "Sure. We can share the same campfire if you want."

"I appreciate it."

"I've got some alfalfa in my pickup." He gestured toward a truck bed that had long ago been detached from the cab and converted into a wagon, like the one in the picture. "If you want to split a flake between your horses, that'd be fine."

"Decent of you. My pack horse is toting oats if you want to treat your oxen."

"No thanks," he said, throwing the stick away as he stood up. "I don't want to spoil them. There's a little spring right down that slope if you want to water your horses when they've cooled down."

She nodded and stepped towards her animals but then stopped and turned back to face Jube. "One other thing. What'd Carlyle promise you as payment?"

He was hoping she wouldn't go there but now that she had he thought it best to answer directly, hoping his openness might mitigate the awkwardness of the situation. "That mule."

Her smile seemed even brighter in the dusky light of the setting sun. "I see. We have a conflict of interest."

CHAPTER TWO

Jube sat on the overturned water pail he used as a camp chair and stared at the green mess Deirdre had offered him as dinner. After she'd built a campfire in the time it had taken him to unharness his oxen, she pulled a couple of avocados out of a saddle bag, chopped them up into a small wooden bowl, including the skins, and added some gooey stuff out of a jar. She then divided the concoction evenly, insisting he share her calories. She had given him the wooden bowl, eating hers in quick gulps out of a tin cup.

He took a bite. It was bad. The gooey stuff had the texture of phlegm and its tart lemony flavor combined with the hot spices disguised any trace of avocado. He watched her as she sat by the campfire scribbling with what looked like a stubby old-time pencil onto a battered yellow pad. She looked up from her writing and noticed there was still gook in his bowl.

"You don't like my food?" She seemed hurt.

"No, it's good. I just eat slow." He took another small bite and forced a yum-yum grin.

She exploded into laughter. "I'm just messing with you," she said as the guffaws dissolved into giggles. "I can't make anything anybody else can stomach, that's for sure. In our camp back in SoCal we have a guy, Joe Reno, who can make the same ingredients taste like a bit of heaven. When I make it, it sucks. I always go too heavy on the spices. I just can't help myself." She laughed again. "If you don't want it, I'll finish it."

He handed her the bowl. The green slime was gone in an instant. He'd never seen anyone eat so fast. It was like she breathed it in, as she had her own portion. She wiped her mouth with the back of her hand and then wrinkled her nose. "You did eat today, didn't you?" she asked, her intense brown eyes beaming genuine concern.

He nodded. "I found a sound can of SpaghettiOs in the ruins of a gas station a couple of weeks ago up at Flagstaff. Opened it this morning for breakfast. It was perfect. Had the sauce and everything. Damn, that was good."

"A can of 21st-century calories?" She shook her head in amazement. "It's rare they're still eatable. It's because you found it up in a cold climate place like Flag. Down in the desert, all the canned food went bad years ago."

She wagged an approving finger at him. "Smart of you to be looking in the gas stations. Some had tiny general stores attached to them. Not many people think of that so they haven't been picked clean by hungry folk like other ruins have." Her brow furrowed. More concern. "So that's all? SpaghettiOs?"

"And four quail eggs."

"SpaghettiOs and quail eggs. Not enough calories." She studied his torso for a moment. He was wearing a fleece-lined deerskin coat, unbuttoned, allowing her to get a good look at his well-defined chest and flat stomach which were covered by a thin T-shirt.

"You've got to maintain muscle mass. That's the key. If you're losing muscle, then you've got to eat more." She sized him up again. "You look all right." She returned her attention to her yellow pad.

"So where's SoCal?" Jube asked.

She struggled for a moment to refocus from her writing to his question. "It's what they used to call southern Pacifica. Part of it is now República land but a good portion is wild." She paused for a moment as she considered what she'd just said. "Untamed is a better word. That's where my people live. I'm a Hussar. You heard of us?"

"Yeah. My brother used to do some trading over in Pacifica. I believe he did business with your tribe. I remember him saying you folks have a reputation for being the best riders."

"We may be. The Vaqueros would have something to say about that. And then there's the Nations." She glanced down at her pad for a moment and then looked up at Jube. "Do you know what Nations means?"

"I thought it was just their name."

"The People of the Nations. You know, like the Apache Nation, Comanche Nation, Hopi Nation, Navajo Nation. For short most people just refer to them as the Nations." The zest in her words showed that sharing the knowledge she had acquired was something she loved. "Did you know that before the Breakdown the Nations were an oppressed people?"

"Really?" He had a hard time believing the powerful Nations hadn't always been a dominant power. He gestured toward her feet. "Those are Nations mocs."

"Good eye. Apache design."

"You know a lot of stuff."

"Self-cultivation," she said boldly. "As I'm traveling I trade for every book I can get my hands on and read them right away. Can you read?"

"My mother taught me the basics," he said, lowering his gaze, a little embarrassed his education was so meager. "To be honest, I don't read that much."

"Yeah, but you learned all that photography stuff. That's

impressive. I love the way different people bring back slivers of the lost technology. The Hussar technician rigged up a TV and DVD player. Powers them off solar panels. We have over fifty DVDs in our —."

A noise Jube didn't hear or a feeling he was unaware of brought Deirdre to her feet in an instant, her rifle in her hands. She levered a cartridge into the chamber and peered into the darkness.

"Did you hear something?" he asked, a little shocked at her lightning response.

"Maybe."

"I think it's one of your horses moving around," he said, reassuring himself as much as her.

"No," she said. "My horses are hydrating over by the spring. There's something up there on the slope."

Jube's camp was nestled at the foot of a rugged mountain that reared out of the earth like an island from the sea. This high chaparral region was dotted by many such formations. The one they were camped by stood alone, not part of a range, and was tiny compared to the huge peaks to the east — more of an overgrown hill — but still formidable in its fierce jaggedness and steep inclines. To the west, the plain inclined gradually down into the Sonoran Desert. The spring was on the west side of their camp.

"Could be a Spirit," she said as she listened carefully. "Danny?" she yelled. A moment later a whinny came from the direction of the flats. "My horse felt it, too."

Jube chuckled.

"What's so funny?" The steeliness in her voice left no doubt that she was definitely serious about communicating with her horse and feeling spirits.

Jube struggled to come up with an answer that wouldn't offend. He was saved from the moment when she changed the subject.

"What kind of weapons do you have?" she asked as if his answer would determine some action she'd take.

"A rifle and a baseball bat."

"What kind?"

"Aluminum."

She gave out an impatient sigh. "I meant what kind of rifle?"

"It's a muzzleloader."

She tilted her head as if the labor of figuring out this eccentric was tipping her brain to one side. "A muzzleloader and a baseball bat? You don't have repeating guns?"

He shook his head. "It's so hard to get ammo these days."

"You can make your own cartridges. That's what I do with my rifle. And my revolver is cap and ball." She drew her handgun and presented it to him as a visual aid to her argument. "All I need is black powder, which I can make myself, a handful of caps and a few pieces of lead—same principle as your muzzleloader except I can get off more than one shot before I reload."

Jube took the revolver, and after examining it for a few moments said, "I guess there're ways to get more firepower but I don't like guns much anyway. I keep the rifle around for game or to put an animal down who's suffering."

"You're a strange one, Jube." She took her revolver back and holstered it. "I'll take the first watch. Get some sleep." The charming campfire attitude was gone. She was all business now, giving him an order as if orders were something she was used to giving.

"Nervous about the Mounties?" he asked.

"I talked to a young girl over in Bisbee a while back." She paused. Jube sensed she didn't like exploring this memory.

"These Arizona Mounties kidnapped her when she was fifteen," she continued, her voice tightening. "Raped her every day for two years." She spat out the words. "When they got tired of her, they were getting ready to hack off body parts for the hell of it."

She tossed him a ferocious look, big eyes blazing, lips taunt with anxiety, face flush with anger. For a scary moment he thought she was angry with him.

"A República patrol raided the Mountie camp and saved her from losing a hand," she said, "but the Mounties had already cut out her soul." Her tone was suddenly soft, almost vulnerable. "She's a walking corpse now." The trembling in her voice was so extreme Jube thought she might even cry, but then nonchalantly she said, "So yeah, I'm a tad nervous," and put her rifle on half cock.

*****

Jube lay stretched out in his pup tent trying to doze off, a tantalizing flood of sleep just behind the dam of conflicted thoughts his mind had constructed.

He couldn't decide what to do about Deirdre. A logical version of himself was telling him this woman was trouble. The convincing way she had threatened him, the blinding quickness with which she handled her rifle, and the surliness of the order to go to sleep all suggested this was a hard, dangerous woman who could turn a girlish vulnerability on and off to deceive fools like him. And that talk about feeling a spirit was weird. The sooner she went on her way, the better.

Another version of himself couldn't stop thinking of her as an attractive woman. When he first saw her, she was a dusty, weather-beaten trail rider, but when he touched her hand, she morphed into a full-blooded woman with a shapely body. As he watched her walk around camp, her every move seemed uniquely graceful and when she sat by the fire, her rich auburn hair turned red by the glow of the flames, he began to think of her as beautiful.

Every once in a while, a cold breeze moved across the campsite, passed over Deirdre, collected her scent, penetrated his tent, and deposited in his nostrils a fragrance consisting of sweat and trail dust which he found surprisingly stimulating.

Soon all his thoughts were about her charm, her skin, her eyes, her hands, her hair, her smile and her smell. When the dam finally broke, flooding his brain with a torrent of sleep, his dream consciousness was utterly dominated by this mysterious stranger.

CHAPTER THREE

As she sat by the dying fire, her Winchester rifle cradled on her lap, Deirdre was preoccupied with the danger posed by the local Mounties. For decades, small towns and tribes had banished hardened criminals into the wilderness. These rough men gathered in isolated mountain ranges and became known as Mounties. This southeast Arizona group was made up predominantly of rapists, some kind of perverse birds of a feather thing. Deirdre was determined to be on keen alert.

Jube's snoring distracted her from her thoughts. She glanced at his compact trail tent. *What sort of man is this?* He was coldly calm when she played the threat. Was he calling her bluff or was he okay with dying? Either way, she found it interesting.

Does he know more about Carlyle's operation than he's letting on? As she reflected on his honest face and spontaneous sincerity, she became convinced he was clueless. Carlyle undoubtedly saw him as a useful dupe.

She liked Jube's look. She guessed his age to be around thirty, maybe a little younger. Clearly of African descent, he possessed a full head of black, tightly coiled hair poking out from under a beat-up broad-brimmed Panama. His face, long and angular, with a sweeping forehead, projected strength, his gentle eyes and easy smile communicated kindness.

She was in the midst of these thoughts when she heard it — a crackling of branches, something large moving through the brush, too clumsy for a mountain lion or a go-shee. When she heard the faint whisper of a human voice, she knew she didn't have much time.

With his muzzleloader and baseball bat, Jube would be close to worthless in the fight so she had to get him out of the way. She needed him alive to find Carlyle.

She crawled into his tent and shook him by the shoulder. He slowly sat up.

"Okay," he said groggily. "My watch?"

She clapped her hand over his mouth.

"Keep quiet," she whispered, removing her hand. "I'm gonna be leading you out of here to a hiding place."

"A hiding place?"

She covered his mouth again, this time with so much force she thought she might have cut his lip against his teeth. "If you must talk, it has to be the faintest whisper." Her own whisper was barely audible.

Jube nodded. She grabbed his hand, led him out of the tent and took him to a small cave she had noted as an excellent hiding place when she rode into the campsite.

"Sit down," she whispered, "and scoot back into that cave."

In the dark, she could just make out that he was looking around, hesitant. She placed her hands on his shoulders and pressed down. "Sit," she commanded in a whisper.

He obeyed.

"Now scoot back."

He did. She heard him grunt as he banged his head on the ceiling of the tiny cave.

"Stay," she whispered. She made her way to the horses, unhooked Danny and the paint, Blue, from the grazing line, grabbed the headstall and offered Danny the bit. He took it without a sound. Deirdre pulled the bridle over his ears, crossed the split reins over his withers, put her left hand on his neck and vaulted onto his bare back, her rifle in her right hand.

Galloping away from the campsite with Blue following, she didn't care if the intruders heard the sounds of the horses running off. That was part of her plan. When the Mounties saw no one was in the camp, they'd assume both travelers had fled and wouldn't look for Jube.

She rode around the foot of the mountain, Danny moving confidently, the light shed by the quarter moon plenty for any horse with one good eye. Blue peeled off at one point to munch on a patch of grass. That was okay. He would only be in the way.

She came upon a brush-covered slope that looked gradual enough to allow her horse to do some climbing. Hoping she was far enough away from her camp that the Mounties wouldn't hear her ascent, she directed Danny up the hill, crashing through the brush.

She was about three-quarters of the way up when they reached an incline too steep for Danny. Off his back in an instant, she climbed as quickly as she could, sliding back from time to time but never stopping the upward push. Just below the crest, she collapsed from exhaustion, her face and hands covered with scrapes from the brush.

She caught a whiff of a campfire to her left. When she regained her breath, she approached the Mounties' campsite.

"You got that shine?" a man asked, his words slurred. She estimated he was about thirty feet straight ahead, behind a stand of bushes. A sudden breeze coming her way brought the stench of sweat, human waste, burnt meat and alcohol.

Edging forward, she peered into a little clearing from the cover of some redshank. Their campfire was beginning to burn out. A man, thick of stature, dressed entirely in grease-stained deerskins, hulked over it while trying to sustain the flames with some fresh kindling. His sloppy movements told Deirdre he was drunk.

"You got that shine?" he repeated.

Another man, this one with a close-cropped red beard, walked into the glow of the campfire. He carried a canteen which he handed to Deerskins.

Red Beard squatted next to the fire. "I do believe they ran away. I heard the sound of hooves making it back up the trail."

"Shit." Deerskins took an angry swig on the canteen and then whined, "I was hoping we'd take that little piece alive and have some fun with her." He sounded like a child who didn't get the sweet he hoped for.

"There'll be others," Red Beard said as he stood and moved away from the campfire. "I'm going down. See what they left behind." He picked up a rifle that lay on a bedroll.

"You do that," Deerskins said petulantly.

Red Beard headed out of the camp.

Deirdre counted the bedrolls situated around the campfire. Five. So there were probably three down in her camp, one headed down to join them and one here in their campsite. She had to be efficient if she was going to pull this off.

She moved through the redshank cautiously so that she was approaching Deerskins from the rear. She edged closer. In a squatting position, she felt her cadences in sync and pushed off with her powerful legs. Before he even knew she was there, her Bowie knife had severed his right carotid. She then sliced his throat, curtailing any cry. He gurgled blood as she pulled out the knife and plunged it into his left breast. One down.

Hurrying after Red Beard, she spotted him descending the hill with big strides. Having to tread softly so he wouldn't hear her, she had difficulty catching up. She was concerned he'd reach the camp before she could eliminate him. If he joined his three associates, she'd be taking on four at once, a situation she hoped to avoid.

He was almost at the foot of the mountain, about fifty yards from her camp, when Fortune smiled. Red Beard sat down on a big rock to catch his breath. There was a depression directly behind him so Deirdre couldn't get the right angle to cut his throat. Her knife penetrated the base of his skull right above the neck. She was hoping the blade entering the brain at that angle would kill him instantly but he let out a faint cry before collapsing to the ground.

"That you, Bishop?" a husky voice called from the direction of her camp.

She sheathed the knife. Her Winchester was on half cock, a round already in the chamber. She thumbed the hammer into full cock position as quietly as possible and advanced.

Two men were ransacking the tents. If they were momentarily concerned about Bishop's little yelp, they'd already forgotten about it. One was a clean-shaven six-footer with broad shoulders tapering down to a narrow waist. The other one was a true giant, over seven-foot-tall, the biggest man Deirdre had ever seen. Probably pushing three hundred pounds, his flowing black beard made him appear even bigger. The third man wasn't in view.

Broad Shoulders looked up, spotted her and reached for a pistol in his belt. It was the last thing he did as her first shot was a direct hit to the middle of his forehead. He went down in a heap. Deirdre levered another cartridge into the chamber, swung the rifle around and expected to take aim at the giant but he was gone from view, weirdly fast for his size.

She paused for just a moment, which was too long. A thick branch from an ironwood tree slammed down on her right forearm. She staggered and fell, firing back toward her attacker with the rifle in her left hand, her right arm now useless. She saw a short man with long blond hair drop the branch, grab his side and dive for cover.

She was struggling to her feet when three hundred pounds of

fury hit her. The seven-footer slammed her to the ground and pinned her arms under his knees. He jerked the rifle from her grip and tossed it aside.

The combination of the body slam and the enormous weight crushing her ribcage had Deirdre gasping for air as his enormous fists repeatedly crashed into her face. She struggled to retain consciousness, panic beginning to take hold. After a few more blows, he wrapped his hands around her neck and began to choke the life out of her. As his strength crushed her windpipe, the panic left, replaced by resignation.

A lifetime of spiritual discipline kicked in. The words she'd repeated so often took over her consciousness, a sort of automatic firewall against philosophical panic.

As children obey their parents, we must obey Fate. Fate brings death to all as an inevitable part of life. Because I see my life as good, I also see my death as good.

As her consciousness began to fade, she felt a profound peace.

Then, suddenly, she could breathe. She sucked in the air and tried to make out what was happening. The giant had something encircling his neck — it was his turn to fight for air. At first, in her woozy confusion, she imagined some kind of constricting snake had grabbed him. Then she realized it was Jube's right arm.

She wriggled violently to get her left hand free but couldn't budge it out from underneath the enormous weight. Jube leveraged the giant's neck, tipping him backwards. Deirdre freed her good arm, grabbed her knife and buried it into the giant's heart. His groan, guttural and desperate, could be heard through Jube's chokehold. And then he was dead.

Deirdre stumbled to her feet.

"I think you better take it easy," Jube said.

"No," she croaked, her voice box damaged. "I gotta get the other one. I landed a round but he was still moving."

She took two steps but her battered brain shut down and she collapsed onto the giant's corpse.

CHAPTER FOUR

The bright blue sky made Deirdre squint. Disoriented for a moment, she quickly became aware of her injuries. Her left eye was beginning to close from the swelling and the pain in her right arm was intense. She smelled vomit and then realized it was her own, splattered all over her shirt. The extreme pain still made her nauseous, although she was pretty sure she had nothing left to puke up.

"How you feeling?" Jube asked, walking toward her.

She could see Danny a few yards behind him, giving her a concerned look. She glanced at her right arm. Someone—must have been Jube—had applied a splint. It appeared he had done a pretty good job. She threw off the bearskin she'd been covered with and started to get up but then slumped back down onto her back.

"You better lay still," he advised, handing her a canteen. "You probably have a concussion."

She gulped down water and then remembered last night's battle. "You saved my ass," she said. It was an observation, not an expression of gratitude. "Did you find the fifth one?"

"Fifth one?" He used his palm to rub some whisker growth at the tip of his chin. "Only three Mounties came into our camp."

"I took out two others up the hill," she said matter-of-factly.

Jube's face crinkled into a grimace. "Shit."

"So did you find three bodies?" she asked, tossing him the canteen.

"No. Just the two."

This news brought Deirdre to her feet. She wobbled a bit before stabilizing. "That means one got away."

"Wasn't four kills enough?" There was no judgement in his tone. He seemed to really want to know how many she needed to kill.

She made no attempt to hide her irritation with his question. "We're going to have a real problem if he makes it back to the Mountie stronghold. They're a vengeful lot."

She walked toward the horses but had to stop to dry heave for a few seconds. She'd experienced pain like this before, so overwhelming it makes a person dizzy and nauseous. She knew she had a rough couple of days ahead, but was determined to get on the move. She had a job to do. After wiping some puke from her lips with the back of her hand, she continued toward the horses, surprised to see Danny saddled and Blue loaded.

"They came back right after the shooting was done," Jube explained. "I figured you'd want to get an early start. Do you think you can ride?"

"If I can breathe, I can ride." She scrutinized Blue's load, lifting up on the panniers, weighing them one after the other with her left hand. "Damn good job."

"I've packed a lot of animals in my time. If you leave now you can get back to Tucson by nightfall."

She shot him a curious look. "Tucson?"

"They have a pretty good doctor there."

"I'm not going back to Tucson." She cocked an eye over her shoulder in a generally eastern direction. "I'm going on with you."

"You got a broke arm, a smashed head and your face looks like a mule kicked you. From the sound of your voice, that big guy messed up your talking box." He touched his own throat and winced in empathy.

She licked her lips as she shook her head. "I got one good arm and a hard head so that takes care of any need for a doctor." Her croaking voice added grit to her words. "And I don't turn back from a mission because I'm not pretty enough. As far as my voice goes, I wasn't planning on doing a lot of talking."

"Well, I'm not showing you the way," he said, his tone firm and uncompromising.

"Why?"

"I'll admit, last night I was leaning towards taking you. I was actually looking forward to the company. But I know now you're a deadly fighter. You just said you're on a mission. I think you want to settle some score about the wagon or something else." His lips curled in a bleak smile. "Maybe you are that killer woman and Carlyle's your next job. If I take you along, it'd be like arranging a hit. That's not my thing."

"Then I'll follow you there," she said with a sneer.

"Then I won't go." He shoved his hands deep into his pockets. "I'll escort you back to Tucson. I was planning on doing that anyway if you couldn't ride."

"You're a strange one, Jube." She tilted her head once more in puzzlement. "What about your mule?"

"Well, aren't you saying it's your mule?"

She threw her good arm up in a gesture of frustration. "Ah, the hell with it. I'll just track them without your help."

He shook his head. "If you was sure you could pick up a week-old track, with all the sandstorms we've been having, you wouldn't have been playing up to me the way you been. You wouldn't need me at all."

She walked over to the fallen cottonwood trunk and sat on it. She made a closer examination of the splint Jube had applied. With what looked like strips from a cotton shirt, he had bound a solid piece of wood to her forearm to hold it still.

"How'd you know my arm was broke?" she asked, waving a fly away from her face.

"When I laid the bearskin on you, I brushed it and you moaned even though you were out cold." His eyes squinted as if talking about her recent suffering hurt him.

She thought his habit of displaying empathy could be an endearing trait in another situation, but right now she found it irritating.

"I cut open your coat sleeve," he continued, "and saw your forearm was kinda crooked."

"Shit."

"I thought it best to set it while you were still out."

"Probably the right move." She recognized the wood and frowned. "You broke down my Winchester and used the stock as a splint."

"Yep. I was careful." He pointed toward the remainder of the rifle which lay on a blanket next to the embers of last night's campfire. "You can put it back together anytime."

"True. But that weapon is over a century old. Probably early 21st. Found it in an abandoned gun safe up in Blythe. Mint condition. You know how rare that is? I can't be using the parts for stuff like this." She looked around and spotted a somewhat straight branch lying under a tree. "Redo it, will you? With that manzanita branch."

He hesitated. "Why should I make it easier for you to kill my customers?"

"While you're doing it, I'm gonna tell you a story. When I'm done, if you don't want to take me to Carlyle, there's nothing I can do about that."

Fetching the manzanita branch, he pulled a hunting knife out of his belt and began whittling off rough edges. He worked on it a couple of minutes, then squatted next to her and started to undo the bandages that held the Winchester stock in place.

"So, what's the story?" he asked.

"For starters, I lied about Carlyle," Deirdre said through teeth grinding in pain. "I'm sorry."

"Don't tell me now he's your long-lost cousin," he said sardonically.

"Oh, no. I plan to kill the son of a bitch." Her voice was hard as granite.

Jube shook his head in disgust as he bit on his bottom lip. "So, you are the hired killer?"

"Nah. It is me they're talking about, but that's just slander spread by Carlyle or maybe somebody else. Some people believe it because I am…" She searched for the right word.

Jube offered some help. "Deadly."

"That works."

She grimaced when a jolt of pain shot up her arm as he unwound the bandage, unintentionally jostling the rifle stock. She took a deep breath and shook her head to take her focus off the pain.

When she spoke, her words were faltering. "They don't want people trusting that I'm out to save those kids he has with him. It's a hearts and minds thing. If I'm a paid mercenary, how can I be up to any good. See?"

Jube removed the rifle stock from her arm, then looked at her face for a long time like he was trying to detect if she was lying. After a moment, he returned his attention to her broken arm. "Go on."

"He grabbed all those kids he's got up there. Some of them were stragglers, orphans." She grunted in pain as Jube positioned and repositioned the branch, trying to find the most effective angle. After a few seconds she was ready to continue. "Most he stole from their families. He's a bad man. He's gonna sell the little folks." She tilted her head back slightly so her chin pointed at Jube. "That's where you come in. He wants photos to show future buyers."

They were both silent as he finished tying off the splint.

"I don't believe you," he said after some deliberation.

"Why?"

"Because you've been lying since we met."

"You think I made up all that about the kidnapped kids?"

"Did you make up all the stuff about Carlyle giving you a wagon with a bad axle and oats sitting somewhere?"

"I've never met Carlyle, and my people grow their own oats."

"So, you made up everything." His voice bulged with indignation.

"Look, I already said I was sorry for lying. I'm not going to apologize for being good at it."

A faint groan came from a clump of bushes up the slope toward the Mountie camp. The revolver was in Deirdre's good hand almost instantly. She stood and advanced cautiously toward the groaning, which now continued unabated. As she neared the source, she heard a male voice call out, "Help me." She looked back at Jube, who was a few strides behind her.

"It may be a trap," she whispered, creeping forward.

She reached a waist-high scrub oak and kicked at a dead branch. It fell aside, revealing the blond Mountie who had broken Deirdre's arm with the ironwood branch. He was propped up against a large rock, his clothes soaked with blood, his face ghostly pale. "Help me," he gasped.

Jube knelt and examined the wound to his side, visible through a tear in his shirt. "There's not much we can do," he said gently.

"There are go-shees up that hillside, behind those junipers." Blondie was shaking with fear and pain. "I can hear them. Finish me off. I don't want to be alive when they start chewing on me."

Deirdre tossed a look up at the junipers. She caught a glimpse of a huge canine that looked like it might be half wolf, half Great Dane, gone from sight in an instant. Deirdre knew that southern Arizona had several big packs of wild canines — wolves crossed with feral dogs — called go-shees.

"I'll tell you what," Deirdre said, holstering the revolver. "I'll put you out of your misery if you tell me what I need to know." Her tone was sharp and demanding.

He nodded weakly.

"Three riders passed through here about a week ago," she said. "They had four kids with them in a wagon. Do you know where they were headed?"

The Mountie struggled to get the words out. He'd lost a lot of blood. "Carlyle's bunch. Their hideout is in the South Dragoons. East slope. Take the South Pass and follow the wagon tracks. You'll find it."

"How many men does he usually have up there?"

"Five, maybe six."

Deirdre turned to Jube. "It looks like I don't need you anymore."

She walked down the slope. Jube caught up with her as she reached the horses. "You're not going to put him out of his misery?" he asked.

She climbed aboard Danny. "Wouldn't waste a bullet on scum like that."

"You can't let him be eaten alive by the go-shees."

"Sure I can," she said as she reined Danny toward Blue. "He's the lowest of the low. I got more respect for the average go-shee. Let that rapist piece of shit be of some use. Protein."

"Well, that's happening either way. But you promised you would finish him before the go-shees got to him."

She looked into Jube's tender, pained eyes and a mysterious emotional spring inside geysered up sympathy, not for the Mountie but for this odd, anguished man standing before her.

Weird, she thought, as she directed Danny up the slope. *To please the guy who hates guns, I have to shoot this asshole.*

When she reached Blondie, she noticed he had pulled out a hunting knife. She didn't know if he planned to use it to fight the go-shees or kill himself. He saw her, nodded, and closed his eyes. She thought he looked peaceful when she pulled the trigger.

CHAPTER FIVE

Bouncing over broken asphalt for miles on end was rough on Jube's back as well as his wagon, but staying on this 21st-century highway was the most direct route to the distant Dragoon Mountains. If things went well he'd make Carlyle's camp by the following afternoon.

He asked himself several times why he hadn't turned back towards Tucson after she rode out. At first, he answered with a lie — *I want that mule*. But after a few hours of jarring over the old road, he couldn't escape the reality of what he was doing. He needed to know if she was telling the truth about the kids. If she was, that would make her a hero and justify the feelings that seemed so quickly to have taken over his entire being.

If she really wants to save kidnapped children, maybe I could help, he thought. And if it was all lies, learning that would be enough to put him off her.

The only thoughts that broke into his speculations about Deirdre were those that had dominated his consciousness for years, memories of his earlier life in Winslow, where he ran a photo studio. He and Norma were happy even though they shared many worries. When he first acquired the photography supplies and opened his shop, he did a booming business. But somebody in La República reclaimed film technology and darkrooms started cropping up here and there. Soon the novelty of his digital photographs wore off as people became reluctant to trade much for photos in general; some fruit and vegetables, maybe a little hardware, occasionally chickens, one time a pig.

They made do mainly on the success of Norma's milliner business. Straw hats were her specialty. The battered Panama he wore was a cherished reminder of the woman who was everything to him. Since her death, he'd been wandering with no aim, no hope, no enthusiasm. It was as if he had died with her, but some cosmic mistake, some perverse momentum kept his body going. All this seemed to have changed when he met the Hussar woman.

The wagon jostled up a bumpy escarpment onto an open plateau dotted with burnt-out tanks, relics of some great battle waged there long ago.

He was so consumed by contemplating the new feeling of being alive that he didn't notice a tent next to one of the tanks about fifty yards to his right. A horse's whinny drew him out of his reflections.

He turned to see Deirdre sitting cross-legged in front of the tank scribbling on her pad. Danny stood a few feet to her left, staring at the oxen. Jube didn't see Blue. He reined his team to a halt.

"You alright?" he called out.

She looked up, smiled and waved him over. "This is a good campsite," she yelled. "These old tanks make nice windbreaks. Great little spring down there by those cottonwoods." She pointed to a gulch where Jube now saw her pack horse drinking from a puddle of water that must have been the mouth of a small spring. "Your animals can hydrate as much as they want."

He didn't respond to her invitation, but sat quietly on his wagon, examining the tanks.

"Come on," she coaxed. "I have venison jerky. You're welcome to share."

Getting down, he led the oxen over to the campsite, parking the wagon next to a burnt-out tank. He sat on a juniper stump. "Camping kind of early, aren't you?"

Ignoring his question, she put her writing aside, reached into a saddlebag by her knee, pulled out a small wooden box and tossed it to him. "My people make the best jerky around. I was saving it for when I ran out of other supplies because it keeps so well, but I can't eat any more of that avocado mess."

The box was made of pine and had a rather elegant buck's head carved into the lid. Jube didn't open it.

"Have some," she commanded, openly irritated that he didn't partake. "What's the matter?"

"Well, it's just that this morning you didn't have much use for me. Now you're offering me your calories again. You're kind of all over the place."

"Whatever. If you don't want jerky, give it back to me."

He opened the box, pulled out a piece and took a bite. After chewing for a few moments, he nodded. "It's good."

"What did I tell you?"

He gestured at the tank behind her. "A lot of those old tanks had green tops. Sometimes it's hard to make out through the rust but they definitely had green tops."

"Green turrets," she corrected.

"Turrets. There's a lot of those busted up green turrets all over Old Arizona."

She craned her head around to look at the tank. "Yeah. They belonged to the Unionists. They were the ones trying to keep the old USA together."

"Who won?"

"Well, there's no more Union so the Unionists definitely lost." She took a bite of jerky and pondered on the turret for a moment. "The other side—the secessionists or separatists or whatever you want to call them—they started killing each other right after they beat the Unionists. That's still going on, all the different people fighting. The forever civil war."

"So why are you stopping so early in the day?" he asked.

Uncrossing her legs, she leaned back on her left elbow, wincing as she positioned her injured arm on her thigh. "I was waiting for you to catch up with me."

"Why?"

"Well, I'm gonna be honest with you," she said, emphasizing the word honest.

"Really?"

She nodded. "I know you don't trust me, but starting this morning, when I told you about the kids, I've been telling you the truth."

She delivered that last line with such conviction he hated himself for wanting to believe her. He decided to fight the urge. "So why aren't you on your way to shooting it out with baby-snatching desperadoes?" He hoped he was projecting relentless skepticism.

"No babies. As far as I can tell, they target kids from ages five or six to around fourteen." She sat up straight, looked at her busted arm and wrinkled her brow. "I need your help, Jube." There was a touch of melancholy in her voice.

"How's that?"

"Going up there and shooting it out with a half dozen gunslingers is chancy under any circumstances but, as you put it, I am deadly." She flashed a big smile. "As I was riding out today, with one wing down, I realized this hawk isn't flying like she usually does."

She picked up her pad and shook it. "Hell, it hurts to write." She slammed the pad back down in frustration.

He stared at her as if trying to solve a mind-twisting riddle. "I'm still not sure anything you're telling me is the truth. I just want to take some photos and get my mule."

"Bullshit," she said, challenging his entire version of things. "You knew what my mission was when you set out this morning. You knew there was a good chance you'd cart your whole kit up there and roll right into the middle of a gunfight."

"What are you saying?"

"You're thinking there may be children in danger," she said, locking her vibrant eyes on his. "And you couldn't ride away from that because you're one of nature's wonders." She paused and spoke with great seriousness, almost reverence. "A decent man."

Those words touched something in Jube; he prided himself on his decency. But did she really see him that way or was she playing him?

She leaned back on her elbow. "Of course, maybe you just like brunettes." She fluffed her hair, which was hopelessly matted with trail filth, flashed a big smile that revealed a tooth missing from her left uppers, and threw her head back like the models in the old 21st-century magazines. The faux-sexy pose, combined with her grime-covered trail clothes and battered features, caused Jube to break out a big, robust laugh. He'd forgotten he could make a noise like that. Deirdre joined in as did Danny with some whinnies.

When the levity died down, she gave him an earnest look. "You won't have to kill anybody. This broken arm means we have to do this with more finesse than gunpowder."

He took another bite of the jerky, his face crimped in an anxious scowl as two versions of himself debated whether he should trust her.

"Let me show you something," Deirdre said, reaching into one of her saddlebags on the ground next to her. She pulled out a folder marked in black ink *Deirdre's Notebook* and shuffled through the loose pages until she came upon a partially deteriorated piece of paper which she handed to Jube. "Read that," she said, stuffing the folder back into the bag.

Something had been printed on the paper long ago, the words faded into illegibility for the most part but Jube was able to make out one line. He read out loud. "Eggs Benedict. Nine dollars and ninety-nine cents."

Before he could ask her why she wanted him to read a restaurant menu from the 21st century, Deirdre grabbed it out of his hand, turned it over and handed it back to him. On the other side was handwriting, jotted down in bright red ink.

"Read it," she commanded.

Now, he understood what he was looking at. This was a letter. He read, this time to himself.

Dear Crazy Hawk. We know you are on the track of the hard men who take the little ones. We have lost children to these desperadoes, twin five-year-old girls, Ruth and Sherry. Our souls have been deeply wounded by the loss of our darlings. We barely have the will to go on. Only the hope of seeing them again keeps us alive. If you were to find them in your travels, we'd be forever grateful if you'd return them to their loving parents.

Joel and Ethel Stein. Tempe, Arizona.

P. S. We're south of the old campus. All our neighbors know where we are. Ask anybody for directions.

He finished and looked at Deirdre. They eyed each other for an intense moment.

She spoke first. "Now if you think I faked that to fool you into—"

"No," he interrupted. "The pain in that letter is real."

"Yeah," she said softly. "That's a good way to put it. The pain is real."

She took the letter back and slipped it into the saddlebag.

"So, they sell the children?" He was just beginning to absorb the seriousness of her mission.

"That's my theory," she said with a nod. "Don't know for sure."

He took a small bite of jerky. "Why are you doing all this?"

"It's personal with me." There was a finality in her tone that brooked no further questions about her motives.

"Why by yourself? You could get help from local law enforcement."

"Local law enforcement?" She emitted a mocking laugh. "If you're talking about the constabularies, they aren't worth much beyond protecting their own turf. Besides, I usually work better alone. So, are you in?" Her question pointed like a dart at the heart of the matter.

"Are you Crazy Hawk?"

"Yep. Nickname. Long story. I need to know. In or out?"

He nodded. "In."

A kind smile graced her lips. "You're a strange one, Jube."

CHAPTER SIX

Around the campfire that night, Deirdre was determined to mine every bit of information Jube had learned from his contact with Carlyle. She was impressed with his observation abilities and his recall.

Carlyle and his men were carrying revolvers and bolt action rifles. *That's good*, she thought. *No automatic weapons.* Jube described Carlyle and the men with him as "born in the saddle types", riding healthy-looking horses. *That's bad. They'll be hell-bent when chasing us.* The most important bit of info came when Jube pointed out that the route Carlyle had told him to use was different from the one the Mountie described. Deirdre latched onto this insight immediately as an advantage. "We'll come at the bastards from opposite directions," she explained.

The next morning, Deirdre led Jube to Middlemarch Road, a rough trail threading between the North and South Dragoons. They detoured into the North Dragoons long enough for Deirdre to pick out a campsite, stretch a grazing line between two cottonwoods, unpack Blue and hook him to the line.

Leaving the North Dragoons, they split up, Jube approaching Carlyle's stronghold from the Sulfur Spring Valley to the east while

Deirdre traveled along the west slope of the South Dragoons.

Her plan was simple. While Carlyle and hopefully the other kidnappers were occupied with Jube, she'd penetrate the stronghold and determine where the children were. If the opportunity presented itself, she'd act right then. If not, she and Jube would rendezvous later that night and plan a rescue informed by her reconnaissance.

She knew Carlyle would have someone on the crest scanning the western approaches, so she chose to travel along the slopes rather than the flats. Because of all the jagged outcroppings beneath the crest, there was no way a lookout up there could spot her. Unfortunately, the western slope was a series of steep inclines with a shale surface that made the footing treacherous.

In spite of the imminent demands of the mission, she had a hard time maintaining focus. Her thoughts kept flowing back to Jube. She didn't understand his motives for helping her.

Why do I care, she'd say to herself and quickly shift her concentration back to the hazardous slope before her, but soon she'd be asking herself again why he had committed so fully to aiding her mission. Her thoughts meandered back to a conversation she had in a Confucian settlement in Payson a few months back. She and the community leader, Nara, sat up late one night debating human nature.

It was Nara's contention that people are born basically good. She used Confucian writings to justify the theory that each individual is born with "sprouts" that, if nurtured, will grow into virtues. If those sprouts are not cultivated properly, humans will be more influenced by the outside world than their inner conscience and lose touch with their original nature. Deirdre argued against what she considered nonsense, testifying to countless experiences that had convinced her of the selfishness and brutality within most humans.

She'd thought a lot about Nara's worldview in the weeks following that discussion. She asked herself why there are people who are selfless and generous without obeying an outside ethos. Her mother for instance. She was always motivated by a loving impulse and not just for her family. She showed compassion to strangers and sometimes even enemies. Where did that come from? What if those sprouts did exist and were so strong in some people that cultivation wasn't important; their original nature would thrive regardless of the circumstances of their lives.

And this man Jube — maybe he was just helping in order to please a woman he found attractive. Or maybe he was actually risking his life to help kids in trouble, kids he'd never met. She knew why she had to pursue these kidnappers. She was driven by hope and revenge, but she couldn't figure out what was in it for Jube.

Something else gnawed at her, a feeling she didn't understand. Why was she so bothered that her plan to free the children would put him in mortal danger? He meant nothing to her; she'd just met him. Certainly, risking this stranger's life was a reasonable gamble to save more than a dozen innocent children. And yet...

Danny started to slip down the shale-covered slope toward a cliff edge. Dismounting on the uphill side, she hoped the sudden weight relief would help but he seemed to be in an uncontrollable slide. Grabbing the left stirrup with her good hand, she dug her heels into the slope and leaned back, hoping her weight might offer the struggling horse some help.

"Move your feet, Danny." It was more an urgent piece of advice than a command. He began churning his legs. Just as his right rear leg poked over the cliff edge his front hooves caught traction and he managed to lurch uphill. Gracefully side-stepping Deirdre, he settled on a ledge and began to munch on a little patch of grass.

Deirdre sat breathless for a moment, surveying her surroundings. There was a gradual incline up to the crest that looked promising. Even though she might expose herself to Carlyle's lookout, she was behind schedule so she had to chance it.

She scrambled up to Danny and mounted. Gleefully, he bounded up the slope to the liberating crest, which was wide enough to supply an excellent trail toward the South Pass. If she moved fast, maybe she wouldn't be spotted.

She was riding into a strong wind so there was little fear that a lookout on the other side of the pass would hear her. Since the terrain on the crest was almost flat and clear of brush, she let Danny gallop.

When she saw a break in the rim ahead, she knew it was the pass. Looking across the chasm, she spotted a lone sentry seated on a flat boulder, puffing on a pipe and staring west toward the ruins of Tombstone. A squat quarter horse was hobbled a few feet away from him.

It looked like she would make it without being seen when the quarter horse became aware of Danny's galloping and began to whinny. It would be only seconds before the lookout turned to see what his horse was reacting to, so Deirdre urged Danny into a full gallop.

She had no idea how steep the slope leading down to the floor of the pass was but she had to take the chance that they could handle it. The sentry had begun to lazily lift himself off the boulder when Danny leapt fearlessly into the chasm.

The slope was so steep that Deirdre had to throw her weight backwards to avoid falling over Danny's head. For a moment, she feared gravity had won and she and Danny would plummet down onto a rocky outcropping below, but the buckskin used a ledge to maneuver to a less radical slope and about a minute later delivered his rider safely to the floor of the pass. She was pretty sure the sentry hadn't seen her.

Deirdre felt her heart racing and took a few deep breaths to settle herself down. She directed the exhausted animal into a clump of oak trees, dismounted and strapped a set of leather hobbles around his front pasterns. He badly needed a breather, and it was better for her to advance from here on foot.

A minute after leaving Danny, she spotted wagon tracks in a dry gulch running south. She dropped down into the gulch and headed toward the stronghold.

CHAPTER SEVEN

A s he set up his picture-taking equipment, Jube was keenly aware of the piercing stare of Tom Carlyle, who, perched on a boulder, resembled a vulture with his gaunt, severe features. Jube's wagon was parked in an open space that was probably a parking lot back in the day. A stone staircase led out of the flat area up a hill to a ramshackle wood frame cabin. Jube glanced at Carlyle, who appeared fascinated with every detail of the operation, particularly the solar generator that powered the printer.

Jube took the camera out of a black bag, checked different readings on its digital monitor and put it down on the open tailgate. Two of Carlyle's men crowded around. Having never seen anything digital, they found the monitor a source of wonder. Because Carlyle had observed Jube go through this process in Tucson, he seemed a little less awed. Nonetheless, he hopped off the boulder and joined the others in examining the camera. It was as if they expected it to spring into action on its own, a picture-taking robot. Jube understood their fascination. The near extinction of the digital world after the Breakdown made what little of that technology that survived a mystery from a magical past for most folks.

Jube reached into a box and pulled out a stack of blank photo paper, each sheet cut neatly to four by six. He carefully placed the stack on a tray in the printer.

"Where'd you get fancy photo paper like that?" Carlyle asked.

"Trade secret," Jube replied as he closed the paper tray.

"So, you ready?" Carlyle asked.

Jube nodded.

Carlyle turned to one of his associates, a short black man who was rolling up the sleeves of his tattered plaid shirt to reveal tree trunk forearms. "Kenny, go get the twins."

"Before you do that," Jube said, "I'd like to see my mule. Remember, you said you'd throw in a saddle, bridle and bit."

Carlyle took off his hat and ran bony fingers through his dirty blond hair as he mumbled something to himself and then spat out an order. "Tac, go get that red mule and put a saddle and a headstall on him."

Tac, a tall, lanky white kid, no more than a teenager, nodded and ran off. Carlyle turned to Kenny.

"You go get those two young ones like I said."

Kenny headed off in the same direction as Tac, toward a section of the stronghold Jube could not see. When he'd driven in, he'd passed through that area so he knew there was a remuda for the horses on the east side of the road and an old metal barn with open-air stalls on the west, the type of structure some folks called a mare motel.

Carlyle strolled around Jube's wagon, peering down into the bed. Something caught his interest and he reached for it. "What the hell is this?" Carlyle held up a rifle.

"It's my gun."

Carlyle checked out the weapon, turning it so he could glance into the muzzle of the barrel, and then gave Jube a puzzled look. "It's a smoothbore muzzleloader. It's the only one you got?"

"Yep," Jube said.

"Why is that?"

"It's all I need. Don't like guns much, really."

Carlyle shook his head as if he thought that was the strangest thing he'd ever heard.

*****

Francine Higgins thought she saw movement among the garbage that covered the pasture. *Was that a coyote?* She was distracted from this speculation when a nine-year-old named Derek sat down next to her and leaned into her side. She put her arm around him as he dissolved into tears while quivering with fear.

She felt for the kid. He was new, brought in with three other kids a few days before. His parents had carved a secure life out of the chaos that was their world and he'd grown up as secure as was possible in those hard days. Then to be suddenly kidnapped, brought to this old steel barn and tossed into one of the open-air stalls was an extreme trauma for this spoiled kid.

Francine pondered the vast difference between Derek's upbringing and her own fractured childhood. She had watched her father cough himself to death when she was seven. When she was nine, her mother ran off with an alcohol peddler leaving Francine on her own.

She thought back on how she'd kept herself alive doing odd jobs and begging, knowing nothing but deprivation for most of her twelve years. *Derek has some fat on him. I've been bone thin as long as I can remember. Of course, this is gonna be rougher on him. Hell, the three meals a day I get here is the best eating I've ever done.*

The other kids looked up to her even though she was not the oldest captive. She accepted her leadership role with enthusiasm. Most folks treated her like trash, but these kids gave her respect. She was tough as nails and they knew it.

She looked around at the others, bundled up in blankets and sleeping bags. There were thirteen presently being held in the stronghold. The twin girls had just been taken away from the mare motel, leaving eleven spread out over three stalls. They varied in ages, from five to fourteen. All were frightened, but none were falling apart. Except Derek.

"Buck up," she said, giving him an encouraging hug. "You have a choice. Be afraid like a little boy or be afraid like a little man. It's all in reach of your doing."

His quivering body told her he was pretty much stuck in little boy mode. She understood why everyone was on edge. There had been a guard change in the last half hour. Kenny, who was easygoing and indifferent to their behavior, had been replaced by Marco, a cruel son of a bitch. They'd all watched him beat a twelve-year-old boy to death when the kid talked back. Carlyle had given Marco a severe beating because whatever his plans were for the kids, cracking open a healthy boy's skull with a rifle butt didn't fit into it.

Francine figured Marco, who was now terrified of Carlyle, was unlikely to repeat that behavior. But the younger kids could only remember the horror of Billy Harris' last moments on earth and trembled in terror whenever it was Marco's turn to watch them.

Their anxiety intensified when Kenny returned and took away the twins, Ruth and Sherry. The children frequently speculated with each other as to why they were kidnapped and where they were headed. So far, they had always been kept together and, except for Billy's murder, none were harmed.

Francine was busy worrying when she noticed something black moving between two stacks of garbage. It had only been visible for a moment, but she thought it might be a hat.

A few seconds passed before a woman wearing a faded black cap appeared from behind a pile of deteriorating tires with a six-inch blade knife in her left hand and a splint on her right arm.

She approached Marco, who sat on an inverted pail staring aimlessly at the kids. Suddenly, his expression changed from bored to vigilant. Francine figured he must have noticed the wide-eyed wonder of eleven children as they gazed at something behind him. He turned in time to see a demon flying through the air, crashing into his chest with both feet. They both slammed to the ground but the demon was on her feet again in a second. As he reached for his revolver, she sprang toward him with blinding quickness. Seconds later, Marco's death rattle could be heard over some terrified murmuring coming from the kids.

The woman pulled her knife out of his chest, grabbed his revolver, tucked it into her belt, removed his ammo bandolier and draped it over her shoulder.

Then she surveyed the children. Several were weeping in horror, afraid they might be the next victim of this death maker.

The woman held a silencing finger to her lips, and the crying ones quieted down as she examined their faces expectantly as if she hoped to find someone in particular. Francine thought she looked disappointed.

"All right. Who can ride a horse?" the woman asked. The question had a gentle tone that Francine found reassuring.

*****

After Jube took several photos of the twins, he insisted on printing some samples. "It's best to see if they're what you want," he advised Carlyle.

He took forever getting the generator going before printing two photos of the adorable twins. Carlyle gazed at the photos for a few seconds, crinkling his nose as he bit on his thumbnail. "They're okay."

The sound of a galloping horse grabbed everyone's attention.

They looked downhill towards the remuda as a saddled, scrawny thoroughbred appeared around a bend, its eyes wide in panic. Jube pulled the twins close and leaned against the wagon. Carlyle and his men scurried out of the way as the animal flew up a slope, passed the cabin and disappeared into a stand of cottonwoods.

"Who the hell put a saddle on that crazy thoroughbred?" Carlyle barked to no one in particular.

Kenny grinned. "Whoever did ended up on his ass."

"Shit," Carlyle moaned. "Go down and see what's happening, Kenny."

As Kenny ran toward the remuda, Tac spotted something. "Look," he said, pointing up toward the rim at a lone rider making his way down the long slope at top speed. "Curly must have seen something."

Carlyle rubbed his chapped lips with the back of a long-fingered, boney hand as he tried to tie together a riderless horse galloping up from the remuda and a hell-bent-for-leather lookout descending from the crest.

He paced nervously waiting for Curly to reach him. Kenny came running back, yelling as best as his breathless state would allow. "They're gone! All of them!"

"What do you mean?" Carlyle growled. "Who?"

Kenny bent at the waist and put his hands on his knees. "The horses," he said between gasps. "And the saddles, too."

"For Christ's sake," Carlyle roared, "what the fuck is going on?" He glared up toward Curly, who was taking forever maneuvering down the massive slope. "Kenny, go check out Marco and the kids. I'm gonna meet up with Curly."

Kenny ran off as Carlyle mounted a rangy quarter horse and started to ride out. After a couple of strides he pulled up sharply on the reins and wheeled his mount around, his face gnarled with suspicion as he addressed Tac, gesturing toward Jube with his thumb. "If he does anything odd, put a bullet in his brain." He loped up the hill.

Tac threw a toothless grin toward Jube. "Don't worry about it. He's paranoid to a fault. Just sit tight and let us take care of business." Then as an afterthought he said, "You should know, though, I'll have no problem killing you if I have to."

Tac looked downhill toward the remuda. "Huh. Those two draft horses are back."

Jube saw the two big animals cresting a distant hill.

Tac looked up toward Curly who was now flying down the last stretch of the slope. "What the hell is up Curly's—."

The hollow sound of the aluminum bat crashing against the back of Tac's skull sickened Jube, but it had to be done. Deirdre had obviously decided to act now rather than regroup for further planning. If he were to save the twins and himself he had to move fast.

The mule, who had pretty much ignored the galloping thoroughbred, now pulled back nervously on the juniper branch he was loosely tied to, his eyes focused on the bat Jube had laid on the wagon bed. Jube pulled a molasses cookie out of one of his bags, crumbled it in his hand and held out the sweet mess to the animal.

Once the mule was fastened to the tailgate, Jube grabbed the twins, one in each arm, placed them gently on the flatbed and leapt up into the driver's seat. He couldn't take the road he came in on; it went right by the remuda and the mare motel, where the entire gang was converging.

Earlier, while he was setting up, he had noticed the terrain to the south was clear of undergrowth but gouged with steep gullies. If his oxen could navigate it, he would be able to intersect with the rough trail that led down to the Gleeson road. It was his only play.

He urged the loyal animals forward. They handled the inclines and declines admirably but were, as ever, extremely slow. The girls huddled together on the wagon bed, wide-eyed with fear, but quiet.

When he finally reached the trail, fifteen minutes had passed. He glanced back at Carlyle's camp. His heart sank when he saw a rider galloping out of the remuda, headed in his direction.

CHAPTER EIGHT

Fortune had smiled upon Deirdre's plan at first. She knew almost immediately where the kids were; while surveying the camp from the top of a hillock, she spotted the twins being led out from the mare motel

On the other side of a dirt road from the motel was the gang's remuda, where seven horses were chomping down on flakes of alfalfa. Four saddles were lined up next to the road, each with a headstall draped over the pommel.

She had four horses tacked up in minutes. After eliminating the guard, she put the little ones on horses—two per saddle except for three tiny boys she put on one rangy thoroughbred. There were still three other mounts available, but two were the drafty geldings drawing Carlyle's wagon in Jube's photo. She couldn't be sure they were broke to riders and there were no more saddles. She knew the little ones needed the security of leather to hold onto.

There was one spare headstall and two of the older children claimed to know how to ride so she put them on a bareback mare and jumped up behind them onto the rump to give them some pointers.

She hoped the two draft horses would follow the herd, which they did.

By the time she reached Danny, who had waited patiently with his hobbles, hydrating at a little creek and munching on wild grass, she was looking around for a local Spirit to thank.

"Thank you, Sister," she called out to a red-tailed hawk gliding over them.

Confident the two bareback riders were in control, she unhobbled Danny, mounted up and led her caravan through the South Pass. Things started to get more complicated almost immediately.

First, the two draft horses she hoped would stay with the herd peeled off and headed back toward Carlyle's stronghold. She was sure Carlyle's people were good horsemen and could probably ride the draft horses even if the animals didn't have a lot of training under saddle. Combined with the lookout's mount, that would give Carlyle enough animals to stage a solid pursuit.

Then the thoroughbred bucked off his three passengers and galloped away. The children were unhurt, but it forced her to redistribute the little ones so that now three of the horses were carrying three passengers each.

She hadn't followed the South Pass east because the descent into the Sulphur Springs Valley was too precipitous given the precious cargo the horses were carrying. It was bad enough she had kids bouncing off flat terrain; she couldn't have them spilling over cliffs.

She hoped to move along the flats west of the Dragoons, take Middlemarch Road east through to the valley and head toward the well-fortified town of Wilcox. When two more little ones took hard spills, Deirdre feared she wouldn't be able to outrun the pursuit. She changed her plan.

She remembered seeing several box canyons below her when she'd ridden along the west slope that morning. After leading her little caravan into one of them, she secured the horses as best she could to a row of scrub oak, positioned the kids up a slope behind some redshank, broke two limbs off a juniper tree and fastened one to either side of her saddle with rawhide ties so they would drag on the ground behind the horse.

She galloped back to the point where they had left the trail. Seeing a dust cloud to the south, she hurriedly rode in circles, hoping to obscure the tracks of the caravan.

When she had done all she could, she cut the branches loose and galloped west. She spotted a crumbling adobe structure, rode to it, dismounted, grabbed her rifle out of the saddle sheath and plopped into an exhausted heap behind the remains of a wall.

She took a moment to stabilize her breathing. Her eyes burning from the sweat dripping off her forehead, her heart pounding like it was about to explode, her arm throbbing with pain, she resolutely drew herself up into a kneeling position and eyed the situation.

The pursuing riders were charging hard, still following the tracks of her caravan. Soon, they'd be at the point on the trail where those tracks would suddenly disappear.

She recognized the squat quarter horse of the sentry. Another rider was on a quarter horse she hadn't accounted for. Only two! She liked those odds and considered moving closer. If she could take out the lead man with an ambush shot, she was sure she could handle the other guy, even with her bad arm.

But when she saw another rider on the thoroughbred making his way at top speed to join the first two, she decided to stick to plan A. The two advance riders stopped to let the other catch up. Soon the three were on the move again.

Deirdre rested the rifle barrel on her splint, training the sights on the second rider rather than the lead. The few times she'd had enough surplus ammo to work on her marksmanship, she'd concentrated on becoming deadly within seventy-five yards.

Now her target was three hundred yards at least. She had little hope of hitting what she was aiming at, not with open sights, black powder, a century-old weapon and firing left-handed, but by shooting at the middle of the group, a stray shot might hit somebody.

The leader slowed down, concerned about losing the trail. She fired.

Her first shot kicked up dust about ten yards short of the third rider. Her second hit right at the second horse's feet. She didn't see where the third shot landed because as soon as she pulled the trigger she scurried to the cover of a boulder where she fired the remaining rounds.

She drew her revolver and squeezed off five shots, then ran back toward the adobe wall, reloading the Winchester as she went. Behind the cover of the wall, she again emptied the rifle towards the pursuers.

She leapt into a gulch and ran into a little clump of oaks where Danny waited vigilantly. Using his rump as leverage, she vaulted into the saddle and rode hard, due west, toward the Whetstone Mountains.

When she penetrated the foothills, she paused on a rise to let Danny catch his breath and threw a look back toward the flats. It appeared none of her shots had drawn blood but her diversion had worked. Carlyle and his men were heading towards her and away from the children.

It was important she didn't get too big a lead. They had to believe they were hot on the trail of the kids and keep pushing on or else they might pause and notice there weren't enough tracks. She reloaded the rifle, squeezed off a few rounds toward the posse, and then rode on.

She came on an old mining road. A band of mustangs had recently passed by, leaving a jumble of equine tracks headed west. They were fresh enough for Carlyle to believe they belonged to her caravan, particularly since the sun was beginning to set; even if he were a skilled tracker, he'd have a hard time discerning mustang tracks from domestic horses in the dusky light.

She followed the hoof prints until she spotted a rocky slope, the type Danny wouldn't leave tracks on. Following her cues, the buckskin scrambled up to the hill, went over the crest and down the reverse slope.

Deirdre dismounted and waited. About ten minutes later, she heard the sound of Carlyle's horses. They were following the mustangs west.

She let herself lean into Danny's flank. She could feel his heavy breathing and wanted to rest him and stretch her weary body out under a nice cottonwood, but she knew that was out of the question.

Even though she'd been mounting for two days with her bad arm, in her present exhausted state, it suddenly seemed very difficult, the pain in the break now excruciating. Danny sensed her discomfort and dropped down on his front knees so that she could climb aboard more easily. She let out a little sob of love for this wonderful animal, dragged herself onto the saddle and directed the horse toward the east.

CHAPTER NINE

Danny started to limp a little after sunset. Deirdre dismounted and checked his hooves. His right front shoe was gone. She couldn't tell much by feeling the hoof in the dark but she was pretty sure he was sore from navigating barefoot over rocky slopes.

Her bond with this horse was too strong for her to push him when he was hurting. She found a spring, unsaddled him, hid the saddle in a small cave and paused to reload.

Weariness drove her to contemplate how nice it would be if the Hussar gunsmiths hadn't converted all the cartridge revolvers into cap and ball. But she understood why that was done. Nobody was producing ammunition anymore. Even when the Hussars developed methods for loading their own black powder cartridges for rifles, they kept the cap and ball technology alive for revolvers so that they'd still have firepower in times of shortages.

After a moment of fantasizing about the luxury of slipping some pre-made cartridges into the chambers of her revolver, she snapped out of her inertia, grabbed her loading kit and went to work.

Sitting on a flat rock with no light, Deirdre poured powder into five of the six chambers, then dropped a cotton wad on top of each charge of powder and a lead ball on top of each wad. She seated each ball firmly in place in the five charged chambers with the rammer. That left the sixth chamber without a load.

Turning her attention to the back of the cylinder, she placed percussion caps on the nipples of the five loaded chambers. Because of the splint and the pain of the break, she was forced to use her right hand to brace the gun and do the more demanding stuff with her left. That caused a couple of fumbles, but she was still able to finish in less than two minutes.

She let the trigger rest on the empty chamber to avoid accidental discharge.

Continuing on foot into the moonless night, she trudged east toward the Dragoons. She hadn't hobbled Danny, wanting him to follow at his own pace. Once they made it back to Blue and her kit, she'd be able to put a fresh shoe on him.

Her broken arm was throbbing and the pain she felt in the back of her head was a piercing reminder of the beating she had taken just two nights ago from the giant Mountie.

She had only one of Jube's tiny quail eggs for breakfast so hunger was gnawing ruthlessly, and she was aware of creatures panting on her right. Probably go-shees. She slapped herself hard on the cheek with her good hand. Go-shees rarely stalked robust, confident humans. They had less compunction about finishing off someone they sensed was near the end. "Look alive," she shouted.

Despite all these sensations, the temptation to sleep was overwhelming. Her anxiety about how the children would survive on that slope in go-shee country kept her from drifting off as she walked. So did the heavy, unfamiliar sense of regret dragging her into a malaise that threatened to limit her effectiveness. "Maybe I'm giving up the idea of ever finding her," she hollered, her words projected toward the go-shees as much as her battered voice box would allow. *Is this true? Are the months of failure eating away at my resolve?*

Her thoughts drifted back to the day she learned her little sister had been taken by a mysterious raiding party. That was a year ago. She'd been relentless in her pursuit of the unknown kidnappers ever since, not caring where she had to go, what she had to do, who she had to kill or what enemies she had to make. She was going to find Mindy and take bloody vengeance on the people who took her.

When her thoughts settled on her kid sister's playful laugh, mischievous sparkle and irrepressible spirit she felt reassured that nothing could discourage her from the search. "So what's bothering me?" she cried out at the go-shees.

She was aware now they were surrounding her, much too aggressive to be friendly Spirits in animal garb. She considered firing a few rounds to scare them off but since a gunshot at night would be heard for miles, and Carlyle might be closer than she hoped, she decided against it. The fear of being eaten alive distracted her for a few minutes but soon the same melancholy settled over her.

She became aware of a vague thought wandering around her psyche. It continued to prove elusive for a few minutes as she struggled to grasp it. Then suddenly the truth of what was bothering her exploded into her consciousness. "I did him wrong," she said to the night.

Feeling woozy, she sat on the ground and asked herself what was it about this one guy that moved her so.

In the last year, she had developed a brutal economy of feelings. She classified every person she confronted while searching for Mindy into one of three categories — ignore, use or kill. She had identified Jube as useful and, if necessary, expendable.

But she was unprepared for a feeling that had been suppressed until now. Affection. There really was a decency to him. His Confucian sprouts were well-developed. He'd committed to helping her rescue the kidnapped children after reading the Stein parents' heartfelt plea.

She'd met a worthwhile person, maybe even a special person. He'd touched her soul and she had probably sent him to his death. This thought made her so sad she would have been paralyzed with regret if she hadn't felt the warm breath of a go-shee on the back of her neck.

She reached for her revolver but stopped when she heard the welcoming sound of galloping hooves. Danny burst into the pack of go-shees, kicking wildly. She could hear the thuds caused by Danny's hooves connecting with go-shee rib cages. When the howls of pain became fainter and fainter, she knew the go-shees were in full retreat. She leapt onto her friend's bare back and seconds later they were galloping toward the Dragoons.

*****

Seeking warmth from the night's cold, Francine slid back closer to the huddled children. She had led them up a slope, sat them under a broad rocky ledge and squatted down holding Marco's revolver, which the amazing brown-eyed woman had handed her. If the bad guys showed up, she'd kill as many as she could before letting anyone touch these kids.

"It's cold," one of the little ones stated through chattering teeth.

"Crunch on in closer to each other," was Francine's only advice. In the mare motel they had been given plenty of blankets and sleeping bags. Each night the guards would build a nice fire that gave them some relief. Now only the clothes on their bodies fought against the cold.

"I never knowed cold like this," Francine said, her voice wobbling a bit because of the shivering of her body. "I always lived in the desert. You can get chills on a night or two down there but this kind of icy stuff. Only heard about it."

"I wish that woman hadn't taken us away from our blankets," Mary, a gangly blonde girl, complained.

"Are you crazy?" said Toney, a rough pre-teen boy. "She saved us."

"It don't feel like it," Mary retorted.

Francine heard movement on the canyon floor. She pointed the gun into the darkness. She'd thought about this moment all night. What if someone approached? At what point would she fire? She couldn't chance killing their savior.

A female voice cut through the night. "Kids, where are you?"

About five of the little ones yelled out various replies. A moment later Deirdre climbed up close to them. "Everybody accounted for?"

"Yep," Francine answered.

"How are you feeling?"

"Frozen," Francine said. "It's a witch's tit out here."

Some of the other children giggled, which caused Deirdre to smile.

"How are the horses?" Deirdre asked.

"Still tied up where you left them," she said. "I think."

"I'm Deirdre, by the way. Sorry I didn't introduce myself earlier but we didn't have a lot of time to chat. I'll learn all of your names as we travel. Here's what we're going to do," she said casually, creating the impression that what she was about to suggest was very doable. "As soon as the first ray of light sneaks over that ridge, we're mounting up. I set up a camp in the North Dragoons. My pack horse is there along with some blankets and enough food for you each to have a bite. You all like candy?"

Mary croaked out a "yes" while most of the others nodded.

"After that," Deirdre continued, "we're headed toward Wilcox. They got a constabulary that'll protect you from the bad guys. Then we'll figure out how to get you all home," she said with such convincing optimism that two of the children squealed with joy.

"Here's Marco's gun," Francine said, extending the revolver toward Deirdre.

"No, you keep that for a while. If Carlyle catches up with us, I may need an extra shooter. I didn't mention it before but it's single action. That means you have to cock it before you fire."

Francine was mortified that all her defense plans would have been useless. She didn't know how to fire the weapon!

Deirdre patted her shoulder. "Don't worry about it. My fault. I should have explained. I'm going to check on the horses."

As Deirdre moved off into the darkness, Francine turned to the other little ones. "That woman's gonna take care of us. We'll be okay."

They all nodded.

*****

Francine couldn't take her eyes off Deirdre as she led the caravan along the Dragoon foothills toward Middlemarch Road.

She was particularly impressed by how many things this remarkable person was keeping track of; she'd be peering toward the plain, looking for Carlyle's bunch, and then she'd throw a glance back at the kids, making sure they were all there, before leaning over to check her horse's gait. He'd thrown a shoe so she was determined to keep the caravan on the softest earth they could find as they made their way toward her camp.

Francine didn't know what had happened to Danny's saddle, but the brown-eyed woman looked so natural and secure riding bareback, she wondered why she ever used a saddle at all.

They crossed Middlemarch Road and headed into the North Dragoons. They were winding along a crooked ridge when their savior stopped the caravan and put her finger to her lips.

Francine looked ahead trying to determine what danger the woman had sensed. It wasn't hard to figure out. Smoke was curling up out of a clump of scrub oak that bordered a deep ledge above them. A campfire.

Still as stone, Deirdre listened for any sound that would give a clue as to who was ahead. After a few moments, the laughter of little children came from the direction of the campfire. Francine thought she recognized those giggles.

Deirdre popped her heels into her horse's flanks and flew up the slope toward the ledge. Francine and the other kids followed.

When they cleared the scrub oak, Francine saw a tall, muscular man with dark skin and a big smile standing by a campfire. To either side of him Ruth and Sherry were cheering wildly at the arrival of their buddies. Behind them, Francine could see a big red mule and a paint. She rode up next to Deirdre. "Is this a good guy?" she asked.

"Yeah, this is a good guy," Deirdre answered quietly.

*****

When Jube had seen the rider coming from the camp, he knew his glacial oxen would be overtaken in minutes.

He jumped off the wagon, mounted the mule, reached down and grabbed the two kids out of the flatbed. After he had situated them both securely, one behind him hanging onto his belt and the other in front of him grasping his right hand, he directed the animal up the steepest grade he could find.

His hope was that the mule could handle terrain a horse couldn't — that the donkey blood, which gave him sure-footedness and agility, combined with the horse blood, which made him fast and powerful, would prove too much for his pursuer. He was not disappointed. The tall chestnut mule scrambled up the steep slope with amazing speed.

A few minutes later, Jube tossed a look behind him and saw the rider, who he recognized now as Tac, riding on a flat below looking for a way to ascend to the ridge. He appeared to be on an unruly draft horse, no saddle and a make-shift rope headstall. The animal balked whenever Tac tried to direct him up or down a difficult slope.

Every time he saw a rough descent or ascent, Jube directed the mule toward it and each time the draft horse fell further behind. He figured Tac wasn't firing because he thought the girls were too valuable to hit by accident.

Jube reached a long descent covered with slick boulders that looked impossible to traverse. He thought of looking for another way down into the Sulphur Springs Valley but heard Tac cursing his mount behind him and pushed Big Red, as he had begun to call the mule, down the daunting slope. He was astounded at the agility of that amazing creature as he leapt from boulder to boulder.

When they reached the flats of the valley, he looked up and saw Tac on a distant ridge riding back towards Carlyle's camp having given up his pursuit of the relentless mule.

Jube rode north hard, cut across Middlemarch Road, made his way into the North Dragoons and found Deirdre's camp. He fed the twins with the supplies there, bundled them in blankets and waited anxiously for Deirdre's arrival. When night fell with no sign of her, he was crushed with despair. In the morning he heard horses approaching.

She appeared at the edge of the campsite sitting bareback on her buckskin. He thought her big grin was the most beautiful thing he'd ever seen.

When the other kids rode into camp and joyously mobbed the twins, she stayed on her horse, watching for a while before she dismounted and walked toward him.

He was getting ready to hug her when she stepped up and planted a kiss on his lips. It was very brief but he knew instantly that those plump lips touching his would replace the texture of her hand as a subject of endless contemplation.

CHAPTER TEN

Tom Carlyle was sitting on the verandah of his cabin cleaning a rifle bolt when he saw the armored car nose over a distant hill. He heard Tac and Curly down in the old parking lot chattering about this incursion. A pickup truck with six well-armed gunmen sitting in the bed followed the armored car and then a retooled pre-Breakdown tank came into view.

The appearance of Kenny on the verandah snapped Carlyle out of his inertia.

"What are we gonna do?" Kenny asked as he bounced on the balls of his feet.

Carlyle put the bolt back into the rifle that lay across his thighs and reflected on his options. Fighting it out with an armored car and a tank was just fancy suicide. Running wouldn't do shit. Those vehicles could go anywhere a horse could.

"We'll just have to hear what he has to say," he muttered, feigning calm.

The armored car rolled into the old parking area, spooking a horse tied up there. "Curly," Carlyle bellowed as he walked down the steps from the cabin. "Move that damn horse."

Carlyle stood in the middle of the open ground. In the distance, he could see the tank being positioned on a hill so its turret commanded a large area. The pickup rolled up to Carlyle. The gunmen jumped out of the flatbed and surrounded him.

Henry Ketchell, large, fleshy, around fifty with a shaved head and a jovial smile, climbed out of the armored car. He approached Carlyle and towered over him for a moment before extending his right hand. "Tom, great to see you."

Carlyle shook his hand which was twice the size of his own. "Hello, Mr. Ketchell."

"Tom, we've been through this before," Ketchell said with a laugh. "Call me Henry."

"Henry."

Ketchell put those enormous hands on Carlyle's shoulders and gave him a little, almost affectionate shake. "I'm here to commend you on work well done."

Carlyle eyed Ketchell's face for a sign of irony but he appeared sincere. "Work well done?"

"Yes." He shook Carlyle's shoulders again, this time with more force. "Those children you collected. Just what my employers need for their program. You showed excellent judgement in selecting them."

He removed his hands from Carlyle's shoulder, reached into a pocket and pulled out a cigar.

"There were a couple of duds," the big man continued while lighting the cigar by stroking a match across his pants leg, "but that'll happen. Selecting subjects for a project like this is as much art as science so there'll always be disagreement. But I think you did a good job." He gestured with the cigar toward Carlyle's cabin. "Let's go up on your porch and have a beer."

Carlyle led Ketchell and two gunmen up the stairs, his mind

scrambling to figure out what the hell Ketchell was talking about. He hadn't delivered any children in weeks.

He fetched two bottles of his precious Mexican beer from inside the cabin and gave one to Ketchell who was getting comfortable in a porch chair. Carlyle pulled up a stool but before he could sit Ketchell snatched the second beer out of his hand. "Damn, Tom, how'd you know I wanted two beers?" He slipped the second into his buckskin coat pocket.

"Henry, cut the bullshit," Carlyle said as forcefully as he dared considering Ketchell was holding all the cards.

"All right." Ketchell took a long chug and wiped his lips with the back of his gigantic hand. "I was in Wilcox this last week trying to sell that town some weapons. They're hopelessly out gunned over there, Tom. How are they ever going to defend themselves against desperate men like you and your boys?"

Ketchell let out a big laugh that Carlyle found unnerving.

"Don't worry," Ketchell said as he exhaled an enormous cloud of smoke. "I'm going to give you an upgrade. You'll still be able to get the better of them in a firefight." He smiled cordially. "But they have a nice cattle breeding program and I need beef for my people, so we made a deal. Anyway, while we were working out the details of how they'd deliver the beef, thirteen kids were brought in, saved from dastardly kidnappers."

His eyes locked on Carlyle's, the cordial smile gone now. "I was standing in front of a saloon when their saviors marched them toward the mission." He took another swig and stared expectantly at Carlyle.

"We got hit by a raiding party," Carlyle explained, picking the words carefully, figuring what he said in the next few seconds would determine his fate. "They took all the kids. Up to this very moment, I didn't know who they was. Wilcox posse, I guess. Never thought they had it in them. They took us by total surprise, Henry."

Ketchell nodded and took a long draw on his cigar. "How many of them you think there were in this posse, Tom?"

"Well, they killed one of my men and got the kids out of here real fast, and when we pursued they laid down a steady cover fire. They definitely had numbers," he said. This was one thing he was sure of. "At least ten. Maybe fifteen."

Ketchell nodded as if he were sincerely absorbing Carlyle's estimate. Then he smiled. "How about one, Tom? A girl in her twenties. Cute kid. Like a little action figure. I guess she had some help from a photographer, but he was just a decoy." He belched. "Sounds like your operation was compromised by one small woman and a lame diversion."

"That's impossible," Carlyle said with earnest conviction mixed with existential panic. "There had to be more than that."

"No. Just the girl. She's a Hussar. Apparently, you snatched her kid sister last year. She's highly motivated to correct that situation. Oh, Tom, you look ill. You eat something that didn't agree with you?"

Carlyle was staring down at the floor planks of the verandah. "All right, I get it." There was quiet resignation in his voice. "I took your gold, your ammo, your supplies and I didn't deliver because one lucky bitch caught us off guard. It looks bad, I guess." He looked into Ketchell's cold eyes. "Do what you're planning to do. I'm ready."

"Fair enough." Ketchell nodded to one of the gunmen who walked to the edge of the verandah and gestured to someone down in the parking lot. A moment later a burst of automatic weapon fire came from that direction. Carlyle figured it for three rifles firing simultaneously. He tried not to show his terror but he was sure he was unsuccessful.

"Good news, Tom." Ketchell finished off the first beer and pulled the second one from his pocket. "You get to start from scratch. We just eliminated those incompetent half-wits you had working for you."

Ketchell walked to the edge of the porch which overlooked the parking lot. When he spoke, his words had a philosophical tone. "Funny, isn't it, how people have strengths and weaknesses. You picked out just the right children, by and large."

He turned back toward Carlyle. "You're also an excellent judge of horse flesh. I saw them, too. She brought in most of your herd."

Ketchell sat back down, puffing intensely on the cigar clenched between his teeth. "And yet you hired brain-dead morons as your associates." He snickered. "At least, that's how I'm going to spin it when I report to my employers. Shit flows downhill, Tom. I'll get a lot of flak when I don't send up enough subjects for their project. You must have known you weren't getting out of this without your hair being mussed. So, there it is."

Ketchell flicked a long ash from his cigar in the general direction of Carlyle. "I killed your henchmen. But I'm giving you another chance." He chugged the rest of the second beer and placed the empty bottle on the rail of the verandah. "They call her Crazy Hawk," Ketchell said between belches. "You heard of her?"

"I heard some talk. She's a hired killer, right?"

"Nah. That's bullshit I spread to discredit her in the little towns. Didn't work. People see her as a hero."

He stood and paced angrily on the porch. When he spoke, Carlyle noticed an exasperated tone he'd never heard from Ketchell.

"We've dealt with her before," Ketchell went on. "She did a similar thing a few months ago in central Pacifica and again last month up by Payson." He stopped pacing and leaned down so his nose was only a couple of inches from Carlyle's. "She has to be stopped. I know approximately where she's going to be and when."

He straightened up and gestured toward the parking lot with the stub of his cigar. "You'll find down there four assault rifles. They're pretty cool. Select fire. You can go between semi and fully automatic. They're a hundred years old, but the organization up north has gotten pretty good at cleaning up these old rifles and putting in new parts when necessary."

He tried to puff on his cigar, realized it had gone out and flicked the stub into Carlyle's chest. "There's also five cases of smokeless ammo. That's a serious upgrade for you. It'll make you and your new gang the deadliest folks on the trail. Also, there's some gold, enough for you to hire good people, restock your herd and outfit a new expedition."

He leaned into Carlyle again. "It's simple," he said quietly, but the threatening tone was unmistakable. "I want her dead. You will deliver her corpse to my fuel dump down in Puerto Penasco. I've seen her, so I'll know if it's her. Do it, and we'll call everything even. Fuck this up, and I will personally lead the charge to find you and skin you alive. That's not an expression. I will tie you down and peel the skin off your body. It hurts, Tom."

"So, where's she gonna be?"

Ketchell sat back down on the porch chair. "I had the pleasure of hanging out with her in a Wilcox tavern a few days ago. I told her about a kidnapping in Gila Bend last week. That's the truth by the way. You're not the only guy doing this. I'm also using Blake Thomas out of Eloy."

"Blake Thomas?" Carlyle couldn't suppress his disdain. "He's an idiot."

"Really? Because he understands something about the job you seemed to have forgotten." The barely muffled rage in his voice caused Carlyle to bow his head submissively.

"He actually delivered kids to me recently," Ketchell continued. "But in a way, you're right. He's not good at judging the talent like you are. What he gave me last year was useless for the program. The people up north assigned them to labor units."

He flashed a smile at Carlyle. "They loved Crazy Hawk's little sister. You hit a home run with that one. Anyway, when Blake and his mob were done with the raid, he headed toward Tecate. I have people there who will take possession of the brats and transport them north. Our girl will be in Wilcox for a few more days. She's busy making sure all the kids are properly channeled to their families. She also offered to take some of them home herself. So, you'll have a few days to find a new crew."

He stood up and looked out at Carlyle's stronghold as if he were sizing something up. "When she's done with getting the kiddies home, she'll go to Gila Bend, I guarantee it. From there, she'll start tracking Blake's bunch. For several days she'll be out in the middle of nowhere, a sitting duck."

He turned to face Carlyle. "Find her and kill her." His voice blistered with the heat of his anger.

"Okay," was all Carlyle could muster in response.

"As a goodwill gesture," he said as he walked toward the stairs, "I told the fine people of Wilcox I'd swing by the villain's lair and blow it up. Round up whatever animals you want and clear out."

He stopped before he descended the steps and addressed one of the gunmen. "Get whatever beer he's got left in there." The gunman entered Carlyle's cabin.

Ketchell smiled at Carlyle. "Sorry, Tom. That's the best beer I've had in a long time. They really know what they're doing over there in … Is it Nogo?"

Carlyle shook his head. "Aqua Prieta."

"Right, Aqua Prieta," Ketchell said as he descended the stairs.

Carlyle followed Ketchell down to the old parking lot. When he saw Kenny, Curly and Tac, he paused to examine their corpses. A sense of loss panged his stomach. He hadn't been close to any of them, but they had shared a few laughs. He would miss Tac in particular. The kid reminded him of his little brother. He became conscious of Henry Ketchell's heavy footsteps approaching.

"Tom."

Carlyle turned. "Yeah?"

Ketchell walked up close to emphasize his towering height. "Even though I gave you an idea where she'll be and when, it's still going to be a challenge finding a sole rider traveling through miles of desert.

You need to recruit the best trackers in the world."

Carlyle blinked nervously. "The Nations? They're not for hire."

"I hear they have some issues of their own with Crazy Hawk," Ketchell said as he opened the door of his armored vehicle. "Maybe you can play on that." He climbed into the cab. "If I were you, I'd give it a try."

He slammed the door shut and gestured to the driver, who wheeled the vehicle around and roared down the dirt road, spooking the horses in all directions when they passed the remuda.

CHAPTER ELEVEN

The draft horse walked toward a goat who had wandered into her paddock. Joel knew the goats were the horse's only hoofed companions and hated to deprive her of this social moment, but he needed to hook her up to the plow.

He was way behind schedule. His field needed to be turned and the lettuce crop planted within a week if he were to benefit from any seasonal rains. The last year he'd gotten an early start and brought two crops to market before the brutally hot weather moved in. He had planned to do the same this year, but everything changed that day he heard the distant sound of galloping hooves. He had been at his neighbor's and ran to the crest of a rise in time to observe six riders galloping away from his house. Even from half a mile away, he could see their brightly colored dresses, Ruth in purple, Sherry in pink, as they were carried away.

When he reached their home, Edith was struggling to regain her feet, one of the kidnappers having sent her sprawling with a slap when she tried to stop the men from taking her children. She looked at Joel with such pained anguish he knew he'd never forgive himself for not being there to stop them—or die trying.

He asked the corrupt Phoenix constabulary for help. They took two days to form a posse, which included Joel. After another day of debate over who would lead the posse, they started a half-hearted pursuit, giving up after forty-eight hours despite Joel's heart-rending pleas.

Ever since he'd returned from this futile endeavor, he could do almost nothing but read scripture by the window, looking out for the return of his children. He had no idea why they were taken. Perhaps it was a mistake, and when the men realized what they had done, the children would be returned. He lied like this to himself repeatedly in the coming weeks.

Edith wept for three days after the kidnapping. On the fourth day, she stopped the tears and started working—cleaning the house, nursing her garden, maintaining the root cellar. Joel understood if she stopped being busy, she'd die of a broken heart.

When the traveling rabbi came to comfort them, he mentioned he'd heard of a woman staying up in Payson who had saved some kids in the same situation. He suggested they write her and so, with Edith having halted her work just long enough to help choose the words, he wrote the letter to the woman with the strange name—Crazy Hawk— and sent it on to Payson with a tinker headed that way.

Joel slipped the collar over the horse's head, applied the harness and led her out of the paddock into the lettuce fields. He backed her into the traces and started connecting her to the plow.

It was a windy day and for a moment he thought he heard the faint sound of a child giggling in the foothills behind him but he didn't turn his head. He'd been checking out every sound for two months now. A hinge didn't creak, a bird didn't scratch at the roof, a pig didn't squeal without Joel thinking it was a sign of their return.

The realization that if he delayed the planting any longer they'd have nothing to trade made him determined to crush his wild imaginings and deal with cold reality.

He was having a hard time adjusting the bit; it seemed too high. The draft horse turned her head to look at something behind her. Joel assumed the animal was checking out her goat buddy and pushed on the side of the horse's nose to get her face forward. The big gal allowed this but swung her huge head back seconds later, prompting Joel to turn and see what the distraction was.

The purple dress registered before anything else. It hovered in his consciousness, suspended like a paper Halloween ghost, devoid of reality. He was sure it was an illusion but when a pink dress appeared on the hill behind the purple one, he decided to surrender to his fantasy. Unforgiving reality was just too harsh. For the moment he was going to believe his daughters were running toward him.

He dropped to his knees, held out his arms and enclosed the dream children in a fatherly embrace. Their little bodies bounced off his chest, his ears were filled with their joyous laughter, and he realized how much he missed the smell of their hair. He gasped at the beauty of the moment and then suddenly understood this was real. His children were home.

The three of them wept their way through the next thirty seconds until it became his one goal in life to bring these children to his wife. They ran across the field, through the paddock and over the fencing that was the last barrier between them and the house.

He let them run on ahead as the emotion of the moment affected his breathing. He watched the girls enter their home. Edith's joyful scream was the most beautiful thing he'd ever heard. He flopped down on a chopping block and thanked his creator.

Joel thought he heard voices behind him and turned just in time to see two riders cresting a distant hill. They were visible for only a few seconds before disappearing as they descended the far slope. One rode a buckskin horse and the other wore a ragged Panama.

CHAPTER TWELVE

During their time in Wilcox, Jube and Deirdre managed to get lots of food, baths and rest. A proper doctor had applied a plaster cast to her arm. With a grateful smile she told Jube that the doctor said whoever set the arm did a good job under the circumstances.

One day, Deirdre invited him to ride out to where she left her saddle when Danny lost his shoe. The doctor had told her to rest her injured voice box so she didn't say much on the ride and Jube was hit by a major case of shyness.

When in town, she spent most of her time trying to organize a punitive expedition against what was left of Carlyle's bunch. Jube was with Deirdre when an arms dealer named Ketchell told her he'd wipe out their stronghold with his tank. Deirdre seemed satisfied with that solution.

Jube admired how quickly she was able to change her focus to returning kids to their homes. Those who had no place to go were placed with foster families. The twins were the last ones due to be taken home. Jube and Deirdre decided to do it together.

Once they were on the trail, things loosened up. Jube told her about his wife. He didn't go into many details as it was still a sensitive subject, but he revealed that Norma had died violently. Deirdre expressed her sympathy, her vocal cords completely healed. She told him about the kidnapping of her sister.

They shared a good laugh when Deirdre made fun of the name of her people. "Back in the day, the armies of Europe had crack light cavalry called Hussars. When I was a kid, I was sure a lot of thought must have gone into picking that name. The old Hussars were great horsemen. So are we. It all seemed so very important. I was so into the history of Hussars I even got a tattoo of a winged Hussar. They were from Poland. You may have heard of them."

Jube nodded as if he knew what she was talking about. In reality, he not only hadn't heard of winged Hussars, he had no idea what Poland was.

She continued. "Then I read the Hussar Chronicles kept by the Grand Scribes. When a Hussar turns fourteen, she gets to read it. Damn, you know where the name came from?" She laughed for a few moments. "It turns out, after the Breakdown, a biker gang by that name ran out of gas in our valley. They hooked up with the horse owners who lived there. That's the origin story of our tribe."

She had a hard time controlling her laughter. When she finally did, she said, "I'm so glad it wasn't the Hell's Angels who broke down. Not nearly as interesting."

More laughter which Jube found infectious, chortling along even though he wasn't sure he understood everything she had said. He assumed the Hell's Angels was another biker gang and the Hussar Chronicles was a history of her people. But he didn't care about that. What mattered was they were on the verge of a breakthrough toward real intimacy.

After dropping off the twins they headed to Gila Bend where another kidnapping had recently taken place. Now they were alone, and Jube began to get nervous, thinking twice before he spoke and three times after. When a couple of his comments didn't land, he clammed up. They rode for hours in silence.

That night was chilly, winter's last gasp before the heat of spring settled onto the desert. They built a nice campfire, and both sat close to the blaze, enjoying the warmth while Jube watched Deirdre scribbling awkwardly with her left hand on the yellow pad balanced on her cast.

He found the well-scrubbed, refreshed version of Crazy Hawk maddeningly attractive. The swelling around her eye was gone and the bruises left by the giant Mountie had faded so much they disappeared completely into the shadowy light cast by the campfire. He was trying to think of something to say to bond them closer, but he was too self-conscious to get anything out.

He wondered what Deirdre thought of him. She was grateful, sure. He'd dragged the Mountie off her and helped her accomplish the rescue. It would be odd if she didn't direct some enthusiasm his way. As to the question of whether she saw him in a romantic light, he was pessimistic. What possible twist of good fortune could have put him in the position to deserve this superstar's affections? She was on another level. It was arrogant to even fantasize about a relationship other than the one they had — trail associates and fellow rescuers.

I can live with that.

Immediately, he knew that was a lie. Call it love, infatuation or obsession; it didn't matter. It was real. She had entered his consciousness as a beloved, one who now dictated his every waking thought, and he had to take a shot at finding out how she felt about him. "What are you writing?" he asked.

She looked up, her forehead furrowed from the efforts of a mind fully occupied. "One minute, Jube, I'm white hot." She immersed herself back into her writing.

Well, that didn't work.

He admired her auburn hair as she bent over her notebook, repositioning it from time to time to get the best light from the dwindling fire. Suddenly, she looked up and took a big breath as if she'd been underwater and was just breaking through to the surface.

"History," she said.

"History?"

"You asked what I'm writing. History."

"You mean like the Hussar Chronicles you were telling me about?"

"No," she said brusquely. "Only the Grand Scribe can add to that. I'm writing about the Breakdown, asking some hard questions, like what was it, and why did it happen?"

"Do you know the answer to that?" Jube's curiosity was in earnest. He'd heard the reasons for the Breakdown debated everywhere, around campfires, in bars, at picnics, and during family reunions, but he'd never heard a satisfactory explanation.

"I've been working on a theory as I travel around," she explained, "figuring in different things I've learned from talking to folks and reading everything I can get my hands on. It's no big mystery why the physical collapse happened."

She waved her hand dismissively as if explaining the physical collapse bored her. "It was brought about by a shit load of disasters — war, climate change, the Great Virus which wiped out millions, the Great Famine, the meltdown of the money system, blah, blah, blah. Then came the Anti-AI Rebellion, which as far as I can tell is a fancy name for when people just started breaking shit. I'm sure you've heard all this before."

He gave her an utterly dishonest nod. He'd heard of a couple of these things, but he wanted to learn her thoughts so he decided not to ask questions.

"The key to my theory," she said, the ardor in her voice intensifying, "is that something else was happening." Her cheeks glowed red with excitement. "There was a collapse of the spirit, some kind of worldwide emotional crisis. I believe it happened after the Cloud of Knowledge disappeared. You know what the Cloud was?"

"I've heard folks talk about it but I never believed in it," he said with a smug tone, hopeful this would make it clear he wasn't susceptible to silly superstition.

"It was real," she said. "They stored all knowledge in the Cloud."

"Was it an actual cloud?"

"I don't think so." Her voice weakened a bit as if she wasn't so sure about the nature of the ineffable Cloud. "It was in the sky though. Something to do with satellites. Anyway, they became too dependent on it. Right before the Breakdown, people were living more and more in Cloud world."

Her voice deepened as she seemed ready to present the essence of her theory. "They carried little devices with them they used to access the knowledge of the Cloud anytime they wanted. Those little devices replaced their inner lives. Pre-Cloud people used an expression to describe thinking about their place in the Universe. 'Soul searching.' But the Cloud-people replaced that with Google searching. It was like the Cloud was part of their spiritual truth, but of course, it wasn't."

Jube nodded. "So, when all the disasters began, and the Cloud disappeared it was like they lost a major part of their lives."

"Right," she said with a big grin, pleased he understood what she was talking about.

"Wow," Jube said. "You've been doing some deep thinking."

"I grew up thinking deep. It's encouraged in my tribe. We're a philosophical people."

He'd been studying her face as she spoke and was still doing this when he realized she was now gazing back at him. Their eyes locked for a moment. She shot him a big smile. He blushed under its radiance. Even after the smile had receded, she gazed warmly at him. Although he loved the attention, it caused him to clam up again, so he was relieved when she chose a new direction for the conversation.

"Tough break you had to abandon your wagon, Jube," she said.

"I didn't mind losing that stuff if it meant I could save those little girls," Jube said, desperate to appear worthy of this attention. From the glimmer in her eyes, he knew his words had landed.

"What are you going to do with your life now? Can you replace your photo stuff?"

He shook his head. "I don't think so. Finding a functional camera, a big supply of photo paper and an old guy to teach me how to work it was an amazing run of luck. It took me a year to find the generator and printer. And the guy who makes the ink and refills my cartridges moved to Silver City. Not on the way to anything. I probably only had a few more months of doing it anyway."

He focused on Deirdre's eyes, which appeared transfixed by his own. "Maybe it's time to rethink who I am and where I'm going. How about you?"

"I'm looking for my sister," she said, her eyes moistening a bit, her tone unequivocal. "That's what I'll be doing till I find her. It's why I'm headed to Gila Bend." She paused as if some thought had just hit her. "You don't have to come with me, you know."

"I know. It seems right though."

She responded with a contented nod. "Maybe I can pick up a clue down there. I'm gonna focus now on capturing one of the kidnappers alive. I'm beginning to think all these incidents are connected and all the kids end up in the same place in the end."

"You mean one person is collecting kidnapped kids?" Jube was surprised by this turn in her thinking.

"Maybe." She picked up a little twig off the ground and started doodling in the dirt as if it was a blackboard that could help illustrate her theory. "They wanted you to take photos. When I first heard that, I thought they needed the pictures to present to different buyers, like some kind of sick child-swapping business."

She tossed the twig into the campfire and scooted closer to him as if this next idea was such a breakthrough she had to make sure he heard her clearly. "But what if all the kidnappers are working for one boss?

One guy or gal or group has commissioned the grabbing of kids and the photos were to confirm they grabbed the right amount or type or look or age or whatever. You see what I mean?"

"I think so."

"Anyway, if I can get my hands on a kidnapper maybe I can get an answer." Suddenly, she stood and glanced at her tent. "I'm bushed. I'm gonna hit the bedroll."

"Okay. I'll take the first watch."

"I was thinking maybe we don't need to keep watch tonight," she said as she walked toward her tent. She paused at the flap door and looked back at Jube. "This isn't Mountie country. If you think you can sleep all bunched up in my tent, you're welcome to join me." She tossed him an affectionate smile and squatted next to the flap. "It's a little nippy and it smells like rain." She then crawled inside the tent.

His first thought was, *I'm definitely going into that tent.* Since Jube had abandoned his wagon he had no tent of his own. When they had camped with the twins, there was no doubt about the sleeping arrangement. The little girls couldn't wait to curl up next to Deirdre in her tent. He had slept under the stars, protected only by a bear skin Deirdre had given him. Now she had offered to share her tent. It was an exciting moment for him.

The time he'd spent with her on the trail had drilled into a sensual spring capped off since Norma's death. Now it was gushing. It got so intense earlier that day he had to teach himself to ride with an erection.

But on reflection, he began to question his interpretation of her offer. Was she motivated by a genuine desire to keep him from getting rained on, or was this an invitation to intimacy? She said it smelt like rain. He sniffed the air. Bone dry. He glanced at the tent. She had left the flap partially open.

A little moonlight was bleeding into the tent so he had some idea where he was crawling when he entered. He tried not to jostle her as he got comfortable. Her back was to him and his first instinct was to face away, but then he reminded himself she had predicted rain when there was no sign of any. He turned toward her, letting his front side brush against her.

After a moment, he scooted a little closer until there could be no doubt he was deliberately making contact. Then he heard it. Raindrops plinking on the exterior of the tent.

Damn, she really did smell rain. He'd misread the situation. She would consider what he was doing as completely inappropriate. Tomorrow's trek would be a tense nightmare as she looked at him in a new light, seeing only a lecher where before she'd seen an honorable man.

He was in the midst of this panic when Deirdre turned toward him and let her face fall onto her folded arm so their lips were almost touching. She opened her eyes, smiled and leaned into him.

They kissed. Her mouth was warm and welcoming. Both picked up the intensity simultaneously. She groaned in pleasure, which increased Jube's excitement as he tried to penetrate her many layers of clothing with his left hand.

Sitting up, she jerked the tent flap open all the way, allowing the moon to supply more lighting. Then she tore off her sweater as quickly as she could get it over the cast on her right arm and flopped down by him again.

He reached under her shirt and felt her back. She rolled on top of him, kissing all over his face as she unbuttoned his shirt. He now had both hands on her bare back and marveled how the skin could be so smooth, the muscles underneath so firm.

She straightened up and took off her shirt. He pulled her down to him, gently kissing her nipples before burying his face into a tattoo of a winged Hussar.

CHAPTER THIRTEEN

It was mid-morning when the four riders rode in tandem into the Verde Valley, the stronghold of the Army of the Nations. Tom Carlyle tossed a look back at his new gang — two men and a woman.

He didn't like or trust any of them but they had reps for being hard riders and deadly accurate shooters, which he needed. They all seemed fine with doing his bidding for gold. Each had well-maintained weapons and Carlyle made sure they had plenty of smokeless ammo. He didn't give his new associates the assault rifles. Instead, he kept one for himself and hid two others and most of the ammo in an abandoned mine in the Black Mountains. The fourth rifle he put into one of the panniers.

By noon, he spotted riders ahead coming toward him. He instantly broke into a sweat. He was right to be nervous. His sister-in-law was Navajo, and from her, he had learned a lot about the post-Breakdown history of Native Americans.

An attempt by a white supremacist group called the Ghost Riders to eliminate the Navajos from northeastern Arizona had caused indigenous people from all over Arizona, New Mexico and Texas to migrate to the area and fight alongside the Navajos.

His sister-in-law proudly explained how the bitter Four Corners War resulted in the defeat of the Ghost Riders. Many of those who'd come to fight with the Navajos, decided to stay. A leadership group was formed that called themselves simply the Nations. Its main headquarters was based in Flagstaff and soon a successful farming and trading network was developed.

Recognizing the need for security, a branch of the Nations set up a powerful military presence based in the Verde Valley. All peaceful folk in Northern Arizona looked to the Army of the Nations for protection. Their reputation as formidable fighters was legendary. It was proverbial among peoples — La República, Trogs, Urbs, Vaqueros, Mounties, Hussars — one didn't mess with the Nations.

The riders were a Nations patrol consisting of ten mounted soldiers. Each wore the Nations armband, a beaded design with a bright yellow sun on a turquoise background. Carlyle explained to the leader that he and his three associates were interested in talking to tribal leadership about business.

As the soldiers spoke among themselves in a language he didn't recognize, Carlyle watched them carefully. He'd never been up close to an indigenous patrol. He'd paged through a couple of books on Indians from back in the day, and he could see that a few members of the patrol had adopted traces of traditional garb — headbands, moccasins, face paint and even a feather here and there. But others wore broad-brimmed hats, a few old baseball caps, blue jeans and cotton shirts. Some wore pre-Breakdown artifacts dug out of ruined shopping centers; some had recently made clothing.

After a brief discussion, one of the soldiers gestured for Carlyle and his group to follow.

The patrol led them up towards Jerome, which for centuries had hung on a mountainside overlooking the Verde Valley. Carlyle could see the boulders on either side of the old highway coming alive with soldiers, armed and vigilant.

As they made their way up the winding road that led from the valley floor to town, they had to clear out of the way of a dilapidated automobile rolling past them down the hill, no motor running, just coasting on gravity. It was full of teenagers who grinned at Carlyle and his posse. He wondered how they'd get the car up the hill again. Maybe they wouldn't.

When they rode into the old town, Carlyle was surprised by how lively it was. In the main square there was an active market selling all kinds of goods, much of it salvaged from the pre-Breakdown world, but a fair amount of new stuff—tools, furniture, toys, jars, boots, art— brought to market from all over Arizona. A spacious produce mart was teeming with activity. Many of the old buildings were crumbling wrecks, but some were well-maintained and housed shops as well as living quarters. Spotted here and there were new buildings built mostly of pine. Solar panels covered many of the roofs, but Carlyle spotted a couple of gas generators.

The patrol stopped in front of a grand old building, probably used as a city hall for centuries. The patrol leader dismounted.

"I'll go get Billy," he said to Carlyle and entered the building. Carlyle and his people remained on horseback, ready to ride for their lives if things went bad. Carlyle noticed one soldier smiling at him.

Carlyle smiled back. "What tribe is Billy from?" he asked.

"Pima," the soldier answered.

"Good to know," Carlyle said with a nod. He was disappointed with that answer. He was hoping Billy would be a Navajo. His sister-in-law had taught him a few Navajo expressions that would make great icebreakers. He didn't know anything about the Pima Nation.

A male wearing a sports jacket walked onto the porch with his hands in his pockets, a cigarette dangling from his lips and a blue cap with the white letters NY sitting on his head. He was young, no more than thirty, but had an air of authority about him.

Carlyle seized the initiative. "Hello, sir. My name's Tom Carlyle."

"Billy Cottonwood." The cigarette stayed on the young man's lower lip as if glued there. "What's up?" His question was neither hostile nor welcoming.

"We're here to talk over an expedition you might want to join. It could be a good thing for everybody."

The Pima eyed him for a silent moment. When he spoke, there was a trace of irritation in his voice. "What are you talking about?"

"On that pack horse is a weapon. I can supply that one and two others I can get real quick if you join us in what we're fixin' to do."

A grin drifted over Cottonwood's face. "Buying Injuns with guns, are you? You got fire water in there, too?"

"What are *you* talking about?"

Cottonwood laughed. "I take it you haven't seen a lot of the old Western movies."

"Movies?" Carlyle said with distain. "Never seen a movie in my life."

Cottonwood shrugged. "Anyway, we've got enough weapons and we're not for hire," the young man said with finality.

"All due respect," Carlyle said softly, "you ain't got weapons like these." He reigned his horse around to face his pack animals. "You're welcome to reach into that pannier on that horse right in front of you and check it out."

Cottonwood glided gracefully down the chipped concrete steps to the packhorse, undid a rawhide loop, lifted the lid of the pannier and peered inside. He nodded, reached in and pulled out the assault rifle. He examined it, working the action cautiously like a man who knew guns but not this particular weapon.

"You got ammo?" he asked. "This rifle is useless without good smokeless. With black powder, it'll jam in a heartbeat."

"I can get you some. And we can hook you up to a guy who can get you more."

Cottonwood returned the gun to the pannier and sat on the second step of the city hall building.

"Well, we can barter if you want," he said. "We'd give up some livestock for that gun. Maybe some gold." Then he shot Carlyle a no-nonsense frown. "But like I said, we're not for hire."

Carlyle nodded. "I hear that and I respect it." His voice was warm and agreeable. "But this particular thing we're doing might interest you."

"Why's that?"

"You ever hear of Crazy Hawk?" Carlyle thought he saw a flinch in the otherwise ice-cool young man.

"What about her?" Cottonwood asked.

"I know roughly where she's gonna be in a few days. We'd like your help treeing her, so to speak."

Cottonwood stood up and eyed Carlyle's little posse carefully. "How many is she riding with?"

"Just some photo boy," Carlyle said dismissively.

"I don't know what that means."

"It means he ain't a problem. It's finding her exact location and cornering her that I need help with."

"What's your issue with her?"

"She took something that's mine."

Cottonwood laughed. "She's a Hussar. That's what they do." He let the cigarette fall from his lips and crushed it with the heel of his boot on the concrete step. "I can give you half a patrol. That's five soldiers. With your four, that makes nine."

"We'll accept the five and be very grateful," Carlyle said, his tone open and sincere. "If you could give us some good trackers…"

"We're soldiers of the Nations. We're all trackers."

CHAPTER FOURTEEN

I t was Danny who let her know they were being followed. He kept wheeling around to put his good eye on the hills to the north of the trail. Deirdre relished the distraction. She was relieved to have something to think about other than her new relationship.

After the first night's lovemaking, she was delighted with everything. The sunrise was prettier, the chicken egg breakfast tasted better and the horses seemed more graceful.

Her sexual experience was limited and she had the feeling that what happened between them the night before was not ideal, but she didn't care. The sense of intimacy with a man she could trust was too valuable to screw it up by worrying about technique.

After a year of obsessing about her sister, she felt a profound attitude change that unblocked her senses and opened her up to her surroundings.

That rosy, blissful feeling was gone by noon the next day when her love of a new-found intimacy was replaced by a fear of that same intimacy. Jube spent the morning talking about his every fear and insecurity. He went into a detailed description of his wife's death;

how a heavily armed band of raiders in trucks, with semi-automatic weapons hit Winslow hard. Their goal was to capture a reservoir of oil the town had built up through the years. When he and Norma tried to help a wounded neighbor get to safety, she took a round to the leg. Jube came to her aid but the force of a mortar blast fifty feet away knocked him unconscious. When he awoke, Norma was dead, having bled out. Deirdre was shocked when he burst into tears, something a Hussar, man or woman, would never do in front of anyone.

It was not all a turnoff. There was an aspect of his vulnerability Deirdre found endearing, but she was turned off by what she saw as extreme neediness.

By the end of the day's ride, she'd resolved to end this as gracefully as possible, but after sharing a skin of Hussar wine, they were again in each other's arms. This time the technique was better. Much better.

In the morning, she was still conflicted. There was something wonderful about what was happening but her fears were building by the hour.

Does he expect me to share feelings with him the way he shares with me? Yuk. Does he think of us as a couple? Are we a couple? He is so not Hussar material. What does that got to do with anything? He never said he wanted to be a Hussar. Do I want him to be a Hussar?

"What the hell is going on?" she said softly to herself as they rode southwest from Phoenix toward Gila Bend.

On her arrival at the Bend, some residents were ecstatic. Her reputation as a savior had spread through the desert communities; the hired killer slander was long forgotten.

She interviewed everyone who knew anything about the kidnapping, got a pretty good description of the four mounted desperadoes and learned they had headed west. A contingent of residents had pursued in an old truck but, gasoline being scarce, soon turned back.

After an afternoon talking with depressed parents about their missing children, she threw herself into Jube's arms. It was a comforting distraction and the only thing about the relationship that made any sense.

The next morning, he readied his mule and the pack horse as if he was going to continue to ride with her on the trail of the kidnappers, even though that hadn't been discussed. She didn't mind the idea but his presumption threw her off a bit. She made stupid mistakes getting ready for the trail, putting Danny's blanket on Blue and leaving her rifle in the ruin of a motel they'd slept in.

They were fifteen minutes out when she realized what she had done. As she galloped back to retrieve the Winchester, she recognized that the new emotions she was dealing with were softening her edge. It was a disturbing realization.

The sign of someone tracking them had brought her back to herself. Now she could be Crazy Hawk—formidable, tough, resilient, focused.

"There's somebody following us," she said.

A concerned Jube turned to look back on the trail. "I don't see anybody."

"Have you noticed how Danny keeps trying to get his good eye on those hills to the north? Don't look!"

"Maybe a fellow traveler."

"Why aren't they using the trail? Why would they be moving through the hills unless they didn't want us to see them?"

The stretch between Gila Bend and Yuma was a true desert, endless stretches of barren earth broken by the occasional saguaro cactus. The temperatures in late March were already breaking ninety at midday. In the summer, the heat would be so severe this terrain would be passable only on camelback or at night. The trail followed the old Interstate 8, which was now hundreds of miles of demolished asphalt.

It had been the target of the Whole Earth, a radical government that controlled Arizona and Pacifica for a few decades after the Breakdown. They were dedicated to destroying 21st-century technology and, in particular, anything associated with automobiles. I8 had been one of their targets. In recent years, travelers, on foot, horseback, camel or vehicle had worn a trail adjacent to the wrecked old highway.

Mountains rolled away into the distance on either side of the road. It was in one of these mini-ranges to the north that Danny and Deirdre sensed trouble.

"Here's what we're gonna do," Deirdre explained. "We'll be west of that small range within an hour. Those hills will still be casting a nice shadow on the west end. We'll head over that way like we want to have an early lunch in the shade. That'll give me a chance to go up and see who it is."

When they reached the shade of the western hills, Danny fixated on something on a ledge above them. Deirdre unsheathed her Winchester and dismounted. The braying of a donkey caused all the animals to stir nervously.

"Could be a wild burro," Jube offered, a little concerned by Deirdre's intensity.

"Could be," Deirdre said, levering a cartridge into the chamber. She spotted movement and pointed the rifle toward a saguaro perched on the ledge.

"You're well within my range," she yelled. "My round will pass right through that cactus you're hiding behind. Show yourself, and I'll hold my fire."

A moment later, Francine stepped out from behind the saguaro.

*****

Francine felt sad when Deirdre and Jube made plans to take the other kids home. She had no family to be sent back to. Derek, the frightened little boy she had cared for so diligently, begged his parents to take her in. Eventually, they did, putting her to work around the house.

Although she had plenty to occupy her mind in her new surroundings, Francine couldn't get Deirdre out of her head. To her, there could be no better role model. She soaked up all that the adults around Wilcox were saying about her hero.

Crazy Hawk was what they called her. There was a rumor she was given that name by the Nations who were bitter enemies of her people, the Hussars. That she was a member of that tribe was the only bad thing the grateful community had to say about her. The Hussars had a reputation as ruthless raiders.

Derek's father, a wealthy Wilcox gold trader, sat at the head of a long table, beer mug in hand, a cigar between his teeth. He was responding to something one of his table companions had said. Francine heard the entire conversation because one of her chores was to fetch beer for the head of the house and his friends.

"I used to live in República territory, down by San Diego," he recalled. "Folks around there know her tribe all too well. They're a collection of outcasts. If you can ride, shoot and steal, they'll take you in, regardless of your past, your class, color, gender, religion. Only other requirement is that you can read." He laughed. "That's right. One hundred percent literacy in a tribe of thieving raiders."

At that moment, Francine decided to follow Deirdre.

*****

"I want to be a Hussar," Francine said after she surfaced from chugging on a canteen Deirdre had given her.

"Why were you up there hiding from us?" Deirdre asked, her tone not so much suspicious as curious.

"I was afraid you'd send me back," Francine said.

Deirdre wore a droll smile. "So, you think you can be a Hussar. Why? Because you don't fall off when you ride? There's more to it than that."

"I know. I can learn to shoot, I don't mind stealin', and I can read!" she belted out triumphantly.

"What do you mean, you don't mind stealing?" Jube asked as he checked Big Red's rigging.

"Hussars are raiders," Francine said as if this was something she'd known from birth. "That's what they do."

Jube turned to Deirdre, his forehead wrinkled. "Your people are raiders?"

"On occasion. We breed horses, make the best wine in SoCal, produce saddles and other tack. We trade all that stuff. We also capture things on raids."

Jube responded to this new data by mounting the mule and staring out into the desert.

"Hussars take good care of their mounts," Deirdre said to Francine, her voice hardened by disapproval. She gestured toward the donkey. "This burro is half-starved. I could give him a little oats, but in his condition it would probably kill him. He needs water more than food and we're twenty miles out from potable water. A Hussar would only push an animal like that in a life-or-death situation. Catching up with us definitely wasn't that."

Francine stood her ground, refusing to wilt under Deirdre's glare. "Okay. I learned something already."

"How did you learn to read?" asked Deirdre.

"My Dad taught me before he died," she said, her voice deepened by honest pride. "It's the only thing he left me," she whispered, looking down at the ground.

Deirdre shook her head, still skeptical. "It's not just that you read that matters. It's what you read."

Francine rushed over to the bags hanging behind the seat of her saddle, pulled out a book and hurried to hand it to Deirdre.

"This was in Derek's library," Francine said, her words bulging with conviction as if the book was the proof of her claims. "I read the whole thing in just the time I was at his house."

"Did you steal that book?" Jube asked.

"I captured it. And the burro and the saddle and the headstall. Captured them all."

Deirdre smiled at Francine's youthful and utterly unjustified confidence. She examined the book. *"Harry Potter and the Sorcerer's Stone."*

"It's over three hundred pages," Francine bragged.

"If you finished it, why'd you have to capture it?" Deirdre asked.

"It's a great, great book," Francine said, her voice cracking with emotion as if the one thing in life she believed in was the greatness of this book. "I'm gonna carry it with me for the rest of my life."

"Reading a kid's book doesn't mean much," Deirdre said, her words slow and dismissive. "Besides, I'm not headed to Hussar Valley. I'm tracking more bad guys."

"Then let me ride along and prove myself," Francine's said with the aggression of a good saleswoman trying to close a deal.

Deirdre scraped some trail dirt off her chin with the palm of her hand as she considered this. "That's not a bad idea."

"That's a terrible idea," Jube said.

Deirdre ignored him, pulled Marco's revolver out of her saddle bag and extended it toward Francine butt first. "Remember what I told you. It's single action. You have to cock before you can pull the trigger. You'll practice tonight when we camp."

Francine took the revolver and shoved it in her belt.

Jube was appalled. "Shouldn't you at least show her where the safety is?"

"It's not loaded. I just want her to get the feel of it. And there are no safeties on revolvers." Deirdre shook her head in dismay that she was with a guy who didn't know that.

"You can't take a little kid after kidnappers," Jube said, his indignation growing.

Deirdre waved her good arm dismissively. "When I was her age, I'd already been on a dozen raids. Let's hit the trail."

Francine approached the burro.

"You're gonna stay dismounted," Deirdre ordered, "and lead that burro on foot for a mile. You'll do that every other mile. At least until he can hydrate."

"Yes, ma'am," Francine said.

Deirdre grabbed Blue's lead line, climbed up on Danny and rode back toward the road. Jube followed, deep in reflection.

Francine brought up the rear on foot, leading the burro by one of the split reins, glancing down from time to time to admire the butt of the revolver sticking out from her belt.

CHAPTER FIFTEEN

They were on the trail for two more days before reaching Yuma. It was a time of anguished conflict for Deirdre. She had always thought that when love found her it would enrich her life, expand her sensibilities and make her wiser. But her feelings about Jube were so complicated and intense that she felt distracted, emotional and in no way wise during the countless hours reflecting on their future together—if they even had a future.

So, when Francine spotted a makeshift poster advertising an ancient movie called *Crazy, Stupid Love* playing in downtown Yuma, Deirdre was curious to try it out. She didn't know how she felt about Jube saying he didn't like the title. "Love isn't stupid or crazy," he said with a weak smile pointed toward Deirdre.

Yuma was a dusty town of scattered homes and businesses amidst blighted ruins. After storing their gear in an abandoned building that had a faded sign with the unfathomable title of Beverly's Tanning Salon, they rode to the theater, tied their mounts in what used to be the lobby and negotiated admission for three. It cost them some deer jerky.

The half-wrecked movie theater could hold a couple of hundred spectators if some of them didn't mind sitting on rubble. On that night, there were about ten other customers. Most of them had brought their own chairs and were sitting in what used to be aisles.

Deirdre found a row that seemed pretty much intact, and the three of them cleared comfortable seating for themselves.

"The roof collapsed," Jube said as he looked up into the night sky. "That would explain all the junk on the seats."

As they settled down to watch the movie, Francine noticed a ring-shaped extension protruding out of the end of the armrest. "What do you think that was for?" she asked.

Deirdre studied the one on her armrest, then pulled her revolver from her belt and let it slide into the ring. The trigger guard and the upper frame caught on the edges of the ring, leaving the handle sticking up at a very accessible angle.

"Cool," Francine said dropping her sidearm into her ring.

Jube had a theory. "I think it was for their drinks."

Deirdre considered this. "Nah. It was for their sidearms."

"For sure," said Francine adamantly. "Why would they need to put their drinks in anything?"

When they had seen the poster, Deirdre had hoped she was going to finally experience a movie on a big screen. But instead, a large flat screen tv sat on a platform in front of the theatre. Deirdre was no stranger to watching movies this way. It was pretty much what they had back in Hussar Valley since Pablo Jones, the chief Hussar technician, had set it up when Deirdre was twelve. Although many older Hussars had seen a movie or two at some point in their travels, most of the younger crowd had not. They waited for the initial Movie Night with hopeful anticipation and the first picture could not have been better suited for young Hussars. *True Grit.*

Deirdre and others in her generation loved that movie. Lines like Jeff Bridges saying "Well, that didn't pan out" became regular catchphrases in their conversations. The long-practiced Hussar technique of charging with reins in the teeth and a revolver in each hand started being referred to as "Rooster Cogburn".

Unfortunately, functional DVDs were harder to come by than books. Long before the Breakdown folks had stopped making DVDs because movies were acquired from the all-powerful Cloud.

Many of the movies took place when they were made, 20th or early to mid-21st, and the Hussar population found that society almost impossible to relate to.

People in those days seemed obsessed with machines and clothing and apparently had no interior life whatsoever. Their entire worldview depended on what other people thought of them, particularly those they imagined they were in love with.

And there were barely any horses in that world—not as transportation, not in combat, rarely even as pets. This made it all seem so ugly and unreal to Hussar youth; attendance started to dwindle for Movie Night. Fewer solar panels were assigned to it and soon the schedule was reduced from weekly to monthly.

Occasionally, a DVD would be found that kindled some interest. *Lawrence of Arabia* was a big hit, but most of the movies brought back from raids were unrealistic adventure stories that could teach Hussars nothing about staying alive or silly comedies about people who seemed tortured by some incomprehensible love obsession.

But Deirdre had observed that every once in a while, a young Hussar would suddenly find those romantic comedies relevant. She found that behavior mystifying and was merciless in mocking it. Now that she prepared to watch a film called *Crazy, Stupid, Love,* the irony did not escape her.

Jube explained that he had also seen movies before. His brother, Paul, had a television set, a DVD player and a DVD of a film called *Christmas Story.* Jube and his wife would go over every Christmas and watch it with Paul, fascinated with this glimpse of what life was like in the 20th century. Paul had other movies but he seldom wanted to use his limited electricity for anything but a DVD of 21st-century people having sex.

Francine was very vocal about never having seen a movie. She was hyper when the TV screen lit up with images. As they rode back to the tanning salon, the young girl couldn't stop talking about what they had just seen.

"How could they live like that? How did they feed themselves? That one guy seemed to sit at a desk for a living. What good does that do? Do you think a world like that ever really existed or was that just somebody's fantasy, like my Harry Potter book?"

Deirdre had read enough books and seen enough of these movies to have figured out some basics about the pre-Breakdown society but she wasn't in the mood to give Francine a lesson on those depressing little cells they called offices.

She was more interested in the bizarre way people in love related to each other. *Crazy, Stupid Love* was aptly named. One of the characters, a spineless man who would have been driven out of the Hussar camp just on principle, threw himself out of a moving car onto the pavement to express his frustration with his wife leaving him. Deirdre had been in enough gas-powered vehicles to know that was extreme behavior.

Is that what love does to a person? She had once thought like Francine, that these movies were just made-up stories that had nothing to do with real human behavior. Eventually, she'd read enough to know this whole obsession with love didn't start with movies. It was a powerful flaw in the human psyche that led to self-destructive behavior and a complete loss of focus.

Later that night, cuddled up with Jube, she was more resigned to her fate. *I may be crazy and stupid, but I am in love.*

CHAPTER SIXTEEN

*D*on't look for things to happen as you wish; but wish the things which happen to be just as they are, and your life will have a tranquil flow.

Deirdre reflected on this passage for a moment. Wishing things to be as they are. It was very much in accord with Hussar tribal philosophy. *Amor Fati* — love your fate — was chiseled into a wood plaque hanging over the Hussar library doorway. The current Grand Scribe, Jeannie, was particularly adamant about this being the cornerstone of a sound philosophical outlook.

Deirdre closed the paperback and examined the small volume. The cover was long gone but the title page was still intact, *The Philosophy of Epictetus*.

She quickly perused the introductory matter and learned Epictetus was a slave of Greek origin who lived in Rome around 100 A.D. When he was freed, he opened a school in Greece. She opened the book to another random passage.

When fate leads me to death, must I die lamenting? If I'm put in chains, must I cry and complain? If I'm exiled, can any man stop me from going with smiles and cheerfulness and contentment?

This reminder to worry only about the things we can control also fit into Hussar teachings, and was an idea Jeannie stressed. It was a call to greet misfortune with courage and resilience, to fortify ourselves with what is always within our reach—our inner world.

"So, you like that book?" a bold, husky voice asked.

Deirdre looked up at the trader, a small man, who sat on a short three-legged stool, beneath an oversized sugarloaf sombrero and behind an old card table piled with his goods, relics from the 21st.

She dropped the book back on the table and shrugged. Deirdre liked the book very much but knew she had to seem indifferent to get a good deal. "It'll make good kindling."

The trader guffawed and rolled his eyes. He was going to be a tough man to bargain with. Deirdre picked up a guitar. It had no strings, and some of the frets were damaged but the body looked sound. She thought she could fix it.

"How much?" she asked the trader. He leaned against his camel which was lying behind him dozing in the twilight.

"What do you got?" he asked with greedy curiosity.

"A skin of wine," she said. "But I'd need you to throw in something else other than the guitar."

"What kind of wine?"

"Dry, red Hussar wine." She eyed him carefully to see if he understood what Hussar wine was worth.

"Two skins."

"Get out of here," she said with a sneer. "For a broken guitar?"

A self-assured grin dominated his face. "Not just the guitar. For the book, too."

"I didn't say I want the book," she said with feigned indignation.

"You want the book. You're a Hussar. My wife reads a little. She told me that's a book of philosophy. All traders know what that's worth to a Hussar."

"Don't kid yourself," she said, dropping the guitar onto the table.

"An old book and a broken guitar for two skins of the best wine in SoCal?"

"I don't know about being the best. We've been getting some good vintages from Temecula."

"Temecula!" She paced in front of the table, agitated. "Come on. Be serious."

"I am serious. I have some customers who prefer Temecula wine."

"Well, then, go ahead and trade your junk for Temecula wine." She started to walk away.

"I want two skins for the book and the guitar," the trader said. "But I'll throw in something else. What do you want?"

Deirdre perused the assortment of artifacts; a revolver frame without a cylinder, a revolver cylinder that didn't fit the frame, four pairs of beige socks in great shape, a bottle of herbal medicine, a hoe, a box of rusty tools, a hunting knife, a stack of girlie magazines, the guitar and the Epictetus book.

"I don't see anything else."

"Well, sorry." He spoke in a clipped fashion as if the negotiation was over. "I want two skins."

Just then the trader's camel let out a loud, low-pitched, melancholic bray. Deirdre studied the creature. "Tell you what. I'll let you have two skins for the book, the guitar and a camel riding lesson."

The trader glanced at his camel and then back at Deirdre. His smugness had vanished. "Why do you want to ride a camel?"

"Just do." She stood square and straight, projecting honest inflexibility. She was willing to walk if she didn't get that camel ride.

The trader looked at her for a long moment and then nodded. "All right. Tomorrow morning. Early."

"Good," she said with a nod of her own. "See you at dawn with two skins of Hussar wine."

She made her way through the sand dunes that covered the plain west of the river to her campsite. Deirdre and her little caravan had passed through Yuma and camped on the west side of the Colorado River because it presented easier access to the water than the east bank.

She found Francine asleep at the foot of a nearby dune and threw a blanket on her. The desert nights could still get chilly this time of year.

Jube walked up leading the burro and Blue. "I'm afraid to let them drink anymore."

Deirdre had dedicated the entire day to the gradual hydration of the animals. "Yeah, you don't want to over-do it," she said. "We'll let them have another session in the morning."

She sat down in front of her tent. "I talked to a tinker who did business with riders traveling with kids who looked scared. They were headed toward Tecate."

"All right. I'll start packing at dawn."

Again, he's assuming he's going with me, she thought, but this time she was very comfortable with the idea; no conflicted feelings.

He tied Blue and the burro to a couple of grazing stakes and took a seat next to Deirdre. "You want me to take Danny down?"

"That'd be nice," she said with a grateful smile. "Thanks."

"When I'm done, I'd love a cup of Hussar wine," he said with a twinkle.

"Sorry. Just promised my last two skins to a trader."

"For what?" he said, not trying to conceal his disappointment.

"A book, a guitar and a camel riding lesson."

He studied her for a moment as if he was trying to determine if she was serious. "Do you play the guitar?"

"No, I'm gonna learn. Every Hussar is supposed to play an instrument. I never learned." She laughed. "They let me slide because I had other talents. But it's time. Just like I'm gonna learn to ride a camel."

"And I'm the strange one."

She gave him an affectionate poke to the ribs. "Go water my horse."

*****

As Jube led Danny toward a flat stretch of embankment jutting into the river, he was thinking about Deirdre's tribe and what being in love with a raider meant to his life. He was worried that maybe it wouldn't work out—he definitely disapproved of raiding—but part of him hoped he could change her.

Later that night, after the desert had cooled, a strong wind kicked up and Deirdre and Jube were happy to crawl under the bearskins. It wasn't long before they were curled up together for warmth and soon there was real heat in that tent.

When they'd finished their lovemaking, Jube lay dreamily imagining he and Deirdre living together on a small farm someplace. In his fantasy he was raising crops like his father did; she was breeding horses and there were lots of kids running around. He looked at Deirdre, who appeared deep in thought. *She may be imagining our future together, too.*

"Whatcha thinking about?" he asked softly.

She took a moment to respond but then gave him a sweet smile. "Nothing important," she said. "Just planning a raid on Temecula. We've got to destroy every grape in that place."

*****

Deirdre plopped her bottom onto the large saddle, which sat in front of the hump and was made up of two vertical posts separated by a sheepskin-covered seat. She rested her feet on horizontal pegs sticking out of each side of the saddle, giving a slight bend to her knees.

"When he gets up, you'll pitch forward for a moment, so be ready for it," the trader said, giving the camel a little kick in the shoulder.

Deirdre did indeed pitch forward and then back as the animal raised first his back end and then his front.

The trader handed her a stick. "His name is Frodo. A pop to the shoulder will get him going. If you want him to pick up the pace, smack him a little harder. He used to be a racing camel so be careful."

She poked Frodo on the shoulder and directed him with rope reins toward a group of rolling sand dunes about a half mile away. The ride was bouncy but not uncomfortable. She poked his shoulder a little harder and he picked up the pace. The faster he went, the smoother the ride. Then she gave him a hard slap with the stick and he took off like a shot.

Deirdre was thrilled with the ride now. Although it was very different from a horse, she felt comfortable enough for her to settle into the seat. She had a grin on her face as the dunes came at her quicker than she thought was possible on such a big, oddly-shaped creature.

When he reached the foot of the first dune, she grabbed the front post, just in case uphill on a camel was going to present problems but he flew up the slope with the same smooth gait.

Frodo crested the dune and descended the other side. Deirdre was having a wonderful time when suddenly the camel turned violently to the right. She shifted her weight, skillfully maintaining balance, and tried to straighten him out but he responded with a violent buck and spun wildly again to the right.

She lost contact with the saddle seat and, using the front post as a pivot, swung round so she was sitting on Frodo's neck. Managing a graceful jump, she landed on her feet and watched the camel run off over a dune and out of sight.

As she walked in his wake, she was exhilarated by the entire experience, blaming herself for the mishap, assuming she had done something wrong. *After all, there has to be a learning curve when changing species.*

She saw movement out of the corner of her left eye and turned to see two riders moving towards her between the dunes. Frodo must have spotted them and, being nervous under a strange rider, spooked.

Deirdre watched as a well-conditioned appaloosa with bright red speckles on his chest drew closer. The rider wore a beaded headband covered with colorful geometric figures. He was stocky with long, flowing black hair and a boyish face.

The other rider sat on a magnificent bay thoroughbred with a bright white star on its forehead. The way the horse strode out, Deirdre was sure it was a stallion. The rider was a small woman with blazing black eyes and brown skin that shone bronze in the desert sun. On her head was a grey fedora and she was wearing ancient army fatigues several sizes too big for her.

Each rider had multiple weapons—revolvers, knives, hatchets— hanging from their waists and saddles. Both wore Nations arm bands. They flanked her on either side.

"Hi, folks," Deirdre said with a smile. There was no response from the somber riders. "Well, I better go see where that camel took off to." She started walking but Fedora directed the bay into her path.

"That your camel?" Fedora asked.

"Yep." Deirdre thought it best to let these soldiers of the Nations think the camel was hers. Hussars never rode camels. If they didn't know she was a Hussar, she'd like to keep it that way. "Bastard threw me. You see that?"

"I saw it. Looked like you didn't know what you were doing," Fedora said with a smirk.

"Well, riding a camel is trickier than you might think." She tried again to walk on but again Fedora blocked her path by maneuvering her mount.

"Those are beautiful mocs," Fedora remarked. "The beading is special." She said this with a little more fire than one would expect in such a simple observation.

For Deirdre the danger quotient just shot up. "They are real nice. I traded a Bowie knife for them."

"You know who makes that design? Apaches." Her intense gaze told Deirdre this meeting had become a hostile confrontation. "We don't tend to trade real nice ones like that. We keep those for ourselves. One way to get them, of course, is to steal them. In a raid. A Hussar raid." She spat out *Hussar* as if saying the word disgusted her.

Fedora nodded to Headband who slipped off the appaloosa and walked toward Deirdre. "We'll be taking your sidearm," Fedora said, revealing a cocked revolver she'd been hiding behind the pommel of her saddle. She pointed it at Deirdre's head.

Headband was right next to her reaching for her handgun when Deirdre spun, slapped his arm away, slid behind him and threw her wiry arm around his neck.

She could feel an enormous explosion of strength from Headband's rock-hard body as he fought to free himself. She knew she couldn't hold him for long but already what she hoped for was accomplished.

Instead of dismounting and helping her associate, Fedora was trying to subdue her frothing stallion who was spooked by the wrestling match in front of him.

Deirdre released Headband and dove toward the stallion's hind quarters, her boot knife in her hand. The blade pierced the horse's rump, just deep enough to be painful but not so deep as to cause a serious injury; already she was calculating how valuable an animal like that would be. The horse bolted, Fedora now fighting to remain in the saddle.

Deirdre turned and saw Headband charging her, drawing his sidearm as he ran. She drew her revolver and fired. The round caught him in the right shoulder and he went down, dropping his gun in the sand. As he reached for the weapon, she leveled her revolver at his heart and thumbed back the hammer. She was readying the kill shot when something unexpected happened.

A thought rose up from the sea of her unconscious, like a whale breaching, and sent waves splattering into the secure, dry vessel of her mind, dampening the usual efficient process that had saved her so often. The thought was simple. *I shouldn't kill him if I don't have to.* A check, a restraint, a scruple. She paused as Headband grasped his gun and struggled to aim it, the shoulder wound limiting his movement. The sound of hooves pounding on sand drew her out of her thoughts. Fedora was charging, her horse now under her command, revolver at the ready.

Deirdre, holstering her weapon, sidestepped the stallion's charge, leapt up toward the rider, deflected Fedora's handgun, grabbed hold of her fatigues and, jerking backwards, successfully unhorsed her. They hit the desert floor with a thud. Neither moved for a moment, dazed by the impact as Headband struggled to level his handgun at Deirdre.

*****

Jube was first to notice Frodo appear riderless beyond the second dune. Within seconds he was on Danny, who was the closest mount. He was concerned that Deirdre might have hurt herself in a fall but that concern turned to anguish when a single gunshot rang out.

As soon as he reached the first dune, he grabbed Deirdre's Winchester from the saddle sheath, dismounted and scrambled up the sandy slope.

Reaching the crest, he spotted some movement on the desert floor; somebody was on the ground, struggling to get up. His heart in his throat, he raced along the crest. Soon he was able to see that there were two people on the ground. Deirdre was the one getting up. The other person, no more than a few feet away from her, was lying still so perhaps Deirdre would be all right.

Then he noticed a third person, about ten yards beyond Deirdre, a man with a headband rolling onto his stomach and pointing a handgun in her direction.

Jube dropped to one knee, worked the lever action and aimed. Never having killed a human being, he was scared, drenched in sweat and struggling to keep his hands steady.

Suddenly, Deirdre was between him and Headband, blocking his shot. She drew her weapon but rather than firing, she charged the fallen man with great urgency, trying to reach him before he fired. A shot rang out. Headband had managed to pull the trigger but missed. Deirdre was on top of him a second later pummeling him with the barrel of her revolver. Jube wondered why she hadn't fired.

*****

Siki felt the vision was vivid and unambiguous. It was one of the Mountain People who had visited her while she was unconscious. He spoke with piercing intensity. "Siki, you must follow the Hawk. The flow of the honey will be stopped."

He said this in Apache, a language she knew well. She took her heritage very seriously and was fluent in Mescalero-Chiricahua.

When Siki regained consciousness, she found herself looking into the face of a man of African descent. He was kneeling next to her, offering a sip out of a canteen.

Tied to a large boulder with the latigo from her own saddle, she took some water and looked around for Nacoma, the Comanche she'd been riding with. She spotted him propped up in a sitting position against the dune. His eyes were closed, but she could see him breathing.

When the African man spoke, there was kindness in his tone. "We can only spare this one canteen. I'll leave it with your friend. Hopefully he regains consciousness soon. His shoulder wound doesn't seem to be bleeding much. He may make it."

Siki noticed the woman standing on the slope of a dune. She knew with certainty now this was the one they'd been looking for, Crazy Hawk, and was just as sure this was the Hawk the Mountain Person in the vision told her to pursue.

"Let's go," Crazy Hawk barked at Gentle Boy, which is what Siki decided to call the lean black man who traveled with the Hussar. The man walked to Nacoma, leaned a canteen against his leg and climbed up the dune past the woman. Crazy Hawk followed. When she reached the crest, she looked back at Siki for a long moment and then descended the other side of the dune, out of sight.

That's one bad white girl, Siki thought. *But she left me alive. Big mistake.*

CHAPTER SEVENTEEN

Deirdre moved the thumbwheel of the binoculars ever so slightly, getting every degree of magnification possible out of the century-old piece of equipment. She was trying to determine if the dust cloud she saw in the lowlands around Ocotillo Wells was generated by multiple riders or a harmless dust devil kicked up by whirling winds.

The run-in with Fedora and Headband forced her to change her plans. No longer on her way to Tecate in pursuit of kidnappers, her destination now was home. It took two days to reach the beginning of the winding mountain trail that would take them up to the Warner Springs plateau and Hussar Valley.

On a rock outcropping a hundred feet above the desert floor she had excellent visual command over the area due east, the most direct route for pursuit. Until she spotted the dust cloud in question, she thought her group had time for a much-needed rest.

When she had returned to the camp from her ill-fated camel ride, all the travelers, except Frodo's owner, had moved on. There was a good chance no one would discover the two for a while. That meant Deirdre and her people would have hours to put rough terrain between themselves and a pursuit.

Frodo's owner retrieved the camel, gave Deirdre her book and guitar and was about to leave, but Deirdre offered him one more trade—a Hussar hunting knife for a jar of herbal medicine. She applied the medicine generously to the shallow wound on the rump of Fedora's bay. According to the Hussar law of spoils, the thoroughbred was now Deirdre's.

She put Francine on the appaloosa, turned the burro loose to join one of the wild herds and ponied the thoroughbred behind Danny, trusting Jube to pony Blue behind his mule. The caravan was on the trail by midmorning. They camped that night in a gulch close to Ocotillo Wells and were on the go again before dawn.

She studied the dust cloud as it moved toward her position. In the blink of an eye, it was gone. "Dust devil," she said.

"So have we made it?" The question came from a ledge below.

Deirdre looked down to where Jube stood peering out toward the vast stretch of desert.

"I think so," she answered as she hopped down to the lower ledge Jube was on. "If they're not even in sight, we should be all right. It's too much ground to cover before nightfall, even for indigenous. Anyway, we have to rest the animals."

She pointed toward the mountains towering to the west of their present position. "If we push up that grade with winded mounts, we'll have horses breaking down before we reach the plateau. They should be ready to go by nightfall. Danny knows the trail so well he can cover it at night with no problem. The others will follow."

"You're sure there's more than those two in the Nations patrol?"

"Their parties travel in groups of five to ten. They break up into detachments of two or three riders to cover more ground when they're searching for something. When the others find Fedora and Headband, they'll pursue."

Jube stared out at the long distance anybody chasing them would have to cover, his forehead wrinkling as he moved his upper teeth back and forth across his lower lip. "I'm not so sure," he said. "They must know by now they messed with the wrong woman. Maybe they don't want any more of you. They'll probably just continue with whatever mission they were on to begin with."

She shook her head. "They threw down on me right away, Jube. It was me they were looking for."

"Why?"

"I know why. Why now is what I'm lost on." She gnawed on a knuckle pensively for a moment. "All that happened three years ago. I thought they had let it pass."

She began to descend a slope toward a flat where Francine was tending to the animals.

"What happened three years ago?" Jube asked as he hurried to keep up.

Deirdre sighed, stopped walking when she reached the flat and turned toward him, her hands on her hips, her feet a little wider apart than usual as she prepared to tell him a tale she knew he wouldn't like.

"We were trying to get back to our valley with a herd of sheep when they hit us."

"They stole your sheep?"

"No. We had captured theirs."

It was Jube's turn to sigh.

"Anyway, we camped about a day out from home," she continued. "Didn't think there were enough Nations around to give pursuit. We were wrong." She started walking again toward the horses, Jube keeping up.

"They jumped us about midnight," she went on. "They took the sheep back, which is fair." She punctuated this last judgment with a philosophical shrug. "But we were gonna fight them, of course.

Firefight broke out. A big Apache named Dequan tried to blast Danny with buckshot. Mostly missed," she said wistfully, "but one lead pellet managed to land."

Jube nodded sympathetically. "His eye."

"Yep."

"So what did you do?" He sounded a little afraid of the answer.

She reached the horses, picked up a brush from a blanket and started grooming Danny. "It took a while for Dan to get right." She kissed Danny on the shoulder. "You worry about infection with a wound like that. But pretty soon he was fine, a better trail horse than most two-eyed horses."

Another kiss, this time on Danny's neck. She turned toward Jube wearing her most intense no-nonsense expression. "Then I went looking for Dequan."

Jube rubbed his face with both hands. "Oh, boy."

"I heard he was in Laughlin," she said, "which is an open trade town. Confronted him on the main street."

She paused. Jube shuffled his feet.

"Shot him through the right eye," she said, "which was just."

Jube stood stunned for a moment before he spoke. "Wow."

"He was carrying a rifle so he had a fair chance." She tossed the brush aside. "I was just faster than him." She squatted down onto her saddle which was lying on the ground a few feet from Danny. "But it gave me a bad rep among the Nations. They're the ones that saddled me with that damn nickname. It was really based on a confusion. My tribe uses the names of raptors for rank. The highest-ranking Hussar is Eagle. The next highest rank is Falcon and so on. I was only a Kestrel then, so it really wasn't an accurate nickname. I am a Hawk now, however, so I guess it works." She flicked her hand in the air to signify acceptance of the situation. "Anyway, that's how I got that name."

"That explains the hawk part," he said with unveiled sarcasm. "I think I can guess why they added crazy."

"Danny's my Soul Horse," she said, standing up and facing him directly. She wanted this point to be crystal clear. "When you learn more about my people, you'll understand what that means."

She picked up a canteen and took a long swig. "Anyway, it turns out Dequan was a captain in their army and very well connected. Cousin of one of their important leaders. They were pretty pissed." Her tone had become surprisingly regretful. "Messy business."

She squinted at a grouping of hills about two miles to the north.

"Huh," she said.

"What is it?" Jube asked.

"They could advance a long way without us seeing them if they used those hills as a screen." She looked back toward the open desert. "But to get behind them they'd have to go out of their way. I don't think they'd spend the time on a maneuver like that. I'm betting the rest of the patrol didn't discover those two until late in the day yesterday. Or maybe not even till this morning."

"So, you believe the rest of the patrol searched for them?" Jube asked.

"Oh, yeah," she said with a hard nod. "They take care of their own."

"Good," he said with a relieved exhale. "I'd hate to think of those two out there just rotting."

Deirdre shook her head in amazement. "You're a strange one, Jube."

*****

Siki watched as Crazy Hawk and Gentle Boy moved off the rocky hillside and disappeared from view. She stood behind a manzanita, peering through the branches, no more than a mile north of her quarry's position.

She put her binoculars in the pocket of her cargo pants and walked back towards a viewpoint that looked over the plain north of the hills. She could see dust being kicked up by the rest of the party as they followed her tracks. They'd catch up with her by nightfall.

It had taken Siki almost two hours to work the latigo up the boulder to a position that allowed her to push up with her legs and jerk her hands loose. Once free, she checked on Nacoma's shoulder wound. Gentle Boy was right. The bullet was still in his shoulder, but it hadn't hit a major artery, keeping the blood loss to a minimum. He was conscious enough to gulp down some water from the canteen but very weak.

Promising Nacoma she'd be back for him as soon as possible, she began walking south toward the prearranged meeting place where the various units, Nations and white, were to rendezvous after they searched their assigned area. She knew that when she and Nacoma didn't show the group would head in her direction. About an hour into her hike, she saw riders coming her way.

When Siki told the others what had happened, Carlyle wanted to go directly after Deirdre. Siki pointed out that if they did that, Crazy Hawk would see them coming miles away. She suggested using the northern hills as cover and taking them by surprise if they decided to rest. Carlyle resisted at first but eventually gave in.

Siki rode on ahead as the advance scout. The others came at a slower pace, swapping out mounts from the horse reserve from time to time.

One soldier was assigned to care for Nacoma. That meant the group riding toward Siki consisted of two indigenous and four whites — seven guns total including hers. The Hawk would be dead by morning.

Deirdre sat in the darkness, watching Jube's shadowy movements as he finished saddling his mule. The run-in with the soldiers of the Nations had changed everything. Now she was bringing her lover home with her, a lover who didn't like guns, disapproved of raiders and fretted about the suffering of the people who tried to kill her.

Jube tested the rigging with a jerk and turned toward Deirdre. "That ought to do it."

She nodded and called into the darkness. "Francine, you ready?"

"Yo." The youthful voice came out of the dark, a little uphill from Deirdre and Jube.

Deirdre walked up to the remains of the fire they had built to cook bacon and began spreading the last fading embers with her foot.

"Don't forget your hat," Jube said.

She turned to see him enter the last bit of light cast by the dying fire, holding out her cap, a sweet smile on his face. Suddenly, he grabbed his left shoulder, his face contorted in terror.

A moment later a rifle report exploded the quiet of the night, the bullet having hit its target before the sound of the shot reached their ears. He collapsed into her arms. She felt inside his shirt. A wound about four inches above the left nipple was spurting blood.

Since she'd met Jube, Deirdre had dealt with many exotic, new feelings. Now, as she looked into his frightened eyes, her emotions were all too familiar.

CHAPTER EIGHTEEN

Henry Ketchell sat on the back verandah of his bungalow, hypnotized by the rippling waves of the Sea of Cortez. He wanted to stay just where he was, on the outskirts of Puerto Penasco, forever. Warm weather, tequila, a seafront home and a couple of beautiful young mistresses. Heaven on earth. He poured himself another drink, took a bite of a taco and downed the shot.

"Good tacos," he said to the woman who had been cleaning inside and was now tidying up the verandah. "I can't leave good tacos out of any description of paradise."

The woman, Nancy, fifty-something and pleasantly plump, gazed at him, unsure how to respond.

"Buenos tacos," he said.

She silently returned to her work.

There was a knock on the front door. He dragged his big frame out of the chair, entered the bungalow through a sliding door, made his way across the living room and opened the front door. Standing on the verandah was his right-hand man, Manny Cepeda, mid-thirties, stocky, with a well-kept handle bar mustache that gave personality to an otherwise mundane face.

"Some guys from La República are here to see you," Manny said, his English strong, his Spanish accent stronger. "They look like they're officials of some kind."

"Federales?" Ketchell asked.

"I don't think they're called that anymore."

"Well, invite them in. I'll open a new bottle."

He grabbed a bottle of Tequila off the island separating the kitchen from the living room and walked out onto the verandah. He looked out at the sea with the bottle dangling between two of his thick, hairy fingers and wondered what they wanted.

La República de Baja de California controlled much of Southern Pacifica and the Baja peninsula. They were particularly strong on the west shore of the Gulf of California which Ketchell stubbornly called the Sea of Cortez.

La República capitol in La Paz was full of honest leaders known for their integrity. He avoided them like the plague. It was the regional governors, mayors and federales, or whatever they were called, who were susceptible to his bribes.

Under their permission, he'd set up a fuel dump outside Puerto Penasco, well protected by armored cars and tanks. He controlled over seventy-five percent of the fossil fuel in República territory, making him the most powerful man in the region. He knew his position depended on the whimsy of his employers up north, the people who had financed his operation from the beginning, but so far he'd been able to satisfy their various odd demands.

Ketchell guessed these visitors wanted a bigger piece of the action. He was curious as to what they had to offer.

There was another knock.

"Come in," he bellowed.

The door opened and several sets of footsteps approached. He turned and was genuinely surprised by what he saw.

Three timid-looking dirt farmers stood before him. Only faded, century old police uniforms spoke of any position of authority. Behind them stood Manny. "They say they are Federales. My mistake," he said.

Ketchell hid the Tequila behind his leg. No need to waste good liquor on such as these. "How can I help you gentlemen?" Ketchell asked in pidgin Spanish.

A tall man with a pock marked face stepped forward, presumably the leader of the Federales. "We have brought you something, Señor Ketchel," he said with bowed head.

"What have you brought me?" Ketchell was already impatient. He liked subservience but not if it wasted his time.

"A body."

Ketchell threw a questioning look at Manny who shook his head to show he didn't get it either.

"I don't understand," Ketchell said, his impatience growing. "Whose body?"

"We don't know. It's wrapped in a sheet of canvas. We were told it would be of great value to you, sir. For your eyes only."

"Who told you that?"

"Vaqueros."

"Vaqueros delivered you a corpse and told you I'd find it to be of great value?" Ketchell was now very interested.

"Yes."

Ketchell smiled at Manny. "You know who this is, don't you?"

Manny nodded. "Carlyle got his girl."

Ketchell dropped the bottle onto a chair cushion and followed the visitors through the bungalow out onto the front verandah where he saw a dilapidated pickup wagon pulled by two burros parked by the porch steps. On the flatbed was something rolled up in a canvas. The stench of a rotting corpse did nothing to dampen Ketchell's enthusiasm.

"Manny, get up there and roll it out for me."

Manny climbed onto the flatbed as Ketchell walked to the back of the wagon and opened the tail gate. Manny pulled up aggressively on the canvas.

Ketchell watched the body as it slammed to the earth at his feet. He stared at the dead face for a moment before he recognized the gaunt, severe features of Tom Carlyle.

CHAPTER NINETEEN

Report on the Investigation into the Activities of Hawk Deirdre Buford for the last nine months of Hussar year 98 and the first four months of Hussar year 99 by Falcon Margaret Hensley. Upon approval by the Grand Scribe, this report is to be appended to the Hussar Chronicles Supplemental Material.

The data included here comes from the testimony of Deirdre herself; a young girl, Francine, who witnessed some of Deirdre's deeds; and several traders and travelers who brought us reports of her activities.

On March 18th of the year 98, Mindy Buford, age fourteen, a Raider Trainee and Deirdre's sister did not return from morning rim patrol. A search party discovered signs that she was taken by six to ten riders.

Eagle Haller thought the kidnapping might be a precursor to a larger invasion and, with Griffin Squadron absent, refused to commit a force for a rescue expedition.

Deirdre was leading a raid on La República with Griffin Squadron at the time. When she returned, she immediately planned a pursuit of the kidnappers with her Squadron. Eagle Haller would not approve this. The Eagle pronounced Mindy a casualty of war, to be mourned as any other deceased Hussar and *forbade depleting the Valley forces for an extensive rescue mission. Deirdre requested permission to search for her sister by herself.*

After much debate in an open forum, Haller permitted Deirdre a one-month search under the provision she did not antagonize other tribes, particularly the Nations, reminding her she was still on probation for taking revenge on the Nations Captain, Dequan, an act considered illegal by Hussar leadership.

To no one's surprise, she did not return by the deadline. There was talk of disciplinary action, even banishment, but word drifted into camp of heroic deeds she performed while rescuing children kidnapped from different tribes and villages.

This built up goodwill among various peoples toward Deirdre and, by association, the Hussars, and goodwill was something we certainly needed after some of our people got out of control on the raid against the Riverside County Urbs. The details of the now infamous Hemet Massacre can be read elsewhere.

Deirdre may have been welcomed home as a hero if not for another unfortunate run-in with soldiers of the Nations. It appears that the mysterious kidnappings are being done by one entity. That entity decided to punish Deirdre for her interference and recruited help from the Nations. They probably agreed to participate because it allowed them an opportunity to avenge the killing of Dequan.

Deirdre was confronted by two of them, who she subdued but refrained from killing, a remarkable display of restraint considering what we know about the temperament of this ferocious fighter.

She attempted to make her way back to the Valley without further conflict. However, she and her two companions were ambushed west of Ocotillo Wells. One of her traveling companions, a man named Jube, was seriously wounded.

According to Francine, Deirdre went berserk because she has a romantic tie with Jube and accomplished a remarkable one-woman counterattack against heavy fire. She killed one of her pursuers, a mercenary named Tom Carlyle, and wounded several more, including two soldiers of the Nations.

She also captured a mercenary, interrogated him, Hussar-style, and received the following information.

1. *He was hired by Carlyle.*
2. *Carlyle's mission was to kill Deirdre and deliver her corpse to a man named Ketchell, who has a massive fuel dump on the east shore of the Gulf of California.*
3. *Ketchell is the organizer of the kidnappings, and he ships the children somewhere up north once they are under his control.*

Deirdre, well known for her dark sense of humor, sent Carlyle's corpse to Ketchell via our allies, the Vaqueros. She then returned to Hussar Valley with her wounded friend, Jube, and Francine, whom she recommended as a prospective Hussar.

Since arriving back in camp, Deirdre has dedicated herself exclusively to caring for Jube as he fights for his life. She also lobbied the forum to support a strike against Ketchell's base. This has been rejected as a suicide mission; that fuel dump is known to be fortified by heavy artillery, armored cars and tanks. Besides, the man she interrogated said the children had been shipped north. In all probability her sister isn't with Ketchell.

What disciplinary action should be taken against her has been debated since her return. One group wants to let her slide since her adventures were not without a certain nobility and even produced some positive results. They argue that she improved our image among many peoples. She showed unusual restraint in dealing with the People of the Nations, at least until her friend was wounded. It would have been against every Hussar norm if she hadn't retaliated against such an ambush.

In addition, she brought back a book, a collection of sayings by the Greek philosopher Epictetus. The Grand Scribe has identified this volume as a valuable addition to our Wisdom collection, something for which all Hussars are grateful.

But another powerful group argues that she is a loose cannon, out of control and dangerous. In their view, she neglected her duties as leader of Griffin Squadron for a year, endangering the security of the Valley for the sake of her sister. Choosing family over tribe is a clear violation of the Code of Lauren.

It remains to be seen what actions will be taken against her, if any. The problem may sort itself out. Those who have spoken with her feel she will again set out to find her sister as soon as the issue of Jube's health has been resolved. Popular consensus is that the Spirits will take him soon. If, at that time, she leaves on another rescue expedition, she will do so without Eagle Haller's permission. This disobedience will undoubtedly trigger her banishment.

CHAPTER TWENTY

Ten heavy machine guns strategically placed at different points on the hundred-and-fifty-foot vessel's bulwark had transformed the factory ship into a massive gunboat.

It'd been a long time since anyone had been able to use the abandoned war vessels that floated aimlessly through the seas, so no one had a naval presence in the Pacific. Ketchell's employers reasoned any display of power would allow them to dominate sea trade and armed this relic from a once thriving fishing industry. It usually sat in the San Francisco harbor, a threat to all competition. When it arrived in Puerto Penasco to pick him up, Ketchell knew his employers were not pleased with his work.

As the ship cruised into San Francisco Bay, he leaned on the balustrade admiring the surroundings. His goal was to enjoy one night in the big city before he headed east.

This thought cheered him up. These excursions north to explain how he was spending the gold given him by the Bees were not pleasant experiences in the best of times. This trip was going to be unusually nasty. The experiments being done with the children were considered of the utmost importance to one powerful faction of the Bees and Ketchell's failure to deliver enough youngsters in a timely fashion was going to have consequences.

He watched as the remains of the once-great metropolis of San Francisco neared. Unlike other destroyed 21st-century cities, San Francisco had retained a personality. It had restaurants, bars, brothels, libraries, parks and even some active office buildings, all bunched around the remains of Fisherman's Wharf.

The rest of the city consisted of bombed-out rubble occupied by violent gangs, but the well-armed San Francisco Constabulary managed to maintain some semblance of order.

Ketchell was anxious to have one night of escapist sensuality in what was left of the City by the Bay. He remembered meeting a blue-eyed bar girl last year who'd perched ever so lightly on his lap for hours. Her rakish smile and the playful way she took his gold were a dear memory for him. He struggled to remember her name. *Yvonne. I think.*

Any hope of escaping into the arms of that young beauty was shattered when he saw a well-maintained helicopter sitting on a wharf. There were probably only five working choppers in all Pacifica and the Bees controlled three of them. About a dozen people were waiting for the arrival of his vessel. Henry searched for a recognizable face. He found what he was looking for.

"Henry, so good to see you," the brown-haired white woman said, extending her hand toward him as he debarked.

"Hello, Major Parelli," he said, taking her hand with a gracious little bow. "I didn't expect such a greeting."

"Well, we're anxious to get a full report. By the way, I've been promoted," she said with a smug smile. "It's Colonel Parelli now."

"Congratulations, Colonel."

She sauntered toward the helicopter. "How was your trip?"

"Fair," he said as he walked adjacent to her. "I hate boats but traveling on a big one like this wasn't so bad."

"Good." She gestured with a tilt of her head toward the helicopter. "How do you feel about these?"

"I guess I'm going to find out."

She flashed a playful grin, enjoying his discomfort. "A virgin? You've never been in the air at all?"

"A hot air balloon when I was a kid."

"This is much more exciting."

"That's what I'm afraid of."

She laughed, displaying more warmth than he expected. Ketchell was accustomed to watching this handsome woman stand with rock-like rigidity over Commandant Walker's shoulder.

The helicopter flight was horrifying. The pilot, a black woman, no more than twenty-five, was so relaxed as to seem indifferent. He refrained from screaming by focusing on the calm demonstrated by the two young women in front of him. *They have total confidence. Either they're idiots or this is relatively safe. God, I hope I don't crap myself.*

He got his mind off his discomfort by observing the land beneath. There were small towns that nature had reclaimed, recognizable only by the occasional church steeple or industrial chimney poking out of the foliage. They flew over some active settlements that appeared to be thriving, perhaps shells of what they once were, but quite lively nonetheless. Several large well-cultivated fields were evidence of disciplined farming in full sway.

Bombed-out tanks and trucks were strewn along every roadside, remnants of the long fight for supremacy that marked the decades after the Breakdown. Most of the traffic consisted of wagons drawn by some beast or other. He saw a couple of fossil fuel powered vehicles maneuvering around horses, mules, oxen and donkeys.

Ketchell was struck by how far he could see in any direction and was impressed with the natural beauty of this area. His travels throughout the west had allowed him to experience the healing of the environment triggered by the obliteration of the industrial world. Air pollution had disappeared almost completely and the forests, wildlife, rivers and lakes were making an astounding recovery from centuries of exploitation.

This area of Pacifica was no exception with its crystal-clear horizon and the glistening blue lakes. That all changed when he spotted a yellow cloud to the east—they were approaching the Hive.

The Bees dedicated a good portion of their resources to suppressing detailed knowledge of their operations. A five-mile no man's land around the perimeter of the Hive, patrolled by a fleet of armored vehicles, kept people from getting too close.

They'd been successful in hiding the extent of their realm. Until this flight, Ketchell had no idea of the size of the operation. He wondered if that's why he was given this helicopter ride, to teach him how powerful his bosses were.

After clearing five oil refineries, they passed over dozens of block-shaped buildings, some with billowing smokestacks. Ketchell surmised these were factories. As they approached the center of the Hive, he was impressed with the elegant skyline of sleek administrative buildings mixed in with tastefully designed housing complexes.

They landed on top of the tallest structure, a ten-story concrete building which Ketchell recognized from his previous visits as the Security Center. It dominated the Hive's skyline, no other building being higher than four stories. When he debarked, he was met by armed guards who gestured for him to follow them towards a staircase that led down to an elevator.

In a few minutes, he was sitting in Commandant Walker's spacious office. Wood floors, wallpaper covered with an eye-popping geometric pattern and a behemoth-sized mahogany desk gave the room an opulent feel from another time.

A door to Ketchell's left opened and the rock-jawed Walker entered. He sat behind the desk without acknowledging Ketchell's presence, offering none of the usual polite greetings. As phony as those pleasantries had been in the past, Ketchell missed them; they were comforting.

The Commandant perused some paperwork, his bushy blond hair looking casually unkempt, a style Ketchell was sure he affected to appear less vain. It wasn't a successful ploy. His vanity was the one characteristic Ketchell always noticed.

Today, the thirty-something had dressed his muscular torso in a tightfitting red pullover shirt. It looked like what a space captain might have worn in a 20th-century sci-fi movie.

Walker looked up and focused on Ketchell's eyes. When he spoke, his deep voice was melodious.

"So, tell me about Crazy Hawk."

Ketchell couldn't conceal his surprise; his eyes widened a bit, his jaw slacked slightly.

The Commandant smiled, his oddly white teeth in sharp contrast to his bronze tan. "You thought we hadn't heard about her, Henry? The talk of every little podunk town in Pacifica and Old Arizona? You're not the only associate we have in those parts."

Ketchell regrouped quickly. "She's a—"

"Hussar," Walker said, finishing Ketchell's sentence. "Mid-twenties, a superbly effective fighter. We have the outline already, Henry. What I want from you is detail, context, understanding. I need to know why she was able to disrupt your operations so thoroughly you couldn't fill our order. Is she Superwoman?"

Ketchell paused as his mind scrambled into damage control mode. "I had the wrong people on the case. I'm going to take personal charge next time around."

"Really?" The Commandant wore a bemused frown. "You think we're going to depend on you again for this? You haven't answered my question. Is she Superwoman?"

Ketchell eyed Walker carefully, trying to spot a note of whimsy.

This had to be a joke. He allowed himself a little chuckle. "No. I don't think she's Superwoman."

"The children we asked you to collect. What do you think we need them for?"

Ketchell was conscious of his breath quickening, a sign of fear he didn't like projecting, but at this point there wasn't much he could do about it. "I know it has something to do with genetics."

"Yes." Walker pressed his lips against the knuckles of the fist he held in front of his face. He let the fist drop with a thud onto his desk. "We use them in a controlled experiment. We're trying to determine if the human race is on the verge of something very exciting."

"Like an evolutionary breakthrough?" Ketchell was winging it now.

"Our geneticists call it a Post-Breakdown Resurgence."

Ketchell could feel a bead of sweat break away from his armpit and run down his side. "So, you're asking if I think Crazy Hawk is an example of that?"

Walker's preposterously white teeth appeared ghoul-like as they bulged out of a forced smile. "Henry, did you know she confronted an Apache captain, Dequan, in a town square?"

Ketchell bobbed his head slightly. "I heard something about that."

"The Hussars converted their revolvers into cap and ball technology," Walker continued, "because they believe if they lose the capacity to make cartridges, they can still defend themselves as long as they can make black powder. A sound theory in these times when supplies are so limited, but there's a problem. That type of handgun is notoriously inaccurate and unreliable. And yet that's what Crazy Hawk armed herself with when she called out Dequan. It was like a duel out of some old western."

Walker stood up and paced behind his desk, his usual stolid face taut with anxiety. Ketchell had never seen him so vulnerable.

"We've talked to witnesses who say he had his rifle cocked in hand before she made a move," the Commandant said as he leaned on the back of his chair, his cold blue eyes locked on Ketchell. "She drew, fired once and hit him square in the right eye. In spite of what happens in those movies, that's very difficult to do, especially with that weapon. Lucky shot?"

Ketchell wasn't sure if the question was rhetorical. He decided a nod was the safest response.

Walker shook his head forcefully. "When I first heard about it, I dismissed it that way. Then a report came in explaining she was on a revenge mission for a wound Dequan gave her horse. A wound to the right eye. A literal eye for an eye sort of thing," he said, his voice swelling in admiration. "A truly remarkable shot. As more data comes in about her adventures, we're beginning to wonder if she isn't something special, unique. We've of course done tests on her sister. Some of those results have been intriguing."

Ketchell smiled. "Yes. I think Crazy Hawk is Superwoman."

Walker laughed. "Of course, if she is, your failure is less egregious. You're quite the survivor, Henry. I admire that. I really do."

He walked around the desk so that he was standing behind Ketchell and put his hands on the big man's shoulders. Ketchell's anxiety level shot up even higher as he recognized this physical contact as a message, a reminder that his fate was in those hands.

"Right now, a squad of our best advisors are headed south to organize an attack on Hussar Valley," Walker explained. "Enlisting enthusiastic allies will be no problem. We'll offer some wonderful gifts and we'll have our pick of tribes. They all hate the Hussars and their raiding ways."

Walker removed his hands from Ketchell and walked back around the desk to his chair.

"We have reason to believe she's back home," Walker said, plopping himself into his chair. "If we can strike quickly enough, we may be able to take her captive. You have been around her, haven't you, Henry?"

"I saw her in Wilcox on several occasions." Ketchell's nerves began to calm. They needed him for something. He wouldn't die that day in the Hive.

"So, you'd be able to make a positive identification?" Walker asked.

"Absolutely."

"We'll transport you south as quickly as possible." The Commandant was suddenly all business, a utilitarian vibe replacing his earlier threatening tone. "You'll rendezvous with our people and be ready to pick her out when the time comes. Once you have her in custody, bring her back here."

Ketchell tilted his head and furrowed his brow to communicate he perceived a problem.

"What is it, Henry?" Walker barked.

"Whether she's a bona fide Superwoman or just one very deadly fighter, she's going be a tough capture."

"Perhaps, but it is Leader's fondest wish that she be taken alive." Then with an indifference that surprised Ketchell the Commandant said, "Our people have orders to do their best to capture her. If that proves impossible, they'll kill her. Either way, she will be eliminated as a threat to our operation."

CHAPTER TWENTY-ONE

Francine's appraisal of Hussar Valley had been, at first, a simple one—paradise. When she rode in that first morning, the last remnant of a spring snow could be seen clinging to survival under the shade of a few towering oaks. The sun peeking over the eastern rim warmed Francine just enough to allow her to concentrate on the beauty of this perfectly proportioned valley tucked away at about 4000 feet elevation amidst the southern peaks of the San Jacinto Mountain Range.

In the two months since she'd arrived, Francine had experienced in detail what made up that first glorious impression. The rolling floor of the valley was covered with a balanced blend of greasewood, conifer, oak, redshank, sumac and sagebrush. In places this foliage was so thick it was impossible to ride through without a cut trail. Other areas were open expanses of fields used for livestock or crops like alfalfa for the horses and grapes for the famous Hussar wine.

She particularly loved the paintings that adorned the many huge boulders so common in the valley. Most were images of wild animals; raptors, bobcats, mountain lions, deer, wolves, raccoons, snakes and foxes. Occasionally she discovered a tableau of raiders in combat.

The Hussar camp was on the east end of the valley where tactically placed earth ramparts protected about a two square mile expanse of rolling hills that were dotted by tents, wigwams, yurts, teepees and other forms of portable protection from the elements.

The Hussars saw the valley as their home. Deirdre explained to Francine that twice in their history they'd been driven out by overwhelming force. Both times they were able to flee with most of their possessions and plenty of supplies because they were always one hard ride away from being a fierce mobile army, ready to counterattack as soon as the invaders of their beloved homeland let down their guard.

On both occasions they won back their land and were unforgiving in punishing the invaders, hanging all they captured. This part of their history led to the commonly accepted wisdom that their survival depended on their mobility. A couple of decades of relative security had eroded this conviction. As she explored the camp, Francine was surprised to find the occasional permanent structure tucked into a grove or behind some of the enormous boulder formations.

Public buildings had been constructed in the last decade, including a clinic and the Eagle Mansion, a large wood frame building inhabited by whoever was serving as Eagle, the highest Hussar rank.

This taste of creature comfort led to a desire for electric power. Windmills were built, captured solar panels were placed around the hills, and the Hussar's resident technical genius, Pablo Jones, developed a method to store enough energy to power a primitive electric grid.

All these developments launched a rancorous debate within the tribe. Two parties formed, the Nomads versus the Homesteaders.

Deirdre was an inflexible Nomad. She felt the building of permanent structures was not only a threat to their mobility but a step toward a shallow materialism that would make them weak and susceptible to collapse. Deirdre explained to Francine that an ideological mainstay of the Nomad argument was that the pre-Breakdown people had lost touch with the elemental—the primeval and inescapable character of nature, including human nature.

Francine's most difficult challenge was the Hussar training. No one questioned Deirdre's opinion that "this kid might make a Hussar," and the young girl was thrown into the grueling process after one good night's sleep.

Her assigned tutor was Frank Gonzalez, a twenty-four-year-old raider who had known Deirdre since they were kids. The first thing he told Francine was that the appaloosa she rode in on was now her Soul Horse. When not doing other chores, her every waking hour was to be spent caring for that animal, and part of the evaluation of whether she was Hussar material would depend on the degree of harmony developed between her and her Soul Horse.

Francine was appalled. The appaloosa, who Deirdre had named Tank because of his stocky build, had tried to buck her off repeatedly on the ride to the valley. She couldn't wait to get off the beast. Now this mean-spirited, green bronc was supposed to be her Soul Horse!

She was issued an ancient bolt action rifle. The Hussar gunsmiths had renovated it into a trusty weapon. She was taught how to make black powder and how to load her own cartridges. She was expected to clean the rifle every day, whether she fired it or not.

To Frank's surprise, she was an excellent shot, on target seventy percent at seventy-five yards in her first attempt. Soon she was at ninety-five percent, a real natural.

The physical training was grueling. Long runs through the valley, climbing cliff faces at speed, handling one-hundred-pound hay bales. Her poor performance in most of these endeavors had convinced her she was not Hussar material.

Every morning at daybreak, she had to show up at the library, a brick building from a previous age packed full of old books brought back from countless Hussar raids.

The Grand Scribe, Jeannie Citino, tested Francine's reading acumen, literacy being an essential requirement for becoming a Hussar. Each morning Francine was expected to read several pages aloud and copy long paragraphs onto a chalkboard. Handwriting was a lost art even before the Breakdown, and the Grand Scribe was dedicated to reviving it.

Jeannie also would conduct lengthy discussions on the importance of having an "interior life", a concept Hussars believed essential to "becoming who you are". Whether it was communing with the Universe through the Spirits, meditating, studying a mystical guide from the past or reading more demanding philosophical works, developing a reflective nature was an essential part of a young Hussar's education.

The library prominently displayed two quotes carved into dark wooden plaques, highlighted with yellow paint. One hung over the front door on the exterior wall, impossible to miss by anyone entering. It read *Amor Fati*. Francine learned that was Latin for "love of fate", a concept central to Hussar doctrine.

The second plaque hung over the same door but on the interior wall and could be seen by anyone exiting the building. *Happiness is no easy matter: it is very difficult to find it in ourselves and impossible to find it elsewhere. Chamfort.*

The ever-inquisitive Francine found a short biography of Chamfort in an old encyclopedia and challenged Jeannie as to "why we're listening to this loser?" He was a French Revolutionary who got into trouble with the men running the Reign of Terror. When threatened with arrest, he shot himself in the face with a pistol in a botched suicide attempt. He spent the last few months of his life in agony with half his face blown off.

When Francine finished reciting these facts, she thought she had exposed a serious fault in Hussar thinking. But Jeannie just smiled and said, "Proves his point, doesn't it?"

An essential feature of Hussar education was the Wisdom Book. After being assigned a book, a young trainee was expected to study it regularly until she was twenty-one.

Picking which books in the Hussar library qualified as a Wisdom Book was one of the most demanding responsibilities of the Grand Scribe. Francine learned from Jeannie that each volume had to simultaneously reinforce a martial worldview as well as a reflective way of thinking. Of course, the selection was limited to the books time and Fate brought into their library.

Some of the more popular titles were *The Meditations of Marcus Aurelius*, written when the Roman Emperor was on a military campaign; biographies of both Richard Coeur De Lion and Saladin, ferocious warriors with deep spiritual commitments; *Beowulf*; novels by Mary Renault and Rebecca Roanhorse; Plutarch's *Lives*; various works of Samurai wisdom; a retelling of a Norse myth by A.S. Byatt and two books by Xenophon, *Cyropaedia* and *Anabasis*.

Francine made a serious effort to have her Harry Potter book included. Jeannie was amused by Francine's argument in favor of the martial and spiritual value of Harry's odyssey but remained unconvinced. Francine was also taught how to interpret a Wisdom Book through the truth of the Code of Lauren. The Code was composed by Lauren Rodriguez, founder of the Hussars, the first Eagle, a great soldier and a wise lawgiver. All Hussars were to memorize the maxims in the Code and live by them.

Francine did not find all of the initiation process hard work. Art was big with the tribe, and she was expected to learn to draw, an activity she adored. A level of competence with one of the musical instruments that could be heard being played throughout the day from different corners of the valley was also required. She had a choice of bugle, guitar or flute. She chose the flute and couldn't wait each day to practice with this rustic wood instrument.

The feature of her new society that fascinated Francine most was the Hussars' ability to communicate with the Spirits. Reference to them was as commonplace as talk of the weather. They believed the Spirits influenced every aspect of their lives and were always present. Frank told her that if she didn't experience them, she wasn't "listening to the Universe".

Meals would be left out for the Spirits, who were evidently particularly fond of hard-boiled eggs. One evening, she saw a coyote eating one of the eggs and mentioned this to Frank.

"Yeah," Frank said, "they'll come in many forms."

The Hussars believed one of the blessings of the Breakdown was that there were now fewer material objects standing between the heart of humankind and the spiritual essence of nature. Francine loved all of this, and when a Spirit in the form of a robin built a nest in a tree next to her tent, she felt very much in touch with the Universe.

CHAPTER TWENTY-TWO

The man asleep next to her groaned; he did that a lot. *The wound must be bothering him more than he lets on,* Deirdre thought.

She meditated on the beauty of his bare back, the taut muscles rippling the dark brown skin, and wondered at the mysterious machinations of Fate. How could a meeting on the trail lead to her finding her soulmate? The philosopher in her struggled to explain it.

A book called the *Tale of Genji* drifted into the Hussar library when she was twelve. She spent weeks reading it during every spare moment, taking advantage of the moonlight on occasion to stay up all night relishing a book that seemed to celebrate moonlight on every page.

This eight-hundred-page novel, over a thousand years old, portrayed a society so exotic and different that it read like a fantasy. However, according to the scholarly introduction, it was a realistic portrayal of 10th-century Japan written by a woman called Lady Murasaki.

Deirdre loved the world presented in the book so much she even begged the Grand Scribe to let her keep it as her Wisdom Book. The Scribe argued that Lady Murasaki didn't have a martial bone in her body and that all Hussar Wisdom Books were required to have a military dimension.

Reluctantly, Deirdre returned the book to the library and adopted a collection of Chinese and Japanese epigrams related to the philosophical and spiritual foundation necessary to become a supreme warrior. That, in fact, was the title of the anthology — *Supreme Warrior: Martial Truths From Eastern Philosophy* by Nicole Karr. Karr was one of the last heroes of the old American Marines, having won the Congressional Medal of Honor in the Second American Civil War. She published this compendium of Taoist, Zen, Confucianist and Samurai wisdom in 2042. It was the perfect volume to reinforce in Deirdre the martial philosophy necessary to be a good soldier.

But elements of Lady Murasaki's worldview never left her, like the idea that when two people meet, and a strong aversion or bond grows between them quickly and inexplicably, it's because they knew each other in a previous life.

Perhaps that meeting on the high chaparral of Southern Arizona revived long-dormant feelings their souls had carried from one life to the next. Deirdre wondered what their relationship might have been in an earlier incarnation. Perhaps they were lovers or brothers, sister and brother or mother and daughter. She smiled as she speculated who would have been the mother.

Deep in sleep, Jube let out a snarling snore, his back heaving as he grabbed a breath. *How wonderful it is to watch him breathe.* She feared she had lost him when he was shot. Now she was convinced he had made it through the worst.

She heard a young voice coming from outside saying, "I have a treat for you, Danny."

Exiting the tent into the morning sun, Deirdre saw Francine

squatting next to Danny who was lying in the grass, his front legs curled up against his chest, his back legs spread loosely onto the grass as the twelve-year-old fed him slices of a chopped-up carrot.

"You're not supposed to give the horses human food," Deirdre said. "Besides, if you want to spoil a horse, it should be Tank."

"Tank hates me," Francine said bitterly as she continued to feed Danny.

"All the more reason you should be spending time with him." Deirdre knew she was coming off like a scold, but the kid irritated her.

"Let the girl feed your horse," a husky voice barked from behind Deirdre.

Deirdre turned to see her father sitting in front of his teepee on a lounge chair he'd captured on the last raid. His red beard blazed in the sun's morning blush.

Deirdre directed a frown toward him. "You gave the kid the carrot, I presume."

He grinned.

Francine traced the line of Danny's haunches with her hand. "It's so great that Danny likes to sleep by your tent."

Deirdre sat down next to the young girl. "He's my Soul Horse."

"Everybody has a Soul Horse but Danny's the only one who wouldn't rather spend the night with the other horses," Francine said with tender admiration.

"Danny and me have been through a lot."

"Danny and I."

Deirdre laughed and looked back at her father. "Listen to her correcting my grammar."

"Jeannie says I'm her best student," Francine said, her braggadocio knowing no bounds. "I passed the reading proficiency test with the highest grade."

"Have you picked your Wisdom Book yet?" Deirdre asked. "She's never gonna let you use that Harvey the Sorcerer thing."

"We'll see," Francine said softly and then corrected Deirdre with a smirk. "It's Harry, not Harvey."

"Francine!" A male voice coming from a distance pierced through the morning air.

Deirdre gestured toward a hillock where Francine's tent sat. "Frank's looking for you. You best go."

Francine walked away with drooped shoulders and flopping arms.

Deirdre waited till she was out of earshot. "I don't know what's gonna happen to that kid," she said as she turned to face her father. "She's afraid of her Soul Horse. And why does she hang around here so much?"

He was stuffing tobacco into a pipe. "Well, for starters, you're her hero and she bonded with you on the trail." He tried to light the pipe from the flame of a candle. "There's something else going on," he said through teeth clenched around the pipe stem. "She's lonely and sees you as a kindred spirit. You both lost your mothers."

"Yeah, well I adjusted long ago," she said, successfully avoiding the nostalgia her father wanted to wallow in. "She better come up with something she can do that's useful or she'll end up a Pedestrian doing latrine duty. Or maybe they'll just drive her out."

"She can shoot," he said, now drawing comfortably on the pipe. "Deadly at seventy-five yards with that bolt action."

"Nah. That kid? She's not strong enough to hold a rifle."

He nodded his head a few times. "I've seen her at the range," he said. "They've already assigned her to emergency perimeter defense. She'll be in the sharpshooter troop by the time she's fourteen."

Deirdre watched her father puff out enough smoke to almost obscure his head. "Where'd you get the tobacco?" she asked.

"Off a dead Trog." He started waving smoke away from his head so he could see her clearly. "I see you got your cast off. How's the arm?"

Deirdre emitted a frustrated sigh. "I've had the cast off for weeks,

Dad. And the arm's fine, thanks."

He let the smoke curl playfully up around his face, enjoying the first smoke he'd had in months. Despite his hulking frame, he looked small sitting in front of his oversized teepee.

"You ought to pass that teepee onto a family who needs it," she said.

"I ain't seen anybody in want of a teepee," he said sharply. "I'm used to this one."

Deirdre knew he was holding onto it because it reminded him of his disappearing family. She wondered if he judged her for not getting Mindy back.

"I'm loving my tent," she said. "It's smaller, so it holds the body heat." She gestured to her medium-sized tent, big enough for two to sleep comfortably; she used it exclusively while she was in Hussar Valley. It was larger than the tent she traveled with but only half the size of her father's mansion.

"I'm glad for you," he said.

Deirdre stood up and straddled Danny, who was still lounging in the grass. "I'm gonna get something to eat. You coming?"

"Nah. I just want to sit here and smoke for a while."

"If you're around when Jube wakes up, tell him I'll bring him back some breakfast."

She gave Danny a little poke with her toe. "Let's go, Dan."

As the buckskin scrambled to his feet, Deirdre settled herself on his back before they trotted off toward Camp Center.

CHAPTER TWENTY-THREE

Danny carried Deirdre through the heart of the Hussar camp. When they passed the Raider mess hall, she slid off the buckskin who continued on to the feed barn where Pedestrians were parceling out alfalfa to the free-ranging Soul Horses.

The mess hall was a fifty-yard-long tent with fires blazing in wood-burning stoves every ten yards, the smoke escaping through aluminum chimneys that pierced the canvas roof.

During the winter, most Hussars congregated around the stoves for warmth but now it was late May, and even though mornings could still be a bit chilly, no one felt the need to warm themselves. They approached the fires only to utilize the stove tops to cook their breakfasts.

Deirdre heard Margaret's booming laugh and smiled, looking forward to some good Raider talk. She went to the food table already prepared by Joe Bond and his staff, something she always preferred to cooking her own breakfast. She truly hated cooking.

She grabbed two hard-boiled eggs, two pieces of jerky, a slice of bread and two apples. As she walked toward her usual table, she pocketed one of the eggs, both apples and a piece of jerky. Her breakfast would consist of the remainder, an egg, a slice of jerky and a slice of bread.

She reached her table as Margaret, age fifty, a tall, robust mountain of a white woman, was in the middle of a tale, addressing a table of listeners. Seated at the table were Margaret's partner, Janie, forty, a well-muscled black woman; Zeke, Eagle Haller's son, a muscular twenty-two-year-old; Alonso, bone thin and middle aged; and Frank, Francine's tutor, a stocky twenty-six-year-old man with close-cropped black hair and a friendly face that Deirdre had loved all her life.

"So, I had one Urb by the throat," Margaret explained, "and couldn't get my damn Bowie knife out of the other one. It got caught on his rib cage or something."

She laughed merrily as she remembered her dilemma. "So I let go of the knife and just start punching the other guy in the face. Well, he starts punching back and that boy could hit. He caught me with a left cross right on the chin—knocked me colder than an icicle." She laughed uproariously.

"When I woke up, his head was resting on my stomach and his brains were all over my face. I learned later Alonso got him in the back of the head with that sawed-off he carries. Shit, that boy hit hard."

She laughed again. The rest of the table joined in with sporadic chuckles but no one was quite as amused as Margaret. She turned her attention to Deirdre. "How's your boy doing?"

"He's coming along."

"I'd say so." A mischievous twinkle danced in Margaret's eyes.

"What's that supposed to mean?" Deirdre asked, her coy smile anticipating what was coming.

"That means I rode by last night coming back from rim patrol and heard the clear sounds of you guys getting it on."

Alonso snorted a muted laugh and Zeke grinned lasciviously. Even Frank, who usually took Deirdre's side in everything, struggled to hold back a laugh.

Deirdre flashed her killer smile. "Yeah. He's definitely coming along."

Everyone laughed and it felt like old times. Margaret gestured toward a crow sitting on a fencepost just outside the entrance to the mess tent. The bird was peering in to see what was going on. "Maybe you ought to thank her."

Deirdre nodded, picked up a piece of bread, broke it into pieces, walked to the tent entrance and dropped the offering on the ground in front of the post. The crow fearlessly plopped down and began nibbling. Deirdre returned to the table.

"Yeah, that's a Spirit. She gave me a little wink."

"It's the Spirits who are getting your man through this," Margaret said as she watched the crow Spirit eat bread. "There's no other explanation."

Deirdre addressed the large woman who commanded so much respect among the Hussars. "Hey, Margaret, if I have to leave for a while can you and Janie keep an eye on Jube, just see how he's doing?"

Silence engulfed the table. Deirdre tried to read the uncomfortable faces. "What's the matter?"

"There's an open forum this Monday to discuss you and him and stuff in general," Margaret explained.

"Really?"

"I don't think you'll be going anywhere for a while," Margaret said, her usual hardy speech now softened.

Deirdre grabbed a half loaf of bread from a large basket at table center and walked away as the others exchanged glances. She stopped after a few strides and addressed Frank.

"How's the kid doing?"

Frank shrugged, his mouth drawn out flat and ambivalent. "She tries hard. Has no feel for that horse."

"I hear she can shoot."

"Yeah. Weirdly good with a bolt action."

CHAPTER TWENTY-FOUR

Jube searched carefully in the tall grass for rattlesnakes. Convinced there were none, he gingerly lowered himself onto the crest of the hillock and faced the lush copse of oak trees that sprawled down the hillside and onto the flats below.

He was high enough to see the full expanse of the valley with its changing colors as a cloud bank moved through the sky, altering the lighting every few seconds. It was midmorning, and the spring warmth was making him drowsy.

He looked down at Deirdre's tent tucked nicely behind the oaks which served as excellent windbreaks along with the hillock. This was the farthest he'd walked since he'd been brought in half-dead three months ago. The pain in his chest had been negligible when he woke that morning, so he decided to venture out on this little expedition. After the exertion, the wound was throbbing, yet he felt a resurgent strength that pointed to a full recovery.

From his perch he could see someone crossing a field from Camp

Center. He recognized the confident, graceful gait of his woman. A nervous sensation crept into his stomach as it often did when he considered their relationship and how he'd become completely dependent on her love.

A garter snake slithered through an open space in the grass less than a yard from his feet. Hussars believed whenever a wild animal came unusually close to humans in a non-aggressive manner, it was one of the Spirits initiating contact and it was important for the humans to respond appropriately. Usually this meant an offering of some kind, food or occasionally some talisman like an old coin or an ancient piece of clothing. *What does one offer a garter snake?*

Before he could ponder much on this, the snake moved off into the grass, out of sight in seconds. Jube questioned whether he could ever believe in that stuff. He knew Deirdre did. It worried him at times that his skepticism about the Spirits might cause a rift between them.

There were other potential conflicts. The raiding lifestyle of the Hussars seemed to him like glorified stealing. He didn't like living off what was taken from other hard-working people.

All the Hussar philosophizing was about fortifying their resolve in times of stress or comforting them when confronting the vicissitudes of Fate. He wasn't a philosopher himself, but he was sure part of philosophy was the struggle to know which actions were morally bad and which were good, but that wasn't a subject that interested Hussars. They had learned from the Code of Lauren that what made the tribe stronger, healthier and safer was right, and anything that threatened the tribe was wrong. They never questioned this simple ethos.

Their casual acceptance of raiding, war and revenge clashed with his innate feelings. Deirdre called it his peaceful "sprout" and seemed to have no problem accepting this very non-Hussar trait. Jube didn't know if he could be as tolerant of the Hussar worldview.

What concerned him most was the part he would play in her life once he was well. She often talked about him working in the clinic. She felt there was a place for him in the Hussar world. He wasn't so sure.

Approaching the tent, head down, Deirdre didn't notice him sitting up on the hillock. He thought about calling out to her but a playful whim kept him quiet.

A moment after disappearing inside, she was out again looking at footprints in the soft soil surrounding the tent. Following the direction of the tracks, she looked up and saw Jube sitting on the top of the hillock with a big grin on his face. She laughed and ran up the slope, sat down next to him and gave him a big kiss on the cheek.

"Out and about, huh?" she said as she emptied the contents of her pockets — the egg, the apples, the slice of jerky and the bread — onto his lap. "How you feeling?"

"I'm okay. Hurts a little but I feel strong."

"Ha. Margaret was teasing me today about how strong you felt last night." She giggled at Jube's confused look. "She rode by coming back from rim duty and heard us getting busy."

Jube still hadn't gotten used to the casual way Hussars joked about sexual relations but it was one of the traits of the tribe he didn't mind and occasionally found charming.

"You were walking back here with your head down so wrapped up in your thinking," he observed playfully. "If I was laying in ambush I could have killed you easy."

Deirdre erupted with laughter. "All right," she said between guffaws. "I'll be more careful around you from now on." When her laughter died down, her words were almost inaudible. "We got trouble ahead, Jube."

"Trouble?"

"An open forum," she said. "The topic is Deirdre and her outsider boyfriend."

"You think it could get bad?"

"I think they know my plans and I doubt if they like them."

He leaned toward her to make sure she understood the seriousness of his next question. "Mind telling *me* your plans?"

She draped her arm over his shoulder. "I was thinking we'd just tent up together and make love forever and ever."

Playful as that comment was, Jube thought a part of her may actually want that.

She plopped back onto the grass, adjusting her head so that a nice clump of crushed grass served as a pillow. "My plans are that you become a Hussar and wait here for me while I search for my sister." She looked at him expectantly. "How's that sound to you?"

"Why can't I go with you?"

"How long did it take you to climb this hill?"

He looked down at the slope he had just ascended. It did take him awhile. "You can't wait till I'm one hundred percent?"

"No," she said firmly. "I've waited too long as it is. But they're not going to let me go. We have strict rules against a Hussar going on a mission not directly related to tribal business." Her cheeks were flushed with anger. "I guess a lot of folks feel I've spent enough time looking for Mindy."

"They can stop you?" He was genuinely puzzled as to why this formidable woman would be slowed down by a forum, which he assumed was just a glorified bullshit session.

"They can make it real hard for me to come back." She rubbed his leg gently. "And I don't think life for you will be that much fun here if they're mad at me."

"I see the problem." After a moment of reflection, he had a proposal. "Maybe it's time for you to strike out on your own."

"It's not that simple, babe. These are my people and this is my valley. I can't abandon all that."

"So, what are you going to do?"

Before she could answer, the shrill sound of a hunter's horn broke the quiet of the summer morning.

"What's that?" Jube asked and glanced up at Deirdre who was

already on her feet.

"It's an alarm." Deirdre's eyes scanned the valley for tell-tale movement.

Horns started blowing throughout the valley from all directions.

"What the hell is going on?" she said and headed downhill. She paused when a lone rider galloped by her tent and up the slope toward her, ponying Danny behind him. A redheaded man in his early thirties, mounted on a blonde mule stopped a few feet from her. Breathless, he spoke with great urgency.

"Trogs are pouring in over the north rim. They got hold of some automatic weapons and smokeless ammo." His words were punctuated by the distant sound of gunfire.

Deirdre tacked up Danny in less than a minute, fastened her gun belt around her waist, hung a holster holding an extra revolver on the pommel of her saddle and slid her rifle into the sheath. She vaulted onto the saddle and was riding off when she pulled up, turned around and called out to Jube. "You can get down alright, can't you?"

"Of course."

Jube watched her for as long as he could but she was out of sight in seconds, Danny seeming to fly over the rolling terrain.

He spotted a ground squirrel about six feet away standing on a large boulder staring at him. He broke off a piece of the bread.

"My woman's riding into battle," Jube said to the little critter. "Bring her back to me, will you, Spirit?"

He tossed the bread on the ground. The squirrel came off the boulder, snatched it, ran off and appeared to dissolve into the earth.

CHAPTER TWENTY-FIVE

Deirdre led Griffin Squadron up Plane Crash Road over the North Rim and into Cooper Canyon. Fifty of the best Raiders rode behind her, each armed with a rifle, two handguns and a slashing weapon—sword, machete or Bowie knife.

Hiroto Kaneko, the previous commander of Griffin Squadron, had trained the unit to function in three capacities; dragoons, light cavalry and heavy cavalry. When going up against a well-armed opponent, as dragoons, they'd ride to a flanking position, dismount and open fire with long guns. The light cavalry capability enabled them to function as pursuit troops against a retreating and disordered army. Against a demoralized or poorly armed adversary, the heavy cavalry training enabled them to unleash an all-out charge using handguns and slashing weapons to spread chaos throughout the ranks of the enemy.

Deirdre reflected with gratitude on Hiroto's last day as leader of Griffin Squadron. He was mortally wounded in a raid against the Urbs and on his death bed recommended Deirdre be appointed his successor, making her the youngest squadron leader in Hussar history. After several years of leadership experience in raids, she had been promoted to Hawk, a position usually reserved for much older Hussars.

Once they cleared the rim, Deirdre led them west through rough terrain to reach an old mining trail that would take them to Anza Road and the rear of the Trogs.

She knew every contour of the terrain and the strengths and weaknesses of each horse so well that she could push the animals just enough to maximize the speed of the advance without exhausting the mounts.

Halting the troop in a meadow, she addressed Ross Meusel, a lanky dour man who served as her second-in-command.

"Have them dismount and rest the horses for ten minutes," she said. "And get Annie up here."

Ross directed his quarter horse back toward the troops, barking orders as he went. Deirdre dismounted and let Danny stroll over to some grass under a majestic oak while she listened to the sounds of the distant battle.

The gunfire was erratic, both sides conserving ammo, looking for a tactical advantage. She was confident that while she was doing her maneuver, Eagle Haller had used the Hussar's superior mobility to move a formidable contingent of Raiders into the path of the advancing Trog army, dismount his force, and set up a defense line on a ridge, or a gully, or a stand of oak or a combination of all of those. That would give time for the infantry regiment, consisting of unmounted Hussars, called Pedestrians, to reinforce the advance mounted troops.

Annie, a rail-thin feather of a woman, rode up to Deirdre on an equally lean quarter horse. Her wrinkled, soulful face told of a long and troubled life.

"Annie, you need to scout the Trogs," Deirdre told her, confident her orders would be obeyed. "Find a weak point in their line. We'll be riding towards you in a few minutes. We won't go farther than Two

Ghost Springs. We'll wait there for exactly five minutes for your report. If you don't show, we'll advance blind."

Giving the slightest of nods, Annie cantered off. Deirdre watched her go with an admiration that bordered on love. Annie was the oldest rider in Griffin Squadron. She claimed she was fifty even though Deirdre was sure she was well into her sixties. She was Griffin Squadron's best scout.

Deirdre removed a canteen from a rawhide loop dangling from her saddle and took a swig. An owl popped his head from behind some oak leaves and peered down from a branch that hung right in front of her. To see an owl in the daytime was rare. To see one this close was unheard of. She nodded to the creature. "Sister Owl, I honor you and ask for success in the coming battle." The owl blinked before disappearing back into the leaves.

Before Deirdre could take another swig, she heard a faint belching sound coming from the battle and then a moment later a sudden increase in gunfire. Or was it an explosion? At this distance, and muted somewhat by the competing sounds, it wasn't clear what was happening. There was another identical belching sound followed this time by the unmistakable roar of an explosion.

She mounted and rode up to Ross, who was stroking his horse's neck as he sipped water from his canteen.

"Mount up," she ordered, her tone suddenly severe. "We're moving out now."

Ross gave her a questioning look. Deirdre was very disciplined about making sure the horses weren't winded when they went into battle. Cutting the ten-minute rest to three confused him.

"You didn't hear it?" she snapped.

He shook his head.

"The Trogs have gotten hold of some kind of artillery. If they know how to work it, our people could be in real trouble."

Because the squadron was advancing earlier than planned, there was little chance Annie would be at the rendezvous point. Indeed, she wasn't.

Two Ghost Springs bubbled up about half a mile from the old Anza road that led over these hills to Anza Valley, the Trogs' stronghold. A row of cottonwoods blocked visibility between the road and the spring. As soon as the squadron pulled up behind the tree line, Deirdre signaled Ross to join her.

"Move ahead at a walk," she instructed. "I'm going on at a gallop. We can't wait for Annie. I'll do my own scout before we commit in force."

When Deirdre cleared the cottonwoods, the Anza Road was visible, no Trogs in sight. The enemy thought their rear was safe and entered the valley with the entire Trog force.

She was about to gallop to the crest when she spotted Annie guiding her horse, Thor, down a slope on the other side of the road. Deirdre crossed the road and met up with her scout as she completed her descent. Deirdre took notice of something very hard in Annie's eyes.

"They have at least two mortars," Annie reported. "They know how to work them. Casualties and panic among our people."

Deirdre now understood she didn't have time to set up her squadron in a dismounted position and open fire; they'd have to engage on horseback, a dangerous operation against a heavily armed opponent. If the charge was detected too soon and the Trogs turned their weapons around—horses make very good targets.

She glanced back toward the springs and saw Ross leading the squadron into view at a walk, just as ordered. She gave him a double fist pump, the Hussar signal to join at a gallop. Seconds later she was surrounded by the entire squadron.

She spoke loudly, her bold tone projecting confidence and urgency. "Annie says our people are taking serious hits from mortars. It looks like the Trogs might break through into our valley. We're the only hope."

She turned to her youngest trooper, fifteen years old, black, lean, athletic and supremely competent.

"Freddie, as soon as you spot a mortar, peel off and attack its crew. Once you disable it, look for other mortars. There are two for sure." She assigned five riders to follow Freddie in this crucial assignment.

Scanning the faces of her squadron, she spotted anxiety, maybe even some fear but no sign of the kind of terror that could be paralyzing. They would perform well and she loved them for that.

Deirdre reined Danny around and rode toward the rim at a walk, her troopers following. When they were twenty feet from where the road descended steeply into the valley, she turned to the riders and spoke. "Go at them from the jump. Rooster Cogburn at fifty yards."

Like a giant mythical griffin, the squadron exploded over the crest and descended into the valley.

As they thundered down the slope, Deirdre noticed that the invaders had advanced further than expected. They were almost at Oak Grove Road, a good mile away. It would take some good luck for the squadron to cover that distance without the Trogs discovering their approach.

When they neared the end of the slope and fanned out onto the flats, Deirdre could make out puffs of smoke coming from a ridge south of Oak Grove Road. This was where Haller had set up his line of defense.

She watched as a direct hit from a Trog mortar sent several of her fellow Hussars flying through the air. Some of the Pedestrians broke ranks and fled in panic. There was a real chance the entire line could collapse from the pressure of the mortar hits.

Deirdre pushed Danny to the limit. She could see the individual Trogs clearly now. For some reason the male Trogs always went into battle shirtless. The intricate tattoos on their backs presented inviting targets. A couple turned to see them coming and tried to warn the others, but it was too late. Griffin Squadron was closing rapidly.

Deirdre put the reins between her teeth, drew both handguns and took aim at the Trogs. The entire squadron was spread out now, all the riders with their guns drawn and reins between their teeth.

The first volley took down twenty-five of the enemy. By the time their weapons were empty, at least seventy-five Trogs were dead or wounded and an entire chunk of the Trog defense was in a panic.

Deirdre drew her Bowie knife, galloped toward a fleeing Trog and, leaning from her saddle, slashed at the back of his neck. Blood spurted upwards and the wounded man collapsed with a scream. This was an important part of any charge; the Hussar Battle Manual called it Naked Blade. The entire squadron hacked away at the Trogs as panic flew down their line.

Halting Danny, Deirdre looked around and spotted a mortar one hundred yards behind the line. Already Freddie and his five riders were galloping towards it.

In a few moments they were hacking the crew to pieces while other Hussars were disassembling the mortar so it could be transported back to the Hussar camp. Some troopers spotted the second mortar behind a clump of redshank. The crew fled in terror when they saw riders thundering toward them.

Deirdre looked west and saw a reserve of Trogs moving towards her position. Things could still go bad if the enemy were able to bring any serious firepower down on her squadron. She feared that the flanking maneuver, the charge, and the successful surprise would be in vain if the Hussars on the ridge didn't realize there was panic in the Trog army.

Throwing a look in the direction of the friendlies, she was delighted to see Frank and her father jogging towards her, followed by a mob of rifle-wielding Pedestrians. In the distance she saw a Hussar charge being conducted against the enemy's right wing which was in full, disordered retreat. The Trog line was collapsing. Her beloved valley had been saved.

CHAPTER TWENTY-SIX

Deirdre stood for a while inside the doorway of the clinic watching her man care for the patients. One moment he was emptying someone's bedpan; the next, he was helping a young woman with a terrible leg wound take a sip of water. Then he was holding down an older man who was screaming as Herb, the camp surgeon, amputated his mangled arm with a hack saw. When the amputation was done and the man had either passed out or died, Jube looked around for his next job. It was then that he saw her.

They embraced in an aisle between two rows of beds, and then both took a step back to examine one another.

"You're okay," he said, his watery eyes revealing he was close to weeping for joy.

"And your wound is bleeding." She gestured toward a red spot discoloring his shirt on his upper chest. She looked around for the surgeon. "I'll get Herb."

"Don't bother him," Jube said softly. "I'll take a break and patch myself up. Someone in the corner over there has been asking for you. Says she's your scout. Bullet's in a bad place," he said, the gentleness of his tone communicating deep empathy. "Herb says it's inoperable."

At first, she thought Annie was already dead, she looked so gaunt and lifeless, but when Deirdre touched her shoulder, the dying woman opened her eyes and reached out her right hand. Squeezing it tightly, Deirdre knelt beside the cot.

"Thor." Annie could only manage a whisper, the Trog bullet having penetrated her lung.

"What about him?" Deirdre asked. Picking up a towel that lay on Annie's bed, she dabbed sweat off her friend's feverish forehead.

"He took some shrapnel in the right front knee, but he can still limp around." Every word was an effort and barely audible but she knew what she owed her Soul Horse. "I don't think he's in much pain. He won't be good for riding anymore but can you just let him graze for a while? You don't have to give him alfalfa or grain. I know that wouldn't be right. Just let him wander free and graze like a retired horse would back in the day."

Deirdre nodded and squeezed Annie's hand a little tighter. She'd learned from cruel experience that dying people found a firm hand grip from a loved one comforting. "I'll see what I can do."

Annie gave a little point with her chin toward Jube who was standing at the dressing station working on his own wound. "He's a special man. You're lucky."

Deirdre smiled and nodded. Annie's feeble grip told her the end was near.

"Do you believe in anything, Deirdre?" Annie asked, her breathing forced.

Deirdre studied her scout's face, trying to understand where this question came from. Annie's eyes were moist and opened wide. Deirdre was unsure whether the cause was pain or fear.

"You mean like the Spirits?" Deirdre asked.

"I mean like things after we die." Her face crinkled into a mystified frown, her eyes even wider now as if she were trying to see the unseeable.

Deirdre placed a hand on Annie's shoulder and rubbed it tenderly. "I have some theories. What about you? Do you believe in things like that?"

"Yes."

Deirdre leaned forward so close that she could feel her lips brush against Annie's ear as she whispered. "You're going to scout the other side for me. Do a good recon and come back and tell me about it. In a dream maybe."

Annie's eyes relaxed, and she smiled. She liked that idea. Within a few minutes her eyes were closed, then the rhythm of her breathing changed. Deirdre knew this was the first of Annie's last few breaths.

On her way to her tent, Deirdre stopped to see the Head Wrangler, Tony Antonelli. She asked if he could let Thor roam for a while. He said if nobody complained and the knee didn't get infected, it was all right with him.

When she arrived back at her tent, no one was around. She'd seen her father wrangling riderless horses after the battle and knew he wouldn't be back until late. Francine was probably on sentry duty.

Glad to be alone, she entered her tent, sat on a stack of bearskins and dissolved into uncontrollable sobs. She gave herself one good cry for every death that moved her. There wasn't time for more than that. There were lots of deaths among the Hussars.

✦✦✦✦✦

It was close to midnight when Jube's wound opened again. This time Herb wouldn't let him return to nursing.

Jube didn't protest; he was dead on his feet. When he left the clinic, he spotted a campfire burning about fifty yards away. There was a chill in the air and he yearned to plop down by that fire and just breathe.

Approaching, he noticed no spots were available among the ring of exhausted Hussar Raiders surrounding the fire, so Jube changed his route, trudging toward his tent, a ten-minute walk. He'd taken about five steps when a female voice stopped him. "Jube."

Turning, he saw a woman he didn't recognize gesturing that she intended to give up her spot for him. He nodded in gratitude and walked back to the circle.

When the heat from the fire hit him, he collapsed in an exhausted heap. He could feel a little stream of blood ripple down his chest from the wound, but he was too tired to check it.

A bearded, gap-toothed young man with an unfamiliar accent spoke. "We know what you been doing in the clinic." He tossed a thankful nod toward Jube. "We're appreciative."

There was a moment of silence, and then someone snorted. In the faint light cast by the dying fire, Jube saw it was an older man named Alonzo, who had visited Deirdre a couple of times. "And we know who your woman is." There were chuckles and muttered acknowledgement coming from all the men and women in the circle.

"She was in deep shit," the bearded man said. "She was about to take off looking for her sister again and she would have been banished because of it. It didn't look good. And she didn't make it no better with her damn pride. Now she's a big hero again. Right?" He was asking the whole circle. They murmured their collective agreement.

"It's the Spirits," Alonzo said as he tossed a branch on the fire. "They've always blessed her, but someone worked extra hard on them this time."

Jube woke at daybreak. He was the only one remaining by the now-dead fire. Someone had draped a deerskin blanket over him. He reviewed the events of yesterday, the terrible battle, the misery of the wounded, Deirdre's heroism and the change in her fortune. He was full of profound gratitude that she had returned from battle unscathed. A ground squirrel sat on a log not far from the campfire. Recalling that he had asked a squirrel Spirit to protect Deirdre, he said playfully, "Did you have something to do with this?" Then he gasped, all sense of play gone. *Did that just happen? Yes. Yes. That squirrel gave me a wink and a nod.*

CHAPTER
TWENTY-SEVEN

Ketchell sat in the tent pondering his situation, his hands bound behind him, iron shackles gripping his ankles. His thoughts drifted to how quickly the Bee mission to the Trogs had crumbled.

At first, everything seemed to be going well. The Trogs had enthusiastically accepted the bribe offered by the Bee advance team — twenty semi-automatic assault rifles, several cases of smokeless ammo, two mortars and a generous supply of mortar shells. They mobilized efficiently and the individuals assigned to operate the mortars were quick learners.

The attack was planned for a Monday morning. Things started to go poorly as soon as the Trog army was on the march. They were undisciplined, some straggling aimlessly, others advancing aggressively, feverishly excited by the prospect of invading the home of the hated Hussars.

The mountain road that connected Anza Valley with Hussar Valley was rugged, with many steep elevation changes that slowed down the advance. Even though they left before dawn, they weren't in position on the rim above their target until mid-morning. Since Trogs had no vehicles or horses, the march exhausted them before the battle began. The Bee advisors were unsuccessful at convincing the Trog leadership they should leave a rear guard on the rim. The entire army poured into the valley at once, disorganized and unfocused. Forward stragglers fired at distant Hussar horsemen who immediately rode out of range. While the Bee advisors were trying to organize the Trog advance, a large force of Hussars had ridden to a tactically advantageous ridge, dismounted and formed an impressive line of defense. They were reinforced about thirty minutes later by a sizable contingent of infantry.

Things still might have worked out for the Trogs and their Bee advisors; the assault rifles and the mortars took a toll on the Hussar army. But at a crucial time, the Trog line was hit hard from the rear by a mounted assault led by...*her.*

Maybe she is Superwoman.

After the Trog army had collapsed, he was found hiding behind a fallen oak. Several Hussars were ready to kill him when Crazy Hawk rode up and ordered that he be taken captive. He shuddered as he pondered what she might have planned.

The flap to the tent was pulled up and the devil herself entered. She sat on the ground in front of him.

"Why were you invading our valley with Trogs?" Deirdre asked with a surprisingly relaxed, unconfrontational tone.

"I was ordered to come down here and join them in the attack," he said openly, anxious to communicate his desire to cooperate. Any thoughts of loyalty to the Bees seemed absurd at this moment.

"By the people who gave them their weapons upgrade?"

"Precisely. The Bees."

"The Bees." She repeated the name with an amused lilt. "Interesting name. You were an advisor to the Trogs?"

"My mission was very specific. They wanted me to identify you."

Her head tilted to one side and a wry smile slid onto her lips. "My corpse?"

"If that proved to be the case," he said clearing his throat. The subject of her death at the hands of the Trogs made him nervous. "They held out hope they could capture you."

"Why would they want that?" She leaned forward.

"There's a faction of the Bees who think you may be some special species. An evolutionary resurgence or some horseshit like that," he said with a big smile hoping to enlist Deirdre into mocking the Bees. "They're watching too many old movies." He laughed. Deirdre didn't.

"Are they the people who have my sister?" Her laser-like eyes reinforced the directness of this question.

"Yes," he said bluntly, hoping that the information he possessed would make him valuable enough to keep alive.

"And she's well?" she asked, her eyes softening a bit as her fear of the answer revealed a note of vulnerability.

"Yes."

She took a deep breath, then let it out in a relieved sigh. A moment later, her laser eyes were back. She scrutinized him for what was probably only a few seconds, but it seemed like an eternity to Ketchell who wondered if that was all she needed from him and now she would gut him like a pig.

She reached for an oversized paperback book shoved under her belt, jerked it free and dropped it in front of Ketchell. It was a 21st-century atlas of the old USA state of California.

"You understand your position?" Deirdre asked, her voice iced with cold efficiency.

"Probably," he lied. He had no idea where he stood with her. "But why don't you spell it out for me."

"You show me where my sister is," she said in a business-like manner. "I go get her. You'll be held here until I get back. If your information turns out to be good, I'll recommend clemency."

"Could you define clemency?"

"A quick death," she said abruptly. "No torture."

"As tempting as that offer is," he said, fighting off a chill of panic, "I think I have a little more leverage than that." He pointed at the atlas. "You want me to show you where the Hive is, right?"

Her bitter laugh ruptured any illusion he might have had that he could barter. "You ran a gang of kidnappers who stole my sister, you sent a posse of assassins to kill me—they seriously wounded my man, by the way—and you just participated in an invasion of our valley."

She paused and looked down at the canvas floor of the tent. He hoped she was talking herself out of killing him right then.

She looked up at Ketchell. "I thought you knew you were going to die. How and when are the only negotiable details. If you don't give me the information I need, I'll turn you over to the skinners. If you're lucky, you'll be dead in three days."

Ketchell spent a few moments fighting off resignation. His sense of pride would have dragged it out a little longer, but the way she gritted her teeth told him he better give her what she wanted quickly.

"You need to untie my hands," he said weakly.

She pulled a knife from her belt and sliced the rope binding his wrists. Picking up the book, he began to page through. After a few minutes he found what he was looking for.

"Here." He pointed at the map. "This is it."

Deirdre dug into her pocket, pulled out what looked like a simple stick and handed it to Ketchell. "Circle it."

Ketchell now saw that a pointy, flint-colored substance was taped to the end of the stick. Putting the point of the makeshift pencil on the map, he drew a circle around a town named Folsom.

"Their stronghold is here. They call it the Hive. It's east of what used to be Sacramento, surrounded by a five-mile wide, heavily patrolled no man's land. Even if you could get close, its fortifications are impenetrable." He looked up at Deirdre.

"My sister is in an unapproachable fortress," she said, her voice hard and piercing. She was no longer trying to conceal the rage that was consuming her. "Is that what you're saying?" She thundered these last words.

"Yes," he muttered, his head bowed.

Deirdre jumped up and walked out of the tent. She returned a moment later and strode in a circle around Ketchell, pausing every few steps to cast ferocious eyes on his wilting gaze.

He was sure this was his end. He remembered an old black-and-white movie he saw when he was a kid. In his head, he paraphrased the last words of the protagonist. *So, this is the end of Henry Ketchell.*

Suddenly, she sat down right in front of him, this time very close.

"How are you on a horse, Henry?" she asked, her tone surprisingly dispassionate.

CHAPTER TWENTY-EIGHT

Francine was awakened by the sounds of Deirdre and Jube arguing. She couldn't make out the gist but several times she heard Jube say angrily, "I don't believe it."

What doesn't he believe?

She crawled out of the tent she had recently pitched not far from Deirdre's and scurried to a better eavesdropping position. She lay down on a flat slab of rock right behind Deirdre's tent.

"It's a stupid plan." The frustration in Jube's voice was clear.

"What are you talking about?" Deirdre's tone was tough and uncompromising. "It's a foolproof plan."

"How can you say that?"

"I'll explain one more time because clearly you don't understand."

"I understand," he said sharply. "You're going to let that sleazebag deliver you to the very people who sent him down here to kill you."

Deirdre let out a little exasperated screech. Francine felt her stomach contracting as the argument escalated. She relished the loving relationship she had witnessed between them during the last three months; now the tension in their voices scared her.

"I told you," Deirdre said. "They don't want me dead. They want to experiment on me or run tests or something. He'll get extra points if he delivers me alive. It's in his interest."

"Listen to yourself. You're okay with them experimenting on you?"

"Of course not. Once I'm in their fortress, I'll be able to contact my sister. Then I can figure a way out."

"What if you're wrong about Ketchell? Maybe he doesn't care what the Bees want." A note of desperation colored Jube's pleading. "You've been such a burr under his saddle it may just be personal with him. He might kill you the first chance he gets."

"Gee, have you met me? I'm not easy to kill. He's a soft fifty-something who lets others do his dirty work. I can survive a few days on the trail with that. Besides, I'm convinced his main focus right now is to get back in with the Bees. They're his source of power and wealth and he's afraid of them. He wants to give them what they want and a living Crazy Hawk is *exactly* what they want."

"What's keeping him from just telling them your plan?"

"He may do that, but so what?" There was disgust in her voice as if she was sick of Jube's unwillingness to see the genius of her plan. "I'll be inside the Hive by then. But I don't think he does tell them. I think the temptation to let them think he captured me will be too much. He certainly won't tell them I captured him and now he's just doing my bidding. That'll make him look ridiculous."

There was a long pause. A big sigh leaked out of the tent. Francine was pretty sure it came from Jube.

"And what about us?" he asked.

"What do you mean?" Deirdre sounded genuinely confused by the question.

Jube took a moment to answer. When he did, the desperation was replaced by sarcasm. "Am I just supposed to say 'Have a nice trip, give my best to your sister'?"

"Not in those words but I'd like you to send me off feeling good about us."

"What is us?"

"I'm not getting it. What are you asking?"

"Was this just a passing thing or are you in love with me?"

Francine was horrified at the long pause that followed. *Tell him you love him.*

Deirdre finally broke the silence. "It's not a passing thing."

"But you can't say you love me." He was speaking so quietly now Francine could barely understand what he was saying but the disappointment in his voice was evident.

Another long pause. Deirdre cleared her throat and spoke in an unemotional voice. "What I can tell you is that you're inside me now. Just like my sister and Danny and my father and Francine."

It was all Francine could do to keep from crying out in joy.

"And when people get inside me," Deirdre continued, "I'll do almost anything for them. Jube, I'll kill for you, I'll die for you, I'll sit at your bedside for days taking care of you. I'll go hungry for you. I'll walk barefoot through snow for you. If you want to call that love, that's okay with me."

She took a deep breath. When she continued there was steely resolve in her voice. "But there is one thing I won't do for you. I won't give up on Mindy."

There was another pause, but this time Francine barely noticed. She was too busy savoring the joy of learning she had a family. That warm feeling didn't last long.

"Let me go with you," Jube said.

"Then it *would* be a stupid plan," Deirdre responded. "Your wound."

"I worked ten consecutive hours in the clinic without much

problem, just a little bleeding. I feel stronger every day. I could go with you."

"Even if I bought that, Ketchell has no use for you. Once I'm 'captured', there's no telling what he might do with you. I'm not taking you into harm's way. That's final."

"What if I don't wait for you?" There was suddenly fire in his voice. The longest pause.

"That would make me sad," Deirdre said softly. "But you have to do what you have to do. Same with me."

Francine found the silence that followed heartbreaking. That seemed to be the end of the discussion. In a few moments, she had learned she was part of a family and then had to listen to that family dissolve.

After she crawled back into her tent, she started crying. When the sun came up, the tears were still flowing.

CHAPTER
TWENTY-NINE

Deirdre was up at daybreak the next day, anxious to get going. Her father, Francine and Jube helped her saddle and pack three horses and one mule. The farewell was efficient and low-key, the way Deirdre liked it. Francine gave her an unusually long hug. The two men were silent, suppressing whatever emotions they were feeling.

After mounting Danny, Deirdre rode up to Jube and said, "Hope you're here when I get back."

"Can't promise anything," Jube said, his voice chilled.

Deirdre cantered off toward the tent where Ketchell was being held.

She had informed Eagle Haller what she learned about the Bees and Mindy and said she was taking Ketchell north to trade him for her sister. He was fine with that. With the goodwill fostered by her battle heroics still fresh, no one had a problem with such a limited mission. The prisoner swap was a simple task; it would either work or it wouldn't. He asked her to compile as much intelligence as possible on the mysterious Bees. She had told only Jube and her father about her actual plan.

Deirdre's caravan consisted of herself on Danny, Ketchell on a mild-mannered quarter horse named Durance, her pack horse, Blue, and a sturdy pack mule, Deja.

She planned to ride east to the Pacific Crest trail. A transportation artery for hardy north-south travelers, the PCT had been maintained in the 21st for hikers and hobbyist horseback riders. She would follow it to the small desert town of Mojave, then pick up old Highway 58, which she heard was well protected by biker gangs who charged a toll to travel that stretch. She figured one skin of Hussar wine would be enough to buy her safe passage through Tehachapi into Bakersfield where she would leave the animals with an ally of the Hussars who owned a ranch there. She planned to catch a ride on a fossil fuel vehicle to Fresno and then onto Sacramento where she'd allow Ketchell to "capture" her.

"It's just crazy enough to work," she said aloud to herself the first night as she worked to put up her trail tent. She laughed. She'd heard that line used sarcastically in an old movie but until now, she didn't get the joke.

She needed a lot of breaks to go her way if her plan was to be successful, but she had to take the chance. The very meaning of her existence depended on her doing everything in her power to get Mindy back. That was why she had to be so tough on Jube. She feared she'd lose her resolve if she softened for him.

She recalled standing next to Mindy years ago as they looked on together at the funeral pyre. The Farewell Ceremony began and several Hussars rode up with torches. Mindy, who was four, called out to the corpse that lay so still on top of the pyre. "You better get up, Mommy. They're going to burn you."

Something about that little voice sliced Deirdre's soul. She'd fallen to her knees weeping, the only time in her life she'd cried in public, while

Mindy hugged her in a consoling way and tried to kiss her tears away with soft, tiny lips.

That day, almost ten years ago, Deirdre had looked into the child's big brown, soulful eyes and knew she'd spend her remaining days on earth protecting the kid. But she had failed to do that.

Her reverie was disrupted by Ketchell's laugh. She looked at the man she had chained to the trunk of a manzanita tree.

"I just figured it out," he said, his red, jowly face sporting an expansive grin.

She seated herself on a flat stone not far from him. "What'd you figure out?"

"Your plan. It's brilliant. Congratulations. I'll be happy to cooperate."

"I'm gonna trade you for my sister," she said evenly. "I don't need your cooperation to do that."

He shook his head forcefully. "I heard you explaining that to the guards back in your valley—the part about a prisoner swap."

His huge smile showed honest delight. "I was thinking the Bees are sniffing around the wrong gal if they're looking for an evolutionary breakthrough. Unless they think Superwoman is an idiot. A prisoner swap! You've got no leverage for that. They don't want me back. I failed them. They're real strict that way."

He studied her as if gauging the effect of his words. She hoped her face was unexpressive. After a moment, he continued. "Just now, it hit me. You want me to turn you over to them so you can be in there with your little sister."

His eyes widened. "You think it'll be easier to break out than break in. And you know something?" His laugh echoed through the box canyon she'd chosen as their campsite. "You may be right. When were you going to tell me?"

She spent a moment imagining the large man's throat sliced, blood spurting from his left carotid. "I was gonna pick my moment, but that won't be necessary now."

"No, it won't. You know what else isn't necessary?" he said, moving his arms so that the chains holding him in place rattled. "Chaining me to trees, binding my hands to the pommel of the saddle. You're right. It's in my interest to go along with your sting. Showing up with you as my captive will give me a fresh start with them. They'll see me as a valuable man again. I'm ready to cooperate."

He rattled the chains as if to emphasize his point. "Why don't you let me loose, and I'll help you finish setting up camp."

Deirdre watched him. He was wearing a self-satisfied grin, triumphant that he had figured out her plan.

"No," she said and went to find more firewood.

They continued on the Pacific Crest trail as planned for three more days. They were still a day's ride out from the desert village of Mojave when it became obvious she'd have to change their route. Massive columns of smoke clouded the northern horizon. The southern foothills of the Sierra Nevada were burning.

By the time they reached Mojave, the sky was black with soot, the air pungent with the smell of burning woodland. The bikers who were supposed to guarantee safe passage were strewn around in various states of chaos, several coughing violently from having breathed in too much smoke. Others were being treated by their comrades for burns. One group was accusing another of starting the fire so aggressively that Deirdre anticipated a fight breaking out soon.

She cared about none of this. Highway 58 was on fire. She needed a new route. Continuing north on the Pacific Crest trail was not an option; there weren't any reliable trading stations along the old trail and she would be out of food in a couple of days.

She'd seen in her California Atlas that in 2025, the publication date, there was a Highway 178 that ran through the mountains into Bakersfield.

She approached a biker sitting exhausted on an old stone bench, his face black with soot. "Hey, brother, you know if 178 is passable?" she asked.

The biker, who had tattoos running up his neckline and onto his face, squinted at Deirdre like he was trying to see through a fog. "What's 178?"

"An old highway that intersects with the 14 north of here. It runs past Lake Isabella into Bakersfield."

He continued to appear lost in a haze.

"I'm asking what condition it's in."

He coughed up some phlegm and spat it on the ground before he spoke. "I have no idea but it don't really matter. Those hills are rotten with Mounties. They'll make passage a real bitch."

CHAPTER THIRTY

Regardless of the threat posed by the Mounties, Deirdre saw 178 as her only option. She pushed north with her little caravan until nightfall. Camping that night in Red Rock Canyon, they reached the crossroads of the 14 and 178 mid-morning the following day.

The ancient highway ran west across the desert floor before winding snake-like up into the mountains, disappearing behind a distant ridge. It looked fine from Deirdre's position, but she knew that meant nothing. In the mountains, overgrowth, floods and avalanches could easily make it impassable. And then there was the problem of the Mounties.

"Cut me loose now." Ketchell's bass voice disrupted her deliberations. "You're going to do it by the end of the day," he said. "You'll need my back for clearing the road and you'll be tossing me a weapon as soon as we smell that Mountie trash."

Deirdre ignored him and glanced at the sky above the mountains. Threatening clouds billowing in from the west formed a grey shroud over their new route. Combined with the smoke drifting up from the south, it was going to be a dark passage.

She dismounted, reached into a saddle bag and pulled out a pair of split reins. As she attached them to Durance's bit, she spoke to Ketchell. "I'm not cutting you loose from the saddle but I'm letting you drive. When we get up there in those hills I'll have a lot to worry about. I don't want to be ponying both you and the pack animals."

She ran the reins back to Ketchell's hands. His wrists were still tied to the pommel. "Durance has a real sensitive mouth," she said. "He'll respond to just a little tug on the left rein or the right, which you ought to be able to do with just your fingers."

She remounted and urged Danny forward, ponying the pack train. Ketchell followed behind. They were up into the mountains within an hour.

By late morning, all signs of the highway had disappeared. Deirdre was picking her way through overgrown brush and fallen trees, often having to detour from the old road to get through. The temperature had crashed down into the forties, not unheard of at this elevation in early June.

Eventually, they met up with the Kern. Deirdre knew from the maps that following the course of the river would take them right into Bakersfield.

As they rode, Durance kept drifting toward the edge of the bank. The Kern was a raging torrent, its flow swelled by the melting snow running down from the higher elevations. If an animal slipped in, the power of the current would carry it out of sight in seconds.

When the sun broke through at midday, she could see the warmth made Ketchell drowsy. He dozed off several times and let the mount wander. Each time, Deirdre barked at Ketchell to stay awake and keep his horse wide of the water's edge.

A line of boulders on the river's edge forced them to ride in single file, Deirdre leading the way. A few deer drew her attention for a few seconds to a distant hillside.

When she looked back at Ketchell, she saw what was about to

happen. She wheeled Danny around and tried to grab Durance's bridle but it was too late; part of the saturated bank gave way and the rear half of the quarter horse slid into the river. The dozy Ketchell was wide awake when he hit the cold water.

Deirdre dismounted and leapt off the bank, grabbed onto the horn of Durance's saddle and cut Ketchell loose from the pommel with her Bowie knife. He dove for land with his now free hands outstretched as she slipped onto Durance and managed to direct him to a slanted section of the bank that made climbing ashore possible.

Once the horse was safely on dry land, she dismounted, shivering from the effects of the cold water, and looked to see how Ketchell had fared.

His teeth were chattering from the bath in the ice-cold water, but he stood stolidly on the bank holding her rifle in his oversized hands, the length of the weapon resting on his thighs as his long arms hung loosely in front of him.

"Your revolver is useless with wet powder," he observed casually. "I thought for a second your trusty steed was going into the river after you, so I saved the rifle."

He smiled and leaned the long gun against a large boulder. "You better change into dry clothes and then get to reloading that handgun. You'll need it if the Mounties figure out we're in their territory. Sorry about going into the river. I got to be more alert. Do you have a change of clothes for me?"

She nodded. "In the left pannier on the mule."

He walked over to the pack mule, reached into the pannier and pulled out a shirt and a pair of pants. He held them up to Deirdre. She nodded. He disappeared behind a big cypress tree that stood about twenty feet from the bank.

Deirdre walked over to Blue, pulled some clothes out of his right pannier and quickly changed. She hung her wet clothes on Danny's saddle.

When she was relatively dry, she lifted her revolver, which was dripping muddy water, and set it on the same boulder the rifle was leaning on. When Ketchell emerged from the cover of the cypress fully changed, carrying the wet clothes, she gestured toward the boulder. "Spread out the wet ones here."

When he was done, Deirdre picked up the rifle and tossed it to him. "I trust you'll continue to do what's in your best interest," she said, then added in full command mode, "Grab my ammo belt off the saddle, climb up that slope and keep an eye out for Mounties."

Ketchell nodded, grabbed the belt, scrambled up to the top of a ridge overlooking the river, and scanned the area for movement while Deirdre worked on her revolver.

She spent a moment speculating whether it was time for Hussars to modify their revolvers to accept cartridges. One of the disadvantages of cap and ball technology was that every couple of days, whether the weapons were shot or not, they had to be cleaned and reloaded with fresh powder to ensure reliable firing. This was particularly pertinent in damp weather. Deirdre knew that when revolvers were saturated with mud and river water, it became urgent.

She took the cleaning aids out of her saddle bag and attacked the drying, cleaning and reloading process with her usual efficiency. Danny stood behind her nibbling on rich spring grass. Durance and the pack animals followed his lead.

She had just finished seating the last ball and had started to place the five caps when Danny neighed, backing away from a boulder that was about thirty feet from the bank and twenty feet upriver. Deirdre became aware of movement to her left.

A moment later, Ketchell fired into a tree-covered slope, also to her left. A shotgun blast erupted from behind the upriver boulder. The pellets missed her entirely. A hail of projectiles, shotgun pellets, musket balls and some arrows, peppered the riverbank. An arrow hit Danny's right hindquarters. He bolted downriver, Deirdre's wet clothes falling off the saddle as he ran.

Durance spooked too but headed upriver, the pack animals following.

Deirdre grabbed her Bowie knife from its scabbard and charged the shotgun muzzle she saw poking through a crevice. Vaulting the boulder, she brought the knife blade down deep into the Mountie's back. He struggled for a moment as she jerked the blade around to penetrate his spinal column. He squirmed and screamed, continuing to do so until she grabbed his shotgun and with one blast turned his face into jelly. She glanced toward the hilly terrain south of the river. Mounties, maybe thirty of them were advancing, each searching for cover to protect them from Ketchell's fire.

Scooping up her revolver, she dove for the cover of an ancient culvert and lay amidst the broken concrete as bullets flew over her. Another crack of a rifle came from Ketchell's direction.

She peered up and saw him wedged between a twisted oak and a cliff face, firing her Winchester toward the Mounties. But she also saw something that confused her — a second rifle. Someone other than Ketchell was using a branch of the oak as a rifle rest and firing on the enemy.

Her first thought was that it was one of the bikers coming up to see the condition of the road. Whoever it was, their timing was perfect. This cover fire was her chance to get out of this mess as she was seriously outgunned; she'd been able to get only two caps in place before the shooting began.

Ketchell and his new ally had not supplied support fire for about twenty seconds. *They must be reloading.* She decided that when they resumed the cover fire, she'd make a break for their location.

A rifle report told her Ketchell had reloaded and was firing again. She thrust the revolver into her waistband and was preparing to make a run for it when she heard galloping hooves coming from Ketchell's position.

Poking her head up for a moment she saw a mule thundering toward her, its rider leaning over, reaching down. *How could it be? Jube!*

She leapt out of the culvert, grabbed his hand and swung up behind him. He turned the mule on a dime and galloped back toward Ketchell who continued blasting rounds toward the Mounties.

As they cleared a rise that took them out of sight of the ambush party, Jube brought the mule to a sliding stop. Leaping off, Deirdre hurried to the crest of the hill. When she got close to the crest, she dropped to her belly and snaked up to get a view of the riverbank.

Danny appeared out of a row of manzanita and strode back toward the Mounties who stood between Deirdre and her Soul Horse. She could see a large red spot covering his right hindquarters. It appeared that the arrow fell out or broke off. He was moving okay so maybe it was a surface wound.

The Mounties spotted Danny and his saddle bags and charged the animal. A moment later, a shot rang out, and one of the Mounties closest to Danny fell. Deirdre turned to see Ketchell taking aim at another Mountie with her Winchester. Jube, kneeling next to her, pumped some rounds toward the riverbank, all in an attempt to give Danny an opening to make his way upriver toward them.

Two Mounties grabbed at Danny, who kept circling, looking for an escape route toward Deirdre. Soon he reared in desperation. One of the Mounties fired when Danny was at the top of his rear and the horse pitched backwards into the river.

Deirdre watched Danny's body rotate as it was whisked away by the powerful current. She felt something snap inside her, deep down where the meanings are.

CHAPTER THIRTY-ONE

After Deirdre left Hussar Valley with Ketchell, Jube had gone up to the hill behind their tent and sat for several hours. When it sprinkled at mid-morning, Deirdre's father, Mark, brought him a poncho. Jube didn't react, staring intently into the cloudy sky, forcing Mark to put the poncho on him as if he were dressing a child. Jube managed a weak "thank you".

After the rain stopped, Francine joined him and, between bouts of weeping, expressed how much she missed Deirdre even though it had been only a few hours since she had left. Jube continued to peer up at the clouds like the answer to some cosmic question was written there. When Francine fell asleep, Jube covered her with the poncho and walked down to Mark's tent.

"I'm going to follow her," he said to the father of the woman he loved.

Mark sat in his lawn chair puffing on a loosely rolled cigarette, bits of tobacco dotting his lips. "She won't like it."

"You're right." He squatted in front of Mark. "Don't care."

"I'm not gonna judge a young man who wants to help my one daughter save the other one. Hell, I'd love to ride with her if I thought my old hips could handle that many hours in the saddle. But I'd just be in the way." He pointed with his cigarette towards Jube's wound. "Just like you'll be in the way if your wound opens up again."

Jube rubbed his face with his hands. "I don't know," he said, his voice breaking a bit. "Hell, I guess there's a fair chance I can't even catch up with her." He stood and looked north. "She travels fast."

He looked back toward Mark and smiled warmly. "I understand now that she can't do anything but go look for her sister. That's who she is. But I can't do anything but follow her and try to help her anyway I can." He paused for a moment and then gave a fatalistic shrug. "That's who I am."

When Jube stopped talking, Mark was well into rolling another smoke for himself. He finished it off, lit it up and then spoke. "All right. You and I will spend this afternoon outfitting you for a long ride."

The next morning, Jube, on Big Red and leading a jack donkey as a pack animal, headed for the Pacific Crest trail. Mark gave him his old Marlin 45-70 lever action rifle and two boxes of smokeless cartridges he'd been hoarding for an emergency.

When Jube reached Mojave, it was obvious Deirdre must have detoured around the fire. Her new route was a mystery. He started interviewing bikers until one of them told him they saw a pretty gal on a buckskin riding north on old 14 with a big guy who appeared to be her prisoner.

Within a few hours, Jube spotted fresh tracks branching off the 14 and followed them into the Sierra Nevada, pushing the animals and himself as hard as he dared. He figured he was close to catching up when he heard gunfire ahead.

✶✶✶✶✶

Her shoulders were slumped, her head hung so low her chin touched her chest. Jube thought perhaps she was curling up her body to protect herself from the wind that hit the caravan when they rode out of the mountains onto the flats. But the more he watched her, the more he was convinced her posture was the result of a spiritual crisis. His head throbbed and he felt a gnawing sensation in the pit of his stomach as his whole being empathized with her suffering.

After the Mounties realized the real goodies were on the pack animals who had bolted upriver behind the wall of cover fire laid down by Ketchell and Jube, they decided discretion was the better part of craven thievery and retreated into the woods.

Jube rounded up Blue, Durance and the pack mule pretty quickly. His own pack mule was hobbled in a field not far from the action. Deirdre jettisoned Blue's panniers and mounted him bareback. This served two purposes. It gave her a mount and the abandoned panniers would keep the Mounties occupied while Deirdre and her caravan maneuvered around them.

They penetrated the woods, followed some game trails and worked their way back toward the river when they figured that they had cleared the Mounties. They were back riding along the Kern headed towards Bakersfield two hours after Danny had disappeared into the rapids.

Deirdre was determined to follow the river as far as possible in case Danny survived and scrambled to shore. After hours of moving along the soggy riverbank, the other horses sinking into the muddy ground and occasionally in danger of slipping into the torrent themselves, Ketchell suggested they break away from the river. It was true the Kern would take them right into Bakersfield but since they were out of the mountains they could make better time by traveling directly toward the town on flat ground without following every bend of the river.

After moving away from the Kern, Jube became worried Deirdre might have given up on more than finding Danny. He speculated on the meaning of the term Soul Horse. Was there truly a profound spiritual connection between Deirdre and Danny? Had she endured some metaphysical catastrophe because she lost the horse that had been her daily companion since she was a little girl?

When Dequan shot Danny's eye out, she had responded by gunning him down in the town square of Laughlin. When Jube had been shot, Deirdre launched a one-woman counterattack that left dead and wounded strewn over several miles. It was reasonable to assume that soon there would be a dozen Mountie corpses floating down the Kern River. Yet Deirdre displayed no appetite for vengeance. She seemed defeated and hadn't said a word since Danny disappeared from sight.

Not long after nightfall, Blue lost a shoe. Deirdre dismounted and without saying a word approached Big Red, circled behind him, grasped the cantle and vaulted herself up onto the mule's rump.

As soon as she was in place, she leaned into Jube. It felt to him like a surrendering collapse. He loved feeling her body next to his but her heaving sighs worried him. Ketchell grabbed Blue's reins and ponied the paint as the caravan continued on.

When they entered the outskirts of Bakersfield, some members of the local constabulary were there to question their intentions in town. Deirdre explained they planned to stay with friends and asked for directions to the ranch owned by the ally of the Hussars.

It turned out it was close. A few minutes later, Jube was banging on the door of a dilapidated century-old ranch house. A sleepy man opened the door carrying a shotgun. Jube showed him a Hussar promissory note that Deirdre had pulled out of her cargo pants. The rancher read it, nodded and showed them to a mare motel with four stalls. He gestured toward bales of hay that were stacked in a three-sided aluminum shed.

"Help yourself to some Timothy," he said.

"Shit," Deirdre murmured just loud enough for Jube to hear. "Danny loved Timothy."

The rancher showed them a field and told them they were welcome to pitch their tents there. Ketchell asked about transport north and the man told them a pickup truck was headed to Fresno in two days.

Jube set up Deirdre's tent while she sat by the campfire Ketchell had kindled. When the tent was ready, she crawled in. Jube covered her with a bearskin and was about to leave when she grabbed his arm and said, "Stay with me, please," in a plaintive voice that broke his heart.

He lay next to her. She put her lips to his ear and said, "Thanks for coming." She patted softly on the bandage over the wound. "No blood. That's good."

Then, to remind him she was still on the job, she said, "You have to be careful of Ketchell. Remember, he doesn't need you. If he senses you're in the way, he'll kill you pretty quick." She kissed him on the lips. "Sweet dreams."

CHAPTER THIRTY-TWO

As the next day unfolded, Jube was amazed at Deirdre's resilience. After breakfast, she spent hours with the surviving animals, washing, brushing, massaging, filing hooves, replacing shoes and chatting with them. Jube heard Danny's name mentioned several times.

He turned in early, in need of a good night's sleep. The night before, he'd been too worried about Deirdre to do more than nod off for seconds at a time. It was summer in the San Joaquin Valley, which meant no covering was needed at night, so he lay down on a bearskin a few feet from Deirdre's tent and drifted off while she was giving the horses their evening meal.

He woke when something jarred his foot. Deirdre was standing over him.

"What?" he asked sleepily.

"What are you doing?" Her face was in shadows so he couldn't tell her mood.

"I was sleeping."

"Why out here?" she asked with an impatience that bordered on indignation. "Don't you want to sleep in there with me?"

"I do."

"Then let's go."

By the time he came into the tent she had a candle burning. She smiled sweetly when he sat down next to her. With a forceful push she shoved him flat on his back and leaned into his face.

"I love you," she said. It was a declaration of faith rather than a romantic sentiment.

"I love you, too," he said and surrendered to her kisses.

*****

The ride to Fresno seemed endless. They sat on the bed of a retooled, century-old truck, breathing in exhaust fumes, bouncing along on roads that hadn't been maintained in a century. It was dull until they hit a particularly angry pothole, and then it became painful for a while until their sore tailbones settled down, and then it would be dull again.

The suffering resulting from the loss of Danny had dented Deirdre's will in a way to allow love to flow unchecked toward Jube. It had to work that way for her to survive.

She spent the entire trip daydreaming about Jube and her. The pick-up truck's diesel engine was too loud for conversation, so her imagination was the only escape. And imagine she did.

She could see kids and lots of horses in their future. In her fantasy, this quiet man didn't protest when she was teaching a little version of him how to ride, shoot and raid. It all seemed so perfect. A constant in this fantasy was the presence of her sister.

*****

When they arrived in Fresno, they all agreed they preferred horses.

The transport let them off in a surprisingly intact residential neighborhood where they set up camp in a pleasant oak grove, probably once a city park.

Ketchell suggested first thing in the morning that they could hook up with a guy named Landsknecht, a local entrepreneur who worked out of a large shopping center called the Mercado. Landsknecht could arrange safe transport north to Sacramento where Deirdre would become Ketchell's "captive".

"Landsknecht? What kind of name is that?" Jube asked.

"An assumed one," Ketchell said. "He's showing off."

"What's he showing off?" Jube was curious about everyone who would be involved with his woman in these next few dangerous days.

"The Landsknechts were mercenaries back in the day," Ketchell explained, "and this gentleman is the most mercenary man I've ever met, and very proud of that. Wouldn't it be wonderful if everyone had a name that summed up exactly who they are?"

Deirdre, who was setting up her tent, emitted a derisive snicker. "So, you'd be Child Stealing Scumbag?"

Ketchell raised an eyebrow as he considered the name Deirdre had given him. "I suppose some might call me that. In a couple of days I'll be The Man Who Brought in Crazy Hawk."

That night, in the intimacy of the little tent, Jube made a final attempt at convincing Deirdre not to go ahead with what he thought was a doomed plan. He was only a few words into his plea when she put a finger on his lips. He understood. He didn't say another word.

In the morning, Ketchell told them they had to pass through the ruined downtown Fresno to reach the Mercado. They should leave as soon as possible. It was agreed Jube would stay with the packs at the campsite. Deirdre told him she'd be back at the end of the day to say goodbye.

After a breakfast of eggs and jerky, Deirdre and Ketchell set out to see Landsknecht. Jube nervously awaited her return.

When night fell and there was no sign of her, he panicked, his heart raging, his bowels churning. He knew something had gone wrong. She would never just change the plans and go north with Ketchell without letting him know.

He tried to make his way to the shopping center in the night, but he fell over rubble twice and was lucky to make it back to the campsite. As soon as the morning light was sufficient to avoid obstacles, he was on his way to find the Mercado.

CHAPTER THIRTY-THREE

Deirdre was so relaxed she had a hard time opening her eyes. When she did, the world was a blur. She drifted back to sleep. Or was it sleep, this dreamy, tenuous consciousness? It seemed like an endless loop of the same memories; a dingy bar named Frederick's, a man in a 21ˢᵗ-century suit smiling, Ketchell ordering drinks and a big fellow with a ponytail.

What was he doing?

Then it hit her. *I'm dead. Something happened in that bar that killed me. What was it?*

Even this line of thinking, a meditation on her recent death, couldn't hold her focus as her addled brain drifted off into contemplating the suit coat that shimmered before her mind's eye. She felt herself shaking her head, trying to jar that image loose.

She opened her eyes and this time she could make out some details; a light blue wall with rectangular objects hanging from it. Someone was sitting across the room but that didn't hold her attention. She fell back into the loop. Ketchell was still ordering drinks. Two beers.

Again, she cranked open her eyes. This time the focus was much clearer. Sitting against the wall opposite was a slender woman dressed like a nurse out of a movie. She wore a loose-fitting light blue cotton top and pants. Around her neck was one of those things healers use to listen to your heart.

Herb has one in the clinic but he never uses it. Hey, I'm thinking about Herb and not about the guy in the suit. Who was that? Was that Landsknecht?

The objects on the wall were quite clear now—framed paintings. Her mind was clearing rapidly as was her vision.

Have I been here before? Why is it so familiar?

There was a dresser with a vase of roses on top. In one corner was a television, and on a nightstand by her bedside she saw an electric lamp.

Though her mind was sharper now, she still had no idea what was happening. She gazed at one of the framed pictures, a pleasant painting of a doe standing before a waterfall.

She noticed that the wall behind the woman was covered with a design, large leaves intertwined endlessly. It was wallpaper! She'd seen the remains of wallpaper on her raids but she'd never experienced it intact, fresh and clean as it was intended to look.

She glanced at the woman in the nurse's costume who was reading a book and sitting in a big, bold chair that sat on…*Oh, come on! Carpeting?* Hussars pulled up old carpeting they found on their raids, repurposing it in various ways, but she'd never seen it like this, new, clean, plush. It was as if she were in a 21st-century movie.

The woman in the nurse's outfit looked up from her book and saw Deirdre's eyes open. "Oh, Sweetie, you're awake," she said, her tone warm and welcoming. "Are those arm restraints bothering you?"

Deirdre noticed metal cuffs on her wrists and chains running away from the cuffs to the floor. Moving her left arm, she felt the cuff jerk on her wrist as the chain ran out of slack.

She glanced at the woman in the nurse's costume who was now standing next to her bed, smiling sweetly. Deirdre could see now she had strong cheekbones and a shock of blonde hair. Deirdre guessed her age as around forty.

"You were thrashing around earlier," the woman said. "We didn't want you to hurt yourself or anyone else. My name's Victoria. I'm the head nurse here. I'll check to see if we can take those things off now." The woman gave Deirdre a reassuring pat on the shoulder and left the room.

Deirdre shook her head trying to clear out the rest of the cobwebs. She knew now she wasn't dead, just drugged. She also knew it was essential to meet the next hour with a clear mind.

She pulled on the chains but they wouldn't budge. Scooting as much as she could toward the left side of the bed, she peered down and saw the other end of the chain was fastened to a sturdy D-ring just visible in the plush carpet. She realized for the first time she was wearing nothing but a hospital gown like she'd seen in a movie.

Ketchell must have taken things into his own hands. In the Mercado, they had entered that weird bar. They were there to arrange transport to Sacramento. Somebody spiked that beer!

The head nurse reentered the room, accompanied by two men, both dressed as nurses, and another man carrying a 21st-century assault rifle like the ones that had been supplied to the Trogs.

Victoria seemed genuinely apologetic when she said, "I'm sorry. They're very cautious here. We won't be able to take the cuffs off just yet." A moment later, another woman in a nurse's uniform came in pushing a wheelchair.

"We're going to take you right now to speak with Leader," Victoria said. "This is the only time she has and she needs to talk to you."

"Who's Leader?" Deirdre asked.

"This young lady is my assistant, Barbara" Victoria said as if answering Deirdre's question. "These two gentlemen are also nurses and the man with the scary-looking weapon is from security."

One of the male nurses undid the right chain from the floor. As this was being done, security leveled the rifle at Deirdre's chest. The male nurse carried the chain around to the other side of the bed and wrapped it around the arm of the wheelchair. The second male nurse undid the other chain and gestured for her to get into the chair.

Although her legs were wobbly, she managed the move without embarrassing herself. When she was seated, the first male nurse wrapped the chain around the chair so that it crossed in front of Deirdre's chest twice.

The other one picked up straps that were attached to the wheelchair and fastened them to her ankles and right wrist. He was moving over to the left arm when Victoria stopped him.

"Can't she have one arm free? That way she could drink some coffee. Clear her head a bit. Leader would like that, I think." The male nurse glanced at security, who nodded. Deirdre's left arm remained free.

Soon Deirdre was coasting down a corridor, the young assistant nurse pushing the wheelchair, Victoria leading the way, a male nurse on either flank and security walking behind. Doors, about fifteen feet apart, lined the corridor on both sides. One of them opened and a good-looking couple in their late twenties came out of a room into the corridor. They smiled at Deirdre and passed down the hallway.

This isn't a hospital. It's more like a pre-Breakdown apartment building.

They stopped in front of double metal doors and Victoria pushed a little square button with an arrow pointing upwards. A moment later the doors opened revealing a small square room about the size of a standard Hussar tent.

As they pushed her forward, Deirdre realized she was about to take her first ride on an elevator. Even in her present situation, she found the feeling of her body being raised by a machine fascinating and was disappointed when it was over in a few seconds.

When the doors opened she was rolled into an expansive room. Deirdre was very impressed with the height of the ceiling. *A horse could rear up in here and not come close to smashing its head.*

In front of her was a circular, shining metal desk. Sitting behind the desk was the most beautiful human being she'd ever seen, except a couple of times on Movie Night. He possessed dazzling dark brown eyes and he was showing off his chiseled build by wearing a skin-tight red shirt. His black skin glistened majestically in the warm light of the room.

He stood up, nodded politely at Deirdre, turned to the massive wooden door behind him, opened it and stood aside as the nurse's assistant pushed her wheelchair in. Deirdre found herself in an office big enough to comfortably stable four horses — more carpeting, delicate lighting, a deep brown oak desk, a huge flat screen television set on the wall and an aquarium full of colorful fish, something Deirdre had only seen in old magazines.

Victoria addressed the handsomest man in the world. "Deirdre could do with a cup of coffee, Perry." She turned to Deirdre, "How do you like it?"

Deirdre wasn't sure of the point of the question. She answered honestly. "Hot."

Victoria chuckled. "Put a touch of cream and a taste of sugar in it, Perry."

Wow, they put cream and sugar in coffee. Luxury.

The male nurses started connecting the wheelchair chains to D-rings embedded in the floor. Perry reappeared with a ceramic mug which he held out to Deirdre's free hand.

She noticed an illustration on the cup's outer surface — a full-color representation of a honey bee. Virginia, Perry and the nurses retreated from the room, closing the door behind them.

After she let the coffee cool for a minute, Deirdre downed it in a few gulps, her mind now clear. She wondered if Ketchell had told them her plan. She decided her original theory was more likely the case, that he would rather die than admit to the Bees he was doing her bidding. That's the way she would play it. She was captured by Ketchell, plain and simple. She'd present a bitter and uncooperative persona, the belligerent captive.

The door to the office opened and a beautiful woman, around forty, walked in. She was six-foot, raven-haired with a lily-white complexion and a well-muscled figure that was accentuated by a dark green figure-hugging shirt.

"Hello, Deirdre," she said as she sat down behind the desk. "I'm the person they call Leader around here."

She sent just a touch of a smile Deirdre's way. "I apologize for the restraints but it's necessary for the time being." Her attitude was soft but not gentle, direct without being harsh. "I guess your head's swimming right now wondering who we are and what you're doing here."

"You're the Bees, my head's fine and I don't give a shit why you brought me here because I'm getting out real soon."

Leader went silent for a few moments, a wry smile lingering on her lips. "Love the confidence but not the self-delusion." Some steel was added to the timbre of her voice. "You're in chains, surrounded by well-armed soldiers who will apply overwhelming force, lethal if necessary, to stop you from leaving us."

She circled her beautiful fingers around a shiny metal cup that sat on the desk, brought it to her ample lips and delicately sipped. "How do you know we're the Bees?"

Deirdre held up her coffee mug, displaying the honey bee toward Leader. "I'm Sherlock Holmes."

"You know who Sherlock Holmes is," Leader observed with a big grin. "Very impressive. It's that Hussar combination of literacy and daring courage that made us so enthusiastic about bringing subjects from your culture into our program."

Deirdre squeezed out a grim laugh. "Well, I hope when my culture comes up here, burns your world to the ground and shoves a pike up your ass you'll still be as enthusiastic."

Leader shook her head admiringly as if she were observing a magnificent sunset or a beautifully crafted work of art. "You really are something. I've been hearing about you for months but rarely do such glowing reports have much truth behind them. Deirdre, the Bees are interested in rebuilding civilization and we'd like you to join us." She was oozing seductive charm.

"Bite me," Deirdre said, her face deadpan.

"That's everyone's initial reaction, rarely expressed so vividly. You'd be surprised how many of the subjects come around. You know why?"

"No and I don't give a shit."

"Because we have a plan," Leader said, her beautiful complexion turned pink from enthusiasm. "It's based on real science and we make a very convincing argument. Do you know why you're not dead?"

"Because my heart is beating. I know science, too."

"You disrupted our Youth Acquisition Program for over a year," she said, her tone suddenly harsh. "You've been a major thorn in our side. We could have simply put a bullet in your brain when you were brought to us unconscious."

"Are you looking for thanks?"

"Of course not. I'm just pointing out that even though you've been a formidable enemy to us, we didn't eliminate you."

"I get it," Deirdre said with a mocking laugh. "You want me to ask why. Okay, why?"

Ignoring the sarcasm, Leader leaned forward and spoke with great sincerity. "Because we think you may be special. Genetically speaking."

"Genetically? So, what are you going to do? Measure my brain or something?"

"Brain size is relevant to our theories. Very acute of you. Perhaps before the Breakdown scientists could measure the brain of a living person," she said slipping into a professorial mode, "but we wouldn't be able to do that unless you're dead. I hope that won't be soon. Instead, we'll be observing you carefully to see just how unique you are."

"It all sounds like a crock to me."

Leader leaned back in her chair and examined Deirdre. "Well, I hope in the coming weeks you will see that we're not the bad guys but instead the last, best hope for humankind."

"Speaking of self-delusion." Deirdre's eyes sparkled with defiance.

"I love your sense of humor," Leader said between chuckles. "I guess you wouldn't be open to working with us because of your loyalty to the Hussars?"

"Among other things."

"Full cooperation with us might protect your people when we expand our operations," Leader said, projecting a willingness to deal.

"My people don't need me to kiss your ass to protect them." Deirdre's indignation was genuine.

"No?" A crooked smile eased onto her face. She finished off her beverage with a long swig and then boldly locked eyes with Deirdre. "Do you know what mustard gas is, Deirdre?"

Deirdre's intensity faded just a tad. "I've heard of it."

"One breath of it is fatal. In the 20th and 21st, it was used as a weapon. We're producing a very effective variation. If we were to release it into select areas of Hussar Valley, we could wipe out your tribe in one day. That would not be our first choice. We'd rather ally with them. They're on a short list of peoples we think can be valuable to us. But if we were to learn that Hussars are incorrigible and friendship isn't an option, we'll just have to exterminate them. Starting with your sister, of course."

CHAPTER THIRTY-FOUR

After the meeting with Leader, Deirdre, still strapped to the wheelchair, was rolled through a tree-lined mall. She was fascinated watching the passers-by hurry to some appointment or other. The clothing they wore, the condition of the pavement they walked on, the well-tended grass in certain open areas, and the newly constructed buildings that bordered the mall, all of it made her feel like she'd taken a time machine back before the Breakdown.

She was taken to a room on the second floor of a cube-shaped concrete building, unshackled and left alone. "Enjoy your apartment," Victoria said as she departed.

It was no more than a fancy prison cell. There were bars on the windows and an iron door with a slot for delivering meals. In one corner was a fully functional sink and toilet, luxuries she had never experienced. There was some reading material, pamphlets explaining the Bee worldview, and a couple of old paperback novels.

The concrete walls were painted blue and the floor was plain concrete. Above a drain in the floor, a shower nozzle jutted out of one wall. There was only one nob to control the water. On the narrow bed lay a neatly folded baggy orange jumpsuit that zipped up the front and a few undergarments. Under the bed she found a pair of sandals.

As she took off the hospital gown and donned the jump suit, she wondered if she'd ever see her own clothes again. She was going to miss those Apache mocs. She loved the way they smelled, leathery and real. The only thing she could smell in this sterile cell was a sharp chemical odor, probably from some cleaning agent. She sighed. This was going to be a tough.

*****

Monotonous days came and went. Decent meals were delivered through the slot punctually at seven am, twelve noon and five pm.

Once a day, a tall, black-haired, pale, broad-shouldered security guard named Burke came in. While another guard stood in the doorway, keeping his rifle trained on Deirdre's chest, Burke shackled her to floor bolts as before.

Victoria would then come in to draw blood. When she was finished, Burke removed the shackles and Deirdre would be left alone.

Focusing on her plans proved difficult, her thoughts repeatedly drifting to Jube. What did he do when she didn't come back? Did he come looking for her? Landsknecht and his men would have been hard on him.

When she wasn't worrying about Jube, she was processing what Leader said about the mustard gas. She wondered if they really had such a weapon and a way to deliver it into her valley. Was that just talk, or was a Bee army marching to exterminate her people? And was her attitude toward the Bee agenda really going to decide the fate of her sister and her tribe?

She needed to contact Mindy. She had expected to be in the general population with some hope of reaching her, but this solitary lockdown led her into uncharacteristic despair.

Some of her gloom was brought on by the lack of fresh air and blue sky, having lived almost her entire life outdoors. Now she was entombed in a concrete box and it was crushing her spirit. All this was compounded by an inability to get a good night's sleep. Ominous, half-waking dreams of Jube in trouble and a buckskin horse being swept down a raging river kept her from real rest.

Deidre reached into the memory of her Wisdom Book which she studied as a teenager, the compendium of eastern warrior wisdom. She remembered a story of a great archery teacher who halted practice one winter day so that he could urinate. His students looked on with horror as red droplets speckled the white snow. Their master was pissing blood. He smiled at their alarmed expressions and said simply, "This is practice, too."

She'd held that piece of wisdom close to her heart for years, understanding its profundity from the first time she read it. The greatest challenges are sacred opportunities to practice being a great fighter, whether enduring battle, sickness, isolation, deprivation or separation. But now as she called on this epigram for inspiration, it fell flat on her consciousness, impotent against what was becoming a serious depression.

She remembered reading a Bible story as a kid about Samson losing his strength when his hair was cut. She wondered if this confinement away from fresh air and nature, the essentials of her previous existence, was trimming her metaphoric hair and turning her into a passive weakling.

After two weeks of this agonizing self-doubt, something changed her perspective. It had to do with her vomiting every morning for three days and realizing her period was late. There was a good chance she was pregnant.

Whether that was true or not, she clung to the idea as a motivation to get out of the swamp of despair she was drowning in. She had to act! One thing was clear; the Bees had plans for her. They weren't going to leave her in this hole forever. They'd move her at some point. When they did, she'd be ready.

CHAPTER THIRTY-FIVE

Two weeks into her stay in her soulless cell, Victoria and Burke arrived for what Deirdre assumed was their regular blood raid, but instead she was strapped and chained into the wheelchair, rolled out of the room, down the hall, into the elevator and out into the mall.

At first, the bright summer day gave her a moment of unexpected joy. *Fresh air and sky. How I've missed you.* But the air wasn't fresh, given the pollution from the Bee factories and refineries, and the sky wasn't clear because of the smog. She had never experienced either of those things and found them disturbing. Her joy quickly dulled into sullenness.

She was pushed down the mall toward a large building marked *HOSPITAL* over the main entrance.

When they passed a small grassy oasis amid all this concrete, something caught her attention. Three teenagers, two boys and a girl, all wearing distinctive leather jackets, were lounging under the shade of a cypress. The boys were sprawled on the grass chatting energetically while the girl stood leaning against the tree. Deirdre recognized her wiry frame and casual pose immediately. It was Mindy.

A security officer positioned by the hospital entrance opened the door and Deirdre was rolled down a long corridor that looked just like one she'd seen in a movie hospital.

Deirdre struggled to mask the extreme emotion gushing up from the deepest chamber of her soul. Her feelings bounced between great joy at seeing Mindy healthy and an intense anger triggered by seeing her held prisoner.

An elevator ride took her up to another corridor where she was pushed through a pair of swinging doors into a small square room, about twelve by twelve. Her wheelchair was parked in front of a table with a thin cushion on top. She observed glass cabinets lining one wall. She surmised that the boxes, bottles and vials she saw inside the cabinets contained medical accoutrement.

Deirdre's mind was racing as she considered the Mindy sighting. What did those leather jackets mean? And who were those boys she was with? She saw a sidearm on the hip of the one closest to the walkway. They must be Mindy's guards. Would she ever spot her sister again, or was this her one chance to make contact?

Victoria, Burke and the other guard debated the best way to secure her to the table. Even though Victoria was whispering, Deirdre's sharp hearing caught "I think you two could get her under control if she got out of hand." The one guard was unsure but Burke seemed to want to impress Victoria and nodded.

Something hadn't occurred to Deirdre until now; none of these Bees had ever fought her. She was drugged in the bar and brought here unconscious. What they knew of her combat prowess were secondhand reports. They were underestimating her.

After Burke undid the chains, she slowly pulled herself out of the chair as if she were weak and disoriented. Burke's overconfidence and the other guard's uneasiness told her their cadences were out of sync and it was time to act.

She flew at the guard who had been tentative about unchaining her and slammed the palm of her hand against his nose. As he staggered back toward one of the glass cabinets, she shoved his chin, driving his head into the cabinet, shattering the glass.

She heard alarmed cries coming from Victoria and Burke and the sound of feet scrambling behind her. She grabbed a shard of glass, spun and buried it deep into Burke's left eye as he charged her. As he screamed, she tore the rifle from his grasp and bolted out the double doors.

Exploding through a door marked *STAIRWELL*, she fled down the stairs. Reaching the ground floor, she thrust open the exit door and found herself facing the grassy oasis where Mindy and the boys were still lounging. She ran towards her sister.

The boys spotted her when she was about ten feet away, scrambled to their feet and reached for their sidearms. She leveled one with a roundhouse kick and slammed the rifle butt into the other's forehead. With her back to Mindy, she readied herself for the pursuers who would be bursting out of the hospital at any moment.

She gestured toward the unconscious boys with a tilt of her head. "Grab their weapons, Mindy. We're fighting our way out of here."

She felt the cold steel of a pistol muzzle press against the base of her skull. When Mindy spoke, her voice was mature and assertive.

"Drop the weapon, Dee. I'd hate to splatter your brains all over this pretty grass."

The hospital main entrance coughed up two guards and a moment later two more, all heavily armed.

"I mean it, Dee." Her kid sister's tone was deadly serious.

Stunned by this development, Deirdre dropped the weapon. Burke emerged from the double doors screaming incomprehensible oaths, the shard of glass still sticking out of his eye socket. When he spotted Deirdre, he charged vengefully.

Victoria appeared behind him and barked an order. "Take it easy, Burke. Confine any injury to the head and shoulders."

It was then that Deirdre understood she was pregnant and the Bees knew about it.

*****

"Well, that didn't pan out," Deirdre drawled as she lay on the blood-spattered concrete floor of the dingy cell. The only lighting was a thin ray of sunshine seeping through a tiny window ten feet above.

"You better do something or you're going to bleed out." The words came from a shadowy corner of the cell.

Deirdre sat up and peered into the darkness. She managed to make out the shape of some creature hunched against the wall.

"My scalp is already clotting," Deirdre said calmly as if reporting on someone else's condition. "My nose stopped bleeding a while ago. I'm still spitting out blood but I'm pretty sure that's from a tooth that's been knocked out—not anything internal. They only hit me a few times and concentrated pretty much on my face."

"Really?" The voice from the shadows seemed surprised.

"Yeah. I'm pregnant. They want my baby for whatever the fuck they're doing here."

Laugher erupted from the shadows, punctuated by a series of sharp, phlegmy coughs.

"Who am I talking to?" Deirdre asked.

"Linda."

"Deirdre."

"I'll give you some good news," Linda said, her voice light and genial. She appeared to be happy to have someone to talk to. "If they want your baby, they're not going to leave you down here long. They're just trying to scare the hell out of you. What did you do?"

"Tried to escape."

"And you're alive?" Linda said with a note of wonder. "Huh. You and your baby must be special."

"What are you doing down here, Linda?"

Linda went silent for what seemed to Deirdre over a minute. When she finally spoke, her voice was somber. "I spoke out against their vision of the future."

Deirdre spat out more blood. "What is their vision?"

"They're trying to develop a master race."

"Like the Nazis," Deirdre said, nodding as if *now* she gets it.

"What do you know about the Nazis?"

"Hitler, the Holocaust. I know a lot of that stuff."

"Wow! I'm impressed. In the two years I've been down here, I've had several cellmates. Not one of them knew who the Nazis were or much of anything about the old world."

"I'm a Hussar," Deirdre said proudly.

"Is that supposed to mean something to me?"

"My tribe believes in education."

"How charming," Linda said with a chuckle and a cough.

Deirdre spat out more blood.

"Here," Linda said. Deirdre could hear the sound of fabric tearing. "Take this. It's a corner of my shirttail. I've been preserving it for an emergency. Kept it as clean as possible. No bodily fluids have touched it. Just regular jail cell filth."

A piece of grey cotton landed on Deirdre's lap. It was roughly a four-inch square.

"Roll it up and chomp on it," Linda instructed. "It'll stop your gums from bleeding."

Deirdre obeyed, shoving the cloth roll toward the back of her mouth and chomping down. "Damn, you hate to lose those big ones," she said through clenched teeth.

Linda laughed, prompting another spasm of coughing.

"Thanks for your help," Deirdre said.

"No, not like the Nazis," Linda said, dragging their attention back to the conversation.

"But what about all that master race bullshit?"

"The Nazis thought they were the master race," Linda said. "The Bees have no such delusion, but they are convinced they can develop the master race through selective breeding."

"So that's why they're grabbing kids."

"Yes. The purpose of the Youth Acquisition Program is to widen the gene pool." She laughed again. No coughs this time. "GISP is actually convinced they're on the moral high ground because they don't discriminate in their kidnapping based on race."

"What's GISP?"

"Oh, sorry. GISP stands for Geneticists In Search of Perfection. They're an extremely powerful faction."

"Wow." Deirdre pondered this information for a few seconds before asking, "So you spoke out against all this and that's why you're down here?"

"Pretty much. I was an ethical advisor to GISP. They told me they were only bringing in homeless orphans. So, at first my criticism was of their selection process. They seemed obsessed with picking good looking people, regardless of their intelligence."

Deirdre nodded. "Yeah, I've noticed a lot of good looking people around."

"But soon it became obvious they weren't just supplying a home for the dispossessed. They were kidnapping children from their families. That's when my criticism became more strident. I was labeled subversive."

Deirdre leaned forward and made sure her next question was understood. "Do they really have mustard gas?"

"They began developing the gas three years ago." A coughing fit interrupted the narrative. When she got her voice back, she continued. "As an experiment, they used it to exterminate a village of Trogs. A nightmarish weapon."

Deirdre spent a moment thinking of the devastating effect the gas would have on Hussar Valley before asking, "Is there a way out of the Hive?"

"By escape? No. The only people who could possibly have access to an exit are those they trust as true believers in the cause of making a perfect, soulless world."

"What's your problem with making a perfect world?" Deirdre asked.

"It's magical thinking," said Linda sternly.

"You're wrong," Deirdre said. "They're on to something. Selective breeding probably is the answer to most of the world's problems. And Trogs! I've killed dozens of those guys. No loss there." Her enthusiasm was a little too large to be authentic.

"Oh, I see what you're doing," Linda said. "That's your strategy, to convince them you're on board with their program? I like it. Method acting."

"Acting? Who's acting," Deirdre said with mock indignation. "I'm buying in. And what's wrong with having a good-looking race? Why would it be so terrible if there were more hot guys around?"

Linda's laugh was loud and unsullied by coughs. "Not quite believable, yet. But keep working at it. You may convince them."

CHAPTER THIRTY-SIX

Case Notes: Deirdre of the Hussars

Case Worker: Victoria Leland

July 9. Tomorrow I'll recommend the Hussar be lobotomized. Yesterday she attacked and injured four Bees, shoving a shard of glass into the eye of Security Specialist Burke.

Cadet Mindy Buford participated in subduing Deirdre and told us that even among the Hussars, Deirdre was considered difficult. By all reports, Mindy is a trusted cadet, putting loyalty to the Bees above any sentimentality about family.

The lobotomy would in no way impede our ability to use her DNA in the program if that's still considered desirable. We could oversee bringing her pregnancy to completion and use her child in our infant development experiments. I am becoming convinced the Hussar woman is emotionally unsuited to be part of our program. Perhaps that is true of her child as well. We certainly don't want overly violent psychopaths entering our gene pool.

July 10. Leader refused my request to lobotomize Deirdre even though I *had the full support of all security personnel. She said I need to try harder to pacify her. She's convinced Deirdre is a key to our program's development and ordered that she immediately be released from the high-security cell, receive full medical treatment for the injuries incurred during her escape attempt and then be returned to her room in the medium-security building.*

This is not over. Commandant Walker is vehemently opposed to such lenient treatment of a woman who seriously injured several Bees.

July 15. A remarkable change in Deirdre's behavior! She asked to speak to me. I allowed it and she proceeded to weep. She begged my forgiveness for the attack of the 8th of July, saying it was anxiety concerning her unborn child that drove her to such an extreme act, but now she's convinced the best way to ensure her child's healthy birth is to work with us. "Give me one more chance" was her oft-repeated plea.

I don't buy it. Even though her tears seemed sincere, I suspect she's just trying to get us to lower our guard so she can attempt another escape. When I reported this change to Leader I also said I thought we shouldn't include her in our program unless we're interested in developing a race of convincing actors.

Leader was unamused and told me to enroll her immediately in the indoctrination class. Commandant Walker would not sign off unless Leader approved a shoot-to-kill order to be executed as soon as she steps out of line.

CHAPTER THIRTY-SEVEN

Mr. Daniels ran thick, well-defined fingers through salt and pepper hair as he paced in front of the small classroom, conscious of his dashing profile and well-conditioned body.

Deirdre thought he looked like an actor from a 21st-century movie but couldn't remember which one. She knew it wasn't Jeff Bridges, the only actor she connected with a name.

Daniels stood at a podium in front of the indoctrination class that consisted of four students. Behind him hung a poster, about four by four feet. Printed on it were representations of two brains of differing sizes. *MODERN MAN* was printed boldly under the picture of the smaller brain. The other brain, considerably larger, was identified as *CRO-MAGNON MAN* in equally bold print.

"Cro-Magnon man's brain was one-third bigger than ours," he explained, pointing at the different brains for emphasis. "As technology made human life easier with agriculture, the wheel, the sail, the printing press, cars, planes, computers, artificial intelligence, our brains became more specialized."

He began sauntering across the front of the class, quite proud of his good looks and sonorous voice.

"That section of the Cro-Magnon brain dedicated to the spatial and instinctual aspects of survival was no longer as important. We didn't need to kill a buffalo with a stick; we could do it with a rifle at five hundred yards while sitting in a lawn chair. When technology forced evolution to take its foot off humankind's throat, the brain started to shrink.

"In the 21st, a head of a corporation could fail miserably and not be punished. Instead, the individual would receive a bonus of millions of dollars. Because money gave these failed executives power, they attracted healthy mates, reproduced and populated the upper classes with idiots.

"The same thing was going on in the underclass of the welfare state where lazy parasites were encouraged to do nothing but propagate. More imbeciles contaminating the human species.

"The good news is that the Great Virus eliminated many of these subjects and by so doing purified the physical strength and resilience of those left.

"What the Great Virus did for the physical nature of humankind, purging an entire generation of those with weak immune systems, the Breakdown did for the psychological side of humanity.

"The report of mass suicides after the disappearance of the Cloud is only one bit of evidence suggesting that many people were simply weak emotionally.

"Those who walk the planet now had ancestors psychologically strong enough to survive those horrible days. With the gene pool purified both physically and psychologically, we may very well be on the verge of an evolutionary rebound of epochal proportion."

Deirdre was bored. She turned aside so the teacher couldn't see her yawning and stared at a bumblebee embossed on the big brass buckle worn by her guard. She glanced up at him. He was well over six feet tall, his bright blue eyes staring out from underneath a sweeping forehead covered by rich auburn curls. His skin was darker than one would expect given the blue eyes. She had no idea what his ethnic mix was but it definitely created a beautiful man.

His name was Richard and he'd been assigned to watch her every move while she was out of her cell. Victoria, wearing the same sweet smile she flashed when talking about the breakfast menu, told her all about it that morning. "Richard has total discretion as to when it's appropriate to terminate your stay with us."

She explained that after an evaluation period, if Deirdre wasn't making satisfying progress, she would be lobotomized. The nurse took obvious pleasure in describing that procedure.

When out of her room, Deirdre wore leg irons and handcuffs secured to an iron waistband, leaving her only enough mobility to work a pencil or a fork and walk ever so slowly.

Daniels was explaining the Bee political structure. "Modeled on the Roman model of two Consuls, the Commandant and Leader share power equally. This gives the Bees the perfect balance between strong leadership and a check on that leadership if it should go astray. Any major policy decision has to be supported by both Leader and the Commandant. If there is an irreconcilable disagreement, the deadlock is broken by a vote of the Elders."

As he droned on, Deirdre took stock of her three classmates. They were all attractive.

One was an Asian girl, late teens, with a breathtakingly smooth complexion and an adorable face so perfectly formed she looked more like an idealized painting than a human being. She wore no cuffs or leg irons and listened to the teacher with rapt attention. Deirdre overheard her talking to one of the other students, telling him this was the third time she'd taken the course. "I just find it so inspiring." Deirdre decided to call her Teacher's Pet.

Behind Teacher's Pet sat a hulking man whose hands, as big as a couple of frying pans, lay palms up on his lap. Deirdre figured he was in his early twenties, Mexican, probably from La República.

The black hair draping over his solid shoulders and framing his angular, rugged face gave him the look of a fierce Aztec warrior. He wore an orange jumpsuit, leg shackles and cuffs similar to Deirdre's. The teacher referred to him once by name—Pagan. Sensing she was looking at him, he flashed her the bird.

Hey, you're not so tough, she thought. *You don't have your own private guard.*

She didn't resent his hand gesture. He'd probably heard she was a Hussar. She understood why República types hated her people. Hussars raided his land on a regular basis. His generally defiant mood would have mirrored her own had she not been pregnant. Since her failed escape, all her waking moments had been dedicated to figuring out how best to steer through the land of the Bees without endangering the little one she was carrying.

Her attention drifted to the labyrinth of mysteries surrounding her sister. First of all, why did Mindy help the Bees in foiling her escape? Was it because she saw it as suicidal and thought the only way to save her big sister was to stop an insane escape attempt? And why did she have a gun? She wasn't just a prisoner. Had she really been seduced by the Bee propaganda?

The teacher wrapped up the lecture, a relief to Deirdre and Pagan but a disappointment to Teacher's Pet, who evidently thought the instructor was the most interesting person she'd ever experienced.

Deirdre decided not to let her have uncontested pet status. When Mr. Daniels walked by she said with enthusiasm, "Thank you, sir. That lecture meant a lot to me." From his self-satisfied grin, Deirdre knew her comment had landed.

CHAPTER
THIRTY-EIGHT

Deirdre's performance as an enthusiastic Bee rookie was masterful. Each day she'd amp up her faux commitment. She was able to seem involved and curious three times a week in the hideously dull indoctrination class.

During a pregnancy check-up at the hospital, a nurse commented on her winged Hussar tattoo: "I wish I could get a tattoo but that's strictly forbidden here. You're lucky they're not talking about removing yours."

The next day, when Nurse Leland came to collect blood, Deirdre begged to get a tattoo of a bee on her upper right arm. She feigned disappointment when Leland informed her of the ban on tattoos. Soon the arm cuffs were removed, and only the leg restraints remained.

When she was being escorted by Richard to the indoctrination class one morning, Deirdre spotted Leader surrounded by a group of Bees.

Walking close on her right side was a well-muscled man, taller than Hussar Eagle Haller, who she knew was six foot four. Sporting a tan that made his skin glisten with a golden hue and a full head of carefully disordered blond hair, he strode confidently next to Leader, in contrast to the rest of her retinue, who hung back in various modes of subservience.

Richard watched him with great awe, informing Deirdre that this was Commandant Walker, co-ruler of the Hive with Leader. Deirdre saw an opportunity.

As Leader's group passed, Deirdre called out and asked if she could speak with her. The members of the entourage glared at the young Hussar with disdain. Leader didn't talk to just anybody and never to a passer-by in leg irons. When Leader peeled off from her group and walked toward Deirdre, there was surprise on the faces of her sycophants. Leader stopped a few feet from Deirdre.

"I just wanted to say thank you for this opportunity," Deirdre said with as much sincerity as she could fake and still seem authentic. "I'm so sorry about my escape attempt. It was a foolish reaction to realizing I was pregnant."

Leader studied her carefully and then smiled. "Yes, it was foolish. You know by now another attempt would be suicide."

"I want my kid born healthy, into full Bee status," she said, tilting her head forward, looking at the ground. "I'm going to do everything I can to make that happen." Then she looked directly into Leader's face and said with shameless ebullience, "I want the little one to be a part of the future of humankind."

Leader nodded and continued on with the rest of her group, but Walker stepped out of the crowd to cast a piercing stare at Deirdre. His fierce eyes contained none of Leader's warmth and enthusiasm but instead radiated suspicion and judgement.

Richard grabbed her arm and led her on toward the classroom. The Commandant's glare made Deirdre nervous, but she was pleased with how the exchange with Leader went.

A few days later, she was permitted to eat dinner in one of the mess halls. The experience was a disappointment. About a third of those who ate there had leg irons, and all wore orange jumpsuits, indicating some level of introductory training. No one wore leather jackets like the one Mindy was wearing, not even the guards who wore khaki uniforms like Richard and Burke. She began to worry she might never catch another glimpse of her sister.

She peppered Richard with questions about the significance of the leather jackets. He told her they were worn by the elite Killer Bees, or K-Bees for short, and were only issued to the most trusted soldiers.

Deirdre managed to work up a few tears as she made a passionate inquiry as to how she could get into that trusted circle. Richard didn't have an answer. He said he'd love to move up to the K-Bees himself, but his guard position seemed to be a frozen career field.

Within two months of her incidental conversation with Leader, Richard disappeared from her life. Victoria told her that the door to her cell would be unlocked every day after lunch, and she'd be allowed to move, independent of any personal guard, from her cell to the indoctrination course, the hospital, the exercise area or the mess hall for dinner. The leg irons would remain on. This "freedom" would last as long as Deirdre kept to her schedule.

The newfound mobility enabled Deirdre to move into the next stage of her plan. She would need allies to pull off an escape. Unenthusiastic inductees were the prime candidates. No one was more obviously disgruntled than her classmate, Pagan. His attitude was so bad, Deirdre figured discussions must be underway among the Bee leadership about "terminating his stay". She needed to contact him soon.

Writing with the handle of a plastic fork dipped in gravy, she scribbled a rough note on a paper napkin. Limited by the supply of gravy, she had to keep it short. It read, "*Let's get out of here. Meet me by the mess hall dumpster at 3.*" All inhabitants of the Hive knew what time it was at any given moment. There were clocks everywhere;

punctuality was considered a high virtue. She folded the napkin into a small square.

*****

"Once the perfecting of the genetic side of humankind is accomplished, and the technology of the 21st is recaptured, we will turn our attention to recreating the human experience, this time making a society without hunger, strife, longing or suffering."

Deirdre was barely listening to the claptrap Daniels was preaching. Her eyes were on Pagan. She had to time her exit so that she was right behind him.

When the class was dismissed, she almost knocked Teacher's Pet over as she slid between the Asian woman and Pagan. Just as he was leaving the room, she reached up and stuck the note between his collar and the back of his neck. He gave her a curious look and went on his way.

The big clock on the square outside the dining room read two minutes to three when she turned the corner and approached the dumpster. Pagan wasn't there. She waited ten more minutes but couldn't wait any longer as she was due at the hospital for an exam at three-fifteen.

This failure to make contact with Pagan bothered her more than she expected. The plan to make allies had kept her positive and proactive but it seemed to have hit a dead end.

She returned to her room profoundly anguished about her child, her sister and Jube. Perched on the edge of a spiritual chasm, she desperately looked for a philosophical handhold to keep her from falling in.

She found it in a passage she had memorized long ago from her

Wisdom Book. *Life is an ongoing succession of one action at a time. A warrior who realizes this truth need not hurry or seek anything else. Live in the present with single-minded purpose and life will become simple and clear.* It didn't magically cure her anxiety but it did give her just enough serenity to fall asleep.

In the morning, she shook off the melancholy brought on by a dream about Danny in the river and focused on the problem at hand, ready to explore with an unfettered mind the first opportunity to act that presented itself.

When her breakfast was delivered, she noticed the corner of a piece of paper sticking out from under the plate of scrambled eggs. Moving the plate, she picked up a bright white envelope. She opened it, took out a folded piece of white ruled paper, unfolded it and saw a message written in bold letters with red ink.

Meet me at 5 pm. Under the staircase leading to your cell is a door. It appears to be locked but the lock is broken. Push hard. It'll open. Close it behind you and go down the steps toward the light. I'll be waiting for you there.

The time for the suggested rendezvous was originally written 5:30 but had been changed to *5pm* by crossing out the *:30* and writing *pm* above.

****

The clock over the front door read two minutes to five when Deirdre entered her building and moved quickly behind the staircase. Deep shadows cast by the stairwell hid anything that might be there.

Running her hands along the plaster wall, she touched a door frame, found a doorknob and turned it. As the note said, it appeared locked. She threw her shoulder against it, jarring it open.

Stepping onto a landing, she looked down and saw a light, presumably at the bottom of a flight of stairs, although she couldn't see the steps in the shadows. She closed the door behind her, felt for the top step with her right foot, made contact, decided to trust the other steps were where they were supposed to be and descended as quickly as her leg irons would allow.

When she reached the bottom, she was standing on the concrete floor of an eight-foot-high, ten-foot-wide tunnel. Electric lights suspended from iron fixtures and spaced every forty feet lit it up as far as she could see in either direction.

Along the walls and on the ceiling was a mass of wiring running in and out of sockets. This must be where Bee technicians maintained the electrical grid. The wiring looked new as did the wooden ceiling but the concrete floor and walls were worn and cracked indicating the tunnel was pre-Breakdown. Maybe the Bees built here to take advantage of the tunnel system.

The first time she looked around, Deirdre saw no one but when she checked a second time, someone was standing in the center of the tunnel, backlit by the ceiling lights, which allowed Deirdre to see their silhouette but not make out any features. It was clear this person was much smaller than Pagan.

She worried she'd stumbled on a maintenance worker and quickly constructed a cover story. Then she heard the rattle of a chain and surmised whoever she was looking at must be wearing leg irons.

The mysterious figure stepped forward into the light. The first thing Deirdre noticed was that the chain was not attached to ankle manacles but in the left hand of a woman with blazing black eyes and skin that shone bronze in the artificial light.

Deirdre recognized her. It was Fedora, the soldier of the Nations she had chosen not to kill and left tied to a boulder. In her right hand was a butcher knife.

"Hello, Crazy Hawk," Fedora said in that same gravelly voice Deirdre had heard that day in the desert. "What do you think? Is it a good day to die?"

CHAPTER
THIRTY-NINE

S iki had been wounded by Deirdre's maniacal counterattack after Jube was shot. Although a round passed through her thigh, it didn't break bone or pierce an artery, but it did necessitate a long convalescence before she could ride.

In that time, she burned with a vengeful fire. It wasn't only the leg wound that gnawed at her. The murder of her cousin's husband, Dequan, the wounding of her friend, Nacoma, the theft of her stallion, and being left tied to a boulder to rot—all of it motivated Siki.

And, of course, there were the words of the Mountain Person. "Siki, you must follow the Hawk. The flow of honey will be stopped."

While still bedridden, she requested a visit from an Apache shaman. When she explained what the Mountain Person told her in the vision, he agreed the Hawk was undoubtedly the Hussar woman but was unconvinced by her theory that the "honey" meant Apache fertility.

"I think it could refer to something else," the Apache shaman said. "The Mountain Person didn't tell you to destroy the Hawk, only pursue her. Perhaps if you do that, the meaning of the honey will become clear."

Siki was disgusted by this analysis. In her mind, destroying the Hawk was a given. She felt the shaman was being political since the Nations leadership didn't want to risk an all-out conflict with the Hussars. His weak interpretation would make it almost impossible to recruit help in hunting Deirdre. She decided to do it on her own.

As soon as she could ride, Siki set out with one goal—to end the earthly existence of Crazy Hawk.

She planned to live off the land in the San Jacinto range while observing the Pacific Crest trail, which she knew Hussars regularly used for moving up and down Pacifica on their raids.

She was riding through the Mojave Desert, not far from where she would intersect with the PCT, when she saw a lone rider in the distance headed north.

She dismounted, scurried onto high ground and focused on the rider with her binoculars. It was Gentle Boy, the man who had left the water for her. Her first reaction was shock. The wound he took from the rifle of the dumb white mercenary should have killed him but here he was.

Maybe the power of the Hussar animal spirits is a real thing.

Either way, she had a clear shot. From the way Crazy Hawk reacted when he was wounded, Siki knew he meant a lot to her; killing him would hurt the Hussar deeply.

She had him in her sights for around thirty seconds but didn't pull the trigger. She remembered how Gentle Boy had left the canteen for Nacoma. Her Apache upbringing had fostered the virtues of gratitude and reciprocity. She couldn't gun down a defenseless man who had shown concern for her survival, so she decided to follow him instead. Maybe he was on his way to meet Crazy Hawk.

Following his tracks from a distance, she kept on his trail through the town of Mojave and into the Sierra Nevada. On the third day, she heard a gunfight in progress ahead of her and guessed her quarry had run into Mounties.

The next dawn she picked up the trail again, but this time she was following multiple equines. Probably five. She felt sure one of those riders was Crazy Hawk.

She lost them in Bakersfield, but by asking around, she learned that a party, including a young Hussar woman, was transported to Fresno in a fossil fuel vehicle.

She reached Fresno a few days later and spent weeks around town asking about Crazy Hawk, trading her horse and some of her gear for food and local commerce tokens. She was determined to stay in town until she learned something about the location of the Hussar.

While passing through the ruin of downtown Fresno one afternoon, she heard someone groaning. Gentle Boy lay in a debris-filled ditch, covered with filth, mumbling unintelligibly. A folder full of papers was held close to his body under his right arm.

She was amazed at how much he had degraded since she'd seen him on the trail. He looked up at her and smiled sweetly for no apparent reason, behaving like the village idiot.

She pulled a knife from her belt. "Where's that crazy white girl?"

"You're looking for Deirdre, too?" he muttered, his tone desperate, his voice weak.

"Don't give me that shit. You know where she is."

"No, I don't." His face was taut with pain as he struggled to focus his bloodshot eyes on Siki.

"Are you hurt?" she asked.

"Only in my soul."

"I have no idea what that means." She pointed the knife at his throat and asked coldly, "Do I have to kill you or are you going to tell me where she is?"

"I don't know where she is," he groaned. "Landsknecht took her.

I don't know where."

He appeared out of his mind with pain, thirst and hunger, irrationally obsessed with protecting the folder full of papers which he squeezed even tighter to his torso.

Now that her threat had failed to produce information, she knew it was her duty to show mercy to the man who'd helped her. She tossed him her last piece of bread and leaned a canteen against his side.

She spotted a red stain above his left breast, pulled open his shirt and saw his wound had opened. Grabbing herbs and bandages out of her travel bag, she quickly cleaned the wound, applied some herbs and changed the dressing.

"We're even," she said. Gentle Boy, who was mumbling to himself, had no clue what she was talking about.

She walked to the Mercado and went from booth to booth inquiring about Landsknecht. It wasn't long before she was directed to Fredrick's.

Inside the saloon, which was bizarrely decorated with pre-Breakdown manikins of lithe female bodies, she asked about Crazy Hawk. A guy with a ponytail got rough with her. She went for his throat but someone clubbed her on the back of the head with something heavy and she was out cold.

Siki woke up a day later in the Hive, leg irons on her ankles, assigned to the labor force. Her daily existence consisted of sleep in a barracks with a hundred other manacled slaves and work in a horrible factory where she was chained each morning to her position in an assembly line.

She learned quickly that the way out of this hellish existence was to appear valuable by working hard and showing self-initiative at every opportunity. Soon she was promoted from being a worker robot in the ammunition factory to a do-it-all handywoman with mobility around the Hive, although she was still forced to wear manacles.

One day, when assigned to clean up rubbish at a construction site, she bonded with a disgruntled Bee trainee named Pagan.

*****

Deirdre knew she was at an extreme disadvantage. She was unarmed and her mobility was limited by the manacles, whereas the wiry figure in front of her had two weapons and no chain on her leg irons to hinder her movement. And, of course, Deirdre had to be particularly cautious about any blow to her midriff.

She quickly weighed her options. There weren't any. That chain would be effective at a distance and the knife would be deadly at close range.

"Do you remember me?" Fedora asked. Her tone was playful, but Deirdre knew it veiled a ferocious anger.

"Yeah. You're Fedora."

"Fedora? Is that what you call me? Ha. My name's Siki. I think it's only right you know the name of your executioner."

"You don't have to do this," Deirdre said, her gaze following Siki as she began to drift toward her right, Deirdre's left.

"You left me to die in the middle of the desert."

"I left you with an excellent chance of survival. Obviously, you made it."

"You wounded my partner and left him to bleed out," Siki said, her voice now quivering with rage. "When you went berserk after your boyfriend got hit, you put a bullet through my leg and wounded another of my people who was riding with us. And then there's my cousin's husband."

"Your cousin's husband?"

"Dequan."

Deirdre shook her head. That incident had caused her a lot of grief.

Siki continued. "Everyone knows he was a prick but he was family." Then with a cold calm that told Deirdre things were about to get very real Siki said, "You're wrong, Crazy Hawk. I do have to do this."

She leapt forward and swung the chain toward Deirdre who dodged out of the way but the iron linkage tore the tip of her ear, sending blood trickling down the side of her head and onto her neck. On her next swing, Deirdre lunged toward the knife hand, grabbed the wrist and slammed her shoulder into Siki's side.

Siki stumbled back, Deirdre continuing to cling to the wrist. She brought her left hand up to the throat of the Apache, who understood the chain was no longer useful in close and, letting it drop, clamped her hand on Deirdre's throat.

Deirdre was stunned at the strength of her grip and decided against a choking match. She swung her legs into Siki's knees, which sent both of them sprawling, breaking Siki's throat grip and Deirdre's wrist hold, forcing her to quickly roll away as the knife clanked against the concrete floor, millimeters from her throat.

She felt the chain underneath her, grabbed it and leapt to her feet as did her opponent. Now that Deirdre had the chain, she knew the skilled Apache would try to close as quickly as possible.

Siki charged, in a crouch, hoping to duck the chain, but Deirdre brought it down from above, crashing the iron links against her skull.

The Apache's face hit the floor as Deirdre jumped with both feet onto her right forearm. The grip loosened around the knife and Deirdre was able to kick it out of her hand.

As Siki tried to stumble to her feet, Deirdre started to swing the chain toward her opponent's neck when an iron grip caught her wrist. She turned to see Pagan hulking over her. She landed a solid kick to his groin. He dropped to the ground with a whimper.

A moment later, Deirdre lay stunned against the tunnel wall. Something had struck her alongside the temple. She saw Teacher's Pet standing beside her, holding a four-foot stretch of rebar. "Stay down," the Asian woman barked. "We're on your side."

Teacher's Pet explained to Deirdre that her name was Yen Thi Vo. Deirdre, who had learned much about different ethnicities in her travels, recognized this name to be of Vietnamese origin.

Deirdre sat carefully feeling her abdomen, pretty sure the little one had come through okay. Pagan stood leaning against the wall, bent over, still recuperating from the kick to his manhood.

Yen examined the note Deirdre had received and then darted a furious look at Siki who sat against the tunnel wall opposite the woman she'd just tried to kill.

"So, Siki, you're not to be trusted," Yen said, her lips curled in disdain.

"That's not true," Siki muttered.

"You changed the time from five-thirty to five so you could get here early and attack a potential ally. Why would you do that?"

"I got my reasons," Siki growled.

"She and I have a history," Deirdre said.

"What history?"

"She's an enemy of my people," Siki replied.

"I have respect for the People of the Nations," Deirdre said, "except the man who mutilated my horse and those who almost killed my man."

"We were after you. It was that idiot white guy, Carlyle, who shot your man, not us."

"And Carlyle is very dead now," Deirdre said, projecting icy indifference.

"Yeah, because you got vengeance," Siki said, looking up at Yen to plead her case. "That's what I'm looking for, Yen. Vengeance. Crazy Hawk here gunned down my cousin in the street over a horse's eye."

"My Soul Horse. Yeah. And it was a fair fight. If he was faster, he could have killed me."

"We're responding to the note you slipped to Pagan," Yen said forcefully, dragging the conversation away from their feud to the business at hand. "Why don't you tell us what you had in mind."

"I want to get out of here," Deirdre said, matching Yen's forcefulness. "Pagan looked so unhappy, I thought he might want to work with me before they shove a stick into his brain."

Yen Thi Vo glanced at Pagan. "I told you that you weren't fooling anybody."

Deirdre laughed. "He was trying to fake cooperation? You got to be kidding me?"

"I know," Yen said. "He sucks at it."

"I hate those fucking Bees," Pagan growled.

The Vietnamese woman smacked his forehead with the palm of her hand. She pointed at Deirdre with her thumb. "Even she's heard about the lobotomies. It's going to happen to you. You're a terrible actor. The only reason they haven't done it already is because you're good at construction. But that will only go so far."

Deirdre grinned at Yen. "You on the other hand should get an Oscar."

"An Oscar?"

"For acting. Very convincing. I totally bought you as the committed wannabe. Taking the course multiple times, that was genius." Yen looked puzzled as she was still trying to decipher the reference to Oscar.

"In the 21st, they gave out acting awards called Oscars," Deirdre clarified.

Yen mulled this over. "Hussars are known to preserve wisdom from the past. Is this an example of your knowledge?" she said with a smirk.

"It's something I picked up somewhere. Forget that," she said, dismissing any more talk of 21st-century pop culture with a wave of her hand. "I contacted Pagan because I need an ally to get out of here."

"Yes, that's my thinking, too," Yen said. "One of us needs to…" She hesitated. "Before I go any further, I need to know if there is an 'us'."

"I'm in," Deirdre said.

Yen turned to Siki who glared back. "What?"

"We'll all have to work together, Siki."

Siki nodded. "I can wait till we're outside to kill her."

"Well, we have an alliance then," Yen announced.

"I'm all warm inside," Deirdre quipped.

Yen smiled. "One of us has to get into the Killer Bees. You know, the ones in the leather jackets. They have unique freedoms."

"So, how do we do that?" Siki asked.

"Well, I think she has the best shot," Yen said, gesturing at Deirdre with her thumb. "Do you know Leader considers you special?"

Deirdre nodded.

"Well, then we work with that." Yen's decisive statement seemed to end the discussion.

Deirdre realized they didn't know she was three months pregnant, otherwise they'd understand that the Bees wouldn't let her into their elite unit until after she'd given birth. Should she tell them? Deceit wasn't an ideal way to start a new alliance, but then these weren't ideal allies.

There was another piece of information she was sure her new friends didn't know. "I'm close to one of the K-Bees," she declared.

"How close?" Yen Thi Vo asked.

"She's my sister."

CHAPTER FORTY

Yen explained she worked in administration and that her access to scheduling, housing plans and personnel files might allow her to orchestrate a meeting between Deirdre and her sister, but it would take time.

And indeed, it did. Days turned into weeks, weeks into months. The indoctrination class, the only place she ever saw her co-conspirators, had almost run its course.

Pagan continued to be a terrible actor, even incapable of concealing that he knew Deirdre, sending her the occasional wink or wave. Yen's performance reached new heights. She was so good at ignoring her that Deirdre began to worry she was cooling to the idea of connecting her with Mindy. Meanwhile, Deirdre continued to play the happy Bee so convincingly that her leg shackles were removed.

After two and a half months of waiting, Yen turned right coming out of the classroom. It had been decided she would always turn left unless she had some news. Deirdre caught up to her at the soccer field.

Yen examined Deirdre studiously. She seemed stuck on Deirdre's midriff.

"Are you gaining weight on the mess hall food?"

"It's the lack of activity," Deirdre lied. "It's messed up my metabolism."

Yen nodded and explained what Deirdre was to do the next day to see her sister.

That night, Deirdre tried to imagine what Mindy's reaction would be. She explored every possible scenario—some were joyous, one was heartbreaking, one deadly. Mindy was not the only uncertain variable. Yen's plan of connecting Mindy and Deirdre included Siki. Deirdre wondered whether the Apache had really resigned herself to delaying the pleasure of killing Crazy Hawk or if she would she try again at the first opportunity.

Around midnight, she heard a sound, sat up in bed and listened intently. There was some scraping and scratching coming from across the room. She grabbed the hand crank flashlight, the only light source allowed after nine o'clock, flicked it on and directed the beam toward the sounds.

A mouse was gnawing on the leg of the stand, finding something delicious about the varnish. When the light hit it, the little creature turned and stared at Deirdre.

She instantly knew it was a Spirit, and this recognition had a powerful effect on her. In this concrete hell, it was almost impossible to listen to the Universe. Her entire worldview was stimulated, guided and supported by communion with nature. The absence of that connection had compromised her understanding of her place in the cosmos. She took a slice of bread off the nightstand, broke off a small piece and tossed it toward the mouse. The little critter picked up the bread and started nibbling on it.

"Help us, Little One," Deirdre whispered. She thought she saw it nod before darting out of sight.

✶✶✶✶✶

The next day, after dinner, Deirdre dropped her tray at the dishwasher's window and walked toward the swinging door. A guard was leaning against the wall not far from the door but took no notice as she breezed by.

The kitchen was bubbling with activity as a dozen workers hurried to clean up after the last meal of the day. She noticed most had leg irons. This was not a job people volunteered for.

Turning left, she walked toward a pair of heavy double doors, stopping when she saw a mouse in her path. Was this a Spirit, perhaps the same one she communicated with in her room?

The little creature darted toward two large burlap bags lying against the wall next to the doors, stood on its hind legs and touched one bag with its forefeet.

It then glanced back at Deirdre for a moment, scurried to the second bag, touched it with its forefeet, and then disappeared under a counter. Deirdre wondered whether this was a communication from a Spirit or just a hungry mouse exploring possibilities.

She pushed through the double doors which took her outside on a concrete platform. In front of the platform, on an asphalt driveway, Siki was waiting. She gestured for Deirdre to hurry.

As Deirdre dropped down to her level, she noticed a wooden table piled high with neatly folded towels and facecloths by the platform. Next to it was a motorized cart with a flatbed.

Siki wore leg irons with the chain attached—probably the same chain she used to attack her. Deirdre admired how she had devised a way to take the chain off and put it back on as the situation required.

"Lie on that," Siki said, gesturing toward the cart. As Deirdre obeyed, Siki eyed her swelling figure but didn't say anything. Deirdre guessed she and Yen had discussed the weird Hussar who could gain weight on what was served to them.

As soon as Deirdre's head touched the cart bed, Siki threw a tarp over her and a moment later she felt the pressure of towels being piled up on the tarp. A small gasoline engine started and soon the cart was moving. Five minutes later she heard Siki call out to someone. "Towels for Barracks 3."

"All right, go ahead," an uninterested male voice responded.

After a minute, the cart came to a halt and the engine went silent. Deirdre could feel the towels being removed and when the tarp was pulled off she was in a barren interior, possibly a basement.

"Damn, they love concrete, don't they?" Deirdre said as she gazed at the walls.

"I guess so," Siki said impatiently, handing Deirdre a key. "See that door over there?"

Siki was pointing at a metal door in the corner of the basement. Deirdre nodded.

"It should be unlocked; take the staircase to the left up three floors," Siki explained with detached efficiency. "On the third floor, go to room 304. Use the key to get in and wait for your sister. They're probably finishing dinner now. The K-Bee Cadet mess hall is close. Some of them will be drifting back real soon."

"You sure this key fits?"

"Yen's been working on this meeting for months. If she says it'll fit," Siki said with unshakeable confidence, "it'll fit."

Deirdre went to the metal door and opened it. As promised, a staircase ran up to the left. When she reached the third level, she opened the door on the landing and walked past four doors to 304. The key worked.

The room looked very much like Deirdre's. The fact that the inhabitant was never locked down made it very different but the design and furnishings were similar.

Something struck Deirdre as odd. The bed was made with meticulous precision. She couldn't imagine Mindy doing this; she was a notorious slob. Maybe this wasn't her room and a mistake had been made.

She looked for something that would confirm she was in the right place. Next to the TV stand was a small dresser. Opening the top drawer, she found several empty pistol magazines. In the next draw were several pair of underwear that could have belonged to anyone. She was about to close it when she noticed what looked like the corner of a stiff piece of paper sticking out from under a stack of underwear.

She moved the pile and looked into the face of her mother. Picking up the bent and wrinkled photo, she recognized it as one Mindy always carried with her. Its terrible condition — folds, tears and water damage — spoke of recent rough times.

Deirdre was stunned by the emotions stirred up by this discovery. Her mother's warm, smiling face surrounded by her ebony hair reminded her of a loss she had struggled to put behind her for years. She had convinced herself that she had moved on but the memories of this brave woman's loving care in the face of war, hunger, cold and chaos caused tears to well up. She felt faint and was aware of something odd happening, a roiling or a yearning as if a vacuum she thought she had filled gaped inside her.

She became intensely aware of all the beautiful moments she had lost with the death of her mother and was especially moved by the realization her child would never know that great woman. She was in the grip of these feelings when the door to the room opened and her little sister entered.

They stood looking at each other for a silent moment. Deirdre decided that if Mindy attacked, she wouldn't put up a fight. Pounding her kid sister in the presence of her mother's image would be impossible.

The silence was broken when a joyous laugh burst out of Mindy. The pretty teenager ran at Deirdre and embraced her in a vice-like hug. "I'm so happy to see you, Sis."

Deirdre's sense of relief was powerful enough to rob her of words, so she quietly reveled in the bliss of being in her sister's arms while taking stock of her changed appearance. She hadn't got a real good look at her when she had spotted her earlier. Mindy had grown quite a bit, now taller than her big sister, her dark brown hair even darker against the creamy skin that had become remarkably pale living in this sterile man-made cave. Deirdre was about to say something but Mindy jumped in.

"I've been hoping for this since the day I had to hold a gun to your head." She covered Deirdre's face with kisses. "I love you so much, Dee." Pulling back, she eyed Deirdre. "You know I never would have pulled the trigger. It had to seem that way so you'd drop the weapon. You were going to die if you went on with that fight."

"Of course, Sweetie, I understand," Deirdre said, trying her best to prevent her powerful feelings from weakening her voice.

"I worried about you a lot," Mindy said. "When I heard you were working with the program I was so relieved. How'd they catch you, Sis?"

"They drugged me."

"That was sneaky. I knew they couldn't take you in a fair fight," she boomed out with sisterly pride. Then with gentle empathy she said, "Hey, I know it's hard to get used to at first, but I honestly believe these people are going to save the world. And you might as well accept being here. Eagle Haller didn't lift a finger to come look for me." There was tangible bitterness in her voice. "Anyway, he sure as hell isn't coming here to help us."

She brooded for another moment before her resilient spirit prompted a laugh. "Damn, Dee, you are breaking so many rules to be here. How'd you do it? It's okay. Don't tell me. They love you. They'll forgive a visit to your sister, who is now a loyal Bee. I made a request to visit with you, but they said I needed to wait until you were a full Bee."

She looked at Deirdre's ankles and giggled joyfully. "Look! They took off your leg irons. That's a very good sign. It means they're real close to letting you in."

Mindy noticed the photo of her mother in Deirdre's hand and her voice turned soft and sad when she said, "She was beautiful, wasn't she?"

"Yes, she was."

"It's forbidden to have pictures of non-Bee family. You don't know what I had to do to hide that. One time I slipped it under my pants and kept it against my butt. Sorry, Mom." The young girl addressed the photo with such authentic feeling that Deirdre felt tears forming again.

"Oh, Dee, it's so wonderful to see you," Mindy cried. More kisses and hugs followed. She playfully wrestled her big sister onto the bed next to her so she could hug her while stroking her stomach.

"How's my niece or nephew doing?"

"You know about that, huh?"

"You're showing a little but I've known for months. I have a friend who works in the hospital. The bigwigs are very excited about your little one. Who's the father?"

"Somebody you don't know. An African guy."

"Cool. You know they have no racial prejudice here whatsoever."

"Yeah, they got that one right."

Still more hugs and kisses.

"You settled in pretty well," Deirdre remarked.

"It was real hard at first," Mindy said, a touch of melancholy tainting her euphoria.

"You're into their whole program? Like the looks thing?"

"What do you mean 'the looks thing'?" Mindy asked defensively.

"Everybody with any position of power or responsibility is kind of beautiful."

Mindy stopped the hugging and sat up in the bed. "Deirdre, they're trying to improve the race through genetics," she lectured. "Physical appearance is part of who humans are. Why shouldn't we maximize the potential of that part of our gene pool?"

Deirdre's mood sank a little. She had heard the same speech word for word in her indoctrination class. Her kid sister was buying into this bullshit.

"I mean it's not like they have death camps for ugly people," Mindy went on. "They find work for them."

Deirdre looked around the small apartment. "Don't you hate living in little cells like this?"

"At first, yeah. But you get used to it. Part of civilization is protecting people from the chaos of nature. That means good solid housing. It's up to each person to make her home attractive."

"You don't miss listening to the Universe? Communing with the Spirits?"

Mindy smiled sympathetically. "Oh, Dee, I went through the same thing. I held on to that superstitious crap for months. In my first room, a crow would land on the windowsill every day and look in at me. I thought for sure it was a Spirit trying to tell me something or offering help. I gave it part of my breakfast for almost three months before I realized it was all nonsense."

"So, the Bees have made you happy?"

"Happy?" Mindy paused, considering her answer. "They've given me a home and a purpose. Maybe that's what happy is." Then she quickly changed the subject. "Hey, did they give you a job yet?"

"No, not yet."

"Well, they will soon. It'll be a shit job at first, but you'll eventually be a Killer Bee, once you have the baby. It took me only six months but I wasn't pregnant and I didn't gouge anybody's eye out," she said with a giggle.

Then her expression morphed from bubbly teenager to serious propagandist. "Dee, give it a chance. These people really have their hearts in the right place. They want to bring back civilization, resurrect the good stuff from the 21st—all that was lost during the Breakdown— and make it all work this time. They're on a noble mission. We're so lucky to be part of it."

*****

Deirdre's mind was spinning as Siki drove the cart back toward the kitchen. Dear sweet Mindy had become a Bee, no doubt about that.

When Deirdre first arrived in the Hive she thought Mindy would be a cooperative escapee. Now she understood the teenager was a loyal Bee. But she refused to give up on her sister. It wasn't like Mindy had made a choice. She was kidnapped and brainwashed and had a great deal of anger toward the Hussars for not trying to save her.

After Siki pulled the tarp off, Deirdre quickly hopped onto the loading dock and pushed through the double doors. The kitchen was empty now. Her eyes fell on the burlap bags the mouse had seemed to be pointing out to her. Walking up to the bags, she noticed one was open at the top. She reached in, pulled out a handful of white powder, smelt it, took a tiny bit into her mouth and smiled.

"Thanks, Sister Mouse," she whispered.

CHAPTER FORTY-ONE

Yen sat on the other side of the tunnel from Deirdre who stood leaning against the wall. Siki was barely visible standing in the shadows a few feet away. Deirdre assumed Pagan was busy with his construction job.

"The kitchen?" Yen asked. "You want to work in the kitchen?"

Deirdre nodded. "It should be an easy job to get. No one volunteers for that, right?"

Yen was incredulous. "I thought you were going to see if your sister could help you get into the K-Bees?"

"I'm not getting into the K-Bees until…" Deirdre hesitated.

"Until what?" Siki asked, stepping out of the shadows.

Deirdre sighed. "Until I have my baby. I'm five months pregnant."

"Damn," Siki muttered. "I knew you couldn't be gaining weight on the slop they're feeding us. I never guessed a baby. I think Pagan had a clue. He mentioned your figure a couple of times."

Yen, who had been pacing irritably, stopped and stared at Siki.

"Saying he thought Deirdre's little belly was kind of sexy doesn't mean Pagan had a clue she was pregnant."

"These oversized jumpsuits they make us wear are good at hiding it," Deirdre said, staring down at her belly. "The Bees know all about it. They're running tests on me three times a week. They have big plans for this kid. That's why I want out of here before the little one is born."

Yen stared at Deirdre's midriff. "Yeah, I see it now. Who's the father? Never mind, I don't give a shit."

Siki changed the subject with a question. "What does the kitchen give us?"

"When I was walking through, I noticed a couple of burlap bags," Deirdre explained. "One was open. It was full of saltpeter. They must use it as a preservative."

Yen looked confused. "Saltpeter. What are we going to do with saltpeter?"

"Somewhere in this industrial inferno," Deirdre continued, "there has to be sulfur. The Bees probably use it in fertilizer or as a pesticide, or maybe even as another food preservative. My people use it for all sorts of things."

"I'm still not getting it," Yen said, but Siki was way ahead of her.

"Where do we get the charcoal?" the Apache asked.

"If I'm in the kitchen I can make as much charcoal as we can grind," Deirdre said. "It's really where can I get the wood.'"

"Pagan can get wood off the construction sites," Siki said, her excitement growing.

"Will you guys tell me what you're talking about?" Yen snapped. "I don't get it."

Siki laughed as she turned toward Yen. "Sulfur, saltpeter and charcoal. Those are the ingredients in black powder. The Crazy One wants to blow up the Hive."

✶✶✶✶✶

Indeed, Deirdre did want to blow up the Hive. But not all of it. She wanted to target the Bee production of munitions. If they could blow up even a part of the ammo plant, which was located inside the inner Hive, it might make a big enough bang to cause chaos, the kind of distraction that would allow her and her allies to escape. Damaging their ammo factory would impair their capabilities in upcoming conflicts; an added benefit.

Yen spent the time she should have been sleeping exploring the underground tunnel system, much of which wasn't used by the Bees.

One section, about fifty yards of tunnel, was walled off on both ends by concrete so it presented no practical use to the Bees. As a meeting place and a location to store materials, it would be invaluable. Maintenance workers frequented the developed tunnel system they had been meeting in, and it was only a matter of time before one of them stumbled onto the conspirators.

Yen explained that the section she recommended got extremely cold in the winter. By the time they had enough materials to start producing powder, it'd be mid-December. Siki pointed out that that could be an advantage. The best black powder, the sort with the most reliable ignition, is mixed with alcohol and then cooled.

It was in this new meeting ground, accessed by a crawl space under the gymnasium, that Deirdre assigned roles in the conspiracy. Yen's responsibility was to chart a tunnel route to the ammo factory. Siki had worked there briefly and was able to single it out from the dozens of factories that clogged the landscape around the center of the Hive.

Pagan, who was busy working construction every day, managed to get to one of their meetings. He explained that obtaining the sulfur would take a while. The construction folks used it in insulation, but he'd have to siphon it off in small amounts so nobody noticed. He was confident that he could sneak out wood alcohol from the various sites where it was used for cleaning tools, paint remover and an anti-freeze for the gas generators. The wood to make the charcoal would be a bigger challenge. He'd have to pick up the odd scrap here and there. Deirdre would make the charcoal in the kitchen and Siki would combine the ingredients to make the black powder.

*****

Case Notes: Deirdre of the Hussars
Case Worker: Victoria Leland

Nov. 11. All tests indicate a healthy baby is on its way. Nothing unusual about mother or child. Deirdre's attitude tends to be upbeat and enthusiastic. She has made believers of many influential people in the Hive. Leader is euphoric over her development, as well as the potential of the fetus.

I remain skeptical. I'm particularly suspicious about the Hussar's request to work in the kitchen. It makes no sense. Leader sees no harm in it. "The girl probably misses cooking," she said. We'll see.

Nov. 23. Deirdre is a terrible cook! The Head Chef, Donna, told me she lacks any instinct for successful food preparation. For me, this raises suspicion as to why she requested a position in the kitchen to begin with. Leader, who seems infatuated with Deirdre, puts a positive spin on everything regarding her.

I must admit the girl does work hard at it. She stays after every meal, experimenting with different dishes. All of them are horrid according to Head Chef.

To allay my suspicions, I've dropped by on several occasions to observe, and indeed she is cooking. And Leader makes an excellent point. If she were up to no good, wouldn't she want to work in the armory or the munitions factory where she would be close to deadly force? Why the kitchen? Why, indeed.

CHAPTER FORTY-TWO

Commandant Walker made his way from the Security Center through the military housing on his way to the Administrative Building where Leader lived and had her office.

He was accompanied by a three-person bodyguard, two men and a woman, all armed with semi-automatic rifles, the weapons that were so ubiquitous in 21st-century America. After Bee scientists had re-discovered the formula for smokeless powder, it was Walker's efficiency in overseeing the collection and refitting of such weapons that gave him prominence in the military.

For the Commandant, the time to launch the conquest of Pacifica was drawing near, the conditions ideal, except for one sticking point. Tension between himself and Leader had developed in the last few months, all concentrated on what he considered her strange obsession with Deirdre of the Hussars.

When Ketchell delivered her to the Hive, drugged and bound, Walker was relieved. His many informants spread throughout Pacifica and Old Arizona had warned him of her growing reputation as a hero.

He feared that reputation as much as her formidable combat skills. A woman known as a successful fighter against a mysterious, ominous power could become a focal point of an organized resistance to what otherwise could be a quick and decisive conquest of Pacifica. He lobbied for her immediate execution.

To his dismay, Leader was fascinated with the young woman and insistent that she may be just what their genetic program needed. When it was discovered the girl was pregnant, Leader was giddy with excitement.

Even a violent escape attempt by Deirdre was not enough to dissolve her enthusiasm. Leader argued that news of Deirdre's conversion to a Bee would be powerful propaganda for capturing the hearts and minds of the many people she had previously helped.

The latest madness coming from Leader's office was that Deirdre was to be made a Killer Bee after the birth of her child. For Walker, this was a line that could not be crossed.

As Walker and his men passed the small park in front of the hospital he gestured to a couple of K-Bees lounging in the grass to fall in behind. He wasn't sure how extreme Leader's reaction would be to what he had to tell her.

*****

Leader wore a subtle smile as she sat at one end of the long table. The Commandant sat on the other end, chin thrust out, arms folded across his chest. At the table with them were Colonel Parelli; the Assistant Leader, Ron Allende; two of the Council Elders; and Victoria Leland, Deirdre's case worker.

"So, my proposal that we should give one young girl full Bee citizenship seems to have caused quite a stir," Leader said, her lovely, mellow voice dripping with irony.

"This isn't any young girl," Walker said. "This is Crazy Hawk. From everything we know about this woman, it would be madness to make her a Bee. Certainly, under no circumstances should she be put in the K-Bee training program."

Passion gave a pink hue to Leader's face. "Commandant, you're right to call her a woman. This is no girl. She's a formidable soldier whose abilities we'd be foolish to take lightly. That's why I want her on our side." She lowered her voice to a mild, semi-whisper. "If this is simply a matter of timing, you do understand we're going to wait until she —"

"No." Walker cut her off. "Not today, not tomorrow, not next year. Crazy Hawk must never be a Bee, much less a K-Bee."

Leader's eyes blinked several times, the enthusiastic pink in her face darkening to angry red. "That's an unreasonable position," she snapped.

"She's already tried to escape," he said, matching Leader's passion with cold logic. "She injured several members of my Security Force."

"She's a formidable soldier. When a fighter like that rebels, people get hurt. However, I firmly believe that she has had a change of heart."

"You're being naive," Walker said.

"Since the escape attempt, she's been a model citizen."

"Just the quick conversion should tell you she's faking it."

Leader stared at her hands, the fingers spread out like she was trying to palm the table. She took a deep breath, folded her hands in front of her, planted her elbows and rested her chin on her knuckles.

"At first glance, perhaps," she said, projecting calm while maintaining a steeliness to her words. "But she excelled in the Orientation Class."

Her argument was methodical now that passion hadn't worked, and the red in her complexion faded to its usual creamy white. "In several meetings I've had with her, she argued eloquently that this is the world she wants her child born into. I believe her. This woman yearns to get a bumble bee tattoo. Tattoos are forever. Her change of heart is sincere and we should assimilate this exceptional talent into our everyday lives as soon as possible. It would be particularly healthy for her baby if, in its first few weeks on the planet, Mom feels secure and part of something. I'm extremely excited about adding that child to our gene pool."

Walker shook his head slowly. "Everything she's done she did to buy time and gain more freedom while she organizes an escape or worse."

"Are you aware that when the time came for a work assignment, she volunteered for the kitchen?"

"Yes, I am aware of that."

"She could have volunteered for the armory or in ammunition production, jobs that would have been much more advantageous to someone planning sabotage. But no, she chose the kitchen."

"And why is that?"

Leader laughed, delighted with Deirdre's eccentricities. "She wanted to improve the food! She has this wonderful technique for giving wood flavoring to soups. It's a traditional dish from her tribe. It was hit and miss at first, but now she seems to have mastered it. I had the pea soup last night. Amazing."

Walker nodded in agreement. "Yes, some of the latest preparations are very tasty."

"Well, there you go. Her first instinct was to give hungry Bees a better soup. Doesn't sound subversive to me." Leader leaned back in her chair as if the issue was settled.

A smug grin slithered onto Walker's lips. "What would you say if I were to tell you I don't think she's a cook at all. If her soups are better, it's because she stumbled on a way to improve the flavor, not because she has any expertise in that area."

"I'd say you're being paranoid." She stirred a bit in her seat, unsure where his argument was going.

Walker placed his long forearms on the table in front of him. "She volunteered for the kitchen because that was part of her plan to disrupt the Hive."

Leader's mocking laugh filled the room. "Are you suggesting she's poisoning us?"

"Not at all." The Commandant nodded towards a member of his bodyguard who opened a door behind Leader and gestured with a wave of his hand for someone to come in.

A moment later, Mindy entered, looking sick with dread, her steps slow and tentative as if she were on her way to the gallows. Walker gestured to an open seat by him. Mindy sat down.

"I don't understand," Leader said, her voice a little deflated. "What are we doing?"

Walker stood, walked around the table and positioned himself behind Mindy. "This young woman is a loyal Bee. She has alerted us to her sister's treachery."

Leader's nostrils flared. "I'm not going to believe a fanciful conspiracy theory that could be the product of a sibling rivalry gone nuclear."

"You're selling Mindy short, Leader," Walker said. "Cadet Buford doesn't want to be tarred by her sister's foul deeds."

"There's nothing foul about my sister," Mindy said softly, her eyes fixed on the tabletop. "She's a great person. Unfortunately, she doesn't understand the good the Bees offer the world."

"Cadet," Leader said, glaring at Mindy, "make your accusation. Now!"

Mindy nodded. "Deirdre can't cook. She was probably the worst cook in the Hussar camp. She's bad at it because she hates it. And there's no Hussar tradition for cooking wood-flavored soups."

"Then what is she doing in the kitchen?" Leader asked, her tone stern but less confident.

"I didn't get it at first either," Mindy went on. "I went by the kitchen a few days ago. She wasn't there but Head Chef Donna was. I asked how Deirdre was doing. I could tell Donna was a bit irritated with how messy my sister's cooking method was but the bottom line was that she was happy because Deirdre got all that charcoal out by the end of the day."

"Charcoal?" Simmering rage sent Leader's voice into a lower register.

"Didn't you know?" the Commandant said, plopping contentedly onto his chair. "A by-product of Deirdre's cooking technique is charcoal—lots of it. I had the Chief Quartermaster do an inventory of our supplies of sulfur and saltpeter. Enough is missing to cause alarm. Charcoal, saltpeter and sulfur are the ingredients in—"

"I know what they make," Leader bellowed, standing up with such force she sent her chair skidding across the room, clattering against the wall. She then stormed out of the room.

Commandant Walker grinned at the rest of the table. "This should be entertaining."

CHAPTER FORTY-THREE

The ghostly face hung in the shadows.

Who is it?

It moved, and a ray of light exposed a feature, an eyebrow. Then a moment later, a cheekbone. It was someone she knew well, someone who was once part of her world, someone who was visiting for a reason, to make a request, perhaps.

Is it dear, gentle Jube? Was he already on the other side, beckoning her to join him?

A split second before light flooded the face, Deirdre knew it was the visage that had peered out to her from that photograph she'd found among Mindy's things. Light illuminated the dreamscape, and she was looking into the compassionate eyes of her mother.

Deirdre was wrong. The specter was not there to ask something of her but to comfort her. This realization triggered an emotional Vesuvius. Hundreds of pent-up feelings burned inside her with lava-like intensity. Her mother embraced her.

It was Deirdre's real-life sobs that woke her. She sat up in bed and struggled to regain composure.

She had come back from the kitchen after breakfast to take a nap. The Bees now trusted her so completely she was allowed to come and go as she pleased as long as she was back in her room for lockdown. She glanced at the clock on the wall. Ten thirty am. She had to get back to her soup.

The woman who could stay in the saddle for twenty hours without dozing was exhausted by a few hours of charcoal production disguised as soup preparation. She used her advanced pregnancy — eight months along — as an excuse for catching some sleep, but there was another reason her nap breaks were tolerated. She had become a very popular character in the Hive because of her cooking.

After a couple of weeks in the kitchen, it seemed impossible Deirdre's cover could last. The food she was preparing was so consistently inedible that she expected to be transferred to a job she could actually do.

It was a metal hat, designed by Siki and built by Pagan which went over the two pots and pushed some of the escaping smoke down into the soup, plus some seasoning advice from Yen, that had saved the plan. The result was a truly delicious smoke flavoring. Hungry Bees were soon clamoring for more.

This unexpected turn of events delighted Deirdre. She was particularly amused by the way Donna was threatened by the introduction of flavor into her kitchen.

Deirdre walked to the sink, ran water into her cupped palms and splashed it onto her face. But then she heard something that caused her to turn the water off, alarmed. A door slammed at the end of the corridor, and booted feet pounded in her direction.

The door burst open. Two soldiers wearing black uniforms and carrying rifles entered and leveled their weapons at Deirdre's chest. A moment later, Leader passed between them, walked up to Deirdre and shot a fist into her throat. Deirdre went down hard, gasping for air. Leader towered above her.

"All right, you treacherous cunt. Where is the black powder?"

*****

Yen Thi Vo waited in the abandoned tunnel for someone — anyone — to join her. She looked at the containers full of black powder lining the wall. Siki had used anything she could get her hands on to store the powder, bottles, cups, canteens, alcohol cans and burlap bags. Yen counted thirty-nine containers accumulated over three months of powder production.

To her eye, it seemed a lot, but she hadn't spoken to any of her co-conspirators in weeks, so she didn't know what Siki's expert opinion was. Did they have enough? Certainly, they'd have to make do with what they had. Deirdre's arrest made that a certainty.

One piece of unground charcoal lay on a bowl-shaped indentation in the concrete floor that Siki had used as a mortar. Lying next to it was the pestle — a stretch of lead pipe with a ball of cement on the end that Pagan had made in the Bee construction workshop. A few feet from the pestle was a near-empty bag of saltpeter and a wooden box full of sulfur.

Yen marveled at how much her co-conspirators had accomplished. Pagan had regularly supplied wood to Deirdre in the kitchen. This had been done openly and with the permission of the Head of Construction who thought it was a good use of scraps.

Getting the saltpeter was easy. On Deirdre's first day working in the kitchen, she captured two large bags and slipped them to Siki on the loading dock.

When Pagan learned sulfur was a key ingredient in mustard gas, he volunteered to do some repairs in the gas factory, a dirty job no one else wanted because they were afraid of the gas. Over a period of days, he smuggled out sufficient amounts of the element. He also wrangled a couple of containers of wood alcohol.

Yen's job had been to figure out how the powder could be placed under the ammo plant. She had been frustrated in this. Even though her position as an administration assistant gave her access to floor plans and old survey maps, neither these nor her own subterranean explorations had revealed a way to get underneath the plant. She found something else she hoped would be just as effective.

Now she wondered if the heroic effort of the four conspirators would go to waste. Deirdre had been caught. Since Pagan had been so open about supplying the Hussar with choice pieces of wood, Yen was sure he would be arrested soon.

A noise came from the crawl space that supplied entrance to their private tunnel. Yen thought for a second about turning off the battery-powered lantern Pagan had purloined from a construction site, then decided to leave it on. If the noise came from her friends, she wanted them to know she was there. If it was the Bees, all was lost anyway and she was ready to meet the consequences with courage and resignation.

A few moments later, Siki appeared out of the shadows and squatted in front of her.

"You heard?" the Apache asked.

"Yeah."

"They got Pagan, too."

"I was afraid of that."

Siki rubbed her cheeks with the palms of her hands. "You have a way to get the powder under the ammo plant?"

"Not the ammo plant," Yen said apologetically. "But I found a way to reach the mustard gas factory."

"Wow." Siki appeared to be mulling this over for a moment, her eyes flickering in the lantern light. "Is that inside the inner walls?"

"Yeah. They like to keep their production of deadly force close."

"I don't know if gas works, though." Siki's words were deliberate and without enthusiasm. "Our black powder will make a nice little boom but we're going need secondary explosions if we want to really cause chaos."

"Listen to this." Yen pulled a piece of paper out of a pocket. "I found it in their literature on this gas." She held the piece of paper close to the lantern so she could read. "Prolonged exposure to fire may cause containers of mustard gas to violently rupture and rocket."

Siki jumped to her feet in excitement. The word "rocket" exploded out of her. "Ha. Good odds the black powder explosion will cause a fire. Rocket!" She was almost yelling now. "We want a distraction. Rockets of poisonous gas flying around will do the trick."

Yen grinned at Siki's wild approval but gestured toward the ceiling. "Keep it low. Remember, there's a strength training class going on right above us."

"We'd have to wait for a day when the west wind is coming in strong, so whatever poison is released will blow toward the Sierra Nevada," Siki said in a loud voice, pretty much ignoring Yen's warning. "Otherwise we run the chance of killing ourselves and a lot of innocent people."

She paced around Yen once and then squatted in front of her.

"They're going to nail me soon," Siki said, suddenly somber. "Lots of Bees saw me picking up the charcoal from the kitchen loading dock every day. But you might have some time."

Yen nodded. "You better tell me everything you know about black powder."

Deirdre lay in the hospital bed, iron cuffs once again around her wrists. Despite Leader's anger, she and the other geneticist Bees were so interested in her delivering a healthy baby they were willing to risk one more month of Crazy Hawk in their midst.

After Leader's violent outburst, Deirdre was taken to a man in the Administration Building, introduced as the Torturer.

At least these Bees are honest about it, she had reflected. Even the Hussars dressed up their torturers with names like skinners or interrogators.

The Torturer strapped her to an iron chair. Scattered around his small office were whips, pliers, knives, long needles, a vice and several electric drills. He was a pock-marked fat man with a bulbous nose and bushy eyebrows.

"The Bees do find work for ugly people," she had remarked, which launched him into a violent rant. He talked about ripping her baby out of her, but other than a few slaps, he didn't do anything when she refused to reveal the identity of her co-conspirators. Even when she promised to slice his throat one day, he just gave her another slap and turned her over to Victoria and a couple of well-armed guards. They were reluctant to rough her up too much. They needed to keep mom healthy.

The militarist Bees saw things differently than the geneticist Bees. She heard some of Walker's men outside her room one afternoon arguing with Victoria, saying they had orders to bring Deirdre to the Security Center immediately. It took Leader intervening to prevent them from dragging Crazy Hawk to what would surely have been her execution.

Deirdre took a sip from the tube attached to a water bag suspended above her. *They want mom to be well hydrated.* The door opened and Victoria appeared. She gave Deirdre a snarl, stepped aside to let Mindy enter and closed the door as she departed.

Mindy stood at the end of the bed, head down so Deirdre couldn't see her face.

"It was me that blew the whistle on you," the young girl said, her voice breaking.

"I figured that. You know I can't cook worth a damn."

"I heard the soup was actually pretty good."

"None of my doing," Deirdre said as she squirmed in the bed to get more comfortable. "What do you want?"

"I know you hate me," Mindy said, tears beginning to flow.

"I don't hate you, Sweetie," Deirdre said gently. "I don't know how to hate you."

Mindy looked up, the tears gushing now. "I don't hate you either, Deirdre. I love you. That's why I couldn't let you destroy yourself and your baby." She paused to take a deep breath. "Because that's what would have happened. There's no way you could have pulled it off."

"Well, Mindy," Deirdre said, the gentleness in her voice now replaced by cold sarcasm, "I guess I really owe you one."

Mindy leaned against the foot of the bed and gazed into Deirdre's eyes. "Look, I think you can still get out of this."

"Stop it," Deirdre said with quiet firmness. "Your Bee friends are going to fry my ass as soon as I pop this kid out."

"Not if you tell them everything," Mindy said, voice clear and bright, a sign of last-ditch optimism. "Tell them who's in on the conspiracy with you and where the powder is."

Deirdre laughed. "Is that why you're here? To get me to talk?"

Mindy moved to a bedside chair and sat down, deflated. "The only way they'd let me see you was if I promised to try. I knew you wouldn't talk. I know who you are."

Deirdre looked into Mindy's deep, brown eyes. They were so like her mother's. "What happened to you, Mindy?"

"I found a cause I care about and people who care about me."

"People who care about you?" Deirdre propped herself on her elbows. "The Hussars didn't care about you? Dad and me, we didn't care about you?"

"I was fourteen years old riding rim patrol by myself," Mindy shot back. "I was grabbed by four scumbags and no one came after me. Not a Hussar in sight."

"I was on a mission, Mindy," Deirdre said. "As soon as I got back I set out looking for you. I did nothing else for the next year. What do you think I'm doing here?"

"Why didn't Haller send anybody?" she asked, barely getting the words out between lips trembling with anger.

Deirdre spent a moment thinking of what she might say to ease the tension but decided to answer the question honestly. This might be her last contact with her kid sister and she wanted to be transparent. "He told me he didn't want to deplete the defenses of the valley in case your kidnapping was a sign of a bigger threat."

This explanation caused Mindy's chest to heave. "They kept me tied to a mule saddle the whole time, for two weeks while they did some other kidnappings. I kept looking for any sign of help on the way. Nobody came." She glared at her sister with a look so savage it made Deirdre's stomach sink. "They sent nobody." She struggled to get her breathing under control, her eyes glowing with rage. "That changed me, Dee. Every night I had to watch that bastard Carlyle stretch out by the fire, so happy and content with what he was doing."

"Carlyle, huh?"

"Yeah. He wasn't the main guy. The operation is run by some creep named Ketchell. I never saw him. But Carlyle, I hate that son of a bitch so much."

"Well, I got some news we can bond over," Deirdre said with a wry smile. "I killed the bastard. And it wasn't fast."

Mindy stared at Deirdre for a few seconds before she allowed herself a smile. "Not hating that."

"Come on, Mindy." Deirdre raised herself up as far as the chains would allow. "Help me get out of here and we'll ride together again, get vengeance on everyone who messed with your life."

"No, Deirdre, the Bees are my people now," Mindy said, her voice suddenly steady, her tone resigned. "Maybe the way I got here was ugly, but what I have with my new family is beautiful. They protect me and they damn sure would come after me if I were taken."

She stood and stared silently at Deirdre for almost a full minute. Deirdre sensed Mindy was trying to lap up with her eyes what she suspected would be the last time she saw her big sister.

When she finally spoke, her tone was strong and unyielding. "They're going to save the world, Dee. They really are. It breaks my heart that you won't be with us to see it."

Deirdre wondered if Mindy could see the disappointment in her eyes.

"I guess it's time to give up on getting me back, Sis," Mindy said.

"Never," Deirdre said with conviction.

Without another word, Mindy left the room.

CHAPTER FORTY-FOUR

Covered with sweat and dirt, exhausted almost to incapacity, Yen made her way through the partially collapsed tunnel.

Every night for two weeks she had made her way down to the labyrinth of tunnels, dugouts, crawl spaces and abandoned basements underneath the Hive. Most of the network had been neglected since the original structures above ground were demolished in some long-forgotten battle.

This would be the last time she did this trek. A strong wind was blowing from the west toward the Sierra Nevada. It had to happen today.

She dragged her weary body along in complete darkness. The batteries in her lantern were as close to exhaustion as she was. Each time she switched it on she was aware the light was dimmer.

Her head bunked against a concrete wall, which meant she had to veer to the left. Groping with her hands, she was able to access a tunnel she knew allowed her to stand. Putting her right hand against the wall, she brought herself to her feet and moved as quickly as she could for one hundred and two strides, having memorized the distance in the fourteen consecutive nights she'd done this trek. She had to push herself hard this time because her tank was almost on empty, every step a grueling effort. When she reached her destination, she flicked on the lantern.

To her left was a network of copper piping, remnants of an ancient water system. She'd already packed many of the pipes with black powder, transforming them into a crisscross collection of pipe bombs. She could hear the machinery working right above her, the night crew producing the horrible weapon the Bees planned to use to eradicate entire tribes that resisted their plans of conquest.

Reflecting on these things motivated her. She was not a warlike person. Before she'd been captured, the main interest in her life was writing poetry. Her mother ran a very successful produce market in San Francisco. A few of her friends called her spoiled because she wasn't asked to help in the family business, but her mother loved her daughter's creative efforts, convinced the world needed a great poet more than another produce hawker.

It was her quest for poetic inspiration that led her to hike out of the city to that inviting ridge line she'd seen in the distance every day since she was a child. She was certain that the view would inspire a wonderful poem. It was there she was kidnapped by marauding mercenaries who sold her to the Hive.

Her loving family, the freedom to express herself, the bustling life of an open city — all of that had disappeared in a flash. For weeks after, she was close to suicidal in her new environment, but the steady positive messages given to her by the Bee propagandists began to influence her. She became a true believer in their cause.

She may have continued in that direction had she not tried her hand at writing a poem about the Hive and its mission. When she presented it to her teacher, she was told it was subversive. If she wanted to write a rousing patriotic song, that would be fine, but her poem had references to depression and loneliness. Even though Yen praised the Bees and their mission, her teacher felt the personal sentiments were too ambiguous and subtle. The Bees loved concrete in their buildings and their art.

Besides, poetry was a distraction, an amusement, not to be taken seriously. They were dedicated to the idea that science was the only meaningful field of study and the humanities, in whatever form, were useless relics of an unenlightened age.

It wasn't long before Yen understood how oppressive and stultifying their rigid worldview was. She continued to put on a happy face at work, but in her free time she withdrew into her own reveries.

She felt the need to find secret locations where she could be alone with herself and her writing. One of these places, a crawl space beneath the staircase in her building, led her to discover the tunnel system under the Hive. It was during the exploration of these subterranean passageways that she planned the resistance.

She took a leather bag off her belt, which held the last of the gunpowder Siki had ground so skillfully. She split it into two piles and left one in a heap at the mouth of one of the largest pipes. The other she scooped up in her hands and, backing up, let the grains seep slowly through her fingers.

When she was finished she had left a trail of powder about thirty feet long. Retrieving the lantern that barely supplied a dim light, she knelt at the end of the powder fuse, pulled from her pocket a wooden match Pagan had made and scraped its head on the concrete wall.

It ignited instantly, the flame brighter than the light projected by the tired lantern. Taking a deep breath, she dropped the match on the gunpowder trail. She knew she should run at this point, trying to put as much distance between the pipe bombs and herself as she could, but she was so exhausted she couldn't move.

Her sense of the poetic was delighted when the lantern battery gave out and only the burning gunpowder moving toward the mouth of the pipe could be seen in the darkness.

CHAPTER FORTY-FIVE

D eirdre heard the explosions as she lay in the dark hospital room. They were gradual and soft at first, like a lion, starting with a low growl building in volume until it roared into a full explosion, shaking the barred windows of her room, followed by the sounds of sirens, bellowing voices and the occasional scream.

Someone would come to her; she was sure of it. Maybe it would be Commandant Walker to put a bullet in her head, or maybe Leader with a lobotomist at her side.

When the door did swing open, it was Victoria and a tall rifle-wielding guard.

Victoria was frantic. "Deirdre, we're going to move you to an underground shelter. That explosion released dangerous gas into the air. There's no telling where it will spread."

Gas! Deirdre couldn't resist a grim smile, impressed with the daring shown by Yen Thi Vo. They wanted to cause chaos. This would do the trick.

Victoria continued. "I trust you understand that at this point, no one would weep if Sergeant Lauder here put a bullet in your brain. Don't be foolish. We'd love to observe your baby's development but please don't think that ensures your safety. We'd sacrifice that child in a minute for our security."

The tail end of her sentence was muffled by another explosion, this one loud and earthshaking. Panes shattered and framed pictures crashed to the floor.

Victoria hurried to the window and gazed out. The secondary explosions, triggered by explosive elements in the factory, were creating more fear than the original blast.

Deirdre shot a look at Lauder and noted confusion in his eyes. Victoria let out a moan as she peered at the growing catastrophe. "There's a fire. Looks like it's jumping from rooftop to rooftop." She turned to Lauder. "We better hurry."

As she watched the two of them move around nervously, Deirdre knew the inevitable outcome of the next few seconds. Frightened people hurrying were red meat for a woman with her skills.

Victoria undid the floor bolt to the left arm chain. She did nothing to secure the arm. Lauder pointed his weapon at Deirdre's chest but was distracted by the horrific sounds coming from outside.

Victoria undid the left leg restraint, then the right leg, and was about to undo the floor bolt holding the right arm chain when she stopped and tossed a searching look at Deirdre.

"What are you doing?" Lauder asked, the tension in his voice revealing a budding panic.

Victoria was at the drug cabinet. "I'm going to give her a heavy dose of morphine. It'll make her more manageable."

"Don't worry about that," Lauder growled. "I'll waste the bitch if she looks at us cross-eyed."

Victoria ignored him and began working with a syringe and a vial. Deirdre knew the time had come.

Lauder was staring at her with hatred, his forefinger moving back and forth from the trigger guard to the trigger. Another explosion drew his attention to the window.

Deirdre leaned on her right elbow and threw both legs toward Lauder, wrapped his midsection with a python-like grip and grabbed the barrel of his weapon with her left hand, shoving it downwards. He fired into the floor. The blast caused the barrel to leap out of her hand, but she was able to slam the heel of her left foot into his nose. As he staggered back she grabbed the rifle and jerked it out of his grip.

Victoria saw what was happening and ran toward Deirdre, loaded syringe ready. In a move she would brag about later, Deirdre fired a burst into Lauder's chest with her left hand while simultaneously landing a straight right to Victoria's jaw, knocking her out cold.

Only then did she notice the syringe sticking out of her arm. The plunger had been pushed, the full dose in her system.

*****

Siki listened to the explosions as she sat on the concrete floor of her cell, waiting, resigned to the inevitable vengeance coming her way.

She was so proud of Yen Thi Vo. *The kid pulled it off.*

A few hours after she had given Yen the lessons in black powder and pipe bombs, Siki had been arrested. She laughed in the face of the Torturer who tried to learn what she had done with the charcoal by pulling out three of her teeth with sadistic brutality.

She allowed herself to scream and cry, and she passed out from the pain twice, but this vicious dentistry didn't get a word out of her. Exhaustion finally caused the Torturer to stop. *Pulling teeth is like pulling teeth.* She chuckled at her witticism.

She could tell by the wavering light pouring through the cell window that the Hive was burning. Gunfire rang out on her level of the jail, lasting less than a minute, which meant someone had decisively ended the firefight.

She heard footsteps approaching her cell. The deadbolt moved, the door swung open and Deirdre, wearing a Killer Bee leather jacket, stumbled in, propped herself up against a wall, saw Siki and smiled.

"Hey, Apache Girl." She then slid down the wall onto the floor in a giggling heap.

Pagan stepped in wearing a guard's uniform, carrying an assault rifle and holding a set of keys.

"Can you walk?" he asked Siki.

"Oh, yeah. He worked mainly on my mouth." Siki stood up. "Is the Crazy One drunk?"

"Nah, when she was breaking out of the hospital a nurse stuck her with some drug."

Deirdre sat up and raised her hands in mock surrender. "Por favor, Apache Girl, do not shoot me." Deirdre laughed and then started puking, most of the vomit splattering onto the jacket, some of it onto the floor. She focused on Siki and frowned. "Sorry, Siki. Didn't mean to mess up your cell."

"She really is a mess," Siki said to Pagan.

"Yeah, it's amazing she made it to the Torturer's room. That's how we hooked up. I was there. She did a real number on that bastard before the drug made her silly."

Siki noticed his hands were badly swollen. "Wow, he messed with your hands big time."

Pagan shrugged. "Yeah, he beat them with a pipe. Left one is useless, but he didn't break the right one. She showed up in time to stop him from doing that."

"Well, thanks for coming for me," Siki said, trying to load the sentence with as much gratitude as she could muster.

Pagan nodded toward Deirdre. "She kept saying 'we can't leave without her'. I thought she meant her sister, but she made it clear she was talking about 'Apache Girl'."

Pagan tossed Deirdre over his shoulder like a rag doll, ignoring another stream of vomit spattering onto his back.

"Remember she's pregnant," Siki said.

Pagan nodded, slung the rifle over his shoulder, repositioned Deirdre so that he was carrying her like a cradled baby and walked out of the cell. Siki followed as they moved through the corridor. Reaching the bodies of three guards, Pagan gestured toward one. "That little guy. Take his uni."

Siki eyed the "little" guy. He was little compared to Pagan but not to her. After a couple of minutes, she had the oversized uniform on, complete with a belt with extra rifle magazines, and was slinging the dead man's rifle over her shoulder. They walked toward the flight of stairs that led out of the subterranean jail. Hearing the cries of other prisoners calling out to them, Pagan paused at the foot of the stairs.

"Should we let them out?" He gestured to the other cells.

Siki nodded. "Yeah. That fire is spreading fast. We wouldn't want them roasted alive. Besides, we wanted chaos, right?"

Pagan walked up to one of the cells and, cradling Deirdre with one arm, used the jailer key he'd stolen off a corpse to open the door and toss the key to the gaunt forty-something woman standing inside. "Let the others out," he growled and rushed to follow Siki who was already climbing the stairs.

The main entrance area to the jail was milling with confused Bees who had no idea what was going on. One K-Bee officer was yelling incomprehensible orders, trying to regain control. Others stared out the window at the burning cadet mess hall, wondering if their building was next.

As Pagan, carrying Deirdre, strode toward the door the officer, now hysterical, screamed, "Don't go out. There are canisters of mustard gas flying around!"

Pagan hesitated, but Siki knew the chances of being hit by flying canisters were slim. It was the escaping gas they needed to worry about. Even if Yen timed the wind correctly, she wondered if that would be enough to diffuse the danger. But there was no other option. This was their chance. She pushed through the doors into the night, Pagan following with Deirdre in his arms.

CHAPTER FORTY-SIX

The sun was just poking its head over the Sierra Nevada when Deirdre ascended the slope of the little hillock that sat in the middle of an open field.

She was surprised how grueling this effort was. She had experienced her pregnancy in the confines of the Hive where she'd learned how to ascend familiar stairwells, but climbing a fairly steep incline at eight months pregnant was a different challenge.

The hillock, more of a large mound, was the highest elevation she could find in this stretch of flat farmland. She gazed toward the north trying to discern some activity coming from the direction of the Hive, which she figured was about fifty miles away from where she stood. There wasn't much to see, just some smoke clouding the distant horizon.

"Worried about your sis?" Pagan called out from where he stood at the foot of the hillock.

"Yeah," she said matter-of-factly and then with a touch of

melancholy, indifferent as to whether Pagan heard her or not, "she wasn't ready to come with us, that's for sure."

Deirdre studied the horizon for a few more moments and then called her report down to Pagan. "I don't see any sign the Bees are coming after us."

"We messed them up pretty good," Pagan said with a grin.

When they came out of the jail, there was no gas in the air, just the usual polluted muck they'd been breathing since they arrived at the Hive, but rumors were spreading about how Bees were collapsing from the gas.

In the chaos, Pagan commandeered a truck. They escaped the inner Hive by simply driving out the main gate, which had been left open as an exit for terrified Bees.

While crossing the five-mile no man's land, the stolen uniforms and the cover of night allowed them to get close to an outlying sentry station. When the station crew approached the truck to ask what was going on, Pagan and Siki sent them scurrying for cover with a salvo from the captured rifles. A few minutes later they had cruised out of the no man's land and were headed due south.

Deirdre eased herself down the steep slope of the hillock. She reached Pagan and leaned on him as if he were a fence post. "Once they get over the initial shock they'll send people."

"We can still get another hundred miles out of that gas tank," Pagan estimated. "I say we put as much distance as possible between us and them. Maybe we can find a road in decent shape and pick up the pace."

She nodded and headed for the truck. Siki got out of the cab and stepped forward to block Deirdre's path. Pagan put himself between Siki and Deirdre. "Come on, Siki, you don't want to do this now."

"It's not about that," she said, her voice troubled, not belligerent. "Killing her can wait. Like you said, she came back for me."

Deirdre shrugged. "Don't make too much of that, Siki. I was under the influence."

Siki ignored Deirdre's dismissive tone. "There's something I have to tell you, Hawk."

"I'm listening."

Siki took a deep breath and released it slowly. "Your boyfriend. Gentle Boy."

"You mean Jube?"

"I call him Gentle Boy."

"What about him?" Deirdre stepped forward, her body coiled in anticipation.

"I ran into him in Fresno."

Deirdre bent at the waist, her hands on her knees. She couldn't bear to hear what was coming next. "Did you kill him?"

"No. I gave him water and my last piece of bread. And I dressed his chest wound, which had opened. He didn't look good."

Deirdre stood up straight and nodded. "All right. I'm on my way to Fresno."

Siki tossed a look at Pagan. He had nothing. She turned back to Deirdre. "I saw him eight months ago, Hawk. The way he looked, I don't think he would have lasted."

"I'm going to Fresno." Deirdre turned to Pagan. "Can you get me there?"

"Pretty close."

"Deirdre, you need to get back to your people as soon as possible," Siki pleaded. "You don't want to give birth alone on the trail."

"Note taken." Deirdre climbed into the truck. "Drop me at Fresno."

*****

They didn't find any better road and Deirdre was keenly aware of the battering she and her baby were taking from the rough broken pavement the truck traversed.

At a trading post, they swapped cartridges for enough supplies to give each of them a few days' calories. Pagan traded his Bee guard uniform for a pair of blue jeans, and Siki swapped her uniform for cargo pants and a hoodie. It was still winter, so Deirdre kept the warm leather jacket but the trading post guy was very interested in the Bee arm patch she had torn off the jacket. She was able to trade it for a T-shirt and a pair of overalls which fit her pregnant shape.

The truck ran out of gas outside the ruins of a town. A sign which lay in the middle of the road told them it had once been called Madera. It was time to part company.

Pagan explained he planned to skirt Fresno on the west and head south. Siki was going to head east first and then south along the foothills of the Sierra Nevada. It was the middle of February, so the Nevada range at a high altitude was going to be very cold, but the old state Highway 58 out of Bakersfield, which ran over the foothills, would be warmer. She was going to use that route to get out into the desert.

"You can come along if you want, Hawk," Siki offered, her tone unexpectantly kind. "I can escort you as far as Mojave. Maybe from there, you could contact your people to come get you."

"You're just looking for a chance to cut my throat while I'm sleeping," Deirdre said whimsically as she flashed a smile toward Siki. She was surprised Siki had softened her stance so much that she was now protective of the Hussar and her child.

"I wouldn't kill a pregnant woman," the Apache said, trying one last time to appear indifferent to Crazy Hawk's welfare. "I'm just worried about the baby."

"Well, I appreciate that," Deirdre said. "Maybe I'll name the kid Apache Girl."

"Don't be a wiseass," Siki snapped. "It may be a boy, you know."

"That'll be okay. I'll love him like he's my own."

Pagan laughed. Siki couldn't avoid a grin.

Deirdre's compassion sprout exploded as she realized for the first time how much the Torturer had taken from Siki. "You gonna be able to eat with no teeth?"

"I still have a few," Siki said. "I'll be alright. I watched my mom feed my grandma for years. I should be able to figure something out. Soft food's the key. That's why I went for the avocados back at the trading post."

Deirdre reached into the faded pillowcase she had picked up at the post, pulled out two avocados and handed them to Siki. "Take mine."

"Mine, too." With his swollen hands, Pagan took three avocados out of a wooden box he'd found alongside the road.

Siki nodded her thanks and added the avocados to the supplies she was carrying in a backpack she had traded for.

The three of them looked at each other for a few moments before Deirdre spoke. "So you think Yen didn't make it?"

Siki shook her head. "Can't be sure, but I got a bad feeling about it."

"Maybe we should do something for her," Deirdre said.

"You mean like a prayer?" Pagan asked.

"Whatever you want," Deirdre said.

Siki nodded, closed her eyes, and started chanting softly in a language that Deirdre assumed was Apache. Pagan knelt on one knee, clasped his hands in front of him and prayed silently. Deirdre listened to the Universe. She heard a swallow's song and instantly knew it was Yen's Spirit. *Thanks, Yen. You were our leader and inspiration.*

A few moments later, Pagan crossed himself, stood, grabbed his kit and walked west across an open field. No more goodbyes for him.

Siki was in an almost trance-like state, still chanting. Deirdre, thinking it best not to bother her, grabbed her pillowcase and rifle and walked toward the old road that led to Fresno.

"Deirdre," Siki called out.

Deirdre turned back with a grin. It was the first time Siki had called her by her name. Up to now it had been Crazy Hawk, or Hawk or Crazy One. "Yeah?" Deirdre said.

"East of Bakersfield the Kern loops north for a few miles. I noticed it when I was tracking you."

"I remember that."

"I'll cross the river and camp in that loop while I build up supplies to cross the desert. If you change your mind, join me. Even crossing the low point of the Nevada in winter could be tough considering how far along you are."

Deirdre smiled again as she nodded her thanks. "I'll keep that in mind," she said and walked south.

CHAPTER FORTY-SEVEN

The twenty-mile walk to Fresno gave Deirdre time to think. Siki was right. She should be heading for Hussar Valley where her people could help bring her child safely into the world, but the Apache's description of Jube as some kind of invalid made it impossible for her not to try to find him.

After seven miles, she sat in the shade of an oak tree. The cool February morning and the sensation of breathing clean air after months of Bee pollution had given her the illusion she'd be able to cover the twenty miles to Fresno in one determined day, but the blisters on her feet reminded her she was cavalry, not infantry, and the little one was consuming a good portion of her energy. Leaning back against the tree, she fell asleep.

She was awakened by the incessant caws of an impatient crow perched atop a tall metal post which Deirdre guessed to be an old telephone pole. She studied the bird.

Is she trying to tell me something?

Almost the moment these thoughts entered her mind, the crow flew away and down out of sight, telling Deirdre there must be a radical change in elevation about fifty feet beyond the telephone pole.

She walked to the edge of an escarpment and looked down to see a family — mom, dad and two little girls — passing over an open field in a pickup wagon hitched to two oxen. She thanked Sister Crow and then yelled out a hello to the travelers.

The man halted the oxen as she hiked down the escarpment, approached them and asked if she could get a ride into Fresno. They seemed keen to help the pregnant young woman, although the way they eyed the assault rifle slung over her shoulder, Deirdre thought they might be acting out of fear.

The lumbering oxen reminded her of the first time she'd met Jube, and the memory caused her to bow her head and stare aimlessly at the wagon floor as she was swallowed up into a morass of bittersweet memories.

When they arrived in Fresno a little after dark, Deirdre insisted on paying for her transport with a couple of oranges.

*****

At the Mercado, she traded the rifle for a pile of Fresno Commerce Tokens, a fry pan, a hunting knife and a few days' rations, including a bag of apples an a half dozen eggs. The burly Asian man she was doing business with was startled to see the assault rifle. Introducing himself as Tom, he stated he was making the deal because that kind of weapon would be a hot seller in his shop, but he couldn't give her what it was worth.

"I've got to figure in the risk I'm taking," he said.

"What risk?"

"Bees. They rolled in today looking for the people who blew up their Hive. Terrorists they called them." He scrutinized Deirdre's face carefully for a reaction. She was pretty sure she maintained a poker face.

"You're lucky you came to me," he continued with a smirk, which irritated her, but she still did her best to project indifference. "There are other traders who would turn you in for the reward. They're offering gold for information but I don't do business with the Bees. Just don't like those guys."

Deirdre took the tokens and the supplies. As she was leaving, the man offered one more piece of information. "You should know they're telling everybody that one of the people they're looking for is a pregnant white woman." Deirdre let her poker face go and shared a sympathetic gaze with Tom before she tossed him an appreciative nod on her way out.

She retreated into the ruins of downtown Fresno where Siki had seen Jube. With its abundant crawlspaces, collapsed roofs and underground passages, this labyrinth of rubble offered shelter from Bee search parties. She would have time to look for her man.

She found bodies—so many that she suspected most of them were dumped there. Enduring the overwhelming stench of death, she explored each corpse with a determined fatalism. If Jube were dead, she'd have no idea for how long, so she needed to check almost every corpse and skeleton. Those still recognizable were obviously not him but bodies that displayed advanced states of decomposition had to be examined in detail.

There was always something—size, clothing, bone structure, skin color if any skin remained—that told her it wasn't him. The few living people she ran into were starved and terrified. No one had seen anyone fitting Jube's description.

She searched for three days, spending each night in abandoned basements cuddled up next to fires she built from wood she'd salvaged from the walls of wrecked buildings.

On the morning of the fourth day, she changed focus. The child inside her was very active and she was using up her food supplies quicker than she anticipated. She constantly felt hungry. She had done what she could to find Jube. Now she needed to care for his child.

She could use the tokens to buy supplies but she was nervous about shopping in the Mercado knowing the Bees had a reward posted for a pregnant woman. Returning to Tom's shop, she asked if he could arrange transport to Bakersfield.

The big man's answer was not encouraging. "The Bees are searching every vehicle leaving Fresno. That's going to be tough."

"I've got to get to Bakersfield." She allowed a little desperation to seep into her tone.

Tom considered the situation for a moment, drawing the back of his surprisingly small hand across his forehead to rid himself of a couple of beads of sweat. "You give me all the tokens you have left," he said, "and I'll see what I can do. I know a guy who might be willing to smuggle you out and take you down there off-road. He's got an SUV."

She had no idea what an SUV was and didn't like trusting a stranger, but she had no choice. She turned over all the tokens.

He counted them. "You haven't spent any. I'll throw in some supplies. You stay here," he instructed, grabbing a wool coat. He left, locking the door behind him.

For two hours she sat in the musty old shop which was nothing more than a concrete block in the middle of the Mercado. At one point, she got nervous. *Tom might be in the process of selling me out for gold.* She was moving toward the exit to see if she could open the door from inside when she heard the dead bolt turn. The door opened, and Tom entered followed by a ruddy-faced boy, who couldn't have been more than sixteen.

"This is Ernie," Tom said. "He's confident he can get you out of town without the Bees finding you. Then he'll go off-road, swing east away from the main highway and head south to Bakersfield."

As soon as it was dark, Deirdre learned what an SUV was—a large vehicle designed for off-road driving. This particular model was completely stripped inside except for the driver's seat. From the smell of pigs, she determined it was usually used for transporting livestock. She sat on the filthy floor and tried to get comfortable.

At first Ernie was friendly enough, bragging about how he converted the vehicle from AI to an old-school carburetor system. "That's the key to getting 21st vehicles running, getting rid of the damn computers."

He liked to talk, so Deirdre just stretched out and got comfortable. But soon the bragging turned to complaining. He wasn't making anything off this job; the tokens he got would barely pay for the gas. He was doing it because he owed Tom.

For all his whining, he successfully maneuvered them out of town under the cover of night. She was optimistic this would work and started thinking about meeting up with Siki at the bend of the river. She now accepted that was the best thing to do for her child.

The optimism didn't live to see the dawn. About three in the morning, the SUV broke down thirty miles north of Bakersfield. Ernie cursed the vehicle for half an hour and then cursed Deirdre for another half hour. He labored on the engine all morning and into the afternoon.

By evening, after many failed attempts, he lifted a bottle of liquor from under the driver's seat and started drinking. Deirdre weighed her options. She could sit in the open waiting for Ernie to sober up enough to fix his vehicle, but that put her at risk of being spotted by a passing Bee patrol, and she doubted he would be able to fix it anyway. Or she could continue on by herself. She set off on foot just as the sun was setting.

CHAPTER FORTY-EIGHT

She walked south as quickly as she could, carefully monitoring the life within her. With a cold front moving in and the coming of the night, finding shelter and a place to cook was a necessity. The baby needed it; she could feel that.

After dusk, she saw a light in the distance and wondered if she should chance approaching it. The temperature had dropped below fifty. The leather coat was doing its job but she worried it might get into the thirties before the night was over. Without shelter, she would be very vulnerable. If it were just her, some old culvert to curl up in would do since it wasn't freezing, just uncomfortably cold. She'd handled much worse. But it wasn't just her any more. She decided to head for the light.

As she got close, she could see the source was a lantern in the window of a house, probably the home of farmers. The family who gave her the ride into Fresno were farmers and very sympathetic to her condition, so she decided it was worth taking the chance to knock on the door.

Moving around the house in the darkness, her hands brushing its stucco walls as she went, she felt the wood of a door and knocked.

A moment later the door opened revealing a man wearing a brown uniform. His right eye was all white, the pupil gone. It was Burke. His face crinkled in a spasm of rage as he recognized the woman who had taken half his sight.

Deirdre's reaction was instinctual and immediate. She tried to run, but it was more like a hurried waddle.

"It's the cunt who fucked up my eye," Burke yelled to someone inside. She heard the slide of a pistol being racked.

She was rounding the corner of the house when he fired. A burning sensation seared her left hamstring, causing her to stumble and fall. The pain was sharp but her only hope was to be quiet in the dark.

Burke appeared at the corner of the house directing the beam of a flashlight out towards an open field. When he was joined by someone else, Deirdre started crawling away.

She heard Burke say, "I'm going to check out that gully. I hit her. She didn't get far. You circle the house."

"I don't have a flashlight," the other Bee said. It was a woman. Sounded young.

"Just keep close to the wall and fire at any movement."

Deirdre succeeded in dragging herself behind the house and took a moment to examine the wound the best she could in the dark.

Moving the leg didn't hurt, but pressing her fingertips around the wound was quite painful. Blood was flowing slowly but steady. She hoped the bullet hadn't hit bone, which would mean she could probably stand up. She tried. Yes. Hunting knife in hand, she waited for the young Bee.

The shadowy figure rounded the corner. Deirdre shot a fist toward what she thought in the darkness was the woman's neck. She missed and connected with the back of her head.

The Bee whirled and fired blindly, the bullet exploding stucco off the wall of the house. Deirdre swung her arm out into the darkness. When her forearm collided with the gun hand, knocking it aside, she leapt forward and grabbed at her adversary. Her left hand found a shoulder and she shoved the hunting knife forward with her right hand.

She knew she had hit the jackpot when the young Bee made a gurgling sound, choking on blood. Deirdre jerked the blade sideways, slicing the left carotid. The woman collapsed, flopped around spasmodically for a few seconds and then all was quiet.

Deirdre reached down and felt for the firearm. She found the pistol in the dirt next to the corpse. She was about to move on when a horrible thought hit her like a hammer. She reached into her bag and, against all caution, lit a match. Her sigh of relief was mixed with a half sob. It wasn't Mindy.

She heard Burke approaching along the side of the house. "Reid, did you get her? Reid?"

The pain in her leg was becoming severe and there was some bleeding, but she was able to walk — more like stagger — through some bushes and down an incline. She thought she could cover some ground before tending to the wound.

She heard Burke yell, "Shit."

The beam from his flashlight has fallen on the corpse, Deirdre thought. *He'll see the handgun is gone and realize I'm armed.*

She took a spill down an incline, this one very steep, into a muddy creek bottom. Using the mud to cake a covering on top of the wound, she knew this would slow the bleeding but not stop it completely.

From the direction of the farmhouse, she heard a door close and figured Burke had retreated inside, afraid of a pistol-wielding Crazy Hawk.

Deirdre tried to escape the cold winds by curling up in a hollowed-out tree trunk. Despite being in an extreme state of exhaustion, she couldn't get any sleep because of the pain of the wound and the blood trickling down her leg as it penetrated the poultice.

She ransacked her philosophical storehouse for some wisdom that would comfort her and found among her anxious thoughts a tranquil memory of her father.

The Works of William Shakespeare had been his Wisdom Book when he was young, although she never saw evidence that he knew much about the plays, the poetry or the history around them. But he had picked up one quote that seemed to be meaningful to him. Before bedding down each night, he'd look to the skies and say, "Fortune, good night. Smile once more. Turn thy wheel." When she had asked him once what that meant to him, he shrugged and said, "It's a nod to luck. No matter how smart you are, or how good a warrior or how deep a philosopher, sometimes you need a good break to get you through."

Deirdre now accepted the profound truth of that naive wisdom. If Fortune didn't smile soon, she would not get through. She found this oddly calming, her fate would be decided one way or another within hours and she was ready to meet it.

Her wound was bleeding freely by dawn, but applying a tourniquet to the thickest part of her leg wasn't a practical option. She pressed on, pausing at a pond to apply another mud poultice. It hindered the flow slightly, but she knew her only chance was to hook up with Siki before she bled out. The Apache would know how to fix her.

Soon the periphery of her vision was darkening as if she were walking through a tunnel, and she was beginning to have difficulty catching her breath even though she was ambling at a mild pace. Eventually, she could only take a few steps before she had to plop down and regroup. Each time getting up was harder than the last.

By midmorning, the tree-lined riverbank of the Kern was visible, about half a mile away. Siki had said she'd cross the river to set up camp in the loop so finding a place to ford was essential but she had no idea where she was in relation to Siki.

Is she upriver or downriver?

All these considerations became irrelevant when she couldn't get up after one of her collapses. She was about two hundred feet from the river, but her legs would not support her.

Crawling seemed futile. Even if she made it to the bank, she wouldn't have the strength to look for a ford and swimming across was out of the question. Her poultice had slipped off allowing the blood to flow unobstructed, slow but steady. The life force that should have been keeping her baby alive was spilling uselessly onto the ground.

In the hope of attracting Siki's attention, she pulled the captured pistol from the pocket of her overalls and fired into a tree trunk until the magazine was empty.

A quarter of an hour passed. As consciousness slipped away, it was a sense of despair rather than resignation that dominated her emotions. All the Hussar wisdom about accepting death as part of life suddenly held no meaning. She wanted to live, give birth to her baby, organize a resistance against the Bees, find out what happened to Jube, watch her child grow, and reclaim her sister.

And then she felt it—a warm breath on her forehead.

She opened her eyes and looked into the beautiful face of her Soul Horse. Danny stood above her, his nose an inch from hers. He whinnied. *This must be his Spirit. He's here to usher me to the other side.* She was now at peace with her fate. Danny would care for her. Her mother would probably be there waiting. Maybe with Jube. Maybe Yen. Maybe her baby.

Danny lay down next to her with his legs curled up under him. It took all her strength to roll onto his back. As he rose up, she peered ahead and saw a woman standing on the river bank. It definitely wasn't Siki. The woman gestured toward Danny to follow her and then flew into the air like a bird.

Deirdre felt herself rising up as Danny flew after the woman she now recognized. It was Annie, her scout, who had died almost a year ago. Soon they were moving like the wind as Deirdre clung to the mane of her Soul Horse. At one point, she was sure she saw the Kern River far below before they ascended into the clouds.

*****

It was singing that woke her up. She pried open her heavy eyelids and saw she was in a makeshift tent, an oft-repaired canvas sheet stretched over three posts. A light rain tapped on the canvas.

The throbbing in her leg and an overwhelming sense of exhaustion were signs her mortal body still roamed a world of pain and suffering.

She looked under a recently dried deerskin that covered her and saw that she was naked. A powdery substance had been streaked across the tops of her feet, her ankles and her lower legs. There was a reassuring movement in her womb. Her baby was alive!

Gingerly, she repositioned herself to get a good look at her leg. It had been skillfully stitched. Surrounding the wound was the same powdery substance that was on her feet.

The singing was rhythmic, intense and passionate. With great effort, she stuck her head out from under the canvas. The camp was in the middle of a small meadow surrounded by mesquite. Siki was doing a shuffling dance, her arms outstretched toward the sky.

"Nice song," Deirdre called out.

Siki turned to her.

"You're conscious." She wore a relieved grin. "It's a song I've heard Apache healers sing. I think I got it right. Figured it couldn't hurt." She gestured toward the tent. "There're two oranges in there and goat's milk. I want you to down them right away."

Deirdre crawled back under the canvas, spotted a canteen, unscrewed the top and let the rich goat's milk flow down her throat. Siki knelt down and looked in.

Deirdre pointed at the powdery substance on her feet. "What's this?"

"Tule pollen. Important ingredient in my tribe's healing ceremony. You were near dead, totally out of it. When I dug the bullet out you didn't even wince."

Deirdre took a break from chugging the milk and nodded. "Danny's Spirit saved me."

"What?"

"Danny was my Soul Horse. His Spirit saved me."

Siki chuckled and gestured toward something. "You mean his Spirit?"

Danny's face could be seen over Sik's shoulder as he tried to get a look at Deirdre, who gasped and moved toward him.

"Take it easy," Siki said.

Deirdre crawled out, stood and wrapped her arms round the buckskin's neck. The rain had dwindled into a cool mist. He let his head rest on her bare shoulder.

After a reverent moment, she checked out his condition. He was too thin and his hooves were in dire need of a trim. A sore had developed where the saddle must have sat for months before he was able to lose it. But the wound on his hindquarters had scarred over nicely and he looked generally healthy.

"He brought you in about mid-morning," Siki said. "You were holding onto his mane, barely staying aboard. Who knows how he knew to come to me. He's been running with mustangs." She gestured to something down by the river. "His harem has been waiting for him."

Deirdre looked toward the river. Three mustang mares stood on the riverbank looking in at the camp.

"I don't think they realize he's a gelding," Siki said with a laugh. "They're definitely in love."

Deirdre nodded. "He's proud cut. He still thinks he's got the jewels and the ladies fall for that every time."

She positioned herself in front of Danny and gazed into his good eye. She was conscious of him gazing back. They stood like that, peering into each other's soul, until Deirdre heard Siki speak.

"Deirdre, you should lie down, get some rest."

Deirdre kissed Danny on the nose and crawled back into the tent. She was in a deep sleep seconds later.

CHAPTER FORTY-NINE

Leader stood at a window on the third floor of the Security Building watching the clean-up activity beneath her. The mustard gas factory had been destroyed by the terrorists and the fires that swept through the Hive seriously damaged several other buildings.

The Administration Building, where her office and apartment had been, was burnt to the ground. Although a strong wind had blown much of the gas harmlessly to the east, seventeen Bees had died of burns, gas inhalation or injuries caused by collapsing buildings. Nearly a hundred others were injured.

She noticed something curious in the chaos below. Men in drably colored tunics tended to some of the injured who were being treated on the soccer field because there was not enough room in the partially damaged hospital. She picked up a pair of binoculars off a desk and observed in more detail.

A barefooted, towering white man with rough facial features, brutishly big hands and a bright blond beard was helping one of the

Bee nurses clean the stump of a woman who'd lost a leg.

She panned the binoculars over the scene and spotted close to twenty such men of different sizes, shapes and colors, all offering aid to the injured. "What the fuck…"

Perry, who sat in the spacious office at a small desk of his own, rushed over to her. "Is there a problem?"

"Who are the men in the strange costumes down there with our wounded?"

"They call themselves the Brothers of Mercy," he said efficiently, delighted to supply this information. "They heard about our tragedy and offered their help."

Leader was disgusted. "Are they religious fanatics?"

"They claim to represent a strain of compassionate love that runs through all religions."

"How do you know so much about it?" she asked with accusatory venom.

Perry wilted under her glare. "They have pamphlets. I gave one a quick glance. Then I destroyed it, of course."

"Who accepted their help?" She swung out the question with such force Perry took a step back.

"Commandant Walker." He dropped his head so that his chin was touching his chest.

Her eyes widened in indignation. She seemed unable to speak for a moment but took a deep calming breath and said, "Set up a meeting with him immediately."

*****

Mindy lay on her cot in the middle of the soccer field, trying to shift her broken leg into a more comfortable position.

The fire had spread to the K-Bee cadet quarters quickly. Two of her friends had been trapped on the top floor. Mindy tried to reach them but had to leap out a window to save herself as the screams of her burning friends pierced her heart. The fall broke her leg below the knee.

As she moved, the pillow supporting her leg fell to the ground. She grunted in frustration.

A thin black man was bent over the adjacent cot helping a burn victim sip water from a canteen. Mindy thought of asking him to get the pillow but was reluctant to make requests of these strange men in the weird clothes.

Grabbing the side rails of the cot, she pulled herself up into a sitting position and reached for the pillow, but she couldn't get it. She tried stretching out her body a bit more but this caused her broken leg to slip off the edge of the cot. The pain erupted up her leg with such intensity she couldn't contain a deep moan. She flopped back down.

A moment later, a huge white man with a blond beard stepped up with the pillow in his hand.

"Here you go. Don't be shy about asking for help."

She nodded. "Under my leg."

She was surprised how gently he used his enormous hands to move her leg and place the pillow under it.

"How does that feel?" His bass voice was full of concern.

"Better."

"What's your name?"

She decided that having some bond with these Brothers of Mercy might be a practical necessity. "Mindy."

"Is that short for Miranda?"

Mindy shook her head. "Amanda." She noticed the black man who had been tending to the burn victim was now standing at the end of her cot.

"What do you want?" she asked, spooked by the man's stare.

"Did you say your name was Mindy?" the man asked, his voice weirdly breathless.

"Yeah."

He turned to the huge white man. "Oliver, let me look at that leg of hers. I'm experienced with broken limbs."

Oliver nodded. "Okay, Jube." He moved to the next cot.

Jube knelt next to Mindy and looked at the rough splint bound to her leg. "I should reset it. It's a sloppy job."

"No thanks," she said and lay back, closing her eyes. Sensing he was still kneeling next to her, staring, she opened her eyes and glared back at him.

He was about to say something when Oliver called out to him. "Jube, when you're done there, I think Ahmed could use your help changing a bandage."

"Of course," Jube responded. He stood and was about to move away from Mindy but stopped and looked back once more. "Are you a Hussar?"

"Why do you ask that?"

"An instinct."

"Well, you're wrong," she said nonchalantly. "I'm a Bee."

Jube nodded and walked away to help with another patient.

*****

Walker was looking at a map of Pacifica when Leader entered his office. He didn't look up until she had nested in a chair in front of his desk, then he sat back and smiled. "So, what's the problem?"

"You've allowed religious propagandists to spread nonsense to our people." Her jaw pushed forward aggressively, and her lips curled in disgust; she was ready for a fight.

"We need them," the Commandant stated calmly. "We've got more injured than we can handle."

"Then let some of the laborers work as nurses."

"We tried that. They're slave labor, not in a big hurry to relieve our suffering."

She pulled a pamphlet out of her shirt pocket. "Have you seen their manifesto?"

"Yeah," he said with a chortle. "It's like they grabbed every cliché about love from the old religions, wrapped it all up in a mangy tunic and slapped a catchy name on it, which isn't even original. It's all pacifist claptrap. It's not going to catch on here."

Leader slapped the palm of her hand onto his desk. "You're violating a principle. We can't allow superstition to be preached. It sets a terrible precedent."

Walker ran his fingers across his jaw. "I need a shave."

"Commandant, you have to take this seriously," she said with inflexible determination.

"What do you want me to do?"

"Drive them out immediately."

"They'll leave when they're no longer needed. That's their thing." He reflected for a moment. "Unless you think it's worth scapegoating them." He smiled broadly as if he'd come upon a brilliant plan. "When we no longer need them, we could blame them for the explosion. A mass execution could bring us all together."

"Don't be ridiculous," she said curtly. "Everyone knows who was responsible for the explosion. Have we found her body yet?"

"No. But we found that Vietnamese girl who worked in your building. She was in a tunnel we didn't know existed, right under the mustard gas factory. Workers discovered her body when they were digging around for survivors. It seems she was in on the conspiracy. A beam crushed her skull. Unfortunately, Victoria met the same fate. We found her body in the hospital under some rubble."

Leader's knuckles whitened as she gripped the edge of the Commandant's desk. "But no sign of the Hussar? I think she escaped."

He let out a big sigh. "We received some intelligence yesterday that suggests you're right."

"What? When were you going to tell me?" Her voice went up a few octaves.

"I'm telling you right now. Security Specialist Burke spotted her. She killed one of our people."

"So, Crazy Hawk is still out there." She slumped back into her chair.

"Let's start the healing process by refusing to call that hyper-violent maniac by her colorful nickname," he said with a dour frown. "It gives her legendary status. And you've got to stop obsessing on her. Burke thinks he landed a round. He found traces of her blood. She might be dead by now."

He nodded toward the map that lay on the desk in front of him. "Let's change our focus. It might be time to launch the campaign we've planned for so long. We've lost the mustard gas element but we're still at maximum production capacity for ammo. We had a few casualties but we have thousands of well-trained, well-armed soldiers who are angry and anxious to get revenge." He gazed at Leader, a slight shine now in his blue eyes. "And I have a very special role for you to play in this operation. If done right, it could lead to a direct confrontation with Deirdre, if she's still alive.'

Leader sat up straight and locked her attention on the map. "Tell me what you have in mind."

CHAPTER FIFTY

Deirdre wanted to get going, but Siki was adamant that she needed rest and nutrition. "First of all, your wound is at least a week away from being healed enough to ride. And the sores Danny has from that saddle hanging on him for months need more time to heal. Besides, you'll never get back to your valley before your little one arrives. It's best we stay here for a while. I can take care of you. I know what I'm doing."

Deirdre was touched by Siki's dedication to bringing her child healthy into the world. She was amused by this change of heart on the part of a woman who had a few months ago pledged to kill her, but she wasn't totally sure it was real.

She sat on a log, watching the Apache strip the branches off a chunky scrub oak. "What happens when I squeeze the little critter out of me?" Deirdre asked.

"What do you mean?"

"Well, you said not long ago that you aren't killing me because I'm pregnant. Soon that won't be the case."

"So, you think after the birthing I'll stick a blade in you and ride off with your baby?" Siki asked with a crooked smile.

"Sounds kinda harsh when you put it that way," Deirdre said, picking up a twig Siki had just stripped from the oak. She idly stuck it in her mouth and began chewing on it.

"No. I no longer want to feel your warm blood on my hands," Siki said, a sardonic edge to her voice.

"Well, isn't that gonna happen anyway?" She gestured toward Siki with the twig. "If you're helping me give birth, my warm blood on your hands is still in your future."

"Hopefully not much." Siki turned from her tree stripping to face Deirdre. "I take it you've never helped out at a birthing."

"No. I was a Raider pretty early on in life. No midwife work for me."

"Well, there's some blood in the afterbirth," Siki explained, "but if I have a lot of fresh warm blood on my hands that means things are going bad. Good news is, you're a strong woman and it looks like everything's working fine."

"Great." Deirdre sucked on the twig as she watched Siki. "What are you doing with that scrub oak?"

"It's your birthing post." Siki stepped back and admired her work. "You'll kneel," she said, demonstrating, "and wrap your arms around it while forcing the baby out." She grunted as if that was all there was to it.

"What?" Deirdre's jaw dropped.

"That's what Apaches have done for centuries."

"Well, Hussars lie down."

"There's no Hussar midwife here. You're going to do it the Apache way."

"Not a chance." Deirdre stood up in defiance.

Siki examined her. "You stood up pretty good there. You must be feeling better. I got something for you to do." She pointed to a bucket a few feet from the oak tree. "There's antelope sage in that bucket. Take it down to the river and fill it up halfway and let the sage soak for a while."

"You don't want me to drink it, do you?"

"Nah. I want you to wash your genitals with it twice a day. It'll make the birth go easier."

Deirdre nodded. "Easier is good." She sat back on the log. "Where'd you find antelope sage?"

"Bakersfield Mercado. There's a nice herb store there. They also had yucca up from the Mojave."

"What's the yucca for?"

"The sharp edge of the yucca leaf is perfect for cutting the umbilical cord. But mainly I want you to start eating the inner leaves every morning."

Deirdre's lips curled in nausea. "Why?"

"It'll speed the birth." Siki looked at Deirdre with disapproval. "Don't Hussars know herbs?"

"Some. We do tend to keep antelope sage away from our genitals, however." Deirdre watched as the young woman continued working industriously on the scrub oak. "When did you shop for herbs?"

"A week ago, when I traded the rifle for supplies," Siki explained. "I knew if you made it, I'd have to midwife you." She threw a smile toward Deirdre that was almost affectionate. "That's why I picked this meadow. It's perfect. It's got the birthing post…"

"Which I'm not gonna use."

"Yes, you are," Siki said firmly. "And we've got a nice fig tree right over there." She gestured toward a tall, stolid tree about thirty yards to the south.

"I'm afraid to ask what that's for."

"I'll bury the afterbirth and umbilical cord down by the roots. A fruit tree has new life every year. You'll want your child to come to new life every spring, too. This bond with the fig tree will help that happen."

Deirdre chomped on her stick for a reflective moment. "That's nice. We've got traditions, too."

"I respect that," Siki said, gesturing toward the river. "There's a raccoon that looks at us every morning down there on the bank. Maybe one of your Spirits. I've been putting a little piece of jerky out for him before I go to bed."

"That's good."

"Anything else?"

"We have a horse ceremony for every newborn," Deirdre said joyfully, stirred by thoughts of Hussar tradition.

"How's that work?"

"The baby is brought to a horse right away and placed at the animal's feet."

"Wow," Siki said with a little whistle. "No accidents?"

"Never. You only leave it there for a few seconds. The point is to establish the bond right from day one."

"Well, we got a horse." Siki gestured toward Danny who was rolling in the sand down by the river as two of his girlfriends looked on. "I noticed one of his mare friends moved on," she observed.

Deirdre nodded. "Yep. It takes a while but they'll all figure out pretty soon he's not going to be the stallion of their dreams."

Deirdre realized Siki wasn't listening but had returned to her work on the scrub oak. A burgeoning moral sprout inside told her to trust this woman. She stood and limped toward the pail of antelope sage.

*****

As rooms cleared in the hospital, the Bees moved the more serious cases into the partially damaged building, but Mindy's broken leg was considered a simple injury, so she was left out on the soccer field.

Jube made sure she had an extra blanket, extra soup and water, the only things he had any control over. The Bee hierarchy continued to use the Brothers of Mercy as a stopgap for their nursing needs but supplied them with only blankets, water and one meal a day of bread and broth.

Jube ate the bread and allowed himself a few sips of water but redirected the broth and most of the water to Mindy, always pretending it was part of her daily ration, which in reality consisted only of eggs, bread and water in the morning and jerky, soup, bread and water for dinner. The fire had destroyed much of the Hive food supply. He also made sure the teenager got his blanket, as the February nights could be harsh.

If she recognized the favoritism he directed toward her, she didn't let on. She seemed indifferent to him. Jube wasn't at all bothered by this. For almost nine months he'd pined to have some contact with Deirdre and caring for Mindy was a way of doing that.

When Deirdre hadn't come back that day nine months ago, he had used the only clue he possessed in an attempt to find her—the mysterious Landsknecht.

He asked at the Fresno Mercado about him and was directed to a sleazy saloon called Frederick's, an establishment standing amidst the rubble of a demolished mall on the north end of Fresno, the one building that had remained intact.

Landsknecht was indeed there, but Jube's questions about Deirdre were not welcomed. He was beaten mercilessly by Landsknecht and his ponytailed bodyguard.

Dumped in a ditch not far from the Mercado, he managed to drag himself back to his campsite, but the beating had reopened his wound, broken a rib and given him a concussion.

Starving people took advantage of his helpless state by crawling out of the ruins of downtown Fresno to take what little supplies he had left. He was only able to preserve Deirdre's notebook and a few bandages for his chest wound.

He caught a terrible flu and was soon so ravaged by fever he was unable to think clearly. Even though his chest wound was now in need of daily attention, he could only concentrate on preserving the notebook, which he held perpetually tucked under his arm.

He tried to make it back to the Mercado to seek help, but dehydrated and feverish, he collapsed in the middle of ruined downtown Fresno. He lay there for two days, clutching the notebook.

The unattended wound would surely have killed him either by infection or bleeding out if a stranger hadn't shown mercy. Jube couldn't remember who it was but he was sure it was a woman or perhaps an angel. She gave him food and a canteen of water and dressed his wound. He would be eternally grateful to that mysterious woman; her generosity kept him alive until the Brothers of Mercy came to Fresno.

They found him, nursed him back to health and recruited him into their number. Their mission was simple. Relieve suffering where they could and preach Love Supreme everywhere.

Fearing he'd never see Deirdre again, this new life with the brotherhood seemed a way to deal with the agony caused by the separation from his love.

Their leader, a mountain of a man, almost seven-foot tall, named Oliver, talked of the Fellowship of Pain, both emotional and physical, that united all living things. Jube began to see a way out of the psychological cul-de-sac in which the separation from Deirdre had trapped him.

If he could relieve the suffering of others, it would, in a way, relieve his own, but it wouldn't be easy. He often felt gutted as he speculated on her fate. At times he was so sad it was difficult to be of use in the caregiving mission of the Brothers. Oliver had saved Jube from falling into a fathomless abyss of depression when he taught him a simple method of contemplation.

"Sit still and try to clear your mind of all painful images from your past," he counseled. "It's true that the torment of these memories is what bonds you with all humanity, but if the pain is what you concentrate on, it will soon produce hopeless yearning and bitterness.

"Since we all know we don't have control over our thoughts — we don't think as much as thinking happens to us — it's essential to have something to concentrate on when we're trying to enter a state of contemplation.

"Try this. Imagine you're above all the chaos, the injustice, the cruelty, the violence, the sense of loss, the loneliness. All of that is beneath you.

"Imagine your consciousness is in the sky surrounded by a dark cloud. It's not a cloud full of facts like the one they worshiped in the 21st but a cloud of unknowing. A place where you humbly accept this heartbreaking existence as incomprehensible but also where you profess your faith that the meaning lies behind that cloud in the heart of the divine.

"You must believe that just beyond the darkness is a compassion-filled light that will illuminate everything and bring you peace. And there's only one way to penetrate the darkness. Pummel it relentlessly with rays of selfless love. Hammer at it for as long as you can and as often as you can with expressions of mercy, giving, sacrifice, caring — always humble in your recognition that without a glimmer of light coming through that cloud, the significance of our existence on this earth will forever be a mystery."

Oliver expressed this with simple sincerity as if he were a traveler telling of a wonderful land he'd visited.

Jube chose to embark on that journey into the cloud of unknowing. Each evening before he went to sleep and any other time there was a lull in the activity of the Brothers, he'd practice pummeling that cloudy darkness with love.

He felt he was making progress when word of the terrible explosion and fire at the Hive reached the Brothers. Oliver led his group to the aid of those hurt by this catastrophe.

When Jube walked into the land of the Bees, he was gripped by an almost unbearable suspense as he wondered if Deirdre would be there.

When rumor reached him that the entire catastrophe was caused by a mad woman named Crazy Hawk who was believed killed in the hospital fire, he was devastated, but the sense that perhaps the meaning of all suffering lay behind that dark cloud drove him to continue his daily contemplation.

The Fellowship of Pain inspired him to throw himself into the role of caregiver. While tirelessly working to relieve the suffering of the wounded Bees, he found Mindy.

*****

Deirdre lay exhausted under the canvas, completely drained, literally and figuratively. A light rain had begun to fall shortly after Siki cut the umbilical cord.

The pain of labor had been intense, but she had expected hours of agony, and it was about an hour and a half and not as painful as she anticipated.

Could the antelope sage mix, the yucca diet and the strange kneeling position have helped? Or was she just lucky? She was too tired to reason it out much further. Right now, her main concern was to get her little boy back into her arms.

She heard Danny's whinny and knew Siki had presented the child to the horse, just as the Hussar ceremony required. A few moments later, the Apache knelt under the canvas and handed the swaddled baby to his mother.

Deirdre examined the little guy. Siki thought he was a bit on the small side, but Deirdre didn't care. This was her child, and as she contemplated the little boy's brown complexion she loved the idea that every time she looked at him, she'd be reminded of Jube.

CHAPTER FIFTY-ONE

Mindy spotted Leader and wondered what business she had down with the wounded. The teenager admired Leader to the point of worship. In her mind, anything that was wrong with the Hive was despite Leader, never her fault.

As she watched the statuesque woman stride across the field she knew everything would be okay because greatness was on the job. When Leader stopped at the foot of her bed and addressed her, Mindy was stupefied.

"Cadet Buford, how are you feeling?" Leader asked in a perfunctory manner.

Mindy tried to answer but felt dry-mouthed. Her nerves got the better of her and nothing came out.

"Come on," the beautiful woman said impatiently. "Your injury was to your leg, not your head."

Mindy forced out a response. "Better, Leader. The pain is still—"

Leader cut her off. "Deirdre was seen alive by a Bee who knows her well enough to make a definitive identification." Her words seemed quiet and steady. She was reporting some facts Mindy needed to know, then suddenly, her tone intensified. "Your sister killed another Bee during the confrontation. That makes close to twenty Bee deaths she's responsible for. What do you think of that?" She shot the question out like a bullet from a gun aimed directly at the young girl's center mass.

Mindy thought about her answer for a good half minute. She wanted to be sure of her feelings. "The fire caused by my sister killed two of my friends," she said. "I heard their screams while I tried to get to them. I'm a Bee. My sister should be considered our number one enemy."

Leader studied Mindy's facial expression, trying to see some crack in her declaration of Bee solidarity. "She was shot in a firefight with our troops," she said, finally satisfied Mindy was for real, "but as you well know, she's tough. If she survived her wound, she's probably given birth to your niece or nephew by now. If we can eliminate your sister and save the child, we will. That baby will be useful to our program. When you can walk, you'll report directly to Commandant Walker. He wants to pick your brain about the Hussars."

Leader was about to leave when something caught her attention. "What's this idiot's problem?"

Mindy turned to see Jube standing at the foot of the next cot, looking dumbfounded, staring at Leader.

"Who knows?" Mindy said. "All of those religious people irritate me. When will they be gone, Leader?"

"Soon," Leader answered coldly. "Very soon." She strode off.

Jube dropped to his knees by Mindy's bed.

"What is going on with you?" she barked.

"Your sister…she may be alive. With a baby."

"What do you care about my sister?" Her strained voice revealed her profound disgust with this odd man. "Listen," she said, a mean edge to her voice, "I know you've been giving me your soup. I took it because I thought it might speed my healing and I want to get out of this bed. But that doesn't mean there is any bond between us. Got it?"

Jube nodded, brought himself to his feet and walked away. Mindy heard him mumbling under his breath, but she couldn't make out what he was saying.

*****

"What are we gonna do about the Bees?" Deirdre asked as she soaked a piece of cloth in the shallows of the river.

"Don't you think we put them on their ass for a while?" Siki was washing out the tin plates from breakfast.

"They were crawling all over Fresno looking for us," Deirdre said as she carried the wet cloth to her baby, who lay in a small depression in the soil, swaddled in a blanket. "And you didn't see Leader's eyes when she realized what we were up to. Pure hatred."

Deirdre picked up the baby, walked to a boulder right behind Siki, sat down and balanced the child carefully on her knees. "Now that we blew up her world," she continued, "she's frothing at the mouth, I guarantee it. I don't think she's gonna wait long to get revenge." She carefully unwound the blanket to reveal the baby's perfect little body.

"I think we definitely ended the mustard gas threat," Siki said, letting the river water lap up against a plate.

"Yeah, probably." Deirdre applied the wet cloth to the baby's bottom. "They still have serious firepower. How many military-ready Bees are there, you think?"

"Yen estimated it at over ten thousand."

"They could put seven thousand in the field and still leave a formidable garrison at the Hive." Deirdre picked up the baby and buried her nose in his stomach. When she came up for air she asked,

"Why do human babies smell so good? Even when they're messy?"

"The Great Spirit made them that way," Siki said. "Or mother nature. Or Darwin, whoever the fuck he was."

Deirdre placed the baby back on her knees and smiled down at the little guy. She rubbed some sand off the baby's chin with her knuckles. He grabbed a finger and held on.

Deirdre laughed. "Look at that. He's wrestling with my finger."

Siki joined in the laughter. Danny trotted over from some grass he was grazing on to check if he was missing out on some fun. Siki stood and stroked Danny's nose.

"Hey, Danny. You miss your mare friends?" Danny nuzzled Siki for a moment and then loped off into a copse of oak trees, out of sight.

Siki turned toward Deirdre. "You worry he might follow his mustang sweethearts?"

Deirdre shook her head. "Nah. I'm what he needs. Only idiots don't go for what they need." She packed into a stare as much meaning as she could muster.

It took a few seconds for Siki to notice. When she did, she gave her head a little shake. "I'm not getting it? Who are you calling an idiot?"

"The Nations and Hussars if we don't form an alliance."

"Oh." Siki sat down next to the baby. "My people don't trust yours. The treaty we had was just to keep you from stealing from us. Danny's back looks totally healed," she said, changing the subject. "How are you feeling?"

"I could set out tomorrow, I think. That's a first-rate papoose you built."

"Yeah, us Patchies know stuff."

Deirdre swaddled up the baby, gave her left nipple to the little one and eyed the formidable woman before her.

"You know," Deirdre posited cautiously, "Hussars say when you make an enemy of a friend, it's a tragedy and when you make a friend of an enemy it's a miracle."

"So, you think we're friends?" Siki said as she lined up plates on a boulder where the sun could dry them off. She turned to Deirdre and waited for an answer to the question, her eyes glittering like bright beads.

"Shit, is this where you kill me?" Deirdre said playfully.

Siki tossed both hands in the air in a gesture of frustration. "It's just that I made such a big deal back home about how I was going to cut you open and make you eat your intestines."

"Damn."

"When you tied me to that boulder in the desert…" She paused as if that memory still stung. "I was out cold for a while…you remember that?"

"I do," Deirdre responded, unsure where this was going.

"Well, before I regained consciousness one of the Mountain People visited me in a vision." Siki's voice became almost inaudible as she spoke of these sacred things.

"Mountain People?" Deirdre asked.

"Spirits who have visited Apaches in visions since ancient times."

"Okay."

Siki ran her fingers through her long black hair as she pondered the imponderable. "He told me to follow you and said the 'flow of honey will be stopped'. For the longest time I thought he was telling me that if I didn't take care of you, you would do something terrible to my people."

"And by taking care of me," Deidre said with a weak smile, "you don't mean helping me through childbirth."

Siki shook her head. "At first, I thought it was the cutting you open thing." She sat next to Deidre on the boulder. "But in the days we worked together in the Hive, I began to realize what the 'flow of the honey' meant. Bees make honey. What do these human Bees make? Oppression and terror. The Mountain Spirit wanted me to follow and ally with you so we could stop them."

There was a silent moment as both women thought over this interpretation of Siki's vision.

"Ever watch any old westerns from the 20th?" Siki asked.

"Sure. Love them. You seen many?"

"Some." Siki noticed the baby's foot sticking out and re-adjusted the blanket to cover it. "My friend, Billy Cottonwood, is really into them. He's got like twenty of those little round things."

"DVDs. Yeah, we got quite a collection back in Hussar Valley. Over fifty. A few of them are old Westerns. Do you like them?"

Siki shrugged. "I'd like them better if the indigenous looked indigenous."

Deirdre nodded. "I know what you mean."

"I saw one where an Apache and a white guy become best friends," Siki said. "They sealed the deal with blood."

"Is that an Apache thing?"

"Nah, it's a movie thing. But I like it."

Baby had finished off his nipple feast and was dozing. Deirdre carried him over to a hollow in the ground and placed him in it. She then walked to her weapons belt which was hanging from a branch of a redshank bush and pulled her hunting knife out of the sheath. She walked back to Siki and sat down by her side.

"How do we do it?" Deirdre asked.

Siki nodded as she recalled the scene from the movie. "They each made a cut on the inside of their wrists and then pressed their wrists together."

"Okay." Deirdre pressed the knife point into her left wrist below the palm of her hand. She handed the knife to Siki who did the same. They held their wrists together.

"Blood Sisters," Siki said.

Deirdre wore a grateful smile. "Blood Sisters."

*****

Siki had anticipated the main problem with the rancher would be questions about why an Apache was picking up the Hussar equines left with him the year before, but that wasn't the issue.

Bees had visited his ranch so he was keenly aware of the risks he was taking dealing with the "terrorists". He wasn't satisfied with keeping only one of the animals as payment, which is what Deirdre had suggested. He wanted both horses and the donkey. She could take the mules, a couple of riding saddles, a pack saddle and some tack. Siki didn't have much leverage to bargain with.

She rode back to their camp on Deja, leading Big Red. Early the next morning, she and Deirdre set to packing Big Red. When they were finished, Deirdre, papoose on her back, climbed on board Danny, who was wearing one of the riding saddles.

Siki had learned that the bikers were once again guaranteeing safe passage through the Tehachapi route but Deirdre didn't trust them. She felt it was likely one of them would respond to the reward and turn them in, so they took the northern route past Lake Isabella.

It was early March, still cold at this elevation with some snow on the ground, which was a mixed blessing. It drove the Mounties down to a lower elevation where they were much less bold with their ambushes because of possible retaliation from surrounding communities, but it made that first night camping a lesson on how to keep a baby warm.

Deirdre put the little one close to her breast and wrapped herself in two bearskins. Siki slept under a light cotton blanket, insisting Deirdre and the baby get both bearskins.

The next day, they descended into the desert, skirting the town of Mojave and hooking up with the Pacific Crest Trail. It was time to part company.

Siki pointed to the snow-capped San Jacinto range to the south.

"That'll be a cold, lonely stretch for you. Maybe I should ride along."

"No. I can do it. I may not be an Apache but I'm not exactly a 21st-century princess."

Siki laughed. "That I know."

Deirdre tossed a look back at the little guy in the papoose. "Besides, little Cochise needs to start toughening up. We've been spoiling him."

Siki cocked her head to one side. "You're naming the kid Cochise?"

"Geronimo seemed too on the nose and Victorio sounds Spanish. Besides, Cochise was not only a bad-ass fighter, he was a great leader."

Siki nodded. "Yes, he was."

"How do you feel about that? A damn Hussar stealing a famous Apache name?"

Siki contemplated on this for a moment. "My family is pretty flexible when it comes to names. My mother called me Roberta. Haven't the slightest idea where that came from. When I joined the Army of the Nations they started calling me Siki, which is the name of a famous warrior woman." She looked east toward her homeland.

"So, are you okay with it?" Deirdre asked.

Siki turned toward Deirdre and nodded, a little moisture in her eyes. "Yeah, I like it." She took a deep breath and paused a moment. Then in her usual strong, gravelly voice she said, "I'll tell my people about the Bees and try to make it clear we need to form a true alliance with the Hussars."

She reined Deja around to the east, raised her fist over her head and yelled "Blood Sisters" as she galloped off.

CHAPTER FIFTY-TWO

Francine, wearing a wool cap pulled down over her ears, heavy gloves and an oversized, patched-up U.S. army coat, mounted Tank and rode toward the north rim.

It was uncomfortably frigid weather with a rough wind whipping over the ridge tops, but she knew the morning rim tour was a necessary duty for a young Hussar. Well aware that it was on this very patrol that Deirdre's younger sister was taken by kidnappers, she was ever vigilant as she made her way up Airplane Crash Road to the rim.

The key to a successful scout was to stay on the highest elevation to eyeball as much of the surrounding area as possible. Steep slopes and bad footing made staying on the ridge crests a challenge, but she did her best to put herself in a position to scan all the approaches to the north side of the valley.

Despite the extreme cold and the demands of her job, Francine was in a wonderful mood because of a recent development. Tank turned out to be a good horse. He still had a mean streak, didn't like people much and seemed to hate other horses, but when Francine sat on him, he was a perfect gentleman. That had been the product of eleven months of sleeping next to his corral, brushing and massaging him every day and getting back on him after countless falls. She was close to giving up when one day he just seemed happy and calm around her. A real connection had formed. Now she was proud to introduce the stocky appaloosa as her Soul Horse.

She was coming off a rise at the west end of Cooper Canyon when she spotted it—movement on the Anza Road, a red scarf or sash blowing in the wind, visible for an instant through the branches of the cottonwood trees around Two Ghost Springs.

She debated her next move. A nearby ridge would give her an excellent view but it was too steep for a horse. Her other choice was to advance to the springs behind the cover of the cottonwoods, but if she could see that sash, maybe whoever was wearing it had spotted her and would be waiting in ambush on the other side of the cottonwoods.

She decided to climb up to the ridge on foot. Sliding off Tank, she grabbed her rifle, hung by a sling from the horn of her saddle, and scrambled up to the ridge.

The second she reached the top she saw the red thing again and ducked behind a boulder. This being the first time she'd had an incident on her patrol, she was breathless with excitement mixed with fear—not the fear of dying; that didn't occur to her. It was the fear of failing her people.

She pulled her binoculars from a pouch on her belt and repositioned herself so she could peer over the boulder but leave most of her body concealed.

Now she could see it clearly. A lone rider on the Anza road, leading a pack mule. She brought the binoculars to her eyes and thumbed in the focus.

The rider was bent over, protecting himself from the wind, bundled up pretty good, no weapons visible. The red thing wasn't a scarf or sash but a pair of windblown ribbons tied to a pack on the rider's back.

Definitely not a Trog—they used horses for protein not transportation. The horse looked brown, the mule red, but she couldn't tell for sure in the dim morning light. She scanned the surrounding area for movement before feeling confident this was a solo intruder.

She scrambled down the hill, mounted up while still holding the rifle and loped toward the cottonwoods, threading her way through the copse until she could see the rider again and waited.

When she felt the timing was right, she urged Tank out from behind the cover of the trees toward the road, putting herself behind the stranger, keeping the butt of the rifle on her thigh, the muzzle pointed toward the sky, finger on the trigger.

Sensing someone approaching, the rider stopped. Francine leveled the rifle toward the stranger, who reined the horse around to face her.

Francine gave Tank a pop with her heels and cantered up to about ten yards from the rider, whose face was hidden by a scarf. "Mister, what's your business in Hussar Valley?"

A woman's chuckle came from behind the scarf.

"Alright, let me try that again," Francine said impatiently. "Woman, what's your business in Hussar Valley? Don't be laughing again. I got a nervous trigger finger."

"That was some good riding with a rifle ready."

"I'm a Hussar. That's what we do. Identify yourself immediately." There was an edgy intensity in Francine's tone.

Tank snorted at the intruder's horse, who whinnied in response. Francine tossed a look at the stranger's mount and saw now, in the growing light, it was a rich buckskin. She focused on the animal's right eye. It was gone.

"Deirdre? Is that you?"

Deirdre's hearty laugh rippled through the morning air. Francine put the rifle on safe and dismounted as Deirdre removed the scarf and grinned down at her. "You made a mount out of Tank. You're right, you are a Hussar."

Francine ran up and grabbed Deirdre's right leg, squeezing it in a desperate hug. "Oh, Deirdre, I'm so happy you're home."

"Hey, I'm not traveling alone," Deirdre said.

Francine stepped back and looked around. "I didn't see anybody else."

Deirdre gestured over her shoulder. "Back here."

Francine moved toward Danny's rear. It wasn't a backpack strapped to Deirdre, but a papoose. The ribbons were for the baby's entertainment.

Deirdre took the papoose off and handed it down to Francine, who rearranged the blankets so she could see the face of the child.

"It's beautiful. Is it Jube's?"

Deirdre nodded.

"You know he set out to follow you," Francine offered.

"I know," Deirdre said with a warm smile. "We made that little guy after he found me."

"Is Jube…?"

Deirdre shook her head. "I don't think he made it. Long story."

"Damn, I liked him." The young girl bowed her head, took a few moments and wiped a tear off her cheek with the back of her hand. "How about your sister?"

"She's still lost," she said, lowering her eyes. Francine thought Deirdre's whole body sunk a little as the thought of her lost sister crushed her. And then with more buoyancy, she said, "Haven't given up on her yet, though. How's my dad?"

"He's okay. Talks too much."

"That's Pops. Do me a favor, give me that kid and ride on ahead. Let everyone know I'm home. I want a warm bath ready by the time I get into camp."

Francine handed the papoose up to Deirdre and walked toward her horse.

While Francine was mounting up, Deirdre rode on to the crest with the papoose cradled in her arms. She looked down at the beauty of Hussar Valley. She spoke tenderly to little Cochise.

"That's where you're going to grow up, Sweetie."

A moment later Francine galloped past her down into the valley, her mission to let everyone know Deirdre of the Hussars was home.

*****

Mindy was getting around pretty good. She let that strange man, Jube, redo her splint and it turned out he was right; it did feel better and was apparently healing cleanly now. He also rigged up a wooden heel stub that made going back and forth from the latrine much easier.

Something else had perked her up. She'd been told she was to travel with Commandant Walker's personal staff in the coming campaign. Her expertise about all things Hussar was considered invaluable by the Commandant. She was thrilled. It confirmed that her loyalty to the Bees would be rewarded.

Her feelings towards her sister were no longer mixed. When it was reported that Deirdre was killed in the hospital fire, Mindy's mood was colored by bittersweet resignation.

Fine, that part of my life is over. But when she heard Deirdre had escaped and may still be alive, she became consumed with a desire for revenge. The cries for help coming from her friends as they were immolated haunted her every day. She was fantasizing about a deadly confrontation with Crazy Hawk when she became aware of Jube's presence at the foot of her cot.

"What do you want?" Her curtness disguised the fondness she was beginning to feel for him. His kindness moved some part of her that her training as a ruthless Bee had not succeeded in destroying.

"The Brothers of Mercy are moving out tomorrow," he told her. "We're not needed here anymore. They're headed for the Bay Area to tend to the sick. There's a terrible smallpox epidemic there."

"Bye-bye," Mindy said, feigning indifference.

"I heard you were going on the campaign," he said.

"What's it to you?"

Unphased by Mindy's rudeness, Jube continued with a steady voice. "I know some members of the Commandant's staff are taking people along to help. Assistants."

"So?"

"I'd like to volunteer to be your assistant." A shy grin edged onto his face.

"Your band of do-gooders going to let you jump ship?"

Jube nodded tightly. "We're all volunteers, free to leave at any time. I've already told Brother Oliver. He gave me his blessing."

His way of speaking was so simple and direct it endeared him to her more. She fought off this soft feeling. "What's going on with you? You're not in love with me, are you?"

"No, of course not. I just like looking out for you. It's hard to explain. How's your leg?" He was anxious to change the subject.

"Good. Better since you reset it." There was just a hint of gratitude in her voice. She spent a second readjusting the blanket on her legs, then with undisguised warmth she said, "Thank you."

"You're welcome."

He began to walk away. She called after him. "Jube."

He turned back.

"I'll ask if they'll let me bring you." She smiled for a moment but then added, "You've got to promise you'll keep that universal love drivel to yourself."

"All right."

He moved to a cot across the field and started tending to one of the other wounded Bees.

✱✱✱✱✱

Henry Ketchell sat on his back porch, sipping a cold Mexican beer and listening to a Mariachi band playing down by the waterfront.

Life had been good since he'd gotten back. The "capture" of Crazy Hawk had a wonderful effect on virtually every facet of his life. Ketchell was the only Bee advisor to make it back from Hussar Valley so his uncontested version of things made him a star among the Bees. Commandant Walker did ask some probing questions about what happened with the Trog attack on the Hussars, but Ketchell was able to bullshit his way through the debriefing well enough to be handsomely rewarded with gold. He was told he didn't need to report back in person for a year.

He guzzled the last drop of beer and yelled for his maid. "Nancy!"

Before the woman could respond, there was a loud knock on the door. "Nancy, get that," he growled.

He was trying to relax. The previous night he and his little army had attempted a raid on a República oil reserve but met with much stiffer resistance than was expected. He and his force were lucky to escape with only a few casualties.

He heard the door open and voices coming from outside. A moment later, an attractive brunette dressed all in black stepped into his sightline. It took a good ten seconds before he recognized her.

"Parelli. What are you doing here?"

"We have a problem." She gestured toward a wicker chair. "May I?"

"Sure." Ketchell's mind raced as he tried to figure out why Walker's right-hand officer was on his verandah. He came up with nothing.

She pulled the chair up so she was right in front of Ketchell's lounge chair and sat down. "It's Crazy Hawk."

"God damn it." Ketchell's bellow must have spooked Nancy

because he heard a plate drop in the kitchen. "You didn't kill her?" he asked in disbelief.

"We felt more could be gained by studying her," she said timidly.

"I knew she was going to be a guinea pig for a while but I thought when you were done with…" He smacked his forehead with both palms. "You didn't try to recruit that killing machine into your world, did you?"

Parelli was obviously made uncomfortable by that question. Ketchell's mocking laugh boomed like a shotgun blast. "So now you want me to fix things? Again?"

"We're going to give you plenty of help this time."

"Good," he spat.

"But first, we need to tap into your logistical skills."

"What does that mean?"

"We plan to annihilate the Hussars and occupy their valley."

"Good. What does that have to do with me?"

"We want you to establish a fully supplied forward base up north of El Centro. Leader will be arriving here with a thousand troops. They will function as a flying column to attack Hussar Valley from the south as Commandant Walker attacks from the north with the main body of the army. Your base will provide Leader's column with logistical support." She sat back with crossed arms, expecting his compliance.

Ketchell sat slack-jawed in stunned disbelief for a few moments before he spoke. "So, when do you expect me to finish setting up this forward supply dump?"

"The entire force will be here within two weeks," she explained with cold efficiency, "as well as the necessary equipment. Of course, we'll be commandeering all your armored vehicles. And your entire fuel reserve must be at our disposal."

Ketchell felt his face turning red with rage but he was able to remain calm enough to speak. "You expect me to establish a fully supplied forward base in the middle of the desert in two weeks?" His voice was breathy as if someone had just knocked the wind out of him.

She stood up. "We have a lot of confidence in you, Henry. Make it happen."

After she left, the sounds of Ketchell cursing everything—his maid, his dog, the fates—could be heard by anyone within two hundred yards of the bungalow.

CHAPTER FIFTY-THREE

The stiffening in his aching legs caused Miguel Pagan to reposition himself in the saddle for the fiftieth time since he rode out of La República settlement of Warner Springs and made his way north on the Pacific Crest trail.

He hadn't been on a horse since he was a kid in San Diego, and even then, he'd never ridden more than twenty minutes at a time, always in a round pen. It'd been four hours since he wrapped his legs around this barrel-shaped quarter horse and no amount of changing position could relieve the aching in his thighs.

He was alone. Some at La República congress in La Paz wanted to send a detachment of infantry with him on this important assignment. Pagan firmly believed that one person approaching alone on horseback had a better chance of making peaceful contact.

He was crossing a dry creek bed when his horse whinnied and spun to his right. Three riders appeared on a ridge to the east and rode parallel to the trail, seemingly uninterested in Miguel's presence as they descended a grade and disappeared.

When Miguel returned his attention to the trail in front of him, a lone rider stood on the opposite creek bank blocking his path. A thick, raw-boned woman, late forties, sat casually on a big black horse, smoking a sloppily rolled cigarette, not looking at him, interested only in picking pieces of tobacco from her lips.

"Good morning," Pagan said. No reaction. He was aware of movement to his left. He glanced over and saw two riders coming toward him out of a ravine. A quick look to the right revealed the riders who had disappeared a few seconds before were now back on top of the ridge.

"Took a wrong turn, didn't ya?" the woman in front of him asked.

"Excuse me?"

"You were proceeding north on the PCT and then you veered off onto the old California Riding and Hiking Trail. You didn't mean to do that, right?"

"I did mean to do that."

"But that turn takes you into Hussar Valley," she said, her brow furrowed in mock confusion.

"Yes, ma'am," he said, his voice dropping to a murmur.

She smiled crookedly. "Wake up this morning feeling suicidal?"

"No, I need to contact one of your tribe who I hope made it back to your valley safely."

"You know a Hussar?" she said with genuine surprise.

"Yes, ma'am. The one they call Crazy Hawk."

*****

Deirdre was on the hill longer than usual that day. It was the one she and Jube once sat on looking out across the tops of the oaks at the valley. Cochise lay on her lap waving his little arms as if he were trying to signal something. Danny was lying stretched out on a sandy ledge twenty feet downhill.

She liked being here thinking about Jube and those days when he was healing, and they'd burn every ounce of his renewing energy making love. As she shuffled through memories, she couldn't imagine ever being with someone else. Maybe that would change someday. Maybe not.

A horrible thought gripped her, a familiar one that surfaced a few times each day. *What if Jube is somewhere suffering right now? What if he's wondering why I don't come to him?* Deirdre might have sat there remembering, regretting and imagining for hours, but suddenly Danny scrambled to his feet, alerted by activity in the Hussar camp. When she spotted Margaret on her big black stallion galloping in her direction she knew something important had occurred. By the time Margaret's horse was bounding up the hill toward her, she was Crazy Hawk once again.

*****

Deirdre paced on the porch of the Eagle House. Pagan sat on a stool a few feet away examining his surroundings, fascinated with the experience of being in the Hussar camp. Margaret leaned against the porch railing, eyeing the hulking Mexican. Cochise was secure in his papoose, propped up against the porch wall, watching Mom's every move.

"This is a pretty nice house, actually," Pagan said.

"You sound surprised," Margaret said.

"Well, to be honest, we're taught in school that Hussars live in holes in the ground like snakes."

Margaret's eyes burned with indignant anger. "We're taught República trash have sex with donkeys. That's why they're all jackasses."

This banter ended when Haller walked out of the house carrying a long roll of paper. Pagan was impressed by the appearance of the Hussar leader, the one they called Eagle. Well over six feet with rugged facial features, jet-black hair, broad shoulders and a narrow waist, the white man seemed the epitome of a fierce tribal leader. Pagan guessed his age as forty.

Kneeling on the porch floor, Haller rolled open the paper, putting the legs of unoccupied chairs on the corners to hold it in place. He turned to Pagan and pointed to the map of Southern Pacifica.

"Show us what you're talking about," he said.

Pagan knelt. "Okay." He scanned the map for a moment. "Right here." He was pointing to a location right in the middle of the desert about twenty miles north of the trading town of El Centro.

Haller studied the map carefully. "Are you sure?"

"I saw it myself," Pagan said decisively.

"So why tell us?" Margaret muttered. "It sounds like a República problem."

"I'll tell you why," Pagan shot back. "If they were only going to attack us they'd just use the base they already have in Penasco."

"He's right," Deirdre said, picking up Cochise who had started to cry. "They're planning a move north."

"They're not there to police Mounties or chase Vaqueros," Pagan said. "Boats loaded with troops and equipment are entering the Gulf of California every day. They unload everything at Ketchell's fuel dump and then it's all transported up to their advance base in the desert."

"So, what's their plan?" Haller asked.

"They're coming after us," Deirdre said.

"Damn, girl." Margaret wore a proud grin. "You really pissed them off."

Haller was less amused. "So, you think they're going to launch an attack on our valley using that station as a base of supplies?"

"Yes." There was not a trace of doubt in Deirdre's reply.

"But there's still something I don't get," Margaret said. "Why does La República de Baja California care about Hussar security?" She pronounced the name of Pagan's country with exaggerated but correct Spanish pronunciation, her tone laden with mockery as well as suspicion.

Deirdre answered the question. "Because Pagan did a good job of telling his people who the Bees are."

"Not just me," he said. "I wasn't the only one of our people who escaped that day we blew up their world. Three others made their way back home. All of us told the same story. It's agreed among our people that the Bees are our real threat. You Hussars are only a nuisance. So, we're giving you a heads up."

Margaret took an aggressive step toward Pagan as her pride flared. "You expect us to ride down there and get machine-gunned out in the middle of the desert. Two birds with one stone, is that it?"

"If we wanted to get rid of you, we wouldn't have to resort to a gimmick like that," Pagan said with a sneer. "Ever watch a mule stomp a snake?"

"You've tried that before," she growled. "How'd that work out?"

"Margaret, stand down," Haller commanded. He addressed Pagan. "She has a point. They'll have plenty of men armed with serious firepower guarding that place. If we attack, they could mess us up pretty good."

"Of course," Deirdre affirmed. "That's why they're out in the open like that. They'd love a frontal assault by cavalry. They'd make mincemeat of us. And there's no way to sneak up on them in force. We'll just have to blow it up."

Pagan chortled his derision. "There's no ready-made tunnel system underneath that place like at the Hive. And a few well-placed pipe bombs doesn't make us explosive experts. As a matter of fact, I don't think there's anybody in La República who could make a claim to being good at blowing things up."

Haller nodded. "Same here. Even if we could find a way to deliver the explosives, none of our people have the knowledge to make a good bomb. Maybe I can get Pablo Jones working on something."

"No," Deirdre said. "We need the help of a sneaky tribe who are experts at demolition."

Margaret threw up her arms. "Now you want to work with the Trogs?"

"The Trogs?" Pagan shook his head. The Trogs' reputation as impossible people to approach was known throughout Pacifica.

"We're offering them an opportunity to blow up technology," Deirdre said. "I don't think they can turn that down."

*****

Commandant Walker walked down the line of corpses, fascinated with the different insignias the bikers wore on their leather coats and vests. He could make sense of a few. Here was a Maltese cross, there a flying horse he recognized as being associated with a 21st-century oil company. Most of the symbols were lost on him.

He regretted having to kill them all, but his campaign strategy necessitated that they capture all available supplies to sustain his army on their march south. Hopelessly outgunned, the Bikers fought bravely in defense of their fuel dump. Being a reasonable man, he would have loved to enlist such splendid fighters as allies, but they wouldn't listen to reason. So, they had to die. His casualties were five wounded, one dead. It was a good day to be leading an exquisite army.

When he reached the end of the row of corpses, he heard groaning coming from behind one of the rocks the bikers had used as cover. He approached and saw the leather jacket of a Killer-Bee bent over one of the wounded bikers, giving him water.

"You! What are you doing?" the Commandant asked curtly.

Mindy looked up. "He asked for water."

"Cadet Buford," he said with avuncular gentility, "don't waste your time and our water on men who refused to surrender when given the chance."

"Yes, sir."

Mindy limped away, her leg still stiff from the injury. The biker continued to groan. The Commandant drew his pistol, aimed at the suffering man's forehead and pulled the trigger. He saw that Mindy had stopped and looked back when she heard the shot.

"That's how you relieve suffering on a battlefield, Cadet," he said as if he'd just taught her how to saddle a horse or fry an egg.

✱✱✱✱✱

As Mindy limped back to her tent she decided she was going to let Jube go. She didn't need an assistant. She knew she'd be a better soldier without him around.

Why had she stopped to help that biker? Her intention was to strip useable ammo and weapons from the dead, not care for the wounded. It was Jube's damn gentle nature infecting her martial spirit that had caused that weakness.

The Commandant had lost some respect for her. She couldn't let that happen again. Jube with his sensitive talk and babble about moral sprouts had to go.

She spotted him darting into her campaign tent carrying something large. She was ready to tell him to pack his bags and hit the road. She jerked the tent flap open and entered. Her field tent was big enough to accommodate a small desk, a canvas camp chair and her cot. Jube was bent over the chair.

"Jube, we need to talk," she said coldly.

He looked up, flashed a sweet smile and gestured down at something. "See what I got?"

A piece of furniture sat in front of the chair. It was shaped like a short, wide barrel and had a cushion on top.

"You told me when you're cleaning your weapons or writing reports your leg begins to throb," he explained. "I think if you raise it up and rest it on this, it'll feel better. Give it a try."

The cushiony tub looked comfortable but that didn't change Mindy's mind. "Jube, I've made a decision," she said, her voice deepening.

"Tell me when you're sitting down." He took her arm, led her over to the camp chair and pushed down on her shoulder.

She sat. He cupped his long-fingered hands under her leg and lifted it ever so carefully up onto this novel piece of furniture. "It's in amazing shape, isn't it? I found it in an abandoned warehouse under a lot of garbage. It's called an ottoman."

He sat down on the ground in front of her. "Okay, go ahead. Tell me about your decision."

Her leg felt so comfortable and his face looked so kind, her resolve to fire him was dissolving like a spring night's snow in the morning sun. She decided to at least try to get him to modify his behavior.

"You've got to stop babying me," she said firmly. "I'm fighting a war. I need to toughen up, not get soft."

Jube flinched. "Oh."

Mindy was sure this rebuke stung him a bit. *Good. He needs to learn what is expected from him.*

"For instance, you're still sneaking your rations onto my plate. First of all, you need to eat more; you look like a scarecrow," she said, gesturing toward him with a judgmental wave of her hand. "And I should be eating the same as all the other Bees. I told you a long time ago you're not fooling anybody." Her voice rose a little as she became truly irritated. "This foot thing is like the last straw. What's it called again?"

"An ottoman."

"How do you know that?" Even this irritated her. *Who knows stupid shit like that?*

"My wife used to collect pre-Breakdown furniture."

"Well, it's just another sign of how you're spoiling me."

"All right," he said with an agreeable tone. "I can stop doing those things but look, Mindy, this is a hard world. It makes it more livable for me if I can help other people get through it. Like today, there was a battle. People died, some were maimed."

His eyes seemed to lose focus as he stared at images his imagination was producing. "I could hear the cries of the wounded and tried go down to tend to them but the sentries wouldn't let me approach the battlefield. I couldn't handle hearing them so I took a walk into Mojave."

He stared down at the floor of the tent, his hunched shoulders and exhausted voice revealing the mood of a man wounded by life. He sat still for a moment and then looked up at Mindy with an animated grin as if he'd just thought of something wonderful.

"That's when I found that ottoman in an old warehouse. As soon as I saw it, I thought it would be perfect for you. And right away, I felt better because there was something I could do for someone."

"You're a strange one, Jube."

Jube laughed.

"What's so funny?"

"Somebody else used to say that to me."

"Not surprised. You really are strange."

He stood and reached for the ottoman.

"What are you doing?" she asked.

"You want me to get rid of this thing, right?"

"Nah." She was a little embarrassed by her shameless move toward creature comfort, but she pushed on through that. "Why don't we hang onto it for a while?"

"Well, that's the last nice thing I'll do for you," he said, barely fighting off a smile. "I promise."

*****

Deirdre and Pagan stood on the Anza road staring at the walled kingdom in front of them. The ten-foot-high wall was made of recycled junk, mostly wreckage from demolished buildings and old cars. One stretch of the wall was anchored by two airplane wings partially buried in the earth.

On top of the wall, which ran for half a mile along the southern border of Anza Valley, half-naked men and women, many covered with ornate geometric tattoos, were screaming violently and brandishing an odd mixture of weapons—black powder guns, swords, bows and arrows and, ominously, the assault weapons the Bees supplied to them almost a year before.

Deirdre and Pagan were on foot. Unless it were in an attack, no Hussar would bring a horse close to Trogs, a people perpetually on the edge of starvation. They considered horse meat a delicacy.

Deirdre tossed a look Pagan's way. His upper lip was working over his teeth as he shifted his weight back and forth.

"Remember, Miguel; we got backup." She knew that was bullshit. The contingent of mounted Hussars just over the rise was there for psychological support only. If the Trogs didn't honor the truce, she and Pagan would be dead before the cavalry could ride to the rescue.

Pagan took a deep breath. They walked toward what looked like it once was the aluminum siding of a building. Wedged into the rest of the wall, it served as a gate into the Trog kingdom.

Deirdre weighed the chances that this mission would go well. On the positive side, the Trog leadership had responded immediately to their request for a truce and a meeting. At night, Frank had managed to hang the message on the steel handle of the aluminum gate. He loved reminding them how the superior mobility of the Hussars allowed them to toy with Trog security.

Two days later, a half-dead Trog slave staggered into Hussar Valley with the answer burnt onto his chest. *Our place. Tomorrow. Noon.* So maybe they really were interested in a deal.

On the other hand, these were the Trogs. Their leadership was in a perpetual state of chaos. There was no guarantee the person who set up the meeting was even in a position of power.

As they approached the gate, it slowly swung open to reveal a mass of Trog humanity stomping their feet against the earth in a steady rhythm. Many made obscene gestures and screamed filth at the two as they walked toward them.

Even though it seemed this mob was without order, a clear path opened and some of them gestured to a brick building about hundred yards inside the gate. After they made their way through the sea of screaming men and women, Deirdre and Pagan climbed the concrete steps to the building.

The door opened and a red-headed man, well over six feet, age about fifty, greeted them with a smile. He was standing just inside the doorway. Like every other male in camp, he was stripped naked to the waist. The complexity of the basket weave tattoos covering his chest and arms was breathtaking.

He gestured for them to enter. Once they were inside, the door was slammed shut by someone outside.

Red Head sat on the dirt floor and gestured for them to do the same. The only light came from skylights directly overhead. Deirdre guessed the original use of the 21st-century building was as a city hall or courthouse; now it was some kind of meeting place. It smelt of human waste and sweat.

Shadows partially concealed men with rifles leaning against the wall behind Red Head. "So, Hussars, explain yourselves," he said, his voice deep and hoarse. "Your message said something about blowing up a military base." His eyes widened with excitement.

"Yes," she said. "You know who the Bees are?"

Red Head shrugged. "You mean like honey bees?"

"The people who gave you those guns your men are holding, they call themselves the Bees."

Red Head rubbed his hands across his illustrated chest and let out a sound between a belch and a grunt. "Them."

Deirdre was unsure of this response. If the Trogs still held any allegiance to the Bees, she may have made a fatal mistake. She was hoping they didn't think well of the people who promised them Hussar Valley and led them to a terrible defeat.

"Yes," he said after a moment of reflection, a boyish smile lighting up his face. "We'll blow up the Bees."

CHAPTER FIFTY-FOUR

A profound sense of outrage made Jube decide to take action. When the army marched down to Mojave, they passed the row of biker corpses. Although Mindy wasn't sharing, other Bees told him how the bikers were slaughtered because they resisted Bee aggression. He also overheard several K-Bees talking about killing men who tried to surrender. One young Bee, not any older than Mindy, causally talked about executing the wounded, laughing about how one pleaded for his life.

When another slaughter occurred in Mojave, he bluntly asked Mindy if she was okay with all of it. She became angry and yelled that his feckless worldview would cause her to give him the boot, but she never acted on that and he could tell she was troubled by what she saw.

As the army moved south, he became even more appalled at their brutality. And the hypocrisy! There were a lot of references in the Bee propaganda about ending hunger, but whenever hungry beggars came too close to the Bee camp, they were gunned down. When children were captured, the Bees sent a select number north to the Hive for indoctrination. The rest were killed.

Another massacre in the refinery town of Palm Springs occurred because the residents resisted Bee attempts to take their oil reserve. In that case, Jube witnessed not only murder but rape and torture.

He found the Commandant's relaxed complacency during the campaign repellent. Atrocities were being committed right under his nose but he was either indifferent or approving.

Jube felt he needed to do something to stop this march of evil. He decided to assassinate the Commandant.

On one occasion, he had the opportunity. Mindy brought him along to a tactical briefing for junior officers. Walker was there to give an inspirational speech after the briefing. Jube sat right behind him.

A young officer sitting to his left dozed off during the tedious briefing. His semi-automatic pistol protruded from its holster, easily in Jube's reach. Jube knew it was Bee policy for officers to carry a round in the chamber. He could snatch the gun, click off the safety and blow Walker's brains out in a matter of seconds—a suicidal act, but destroying this evil would be worth the sacrifice.

It wasn't a desire for self-preservation that stayed his hand. It was an overwhelming need not to be part of the endless cycle of violence. There was no hope that the Bee threat would disappear if Walker were eliminated. The second in command, Colonel Parelli, seemed every bit as indifferent to the army's cruelty as her boss. If the Commandant were gone, she would continue to lead the army south, perhaps with even more brutality.

No, his value was not as an assassin. He'd remain with the young girl, trying to turn her away from this darkness toward a life-affirming light. He owed this to Mindy, Deirdre and the Universe.

*****

The tears wouldn't stop. She'd been crying for two hours. Deirdre wondered if there was ever a case of someone stuck in a state of perpetual weeping.

Every time she thought she could stop, she'd think of the dream, and it would start all over. Soft, gentle tears would morph into deep chesty sobs before easing into childlike weeping. This cycle repeated itself again and again.

The dream had been exquisitely beautiful at first. She was with Mindy, Jube, her Mom and Dad and Francine. Mindy was around ten and full of that sparkling spirit that had made her such an irresistible little girl.

Sometimes they were all in Hussar Valley picking grapes, sometimes riding together and sometimes just sitting around being with each other. A little boy would run into the dream and she knew it was Cochise at varying ages. He fit perfectly into this happy family.

Then, suddenly, Mindy was holding a knife to her mother's throat. It made no sense. Mindy adored their mother, but there she was, ready to murder what she loved most. Deirdre tried to plead with her, as did Jube and little Cochise. The knife in Mindy's hand became a revolver and she shot Jube between the eyes.

A moment later, the gun was a knife again back at her mother's throat. Deirdre charged at Mindy in rage but something drew her attention to her mother's peaceful eyes. "Do not kill your sister, Deirdre," her mother begged.

She woke up the next moment. What horrified her most about the dream was not the morbid violence or the threat to her loved ones; it was that final command. It broke Deirdre's heart that her mother's Spirit had to visit her oldest daughter in a dream to deliver that message.

It was Cochise who brought her out of her seemingly inconsolable grief. His hungry cries drowned out her own. Picking him up, she offered her right nipple. As he suckled greedily, she calmed herself and considered the present situation.

Reports had been coming in for weeks of the Bee advance south through the San Joaquin Valley, east through the southern Sierra Nevada into the Mojave where they captured a couple of oil refineries and an oil reserve in Palm Springs.

After slaughtering much of the population of that desert town, they headed west, sacked the thriving community of San Bernardino and then went south along the old I15 corridor. The latest word was that a force of approximately five thousand heavily armed troops with tanks, transport trucks and artillery had occupied Temecula, a day's march from Hussar Valley.

She'd heard nothing from Pagan about his mission with the Trogs. Unless they could at least slow down that column coming up from the south, annihilation seemed the inevitable fate of her people.

She'd sent several messengers to Arizona to report to Siki on the Bees and their bloody march. She received back a promise from the Apache that she would continue pleading with tribal leadership to make a move, but there was no sign she'd been successful thus far.

Some of the Hussars who understood the dire situation argued the tribe should flee now while they could still get out of the valley, but most agreed with Deirdre that their duty was to fight for their paradise.

She looked down at the little face at her bosom. "Cochise, we'll know our fate soon. I pledge to you I will do everything within my power to preserve our home and, with the help of the Spirits, we may pull this off."

But she knew there was one thing she would not do in the coming battle. She couldn't disobey the edict delivered by her mother's Spirit. She would not kill her sister.

*****

Henry Ketchell turned to look at the line of vehicles extending back across the desert floor. The rumbling thunder of their engines made him nervous. Had he assembled enough fuel in the desert to supply this mechanized column?

The woman sitting next to him seemed to read his mind. "Lots of vehicles, Henry," Leader said.

Ketchell turned toward her and took in the sweeping forehead, the chiseled jawline, the heart-shaped lips and the milky white skin—all framed by billowing raven black hair. Several times since she had arrived, Ketchell had been struck dumb by her stunning features and now, as they sat in the rear seat of his specially designed armored vehicle driven by Manny Cepeda, he knew he should say something, but uncharacteristic shyness stopped him.

Leader took advantage of the void in the conversation to add a comment. "I'm sure you've already stockpiled a lot of fuel." The way she was able to make that simple statement so threatening impressed Ketchell. He got the message. He'd better have enough fuel at his forward base or there'd be consequences.

He eyed her exquisite profile, marveling at her profound beauty and ruthless determination, traits he found wildly sexy when blended so seamlessly. He'd heard about this woman for years but had met her for the first time only two days ago.

Now they were at the head of a column of twenty armored cars and twenty troop transport trucks. A stack of metal gas containers glistened on the horizon. "We're coming up on the supply base now," Ketchell said.

The base was one square mile of tanker trucks, gasoline containers, boxes of spare parts and tents. The perimeter was well fortified by earthen ramparts. Every fifty yards a unit of well-armed Bees were entrenched directly outside the ramparts with a clear avenue of retreat back into the base if necessary.

"Impressive defense," Leader said as they entered the main entrance. "But why out in the middle of the flats? Why not use some of the foothills to enhance your position?"

"Our advantage is superior firepower," said Ketchell, relieved he could hide behind his tactical expertise to appear confident to this formidable woman. "My guess is that if anyone's coming for us, it'll be Hussars. Their tactics are based entirely on stealth."

He pointed toward the base of a mountain range about three miles away. "Those foothills would give them a chance to sneak around without being spotted. This position out in the open makes a surprise attack much more difficult. If they want to launch an attack out here, we'll cut them down like wheat at harvest." He punched this last statement with all the testosterone he could muster.

She looked around for a moment, pondering this line of thinking before nodding. "All right. Have you planned a defense for our supply line?"

"I've dedicated five armored cars to patrol the area between your column and the base." He was lying. He had only assigned three vehicles to that mission, but the moment called for bravado.

"Of course, the farther we go, the longer the lines will be to protect," she said with a frown. "I'll dedicate two of my vehicles to help out."

"Good," he said, slightly deflated by her dissatisfaction with his fictional five armored cars.

Her face flushed a bit as she considered the mission ahead. "I'm excited.," she said. "We'll be feasting on horse meat soon."

CHAPTER FIFTY-FIVE

Jube continued to soften Mindy's heart. For all her ferocious dedication to the Bee cause, he felt she was, in essence, an unhappy, confused teenager. She wanted desperately to love her new world and tried to be uncritical of the brutality of the campaign, struggling to keep her focus on the future they were working to achieve.

In some ways she was successful in talking herself into accepting the carnage as necessary. Jube had seen enough of the Hussars to know that she had grown up in a culture that was comfortable with violence; the Hussars occasionally even committed vicious acts, some of them verging on atrocities, in order to capture goods and protect their home. It wasn't difficult for Mindy to see a more meaningful version of combat as superior to the Hussars' self-interested brand.

This idealistic dedication, melded with the desire to avenge the death of her friends, could have, unchecked, created a merciless warrior. But there *were* checks. There was Jube and his alternate vision of the world, and he sensed her feelings about the Hussars were deeply conflicted.

Was her resentment toward Haller and Deirdre really enough to make her accept the Bee attitude that her former tribe was an enemy deserving extermination? And there were the dreams.

She often woke up at night moaning. Jube, whose tent was always nearby, was quick to check on her, and she was open to his soothing voice and healing words. She usually just thanked him for his attentive care and tried to return to sleep, refusing to share what the dreams were about.

One night her discomfort in sleep was so severe she cried out in what sounded like agony. When he rushed into her tent, she was sitting on the edge of her cot, shaking.

"Mindy, you need to talk about what's bothering you. Get the demon out of you." His tone was soothing but direct. "It's like your soul is overflowing with some pain that has to be expressed. Give it a shot. What's going on?"

She relented and told him of a recurring dream she'd been having about her mother crying. "Hussars believe that Spirits visit us with messages when we sleep," she explained, "but the Bees taught me dreams are just a bunch of images our mind shoots off when it's unconscious, like a mental charley horse it has to work out."

She made several rationalizations which Jube thought were attempts to integrate her role of bloodthirsty crusader with her inner world, which was permeated with warm, emotion-filled memories of life with her mother, sister and father.

He put a hand on her shoulder and squeezed gently. "Is it possible, whether it's your mother visiting or your own conscience speaking, that the dream is something you should listen to?"

"My mother was a great woman," she said. Jube thought he heard a suppressed sob underneath the cool surface of her response.

"I'll love her till the day I die," she continued. "It's only natural that some part of me would rebel against a situation that would give pain to her if she were alive. But it's not her Spirit speaking to me.

That's superstitious bunk. It's certainly not my conscience. My sister attempted to destroy my world. She succeeded in murdering my friends. When I kill her, my conscience will be clear."

They had a half dozen conversations like this on the trek south from the Hive. Each time, Jube felt he was close to snatching Mindy out of the pool of venom she wallowed in, but each time her resolve to be a true K-Bee would win out over the conflicting need to be a human being.

Jube's focus began to shift. He no longer believed he could turn Mindy. Instead, he started planning a way to leave the Bees and rejoin Deirdre in Hussar Valley.

*****

The mild June desert night made Pagan drowsy as he looked down at the Bee supply base from his position on a mountain peak. Every night for two weeks, Trog patrols descended toward the base, which was about two miles away, while Pagan and his small detachment of República soldiers stayed on the peak.

Each morning he'd get a report from the Trog mission leader, a wild-eyed illustrated woman named Kelly, that progress was being made, but she refused to estimate when the big day would arrive. During the daytime, his República men and the Trogs would hide in caves and gullies, awaiting nightfall.

Pagan had to give the Trogs credit. Whatever they were doing down there each night, it was sublimely covert. The Bees never detected them nor did Pagan ever realize they had returned until he noticed a few in the gully next to him. But did they really know what they were doing?

Time was of the essence. He had observed Bee reinforcements

pouring into the base the first few days he was there but recently that influx had been reduced to a trickle. Whatever operation was planned, it was fully manned and ready to go.

He estimated a thousand Bees made up the force and they would probably set out any day. If some dent weren't put into their supply before the advance, the column would have plenty of fuel to reach Hussar Valley.

There was another problem. The tension was growing daily between his twenty República troops and the twenty Trogs, the mutual hatred being so deep between the two peoples that he was afraid violence would break out any moment.

From La República's point of view, the Trogs were heirs of the Whole Earth Government that had destroyed so much of the infrastructure and had sent out brutal death squads to execute all who weren't obeying the Whole Earth back-to-Eden worldview.

From the Trogs' perspective, La República de Baja California represented just another attempt to revive the air, water and soil pollution that came so close to destroying the world a century before.

All this tension had pushed Pagan close to the breaking point. He was a construction guy who had leadership thrust upon him. Because the Bee torturer had injured his hands and seriously limited his ability to do construction, he tried to embrace his new role.

When he returned to La Paz after his visit to the Hussars, La República leadership was very impressed that he had not only shaped an alliance with the Hussars but with the Trogs as well. The enthusiasm for his diplomatic brilliance spiked, and almost overnight it was decided he would coordinate the Trog mission to blow up the Bee base camp. He pointed out he had no military experience, but this fell on deaf ears. He was the man of the hour and was expected to step up to the challenge, but he hardly shared their confidence.

Now he was sitting there on a barren peak, quickly running out of food and water, waiting for the crazy tattooed people who never listened to a word he said to blow up a base on which sat a formidable military machine capable of crushing his puny forty-person unit in minutes if they were discovered. He felt way out of his league.

Pagan tired of waiting for the Trogs to return from their nightly foray. He laid down and was asleep in seconds. He was awakened by something small hitting his face. Sitting up, he saw Kelly by the quarter moonlight, squatting on a ledge beneath him and tossing pebbles in his direction.

"What are you doing?" he asked, giving his cheek a little slap to chase away grogginess.

She ceased her pebble bombardment. "It's over."

"What's over."

"This mission."

The base was visible in the distance behind her. Pagan could see nothing that would suggest the mission had been accomplished.

"What do mean? Did you blow anything up?"

She shook her head and grinned. Her teeth were black with some gooey substance Trogs liked to chew.

"So, you're quitting?" he said angrily. "Is that what you're telling me?"

Suddenly, a blinding flash back-lit Kelly. The thunderous sound of the explosions that followed caused Pagan to cover his ears. He watched as a series of secondary explosions destroyed the Bee base.

His eyes met hers again. The black teeth were prominently displayed as she grinned triumphantly. "Like I said, the mission is over."

CHAPTER FIFTY-SIX

T he weapon was a refitted assault rifle from the 21ˢᵗ. Deirdre nodded her approval. *This will do*, she thought, handing the weapon back to La República soldier standing before her.

Five hundred well-trained and fully armed blue-clad soldiers had been waiting in Santa Isabel for news of Pagan's mission. When word came of the utter demolition of the southern Bee supply base, the unit, part of the Fuerzas Especiales de La República, marched north, arriving in the valley on a warm summer afternoon.

The commander, an angular, uniquely tall woman named Sandoval, towered over her troops as she presented the unit to Eagle Haller. The Eagle had asked Deirdre to join him in the inspection.

Afterwards, they met Margaret on the porch of Eagle House and over coffee the three of them made plans to defend against the coming invasion. Their roles were clearly defined by their talents. Deirdre had a genius for strategic and operational planning. Haller's vast experience defending the valley made him the obvious choice to supervise tactical planning. Margaret's bulldog drive made her the ideal hands-on commander who would put the plans into action when the time came. When the fighting started, Deirdre was to retain her position as commander of Griffin Squadron and the Eagle would command any troops held in reserve, including the Pedestrians.

They had mixed feelings about the arrival of La República soldiers. They were pleased with the apparent high quality of the troops and delighted to see they were armed with assault rifles and a supply of smokeless ammo, but when Pagan told them La República was willing to commit troops to the defense of the valley, Deirdre and Haller were thinking more in terms of thousands, not five hundred.

The government in La Paz was reluctant to strip too many forces from their own defense, understandably concerned the Bees could just bypass Hussar Valley and attack La República. Still, these fresh troops supplied the Hussar army with a unit armed with weapons the Bees weren't expecting to face when attacking Hussar Valley.

La República had received the rifles a few years before in a trade with the Hive for beef, an irony Margaret found delicious. "They'll be facing their own guns. Sweet."

"How many mortar shells do we have?" Haller asked. He was referring to the shells and mortars captured when the Trogs invaded their valley.

Margaret shook her head. "We have two mortars and six shells and nobody who knows how to work the damn things."

"Forget the mortars," Deirdre said. "I got a better idea. I was riding out on the south rim last week and I saw mustangs."

Margaret nodded. "Yeah, the Coyote Canyon herd has been drifting our way. Looking for some fresh grass, I guess."

Deirdre's eyes glowed. "Last report we got from our scouts said the Bee front line is right on that dry creek bottom which is adjacent to the old potato fields."

It took Margaret a moment and then she smiled. "And those

potato fields are now covered with some nice grass. Good eating for that bunch."

The Eagle couldn't hide his impatience. "Is this the right time to be worried about hungry mustangs?" he growled.

"No," Deirdre said as she poured herself a fresh cup of coffee. "But if we drive that herd up the creek bottom to that field, they'll probably hang around there for a while."

Haller shook his head and lifted his hands in frustration. "What are you talking about?"

"I want the Bees to get used to the sounds of horses."

Haller was quiet for a moment, his heavy eyebrows moving up and down as he pondered this. He nodded. "Good idea."

"I'm worried about the Trogs." Margaret was referring to a unit of Trog infantry that marched into camp a few days earlier and proclaimed their willingness to join the allies in the upcoming battle. "They're undisciplined and unpredictable. They didn't bring many of their rifles. I don't know how useful they're going to be."

Haller shrugged. "Who knows with them? I was talking to one of their main guys. He said they were working on a big surprise for the Bees, whatever the hell that means." He turned to Deirdre. "Any word from the Nations?"

"No. We may not hear anything until they act. If they act."

"Any guess as to what route the Bees will use?" he asked.

Deirdre nodded. "They'll come up 79 and turn onto the old Santos Road. Oak Grove Road is too steep and twisty to move large motor vehicles."

Haller leaned forward, his solid features softened by worry. "What are our chances?"

Crazy Hawk took a swig of coffee. "When you add República and Trog troops to our people, we can field close to two thousand combatants. Our scouts estimate the main Bee army at three times that many. They have tanks, artillery and armored cars. We have horses."

She winked at Haller. "They don't stand a chance."

Another wrinkle formed on Haller's heavily lined brow.

*****

Mindy had the armored car drop her about a mile from the lip of the North Rim. Early that morning, the Bee army had left five hundred soldiers to hold Temecula as a supply base and marched south toward Oak Grove. They were in place and in the process of setting up camp by mid-afternoon. It was then that Mindy recruited a car to take her close to the valley.

It was a rugged walk uphill from there and her leg was still hurting but she was driven by curiosity and the desire to prove her worth to Commandant Walker. She detoured away from the road and made her way up some rocky slopes, concealing herself the closer she came to the crest.

She knew this area as if a map of the valley were engraved on her brain. She also knew the Hussar patrol habits. If she found a location to observe activity in the valley for an hour, she could still make it back to where the car would pick her up without being seen.

A flat ledge sticking out from the rim had a large boulder towards its tip. She nestled behind it, took off her Bee campaign hat, and took a position that allowed her to peer through a crevice wide enough to hold her binoculars.

Her homeland looked particularly beautiful in the dusky light of the setting sun. The patches of dark green oak mixed with broad squares of horse pasture, vineyards and some vegetable farms, all situated before the backdrop of the South Rim peaks, took her breath away. She was suddenly very sad. So much joy, hope and pride had died the day she was snatched from this paradise.

No, she corrected herself. Joy did die that day but hope died slowly in the ensuing days, weeks and months as no one came for her. Finally, pride in her tribe disappeared as she identified more and more with her new Bee friends. She began to despise the Hussars who had given up on her.

She moved her field glasses off the boulder and swung them to the east. She could barely make out the distant roof of the Eagle House jutting up above the tops of some oaks. That would be her target. Capture that building and kill the Eagle, and this beautiful valley would belong to the Bees. She hoped that if she used her knowledge of the valley in a way that impressed the Bee leadership, she might be given a position of authority in the power structure that would rule the new Bee colony in Hussar Valley.

She heard a noise behind her. Turning, she saw a riderless horse standing at the other end of the ledge; it was Danny. Drawing her sidearm, she scrambled to her feet, swiveling her head around in a desperate attempt to spot her sister. This went on for about a minute, with her crouching on one side of the boulder and then kneeling on the other, trying to put cover between her and the phantom that rode up on that animal.

"Mom visited me the other night." Deirdre's unmistakable voice came from a ridge due west from where Mindy stood.

The sun was behind the ridge line, blinding Mindy to her sister's location — a classic Crazy Hawk move. The young girl maneuvered quickly to the east side of the boulder and leveled her pistol toward the ridge. Silence.

Okay, she wants a response. "You had a dream about Mom. So what? I have them all the time. They don't mean a thing to me."

"It breaks my heart to hear that."

Mindy was indifferent to the pain behind those words as she realized the voice was now coming from below the tip of the ledge.

She laid down on her stomach, slithered toward the edge and saw the lip of a narrow rock promontory right below her. She knew she ran a chance of re-injuring her frail leg but she had to risk it.

She jumped down to the lower ledge. Her leg buckled underneath her and she landed hard on her rear, but she could still level her handgun. Deirdre was gone.

"Damn, you're fast," Mindy yelled.

"I'm not going to kill you." The voice came from above. Deirdre was now up on the ledge Mindy had just left.

"Well, isn't that sweet."

"Not sweet," Deirdre said precisely. "Obedient."

"To who? Haller?"

"Not Haller." The sadness in Deirdre's voice didn't go unnoticed by Mindy. "Mom."

A bitter laugh erupted from Mindy. "You are a sentimental idiot, aren't you? I'll have no problem killing you. Two of my friends died in that fire you started."

"I'm sorry to hear that." Deidre's tone was ripe with genuine sympathy but Mindy wasn't listening. She was focused on a slope on the far side of the ledge from where she sat. She saw signs of where Deirdre had scurried up to the upper ledge. She stood and put some weight on her bad leg. It hurt but held.

Her sister had just said she wouldn't kill her; it was worth chancing a climb to where she was, so she moved up the slope as quickly as she could. When she reached the top, Deirdre and Danny were gone.

*****

Life was good the first full day at Oak Grove for Walker. The oak trees smelt sweet, like his mother's almond cookies, and the thunder of his mechanized war machine was sublime music to his ears. He spent most of the morning joking with junior officers about the coming battle. There were lots of cracks about horse burgers. The entire mood was one of unbridled confidence.

The Commandant had ample reason to be confident. He'd planned and implemented an almost perfect campaign of conquest down the spine of Pacifica, successfully capturing every resource he needed and efficiently pacifying any resistance. He was a day or so away from crushing the most formidable tribe in the area, which would undoubtedly cause many others to surrender to his threats.

A few days before, he'd received a report that Leader's base of supply was established and she would be ready to move soon. The pincer movement on the valley would eliminate the Hussars permanently as a problem. He needed only to solidify his position here in Oak Grove and wait for a sign from Leader. It was agreed that flares were the best way to accomplish this and he had scouts on top of Mount Palomar with their eyes riveted toward the southeast.

A problem came to his attention when he was informed that a supply truck expected from Temecula had not arrived. The army was running out of certain foodstuffs and the cooks were complaining they needed more as soon as possible if they were to serve sufficient meals.

Marching out of Temecula the day before, there had been very little concern about resupply since Temecula was less than an hour's drive from Oak Grove and the old 79 was in good shape.

He'd left five hundred infantry, two armored cars and a tank behind to protect the supplies. Surely this was enough to keep his line of supply open considering there was no large hostile army in the area to threaten such a garrison, except the Hussars themselves, and they wouldn't be foolish enough to deplete the strength of their valley defense to raid Temecula. That would just make his job easier.

Furious about the tardy food delivery, he sent an armored car back toward Temecula with instructions to shoot the food truck driver on the spot. Three more hours passed, and still no sign of either the truck or the armored car.

His attention was drawn away from the food truck around four in the afternoon when his Palomar lookouts came to inform him they had spotted a vehicle approaching speedily from the south. It looked like a Bee command car.

Ten minutes later, a battered jeep arrived holding four exhausted Bees. Walker recognized them as junior officers from Leader's army. They reported that the southern supply base had been blown to bits by saboteurs. Leader was missing and her army had dissolved into the desert.

Walker was still stunned by this news when he was informed that a tractor was approaching from the north. The ancient farm vehicle chugged into camp, driven by one of the occupants of the car that had been sent to check on the food delivery.

The young man had a bad shoulder wound but managed to report they'd found no sign of the food truck, so had entered Temecula. They were about two hundred yards from the supply center when they were ambushed by a large force. The attackers seemed to possess the weapons of the garrison. Most of the crew of the armored car were killed or captured. He'd made it to the outskirts of town, where he'd commandeered the tractor.

Walker was shocked into silence. It was Parelli who thought to ask the key question. "Who captured Temecula?"

The young man did not hesitate. "Soldiers of the Nations. A lot of them."

"The Nations?" asked the startled Parelli. "Are you sure?"

"I grew up in Old Arizona," the young man replied. "I know the Nations."

Siki made several passionate speeches in front of the Tribal Council in Flagstaff in an attempt to get them to authorize a substantial Nations mission into Southern Pacifica. The Council was not unmoved by her vivid description of the Bee threat, but most of the members thought of it as a local Pacifica problem, outside of the Nations purview.

Siki was close to despair when a group of Navajo traders came back from Pacifica with disturbing details of what they'd seen there—overwhelming force directed against even the slightest resistance, entire communities exterminated, and confiscation of everything that could feed the Bee war machine. The mood in the Council began to change.

The next day, two survivors of a diplomatic mission sent by the Council to the Urb center of Los Angeles rode into Flagstaff. The party had been eight strong, with three diplomats and a five-person bodyguard when they'd left Flag. Only two survived an ambush by a Bee death squad. The attack came for no apparent reason.

With some of their number now victimized by Bee aggression, the Council began discussing their options. After two days of debate that Siki found torturous, they decided to send a large Nations force to Pacifica to aid the resistance against the Bees.

Billy Cottonwood was appointed commander of this force. He chose Siki to be a member of his staff, valuing her knowledge of the Bees as well as her reputation as a fearless fighter. Within a week, Cottonwood was able to assemble a thousand mounted soldiers in the Verde Valley and began the march toward Pacifica.

Crossing the Mojave, they ascended to the San Jacinto plateau via the old 371 Highway out of Palm Desert, then descended down into Hemet, where they were only a few miles from Temecula which, according to their advance scouts, was the Bee's main base.

They had reason to believe their presence would not be leaked to the Bees since the local populace seemed unanimously horrified by Bee atrocities and welcomed a force that might oppose the invaders.

When scouts reported a few days later that most of the Bee army had advanced toward Hussar Valley, leaving only a small force to guard the supplies, Cottonwood — at the urging of Siki — decided to act.

The attack began at dawn. The element of surprise was complete. The Bee garrison was caught completely off guard. Temecula was in the hands of the Nations by noon.

CHAPTER FIFTY-SEVEN

Rumors of trouble rippled through Walker's camp at Oak Grove. Many of the rank and file didn't know what was happening but they could see concern on the faces of their officers and the camp was abuzz with theories, predictions and fatalistic pronouncements about the fate of the expedition.

The Bee army had never been tested. They'd fought inferior forces or simply slaughtered the defenseless. Now, on the eve of a real battle, with things not going in their favor, there was unrest in the camp.

A fistfight broke out over a canteen. A heretofore relaxed unit commander could be heard screaming at his troops for a mistake during a routine drill. Sentries, who, the day before, thought their biggest problem was staying awake for their shift, were now so awake that on two separate occasions, they had fired at a mustang herd grazing about a quarter of a mile from the Bee encampment. Both incidents caused the camp to scramble toward full alert status before they were told to stand down. In short, everyone was nervous.

Jube hoped these changes in the army's focus would increase his chances of leaving the camp without being stopped. About nine pm, he reached into his tent, grabbed his knapsack and was about to walk away when he realized by the lightness that something important had been removed.

"Looking for this?"

He turned to see Mindy standing at the entrance to her tent holding a large folder bulging with loose papers. Scribbled onto the folder in black ink were the words *Deirdre's Notebook*.

"We have to talk," Mindy said, retreating into her tent.

When Jube entered, he found Mindy sitting on her cot, the notebook cradled on her lap. "Have a seat," Mindy said. He sat on the ground inside the tent flap.

"You're the father of my sister's baby," she said as if she weren't at all surprised.

He nodded.

"I've suspected for a while now," she went on. "She told me the father was black, and it explains a lot about your interest in me. I confirmed it the first day we were in Temecula when you were setting up my tent. You left your knapsack with my kit. I looked inside." She gestured at the notebook. "She's a pretty good writer."

She tossed it down in front of him, the yellow pad and other loose papers spilling out of the folder onto the floor of the tent. "Go ahead. Take it." Jube meticulously put everything back into the folder.

Mindy laughed. "I assume you're on your way to die with your girlfriend."

"That's one way to put it."

"It's the only way to put it." Mindy's eyes sizzled. "You might see some hope now. The Nations have captured Temecula, and Leader's column has been wiped out. So what? We still have tanks and armored cars and assault rifles. And we outnumber the Hussars by a wide margin and we've got a real good reason to do this right now. We're getting hungry. Tell Sis her scalp is mine."

Jube thought of making one last attempt at turning her, but peering into those hate-filled eyes caused him to sling the knapsack over his shoulder and leave the tent.

He walked toward one of the perimeter outposts where two guards were in a whispered conversation with three other soldiers. They were so involved in their discussion, Jube hoped he might glide by without being noticed, but one of the guards, a short woman who balanced the butt of her rifle on her hip, noticed him. She gestured with her chin as if to say, "Explain yourself."

"I'm gonna shit in the woods," he said. "That latrine is getting pretty ripe."

She nodded. He strode out of the camp and disappeared into a copse of oak, picking up the pace when he was sure he was out of sight.

He thought he heard footsteps. Ducking behind a tree, he waited to see if anyone would emerge from the darkness into the moonlight. Nothing. He decided it must have been a deer or a coyote and was about to walk on when a man's voice addressed him.

"Anxious to see your kid?"

The voice came from in front of him, not from the direction of the camp.

"Who's there?" whispered Jube. He was hoping it was a Hussar scout.

Burke stepped out of the shadows into the moonlight, a rifle trained on Jube's chest.

*****

Mindy woke around midnight, aware of someone standing over her. She sat up and reached for her sidearm but it wasn't on the camp chair where she'd left it. Someone turned on her lantern and she saw Burke a few feet in front of her, his rifle pointed at her forehead.

"Commandant Walker wants to talk with you," Burke announced.

Mindy froze, unsure what her next move should be. Burke ended her indecision by grabbing her by the scruff of the neck, dragging her off her cot and tossing her out of the tent. She sprawled into the dirt. As she scrambled to her feet, she realized she was surrounded by five guards, all training their rifles on her center mass.

As she walked through the camp toward Walker's command tent surrounded by armed guards, she searched every crevice of her mind looking for an explanation as to why this was happening.

It wasn't until she entered the tent and saw Jube that she figured out what was going on. The enormous tent was large enough to comfortably accommodate Parelli, Burke and the Commandant's four-strong bodyguard. The Commandant was seated in a canvas chair with Jube kneeling on the ground facing him. Burke positioned Mindy directly behind Jube. The others were standing in a semi-circle behind Walker.

"What is your defense, Cadet Buford?" Walker asked.

Mindy could see that his face was haggard and taut. He was not handling the recent events well. She understood she better get this right. "Sir, I don't know what I'm being accused of," she said with faux boldness, hoping that confidence in her innocence would be convincing.

Parelli spoke. "Burke, repeat what you told me."

"I've been keeping an eye on her since the campaign began. After all, she's Crazy Hawk's sister. I've always thought these two," he gestured at Mindy and Jube, "were weird together."

"I don't give a shit about their relationship," the Commandant said curtly. "What are you accusing her of?"

"Well, when she returned from her reconnaissance the other day, she was agitated. I thought she might have had some contact with her sister."

"Get to the point, Burke!" Walker barked.

"Tonight, I overheard a conversation between them. He said—."

"A summary is what we need," Parelli said, trying to prevent Walker from gunning Burke down in a fit of impatience.

"She told him he could go join the Hussars. If you look in that knapsack he was carrying, there's a folder marked *Deirdre's Notebook*. Inside are a bunch of pads with writing on them. He's been carrying it with him the whole time. And now Cadet Buford said it was okay for him to take it with him when he went over to the Hussars."

Walker turned, his eyes wide with indignation, toward Mindy. "You let a man sympathetic to your sister leave our camp and join the enemy—with the knowledge he has of our troop strength and defensive placements?"

"I used bad judgement, sir." Mindy bowed her head for a few seconds. Then she looked directly at Walker and spoke confidently. "As far as Jube telling them anything about our position, I guarantee you, Hussar scouts are crawling all over these hills. We just don't see them. They had a good idea of our troop strength and our positions the first night. There's nothing else Jube could have told them."

"That may or may not be true," Parelli said. "But now I question whether your sympathy is with us or with your sister and the Hussars."

"Colonel, on the day of the attack, I will kill more Hussars than any other Bee," Mindy said boldly. "And I will dedicate myself to eliminating my sister as a threat to the Bees."

"And him?" Walker nudged Jube with his foot.

"Allowing him to leave was wrong. I understand that now. I'm very sorry."

"No need to apologize," Walker said. "Just prove your commitment to the Bees. Execute Jube. Now."

There was a long pause as everyone waited for Mindy's reaction. She stood staring at the ground, her hands clasped in front of her.

Finally, she nodded and spoke with icy calm. "I'll need a weapon."

Parelli drew her pistol from her side holster, pressed the release, let the magazine drop into the palm of her other hand and offered the weapon to Mindy. "There's a round in the chamber."

Mindy took the pistol and clicked off the safety. She moved in front of Jube, who looked at her with those big compassionate eyes that almost seemed to say, "It's okay, I understand."

This infuriated her. She leveled the pistol at his forehead, placed her finger on the trigger and began to squeeze. When the gun fired and the recoil jerked her hand, she was surprised how frightened she was.

*****

Francine dragged the captured Bee along a ridge line by a rope tied to his neck, his hands bound behind him. A bandana tied around his face kept a rock that was shoved into his mouth in place. Freddie followed, kicking the young man in the ass every few feet.

Francine reached a cliff face and looked down, examining the drop-off in the moonlight. "This will do," she said.

Freddie nodded, took the rope from Francine and tied it around a nearby cottonwood sapling. When he was done, Francine kicked the young Bee in the back of the knees. He collapsed and began to slide off the cliff edge, his eyes bulging in fear. She caught him by his shirt collar and pulled him back from the edge.

"Okay, it's simple. You tell us what we need to know or Freddie shoves you off this ledge with that rope tied to the tree and your neck. It'll take a while, but you will suffocate."

She reached up and pulled the bandana off his face. The young Bee let the rock fall from his mouth and sputtered something unintelligible.

Francine laughed. "I have no idea what you just said, but who cares. I haven't asked you anything yet. We've been observing your camp from our hidden positions. As a matter of fact, Freddie and I were a few yards from your sentry post for hours. Didn't have a clue, did you?

"Anyway, we heard a shot. Next, we saw two people being led out of a large tent, their hands tied behind them, kinda like you right now. My associate tells me one was Mindy Buford, a friend of his. The other was a friend of mine—Jube. You've got about ten seconds before Freddie here kicks you off this cliff. Start talking."

"I don't know what the original problem was," the young man said, his voice trembling. "But I heard that for some reason, Cadet Buford was told she had to prove her loyalty by shooting Jube. Then I guess she was given a pistol and instead of killing him, she shot into the ground."

"What's gonna to happen to them?" She put her face up close to the kid's, her lips almost brushing his.

He was so scared he could barely gasp out an answer. "They're gonna be hanged. At dawn."

"Francine, we gotta move fast," Freddie said, jumping to his feet with great urgency. "We need to tell Deirdre this."

"I've got more," the Bee said.

Freddie laughed. "Listen to him. He's a real songbird. He'll be giving up his mother soon." He placed his foot on the back of the Bee, ready to shove him off the cliff.

Francine slapped his leg and shook her head.

"Keep talking," she said to the Bee.

"There's panic in camp," he continued. "And most of the Bees who were recruited by being kidnapped don't like the idea of Mindy being hanged."

She nodded. Deirdre had told her a lot about the Bees and she had some sympathy for this kid.

"Good to know," Freddie said, pushing the boy toward the cliff edge.

"I don't think we should do that," Francine protested. "Deirdre wouldn't like it."

"What are you talking about?" Freddie asked with a frown. "She wouldn't like us hanging a Bee when they plan to hang her boyfriend and sister? I've seen her do a lot worse for less of a reason."

"That was the old Deirdre. She's changed."

Freddie shrugged. "We can't let him go. He'll run back and tell them we know about the hanging. Get them all on their guard."

"I won't tell, I swear," the frightened Bee promised.

"Shut up," Freddie growled. "You just gave up more info about your friends than we asked for. Do you think we'd trust you to keep quiet for us?"

"We could tie him to the tree," Francine suggested. "And just leave him."

Freddie thought about it for a moment and then nodded. "Okay."

CHAPTER FIFTY-EIGHT

Mindy dozed off for a few seconds at about four in the morning but woke up almost instantly. Nothing about her present situation was conducive to sleep. She was tied with a rope to the trunk of an oak tree. Burke's words were circling her consciousness in a loop. "This is the tree you'll hang from," he had said, "and this is the rope I'll use."

But what tortured her mind the most was her deeply conflicted feelings. The evening before, her world turned upside down—again! When she took the pistol out of Parelli's hand, she was quite sure she would prove her loyalty to the Bees with a quick and efficient execution. A moment later, she understood she had no idea who she really was.

"Hey, Jube," she said, breaking the ominous silence of the night. He was tied to an adjacent tree which she could see in the moonlight. He was on the other side of the trunk.

"Yeah?"

"What you thinking about?"

"Your sister," he said, his voice soft and sad. "How about you?"

"Different stuff. Not my sister." She thought for a moment. When she spoke, her words caught on the horror of what almost happened. "Did you think I was going to shoot you?"

"Not for a moment."

"Really? How could you be so sure?"

"I know your compassion sprout is growing." He spoke as if that sprout was a tangible thing he had seen with his own eyes.

Their conversation ended when Burke, accompanied by two heavily armed Bees, strode up to Jube and started undoing his ropes.

"Got to get you ready for the hanging." There was a happy lilt in the one-eyed man's voice. "It's happening at dawn. Or as soon as Commandant Walker gets here."

A moment later, two more Bees approached rolling barrels that Mindy recognized as ones taken from the biker fuel dump.

Shortly, Mindy was standing on top of one of the barrels, Jube on the other. Both had their hands tied behind their backs, nooses around their necks, the ropes running up to a heavy branch above them. The ropes were pulled taut enough that both stood on their tip-toes, the wobbly barrels being the only thing keeping them from asphyxiation.

"You guys ever seen a hanging?" Burke asked.

Jube didn't answer. Mindy muttered, "Yes." It was the Hussar method of execution.

"Well, then you know it can be real slow," Burke said. "Seeing a well done execution of traitors will inspire our troops. You guys stay still. Those barrels are none too steady." He walked away, whistling a tune.

✱✱✱✱✱

Bee Cadet Herm Stockton woke up twice during the night. He wasn't sure what it was that stirred him each time. Maybe some noise or just general worry. The news that an enemy force had captured their supply base had spread through the camp the day before and his officers had said nothing to quell the subtle panic that gripped most of the troops.

The good news was that his unit was ordered to remain in their perimeter position. That meant he didn't have to watch the hanging at dawn. He knew Cadet Buford, had a little crush on her, and didn't relish seeing that.

He picked up his rifle, wormed out of his pup tent and walked over to an oak tree. He leaned the rifle against the tree and unzipped. He could barely make out some motion off to his left near where there was a machine gun emplacement. Other than that, everything was still.

A horse whinnied out toward the east. *Mustangs.* He didn't get a piece of the last one that was slaughtered. He'd be in line next time for sure. Objects around him that were shrouded in darkness seconds ago were now becoming visible as the pre-dawn announced the coming of the sun.

He was zipping up when he heard horses' hooves. He glanced to the east, expecting to see the mustangs frolicking. Instead, dozens of armed riders appeared in the dim morning light, galloping directly toward him. One of the machine guns fired a burst, but a moment later two riders gunned down the crew with revolvers. He heard shots all down the line. Most of the firing was coming from the charging riders.

Herm grabbed his rifle, but it was too late. One of the Hussars, a woman he'd seen back in the Hive, the one known as Crazy Hawk, was on top of him, her revolver leveled. She pulled the trigger. He felt a stinging sensation in his right shoulder and fell back into some buffalo grass, where he lay stunned for a moment.

He regained enough composure to evaluate his wound. It was painful but he thought he could move. Horses were thundering by him as he maneuvered behind the cover of the oak tree.

A cacophony of gunfire, screams, orders and the pounding of hooves filled Herm with a feeling of dread. He watched Rick Carey, a fellow cadet he was close with, running for cover. A Hussar rode up behind Rick wielding a machete and, with one powerful stroke, decapitated him.

The head rolled up to Herm's feet. The eyes staring up at Herm were wide with horror and seemed very alive. Whatever training he had evaporated and in full panic mode, he ran towards the main camp, where he hoped to find safety. He'd become separated from his rifle but he didn't care; he was too scared to use it now.

As he ran over the battlefield, he tripped over logs, mounds and bodies. When getting up from one fall, he saw a Hussar charging toward him, a butcher knife poised to split his head open. Herm dove aside and felt the blade slice a wound into his back.

Bleeding from both his shoulder and back, the pain becoming more intense by the second, his fear grew to delirious proportions. He could muster no resignation in the face of his impending death. He screamed in pain and fear as he picked himself up and ran.

He spotted a comforting sight; a Bee unit advancing in good order, well led by competent junior officers and supported by a tank and an armored car. He staggered aside to let the tank by, made his way onto a hillock and turned back to the east to watch the slaughter of the enemy.

What he saw shocked him almost as much as the initial appearance of these ferocious warriors. The riders rode past the tank, indifferent to having such a killing machine in their rear. The tank turned its turret in their direction but suddenly a withering round of automatic weapons fire tore into the infantry supporting the tank.

This was something Herm hadn't expected. The Bee troops were told that the Hussars had only antiquated black powder weapons. Blue-clad men and women could be seen advancing from the same area the riders had emerged from, running from boulder to tree to gully. The tank turned its turret back toward this new threat.

When several of the blue-clad fighters approached him, Herm dropped to his knees and threw his arms in the air. A tall, angular woman grabbed him by the back of his collar and dragged him toward a ravine where other surrendering Bees were being collected. The woman yelled an order in Spanish and a chubby man in the same blue uniform shoved Herm onto the sand of the ravine bottom where several other blue-clad men were acting as guards. They were communicating in Spanish. Herm realized these were República troops.

He heard an odd sound coming from the north. Turning, he saw further down the ravine a ghastly collection of shirtless, tattooed men stomping their feet and reciting some unintelligible chant in flawed unison.

One of them, a muscular, red-headed giant, jumped out of the ravine and, with a swinging gesture of his tree trunk right arm, signaled the rest to follow. Now in the brighter light of the morning, Herm could see most of these freakish warriors carried short sticks with what looked like tin cans attached to the end.

They started running with reckless courage at the tank. Some were cut down by the tank gunner, but others were able to throw those funny looking things at the treads. He flinched as one after the other exploded. Soon the tank was disabled by these explosions and sat still, swarmed over by the tattooed men. Herm was grateful that his military career was over.

CHAPTER FIFTY-NINE

When Francine and Freddie reported what they had seen and heard, Deirdre sat stunned for a few minutes. The joy of hearing that her man was alive was darkened by the knowledge that he was in the hands of monsters who planned to execute him and her sister at dawn. After she had collected herself, she argued adamantly that a Hussar attack must happen in the pre-dawn glow.

Haller resisted for a few minutes, wanting to stick to an earlier plan built on the belief that Bee morale would disintegrate more each day as they dealt with the severing of their supply line, but Deirdre's wild eyes told him he better let her try to save Jube and Mindy or deal with the consequences.

The tactical plan was simple. Under Margaret's command, five hundred horsemen would charge the enemy line at daybreak, bypassing any armored vehicles. A wave of three hundred República infantry would follow, and then all five hundred Trog troops armed with the new toys they had developed for the occasion—powerful, weirdly shaped hand grenades. Hopefully, they could disable armored vehicles with these explosives.

Held in reserve under Haller's command were four hundred mounted Hussars and two hundred República infantry. All told, the attack consisted of eighteen hundred committed troops, with six hundred in reserve. The only troops left in the valley were the poorly armed Pedestrians. The fate of the homeland would be decided here and now. Surprise and superior morale had to be fully exploited since their army was outnumbered by the well-armed Bees three to one.

Griffin Squadron, a hundred strong, with Deirdre in command, would be the vanguard of the attack. She ordered all her troopers to key on her. She hoped to disrupt as many perimeter Bee units as possible, but her primary goal was to stop the hanging.

*****

Deirdre galloped past the tank and steered Danny toward a group of Bees who were milling around in confusion about a hundred yards ahead. She guessed this was the crowd gathered for the morning execution, caught completely off guard by this pre-dawn attack and now desperately looking for leadership.

She pulled up when Ross Meusel yelled something she couldn't make out. He was pointing toward a distant oak tree. Jube dangled from one of the branches, kicking wildly as the noose choked out his life. A few feet from him, Mindy struggled to maintain her balance on a wobbly barrel. Burke was standing between the two of them.

Deirdre's heart exploded at the sight of Jube and Mindy in mortal danger. Danny's galloping morphed into full extension, racehorse-style flying when he felt the tension of Deirdre's legs squeezing his haunches.

They covered the fifty yards to the hanging tree in seconds but not before Burke had kicked over Mindy's barrel. There was no time for Deirdre to deal with him, but Freddie, who was right behind her, fired a round into Burke's heart, collapsing him into a lifeless heap.

Deirdre, knife in hand, reached Mindy first and slashed at the rope, hoping one stroke would do the job. Yes! The rope was severed and the young girl fell to the ground.

Jube's legs had ceased kicking. She leapt off Danny's back, caught the rope just above Jube's head and slashed it in two. Both of them fell to the ground.

Deirdre scrambled to a kneeling position and looked into his his face. He lay still for a few seconds before gasping for air. She knelt cradling his head in her hands for a loving moment before she heard Freddie yelling.

"Deirdre, we're all jammed up!"

Deirdre stood and saw that some of her squadron were dismounting and pulling long rifles out of their saddle sheaths. She looked around. Hundreds of rallying Bees surrounded Griffin Squadron. Hopelessly outnumbered and with nowhere to ride, total annihilation seemed inevitable.

*****

Commandant Walker was shaving in order to look sharp for the hangings when he heard the gunfire. He threw on his shirt, picked up his sidearm and ran out of his tent.

His troops had crumbled into disorder quickly. He spent only a moment in disgust before running to a crowd of frightened young Bees and, with a few forceful orders, turned them back into soldiers.

He walked toward the sounds of the battle, a troop of twenty rallying behind him. Others looking for leadership followed, and before he marched two hundred yards, he had hundreds of Bees under his direct control.

At first, his confidence was a pose. He had to fake it because he had no idea what was happening anywhere on the battlefield. But it wasn't long before he realized a unit of Hussar cavalry, no more than a hundred, were isolated from the rest of the attacking force. If he could eliminate that detachment, it would reverse the process of disintegrating morale as well as seriously cripple the already outnumbered enemy force.

He bellowed commands to two platoon leaders while others showed initiative by taking tactical positions that would block the Hussars' escape.

Soon his troops were assembling in a semi-circle around the Hussars, who were now engaged with Bees coming from the opposite direction. He saw Parelli in the distance, rallying troops and sending them to attack the isolated enemy unit.

He caught a fleeting glimpse of Crazy Hawk amid the trapped troopers and knew the next few minutes would decide the battle. It wasn't an ideal enfilade. Some of his people could die in a friendly crossfire. But he was so sure the battle would end quickly once Crazy Hawk and her squadron were eliminated. He decided to accept the risks from the crossfire and move aggressively.

Most of his troops were in place, ready to initiate the massacre when he heard the first explosion. Several of his soldiers flew into the air, one of their mangled bodies landing with a thud in front of him.

There was another explosion. He pivoted and saw hundreds of shirtless, tattooed men on a ridgeline throwing bizarre looking grenades at his troops. The effect on morale was almost instantaneous. Some of his men dropped their weapons and ran. Others turned away from the surrounded Hussar cavalry to fire on the Trogs.

Now that Walker's force had been distracted, the Hussars could address Parelli's units exclusively. Soon Parelli's advance was stalled as her troops scrambled for cover.

But Walker felt his troops still had the edge. He could see that the Trogs were running out of grenades, and some were unarmed once they had thrown their little bombs. Some of the grenades appeared to be duds, and standing on the ridgeline, the Trogs were easy targets for his men. Several Bee platoons concentrated their fire on them, and soon the Trogs were in complete disorder. Some fled, others charged recklessly toward the Bee line only to be quickly gunned down. Now his troops could turn their attention back to the trapped Hussars.

Then he heard the pounding of hooves. He spun to see that Deirdre's detachment had remounted and was galloping toward a hole that had opened in the Bee line. The trapped troopers were about to escape.

He ran to head them off, several Bees following. He fired at Mindy and missed as she rode away. He turned to see a buckskin horse almost on top of him. He saw Deirdre's burning eyes as a slash from her Bowie knife severed his throat. Commandant Walker fell to his knees. His campaign ended a moment later when a bullet entered his brain.

CHAPTER SIXTY

The twenty-foot-high boulder seemed so peaceful and unhurried, in such stark contrast to the chaotic battlefield Haller had just left, a serious wound to his chest incapacitating him. As he felt his lungs fill with blood, he knew he would be dead soon.

As ruthless as he had been as Eagle of the Hussars, Haller had studied enough of the tribal wisdom to find consolation in the beauty and quiet of that boulder. It suggested a primal stillness at the heart of the Universe. He would soon be a part of that stillness, and that was okay.

He heard hooves pattering on the rocky terrain and a few moments later, Margaret leaned over him to examine the wound. She tossed him a look that was full of empathy but not pity, and he loved her for that.

"They broke, Eagle," she said, sitting next to him in a gesture that implied she'd stay with him till the end. "The entire Bee army threw away their guns and ran. Turns out they were bullies. They'd never been in a battle against a real army. As soon as it looked bad for them, they collapsed. You'll go down in history as one of the great Hussar leaders."

Tom Haller heard the words but only cared about the boulder. As his vision weakened, the nob on the top of the gigantic rock began to resemble the head of a giant looking down on him. He smiled as he closed his eyes for the last time.

*****

When it became apparent the Bee army was on the run and the Pedestrians were securing the battlefield, most of the Hussar Raiders were determined to use the Naked Blade tactic to slaughter as many of the fleeing invaders as they could.

The pursuing troopers were surprised, some even angry, when Deirdre rode out to head them off. She ordered them to return to the battlefield immediately and reassemble in units, explaining to a few that a pursuit that was too aggressive could disorder the Hussars and encourage the enemy to regroup.

She didn't really believe that. She understood that with the Bee leadership dead on the battlefield—Parelli had been killed minutes after Walker had gone down—the fleeing Bee troops were just a bunch of scared kids trying to get to safety. Most of them had thrown their weapons away. Many of them had been kidnapped like Mindy and Yen Thi Vo. She wanted to give them a chance to get home, her compassion sprout in full blossom.

Once she had convinced most of the Hussars to head back to Oak Grove, she started looking for her sister and Jube. Mindy hadn't joined Griffin Squadron when they regrouped for another charge. Deirdre understood, of course. The morning before, the kid woke up a proud Bee. She wasn't ready to fight her friends so soon after.

She must be pretty confused, Deirdre thought as she rode back toward the valley.

She stopped first to the field hospital the Hussars had set up in a small canyon north of Santos Road. She was very concerned about Jube. He'd been hanging by his neck for longer than was healthy and was very shaky when Freddie had helped him mount up.

She was also concerned that if he were capable of moving, he would want to help the wounded on the battlefield. She had instructed Freddie to drop him off at the hospital, but when she reached that large tent, Jube was not there.

She was riding up Old Santos Road toward the valley, speculating about all the bad things that could have happened to Jube, when she saw Mindy.

The young girl was sitting on the horse Francine had brought for her, right in the middle of the road, oblivious to the activity around her as wounded Hussars were being transported back to the valley in a variety of horse drawn vehicles. Her eyes were closed. Deirdre dismounted, walked up to her sister and rubbed her leg affectionately. "Welcome home, Mindy."

Mindy opened her eyes. Deirdre could see she'd been crying. She looked down at Deirdre and offered a wry smile. "Is this my home?"

"Of course it is." Deirdre reached up her hand but Mindy didn't take it. "It'll take a while but you'll fit back in."

Mindy laughed. "I know Hussars." She shook her head. "They'll never forget. I was riding with the devil as far they're concerned."

"Well, if anyone gives you shit," Deirdre said with steely assurance, "they'll have me on their case."

"Yeah. And when you have Deirdre on your case," she said quietly, "you definitely have someone on your case."

"Come on," Deirdre said. "Let's ride back into the valley."

She moved toward Danny but her sister stopped her. "Dee." Deirdre looked back at her sister. "I'm …" Mindy's voice snagged on a sob. "I'm sorry."

Deirdre vaulted onto Danny and rode up so she could hug Mindy from the saddle. "You never have to say that to me. I understand what you've been through."

A captured Bee vehicle carrying wounded Hussars approached. While clearing the road for the armored car to go by, Deirdre and her sister were separated. When the vehicle passed, Deirdre saw that Mindy had left the road and was making her way back into the foothills on a game trail. She decided to let the kid be by herself for a while.

*****

Jube had been working in the Hussar field hospital ever since Freddie dropped him off. He was supposed to seek treatment for the rope burns on his neck, but instead he immediately started tending to the wounded.

It wasn't so much the physical fatigue that caused him to dress one more wound and walk out of the tent. It was the emotional drain of seeing so much suffering, combined with the fear that Deirdre, Mindy and Francine were still in danger. He hiked toward the valley, thinking that was the best place to learn everyone's fate.

He was climbing a steep grade when all the stress—physical, psychological, spiritual—forced him to collapse into a sitting position on a slope, his feet downhill, his back propped up against a jagged boulder.

He began the contemplation process Oliver had taught him. He rose above the agony of the battlefield, the hospital and his own fears and entered the cloud of unknowing. He pummeled the darkness with rays of love and for the first time since he had started contemplating months before, a beam of light pierced through the darkness.

Then another beam brighter than the first, then another and then the entire cloud dissolved into a burning, brilliant illumination that sent divine light into every recess of his consciousness.

Suddenly, he knew that everyone on that battlefield, and every battlefield, was part of the divine underpinnings of the cosmos, spiritually linked forever. He began to cry.

He sobbed uncontrollably for all the pain he had seen and experienced. He cried for Deirdre, Mindy, all the dead and broken people, his wife Nancy, and himself.

For months he had practiced driving all anger and bitterness out of his soul to create a void for Love Supreme to rush in. Now all he had room for in his heart was tender compassion for every living thing. He was simultaneously jubilant that he understood that all was One and heartbroken that this consciousness was not universally shared.

He bent his knees and let his arms hang over them, his feet planted in the dirt, his hands dangling lifelessly, his chin drooping onto his chest. He was almost cried out when he felt it — two hands had grabbed his.

He recognized the strong, warm touch immediately. He looked up into the radiant eyes of his true love. She began kissing the tears from his cheeks, and now his heart broke all over again, this time with joy.

CHAPTER SIXTY-ONE

She couldn't figure out who was more fascinated with who. Jube lay on his side staring at Cochise who, in turn, could not take his eyes off his father. Jube reached out and stroked the baby's cheek and the little guy waved his arms around while propped up in his new papoose. Siki, who had arrived from Temecula late in the evening with a detachment of troopers, had brought a bigger and better papoose for her blood sister's baby.

Jube, Deirdre and Cochise had slept through the night in each other's arms. Deirdre understood now why pre-Breakdown families loved cameras so much. She used to think it was a sign of the kind of sentimentality that made them soft, but she would love to have a photo of this scene.

She heard a commotion outside their tent. At first, she thought it was nothing but revelers. La República soldiers, as well as the few Trogs who had survived the battle, had started celebrating with the younger Hussars in the late afternoon. When Siki showed up with her

Nations troopers, the place really started jumping. They partied late into the night.

She realized this wasn't revelers when she heard a familiar male voice yelling something about Mindy. She threw on a shirt and was pulling up her cargo pants when she stepped out of the tent and spotted her father ranting a few yards away. Margaret was trying to calm him down.

"Take it easy, Buford," Margaret said. "I'm sure she's just going out for a ride."

"With a loaded pack horse?" Buford yelled. Deirdre stepped up to them and asked what was going on.

"Mindy," her father answered. "She's leaving."

Deirdre made her way through the crowded camp toward the saddle barn. She'd never seen so many people in Hussarville. Soldiers of the Nations and La República were socializing with Hussars like it was a normal thing to do. The Trogs hung in the background, watching, anti-social as ever, but at least they weren't blowing anybody up. This would have given her a lot of hope for the future if she weren't so worried about what was happening with her sister.

When she reached the barn, Mindy had a roan mare saddled with a fully loaded pack mule alongside. "Mindy, what's going on?" she said. "Where you going? You okay?"

"I'm fine," Mindy said as she inspected the cinch on the pack animal.

"Has anyone said anything to you?"

"No," she said with relaxed indifference. "Everybody's been nice, and Dad's been spoiling me rotten. It's been okay, considering."

"Considering what?"

"I was with their enemy just a few days ago," Mindy said with a shrug. "You got to admit that's weird."

"So, you're leaving because it's weird?"

"Look, I need to figure out who I am," Mindy said with a frown.

"It'd be great if all this hadn't happened—I was never taken, I never met the Bees and I just grew up a Hussar. But that's not the way it played out. I just can't come back here and make believe nothing's happened."

She climbed onto the horse. "Don't worry, Deirdre. You'll see me again. I've got to hug that nephew of mine some more."

With that she cantered off toward the east, ponying the mule behind. Deirdre stood watching her ride away, trying to understand what the hell just happened.

"Somebody told her something," a young voice offered.

Deirdre turned to see Francine leaning against the barn wall. "Who?"

"One of the Bee prisoners," Francine explained. "I don't know what he said, but once she talked to him, she was in a big hurry to get out of here."

*****

Leader and Ketchell reached the spring a few hours before sunrise; it saved their lives. They had been staggering around in the desert since they escaped the catastrophe at the supply base. Another day without water would have killed them.

Leader watched the sun come up and took another sip from her canteen. The spring sat in a shallow depression, but she had climbed to high ground to watch the sunrise. She'd never had proper respect for the sun. She wouldn't make that mistake again. It looked so harmless now as it cast a subtle light across the desert, but she knew in a few hours it would be a deadly force capable of killing anyone who didn't honor its power.

She became aware of movement to her right and turned to see a rider approaching, leading a pack mule. Weakly, she searched for the knife, the only weapon she had left, and then remembered she left it down by the spring. "How pathetic," she said aloud. Turning to the rider, she resigned herself to whatever was to come.

It was light enough for her to make out details of the figure who sat on the horse, a young woman. The rider came to a stop a few feet from her and dismounted. Leader recognized her as Cadet Buford.

"Did we take Hussar Valley?" Leader asked with breathless anticipation.

"Nah," Mindy said as she walked around the back of the horse and reached into a saddle bag. "The Bees got whipped. A lot of them died, more ran away. My sister killed the Commandant. She's tough," she said with pride.

She pulled a small leather satchel out of the saddle bag and tossed it onto Leader's lap. "Deer jerky," Mindy said. "Hussars make it real good."

The sound of approaching footsteps brought their attention to Ketchell, who was climbing the slope from the spring. "Did I hear someone say something about jerky?" Leader pulled out two pieces and gave one to Ketchell, who immediately ripped off a piece with his teeth.

"How'd you find us?" Leader asked.

"I used to be a Hussar," Mindy answered. "We're good trackers. Not Nations good, but good all the same."

"Damn, this is tasty jerky," Ketchell said, squatting next to Leader. He took a swig out of his canteen and then flashed a grin at Mindy. "My name is Henry Ketchell. Many thanks for the nutrition."

Mindy stared at Ketchell for a long moment. "What did you say your name was?"

"Ketchell. Henry Ketchell."

"Did a guy named Carlyle snatch kids for you?" she said as if she were just curious.

Ketchell suddenly looked uncomfortable. "Carlyle? I don't remember that name."

The quickness with which Mindy drew her pistol and fired the bullet into Ketchell's chest seemed superhuman. Leader covered her face with her hands. She expected to be next. From between her fingers she could see Ketchell's corpse slide down the slope toward the spring.

"Relax, ma'am," Mindy said in a soothing voice. "I'm not going to hurt you. I admire you. I just been waiting to kill that son-of-a-bitch for such a long time. A Bee who was with you in the desert told me you two might be out here. When I heard that name, Ketchell, I knew I had to meet him. Briefly." She chuckled. "Don't worry, ma'am. I'll get you back to the Hive safely."

"So you're still a loyal Bee?"

Mindy shook her head. "Nah." She stared off into the desert for a few moments and then shrugged. "Let's just say I'm a work in progress."

✳✳✳✳✳

Deirdre woke around midnight. Jube was snoring but that wasn't what woke her. She checked on Cochise and he seemed to be sleeping off a busy day of being hugged and kissed by dozens of Hussars and a few soldiers of the Nations.

It'd been weeks since Siki and her detachment returned to Arizona, but the Apache had suggested that to keep the delicate peace alive a squad of Nations troopers should be permanently assigned to Hussar valley and a contingent of Hussars should transfer to Jerome. The Jerome Hussars would be under the command of Billy Cottonwood, the Nations troopers assigned to Hussar Valley would take orders from the new Eagle, Margaret.

"It's just crazy enough to work," Deirdre had said to Siki, who didn't get the joke, but from what she had observed so far, the new arrangement was working, which made her love Siki even more.

Jube's snoring crescendoed into a roar. She wondered why she loved his snoring so much. *Proof of life*, she thought with a giggle and walked out of the tent into the warm summer night. She knew she wasn't getting any sleep for a while. A dream had woken her and she didn't want to return to it.

Danny was sleeping in the sand next to the tent. She could hear him stirring as he reacted to her movements but he didn't stand. She walked toward him in the dark, and when her toe bumped his side, she lay down, cuddling with his torso, her head on his flank, her calves resting on his front legs, her heels in the sand. She reached forwards and searched for his ears, found the left one and stroked it as she listened to his content breathing.

There was no moon. The Milky Way dominated the night sky. Deirdre let herself be absorbed by the beauty of this remarkable sight and for a few moments, nesting in the contours of Danny's body, her man in her tent with their child, her tribe thriving on the new peace, she was content with her world.

It didn't last. The dream snaked its way back into her consciousness. It was a simple one. Her mother alone on a distant ridge, raising her arm towards Deirdre, who couldn't tell whether this was a friendly wave or a beckoning gesture. She couldn't move because of some inexplicable dream logic, so she just stared helplessly at the woman on the ridge.

An unusually warm breeze caressed the left side of her face. It felt like her mother's breath, a phenomenon she'd experienced hundreds of times as a little girl snuggling with that wonderful woman on cold winter nights.

Are you close, Mom? Maybe the woman on the dream ridge was just saying hi. She liked this idea; it relaxed her. She was aware that her breathing had synced with Danny's. Sleep began to fog her brain. Soon she was dreaming she was a centaur. It was glorious.

ABOUT THE AUTHOR

R.J. Stewart is best known for writing the Duane Johnson movie, *The Rundown*, the Pierce Brosnan classic series, *Remington Steele*, and developing, writing and producing the Lucy Lawless ground-breaking series, *Xena, Warrior Princess*. He's worked with Kevin Costner, James Garner, Charlie Sheen and Rebecca DeMornay. He presently lives on a San Diego County horse ranch with his wife, Kat O'Connor. Various horses and dogs have been kind enough to share their ranch with R.J. and Kat, including Danny, a beautiful palomino who inspired the creation of the buckskin character in *Crazy Hawk,* R.J.'s first novel.

NOTE TO THE READER

Thanks for reading my book. Check out the Hovartus Books website.
Hovartus.com. If you'd like to reach me directly,
email me at rjs@hovartus.com.
-RJ Stewart

www.ingramcontent.com/pod-product-compliance
Lightning Source LLC
Chambersburg PA
CBHW032113310726

48972CB00001B/212